LAMBERT, D.

NIGHT AND
THE CITY

BY THE SAME AUTHOR

Novels

Angels in the Snow
The Kites of War
For Infamous Conduct
The Yermakov Transfer
Touch the Lion's Paw (filmed as Rough Cut)
Grand Slam
The Great Land
The St Peter's Plot
I, Said the Spy
Trance
The Red Dove
The Judas Code
The Golden Express
The Man Who Was Saturday
Vendetta
Chase
Triad

Autobiographies

The Sheltered Days
Don't Quote Me But
And I Quote
Unquote
Just Like the Blitz

THE NIGHT AND THE CITY

Derek Lambert

F/340342

HAMISH HAMILTON · LONDON

HAMISH HAMILTON LTD

Published by the Penguin Group
27 Wrights Lane, London W8 5TZ, England
Viking Penguin Inc, 40 West 23rd Street, New York, New York 10010, U.S.A.
Penguin Books Australia Ltd, Ringwood, Victoria, Australia
Penguin Books Canada Ltd, 2801 John Street, Markham, Ontario, Canada L3R 1B4
Penguin Books (N.Z.) Ltd, 182–190 Wairau Road, Auckland 10, New Zealand

Penguin Books Ltd, Registered Offices: Harmondsworth, Middlesex, England

First published in Great Britain 1988 by
Hamish Hamilton Ltd

Copyright © 1988 by Derek Lambert

1 3 5 7 9 10 8 6 4 2

British Library Cataloguing in Publication Data

Lambert, Derek, 1929–
The night and the city.
I. Title
823'.914
ISBN 0–241–12242–2

Typeset by Wyvern Typesetting Limited, Bristol
Printed and bound in Great Britain by
Richard Clay Ltd, Bungay, Suffolk

For Beryl Kranz from another city

Author's Note

I had intended to make a list of those who helped me to write this novel but ultimately I realised that detailed acknowledgements would only detract from appreciation to an organisation that restores faith in that sometimes elusive quality, human decency. It is called Special Olympics and it enables those deemed to be mentally handicapped — although who is to say what visions they perceive? — to compete in their own Olympiads. The motto of these games is: "Let me win. But if I cannot win, let me be brave in the attempt." And it is my belief that many of today's sportsmen who, superficially, have normality on their side could learn a lot from the endeavour of the competitors. Their address in the USA is Special Olympics, 1350 New York Avenue, N.W.; Suite 500, Washington, D.C. 20005; and, in the UK, Special Olympics, Willesborough Industrial Park, Kennington Road, Willesborough, Ashford, Kent TN24 0TD. The others who helped me know who they are and I thank them.

When a man is tired of London he is tired of life; for there is in London all that life can afford
— Samuel Johnson

Hell is a city much like London
— Percy Bysshe Shelley

PART ONE

CHAPTER 1

———— ◆ ————

The beer breath of the venerable pubs warmed the young man's cheeks as he hurried through the dark, snow-flying streets of Liverpool. He was eighteen years old – nineteen tomorrow, Christmas Day – and he wore his worry like an undertaker's coat.

Head down against the snow and the last-minute shoppers, he passed first the Crown, then the Vines – the Big House to Liverpudlians, all mirrors and mahogany – before bearing right towards the bright stores, Lewis's and the Army and Navy.

Outside the Central he hesitated. The noise of revelry beckoned and the warm smell of ale was already balm. He thrust his way to the bar, ordered a pint of bitter and, leaning against a green pillar, surveyed the festivities.

The pub which had retained its Edwardian splendour, even a cupola inside its cavernous saloon, was, like the city, host to success and not a little failure. Those bountifully employed were investing their expense accounts in office relationships, the unemployed were blowing their benefits.

Decorations trembled in the body-heat of office parties; gas flames danced on a fake coal fire; two girls with smudged lipstick and streaked hair exposed legs sheathed in black net for a young man in a sharp suit holding a Polaroid camera.

"Merry Christmas," a voice said. "You look as if you could do with one."

Martin Renshaw turned. The young man behind him was tall and skinny with a flour-white face and long, dank hair; he wore a black overcoat with moulting lapels and a glass bead in the lobe of his left ear. Despite the throng around him he seemed isolated.

"I've got problems," Martin said.

"Join the club. Mine are right behind me. Don't look, it's all a question of accent." His speech was staccato, vowels sooty. "What are your problems? Keep talking."

"How would you like to celebrate your birthday on Christmas Day?" No need to tell the stranger that he was contemplating leaving home.

"In good company." The bead in his ear glittered in the light reflected from an engraved mirror. "Should grow a beard. Perform a few miracles. Which is what we might need any minute now."

A middle-aged man, his face grazed from recent warfare, had moved away from the bar and was standing behind the stranger studying him with owlish intent.

"Two lots of presents," the stranger said. "Can't be bad."

"Lucky if I get one." Martin's Scouse accents weren't fierce but he liked to listen to them in the company of strangers from foreign parts of the land.

"Nearest and dearest skint? No need to be these days. DHSS. Denis Helps Sad Sinners."

"Denis who?"

"Thatcher. The power behind the throne. How do you think he can afford to play all that golf? The old DHSS! There's always a wheeze, cully. So when are you coming down to the Smoke?"

"How did you know I was thinking about it?" asked Martin, who had been agonising for weeks.

"Obvious. The Great Divide. Ninety per cent of jobs lost in ten years in the North, six per cent in the South. What's your poison?"

Martin asked for a pint of Walker's, the stranger ordered a large vodka and soda with ice and lemon.

Martin waved his pint at the assembled company. "They're not on the breadline, are they?" defensively. "Liverpool's still a wealthy city," which was true unless you lived in an industrial wasteland where men exchanged their pride for benefits.

"Wealth? Jewel box in a derelict house." The stranger stuck out a bony hand. "Prince is the name. Song of the underworld – 'Some Day My Prints Will Come'."

The man with the grazed face said: "So Liverpool's a decayed

4

house, is it?" His accent was Scouse with a faint lilt from the Welsh valleys.

"Derelict not decayed."

"There's a difference?" He wore an imitation sheepskin jacket that had been slashed many times with a knife. "What would you know about it, a Cockney. Come to gloat?" He turned to Martin. "Got a cigarette?"

"I don't smoke," Martin said, knuckles polished around his glass of beer.

"What do you do then? Keep fit, is it?"

Prince handed Martin a £5 note. "Get a round in, cully. I've got to pay a call." He headed for the lavatories.

The drunk finished his beer, handed Martin the empty sleeve and said: "Make mine a Scotch and a chaser this time."

"You're not drinking with us."

"I am now."

"Sorry," Martin said, bracing himself.

Prince, fingering the bead in his ear, said: "There's a wallet in there lying on the floor."

"Did you pick it up?" Martin asked.

"I'm not a tea-leaf," Prince said indignantly.

The drunk belched, massaged his belly and made for the lavatory.

"Come on, cully, while the going's good." Prince grabbed Martin's arm and propelled him towards the door.

"What about the wallet?"

"What wallet?" Prince winked theatrically.

*   *   *

Outside, the wind had dropped and the snow hovered in soft flakes in front of the shops in Ranelagh Street where the rich paid with credit cards, the poor with Christmas club savings.

Martin loved his city: its tight-roofed alleys where the songs of John, George, Paul and Ringo were still imprisoned; the new oasthouse of the Catholic Cathedral (the Mersey Funnel) peering along Hope Street towards the brooding pile of its Anglican neighbour; the Georgian terraces of Rodney Street where Gladstone once lived; the baronial majesties of St George's Hall and Landseer's Lions and the Liver, Cunard and Port buildings guarding the pier-head and the red Ribble buses and the comedians and footballers and the salt-and-stout smells of the Mersey.

But he had to leave.

In 1981 mobs had rioted in Liverpool 8, beating anyone who got in their way and putting out the eyes of tired old buildings. Nothing racist as some observers had suggested because Liverpool had long been home to blacks, since the days of the slavers, and to Chinese, Indians, Pakistanis, Jews, Arabs, the Welsh descendants of quarry workers and, of course, the Irish, who sailed across their sea to escape from poverty and the English. No, Liverpool was an integrated congregation worshipping at the altars of Liverpool or Everton football club, and the reason for the violence was far more simple. Frustration. And that was why Martin had to go.

Martin had once heard a woman radiant with good works proclaim: "There's no such thing as poverty these days." Take a walk through Liverpool 8, missus. Sleep in a squat, forage in a rubbish tip, haunt the job shop.

"Got a job?" Prince asked, guiding Martin into Church Street shopping precinct. Canned carols chased each other down the arcades, a man with a ruined face sat on a wall skirting a flowerbed, drinking from a green bottle. The snow fell steadily and Prince's clothes-hanger shoulders were weighted with it.

"I quit yesterday," Martin told him, remembering the zealous contempt on his father's face, the distress on his mother's.

"Lousy job?"

"Humping furniture," Martin said. "Two quid an hour."

"And you with your education!"

"You can tell?"

"Even with that Scouse phlegm of yours," said Prince, who wasn't machine-gunning his words quite so explosively now that he wasn't threatened. "What were you, a drop-out? College education, snotty parents, teach-'em-a-lesson, university of life?"

"My old man lost his job and I had to help support him and my mam."

"Bit of a martyr, are we?"

"What do you do?" Martin asked. "Mug old ladies?"

"Let's have a wet," Prince said, guiding Martin into the

6

Beehive on the corner of Paradise Street. It was crammed with festive drinkers but they were marginally different from the customers in the Central; the Beehive's clientèle was more homely, and one wall was lined with books, novels by Mazo de la Roche, A. E. W. Mason, J. B. Priestley, Edgar Wallace . . .

"My round," Martin said.

"If you insist, cully."

"So what *do* you do?" Martin asked.

"Financial adviser on DHSS benefits. You'd be surprised how many people underclaim. I put them on the right path. And what better place than Merseyside? You know what they say, when Britain catches a cold Liverpool catches pneumonia."

"People actually pay you to fiddle claims?"

"Who said anything about fiddling? Strumming a few chords maybe. I've got a hobby, too. Lucrative in a way . . ." He stared speculatively at Martin, deep-set eyes glittering in his starved face.

"Horses?"

Prince shook his head emphatically.

"Dogs?"

An even more vehement shake of the head. "Trains," he said. He smiled, revealing sharp teeth. "I'm going for the Guinness Book of Records. Seven thousand, three hundred and twenty-nine miles without buying a ticket. Going for the ten thousand. Must be a record," speech clipped at the prospect.

"How can you prove it?"

"Have to take my word. If they don't . . ." Prince shrugged eloquently. "I'll print my own leaflet."

"Condemning yourself?"

"And British Rail. Look." He pulled a mauled copy of the *Liverpool Echo* from the pocket of the funereal overcoat. The headline read BR SEEK £10 SPOT FINES FOR FARE DODGERS. "Admitting they're fighting a losing battle." He delved inside the coat, brought out a bulging wallet and extracted a cutting. "My rival," he said.

Martin read the clipping. RAIL "HOBO" WHO KEPT GET-TING THERE FREE.

A former advertising executive admitted yesterday that he travelled thousands of miles by train without paying a penny.

In 19 weeks a modern hobo from Birmingham was

7

approached by a BR ticket collector only 11 times as he criss-crossed the country.

He said: "I lived on British Rail for the whole 19 weeks except when I returned to Birmingham for my fortnightly £59.40 dole money."

"Got to admire him," Prince said. "Have to go to Birmingham to see what he's clocked up. Might be able to help him, too. Fifty-nine quid? Pathetic."

"What do you charge for your services?"

"Modest, very modest." Prince took a £20 note from the stuffed wallet. "First week's profit over and above what they were already drawing. Can't say fairer than that. Beer?"

"A half," Martin said, tongue thickening in his mouth. He went to the lavatory and peered into a mirror. Half poet, half pirate, according to Joanne. The whites of his grey eyes were pink and his black hair curled with sweat. He combed his hair with a gap-toothed comb, straightened his reefer jacket and returned to the bar. The noise came at him in waves.

Prince, glass in hand, was examining the books on the wall. They reminded Martin of summer evenings. He said: "Prince of what?"

"Just Prince."

"No first name?"

"Just Prince." He handed Martin the pint sleeve which had been topped up with the half.

"So what does your girl think?" Prince asked.

"About what?"

"You taking off for the Smoke."

"She doesn't know," Martin said. Nor do I, he thought.

They had discussed it one afternoon in Sefton Park before the snow came, watched by cruel-eyed mallards on the lake and lonely men walking their dogs. She had taken his arm as though trying to anchor him. And he had felt the breeze finding its way to the greenness from the Mersey that was stirring her auburn hair and he had felt her warmth and urgency as she advised him to stay where his roots were, to study at night . . . But he had seen another Joanne too; ten years older, mistress of a small household complete with mortgage, agreed friends, Sunday-washed second-hand car, reluctant indulgence towards masculine failings such as football and the occasional drink-up. Martin had observed how many husbands were gently mocked;

8

sometimes wives even spoke for them in their presence.

That evening Joanne, Liverpool-Irish, sensuality and purity, both inherited from Dublin, locked in combat, had made love for the first time in her father's gaunt house in Bootle; and as the sensuality had briefly triumphed he had almost settled for the computerised future. Almost.

Prince said: "Day after Boxing Day. Merseyside Pullman. Leave in style. Forget the 00.15 overnight, the scroungers' special. Five past seven, platform 8."

"You'll be on it?"

"Back to base," Prince said, "to count the pickings. And to pick up my own benefits. Advise myself – one of my best customers. And I miss the Smoke. Know something, cully? Go anywhere outside London and you're a foreigner. But not in Aldgate, not down the Clerkenwell Road, not in Peckham, Purley or Penge."

"Not in Liverpool," Martin said.

"A Cockney in Scouseland? Pull the other leg, it's got bells on it. You saw what happened in the boozer . . ."

"He was drunk," Martin said.

"Drunk or not, he picked on the accent. Like it or not, we're divided, a land of tribes." He chewed the rind of the lemon experimentally. "What's her name? Sharon, Sheena . . . Clare . . . Getting close?"

"Joanne," Martin said.

"Irish? Tamed? Wild ways squeezed into a church pew?"

"Close," Martin said.

He gulped beer and heard it splash in his stomach. The smell of cigars was strong in his nostrils. Beside him, beneath the umbrella of tobacco smoke, a perspiring young man whose shirt-tails had escaped from his trousers, was kissing a girl with ringlets. Martin longed for Joanne. How could he leave her?

"My father comes from London," Martin said.

"Then he should go home."

"He came here when he married my mam. Liverpool was a busy place then. Before the ships sailed away."

"He should have sailed with 'em."

"He's too honest."

"What's that supposed to mean?"

"Whatever you want it to mean." The sweat was cold on his face and his voice was loud in his ears, Scouse a saw cutting

9

metal and shedding sparks, hard and true and in . . . can . . . descent.

He said to Prince: "Do you believe in Father Christmas?"

"Of course."

"And the world is flat?"

"Whatever shape you want it to be."

"What made you a philosopher?"

"Questioning everything. Stars millions of light-years away. Believe that and you'll believe anything. Just explanations, cully, of things we don't understand. Courage . . . What's so fantastic about courage? Graveyards are full of heroes."

"Time . . . to . . . go," words trailing behind his tongue.

"Don't forget. Thursday, 7.05. You'll see, there's . . ."

". . . always a wheeze."

Outside Bing Crosby was dreaming of a white Christmas through the loudspeakers. Likely to get his way this year, Martin thought, and laughed. And as he made his way to the bus station it began to snow again and the flakes joined the blizzard of his thoughts and, touching his cheeks, turned to tears.

*   *   *

His tiny room glowed with pale blue light and Martin, struggling to vault the bar of pain in his skull, remembered gradually that he was nineteen and that Jesus would have been nearly 1,990 years old.

Naked save for his Marks underpants, he swung his legs from his bed, drew the curtains and let in the light. Snow was still falling, hesitantly now, white moths chasing each other across the waters of the Mersey where tall ships had once rested.

Such ships. In his childhood they had sailed in his dreams, unfurling their sails in the sepia print on the wall after his mother had switched off the light. Sitting on the edge of the bed, he closed his eyes and the tall ships sailed back, and steamships laden with sugar and spice and tobacco and orchids followed them home; and packet ships departed, taking with them nine million emigrants to America, Canada and Australia. When he opened his eyes there were only two ships out there, both ferries.

But the rooftops were still as they had been in those teeming

10

days – a staircase, white-carpeted today, descending to the broad estuary and its once-vibrant docks. One push and the terraces of Dingle, cardinal red and as pert as robins, would tumble down the precipitous streets into the water. Martin yawned, put on his plaid dressing-gown and went downstairs to make the tea and warm the mincepies.

While the kettle boiled in the tiny kitchen he counted the Christmas cards on the mantelpiece – fourteen, eight of them crusted with glitter-frost. Paper-chains linking the four corners of the living-room moved in an imperceptible breeze; the baubles on the imitation tree spun points of light beneath a bald fairy. Cold reached his anaesthetised nerve-endings and he switched on the electric fire, two bars because it was Christmas. The double-bed creaked above the parlour. How was he going to tell them? Today of all days.

He made the tea, one tea-bag for two mugs, and snatched the mincepies from the oven. He placed the tin tray on which a picture of the Queen and the Duke of Edinburgh at the Coronation was just discernible and called out: "Merry Christmas," adding, guiltily, "and a happy New Year."

"Happy birthday, dear," from his mother, a mumble from his father. *Where the devil were you last night?*

He returned to his room, to Everton FC, arms akimbo on the wall, a programme for *Educating Rita* autographed by Willy Russell, a photograph of Liverpool's last tram, No 6A in 1957, a pair of boxing gloves said to have been worn by Nel Tarleton – "Who was the last person to box Tarleton?" Answer: "The undertaker" – and a reproduction poster of the Beatles in the Cavern. He stared through the confused snowflakes at the blurred outlines of Birkenhead, Tranmere, Rock Ferry and New Ferry across the water. How could he leave?

He shaved in cold water. His skin was tender, eyes still as pink as a white rat's. He cut a swathe through aerosol foam; his skin bled a little. A seepage of truth? There were jobs of a sort on Merseyside; there were night schools. Or was it the confines of this claustrophobic home that he wanted to escape? His father's martyrdom, his mother's reproach.

He stung his cheeks with Imperial Leather aftershave. Floor-boards creaked in the next room. A murmur of voices, his mother's tight with Christmas secrets. A pigeon landed on the window-sill and, throat pulsing, peered into Martin's room; its

11

eyes reminded him of the mallards in Sefton Park.

After lunch Joanne was picking him up in her father's car. He would discuss it with her after they had made love – no sense in jeopardising that – and perhaps postpone any agonising with his parents until Boxing Day.

He washed and towelled his face, dressed in jeans and grey sweater, and went downstairs for the first rituals.

His father, fifty-seven, with a grocer's face and grey, Brylcreemed hair, was sitting at the gate-legged table rolling a tobacco-starved cigarette; his mother was in the kitchen frying bread and bacon. The presents, packaged in last year's wrapping paper, waited beneath the tree.

"Happy birthday, lad," his father said. He stared at Martin's face. "Sup a few last night?" He lit his thin cigarette.

The smell of its smoke beckoned scents from Martin's childhood. Shag tobacco on the jackets of the dockers as they entered his father's shop on the corner of the terrace; Tizer and carbolic soap and custard powder. And he remembered his father cutting yellow cheese with wire, slicing bacon dangerously with his razored wheel, weighing, always weighing, portions which got lighter and debts deeper as the strikes continued and the container ports took away the business. And, playing ollies on the cracked pavement outside, he saw, but didn't comprehend, the bleakness on the faces of the dockers as they strode away, departing eventually to the chain stores, leaving Renshaws to rot with its food.

"I had a few pints," Martin said.

"Wonder you can afford it. But I suppose you'll be earning good money now you're unemployed."

"Why shouldn't he have a few drinks on Christmas Eve?" Martin's mother demanded from the kitchen. Her voice was pure Scouse, incisive and catarrhal as though the wet winds from Ireland had clogged the nostrils, drowned the final g's and left the wit. His father's London vowels were still intruders.

"So what are you going to do now, lad?" his father asked. He had been out of work for six years and had an unused air about him.

"I'll have to think about it," Martin said.

"But not today," his mother said emerging from the kitchen, wiping her fingers down her rose-patterned apron. Perversely she had grown plump since hardship had lodged in the house;

her grey, watch-spring hair was jaunty but her eyes were old beyond her years, glazed by her husband's unremitting honesty. "Anyway, it's time to open the presents," she said. "Will you ever forgive me," to Martin, "for having you on the twenty-fifth?"

"You could have waited a couple of days," Martin said, smiling.

The Navy sweater with leather at the elbows and shoulders was for his birthday, the Sony Walkman for Christmas. From Joanne a Pears Cyclopaedia and a striped tie. He gave his mother a shawl, supposedly woven in Cyprus, his father a book-token for £5; his parents gave each other gloves.

After breakfast Martin ran through the snow to the privy at the end of the yard, currently pivot of conversation in the Renshaw household because indoor lavatories were being installed in many of the little houses separating the Mersey from Toxteth whether the tenants wanted them or not. Martin had never complained because the privy had been part of growing up — arse ice-cold, squares of newspaper threaded with string, tortoise hibernating in a shoebox.

"Make the most of it while you can," his father said when he returned. "A couple of weeks and they'll have us in a hostel while they install the new one. And then the rent will go up, mark my words. Eighty-three p a week we pay now; some reckon it will be £16 when we're allowed back. Who's ever complained about soil at the end of the yard?"

"You'll have to apply for more benefits," Martin said, thinking about Prince.

"You know what I think about charity."

"Perhaps you should ask mam what she thinks."

"Your mam and I think alike."

His mother said: "Your father's got his pride."

Martin said to his mother: "You shouldn't have to work at Littlewoods."

"Your father draws what he has to. No more. And," smiling festively, "let's all have another cuppa and then I'll get the bird in the oven."

Another rite, the annual tussle with the recalcitrant turkey, while the pudding steamed imperturbably in a saucepan with a bobbing lid.

His father switched on the radio. The news which yesterday

13

had been threatening global conflict in the Middle East was as harmonious as a carol.

While Martin read yesterday's *Echo* his father perused the council's *City Magazine*. Martin had already seen it. *A Matter of Life and Death*, hints on how to stay warm in winter. Eat more, wear warm clothing, keep active.

Don't leak heat, the article urged, recommending draught-proofing and projecting a homily on how to prevent pipes bursting which was practical enough unless you were an eighty-four-year-old woman drawing £39.35 a week and living in a council flat spending 11.5 p an hour on a two-bar electric fire which kept the room temperature at 49 degrees Fahrenheit. Martin who worked voluntarily with old people knew about these things.

His father leaned forward and switched off one bar of the fire.

Martin said: "You can get a grant from the council to insulate the house. Sixty-six per cent of the cost up to £69."

"You know what I think about grants," his father said.

"Maybe you could get mam to fiddle a football coupon for you," Martin said.

"Maybe you should get another job. Repay some of the money we spent on your education."

Martin, sipping sweet tea, turned a page of the *Echo*. A whole page was occupied by intelligence from the Department of Health and Social Security explaining how old people could draw extra money for heating. How many would bother to fill in the form? How many would admit that they had less than £505 in the bank? What old people resented more than the cold was the intrusion.

Martin, only recently aware of inequality, knew that no government should have allowed conditions to deteriorate to the point where the infirm had to fill in forms to stay alive.

What did they think of monetary policies?

We spent on your education? His mother more like: it was she who had wanted him to go to university. "A degree ..." uttered with awe. But the loss of the shop in the wake of the abandoned docks had put paid to that.

His mother said: "What's on telly?"

Martin said: "The Queen's speech, *Guns of Navarone*, Cilla Black."

14

"How do you know?"

"Is the Pope a Catholic?"

Martin who had turned down an invitation to play five-a-side football to stay at home stood up, unsure how to pass the time. In the kitchen his mother remonstrated with the turkey; church bells pealed. He ducked his head and walked into the miniature dining-room and back again.

His father said: "Don't let us keep you."

"I'm sorry." Martin sat down, aware that at some future date he would miss this snugness.

Should he broach the possibility of departure this evening?

At midday his father produced a half-full bottle of port and a small, flat bottle of whisky, the sort you find on a park bench wrapped in brown paper.

"Whisky?" His father looked at him doubtfully.

"Just a drop." Which was what he got.

His father poured himself a meagre measure of Scotch, his wife a glass of port, and returned the bottles to the cupboard beside the fireplace for New Year's Eve. He lit a Hamlet and, when it was drawing, they raised their glasses.

*   *   *

Joanne drove north in her father's rusting Fiesta along Sefton Street, past the atrophied docks, Brunswick, Coburg, Queen's, King's ... seven miles of them, past the city's badge of pride, the refurbished Albert Dock with its Maritime Museum, and the pier-head and the Liver Building with its eighteen-foot-high Liver birds – cormorants, according to some – and the tunnels under the Mersey ...

Just before the container port at Seaforth she turned right down Knowsley Road, wheels skidding on the snow. In a couple of minutes they would be there; Martin, anticipating sex, shivered.

The Catholic in her, he suspected, would have preferred to wait until they were married, or engaged, and occasionally he wondered, unworthily, whether she regarded sex as a nuptial bond. Thank God for the liberated Celt in her that, when aroused, trampled on convention.

She smiled faintly, biting her bottom lip, as she turned into the terrace street of tall houses where she lived, reminding

15

Martin of her mother, a tall woman, almost angular, reddish hair matured with grey, who sometimes smiled secretly contradicting the resolution that a drunkard's wife must display.

Joanne parked the Fiesta in front of a soiled hedge of privet sealed in white; even the gloomy-eyed houses had regained a modest dignity in the snow, wounded roofs bandaged, neglected gardens tranquil. A snowman with pebble eyes, a carrot nose and a pipe stared at them but the street at this time between dog and fox was lonely.

Behind the curtains of No. 14 Martin saw the winking lights of a Christmas tree and thought for one alarming moment: "Christ, they're still here." But Joanne, smiling her mother's secret smile, shook her head: they were visiting in Speke. But for how long? Joanne slid the key into the lock and the front-door of the house opened; it smelled of indoor plants, spice and stale booze.

Joanne drew the curtains. The room was tall and unlived-in, even at Christmas: the Kellys lived in the big warm kitchen. Christmas cards were on parade on the mantelpiece. Was it blasphemous to fornicate on Christmas Day? On the russet cushions of a sofa that looked as though they had never been sat upon, far less laid upon? It *is* my birthday.

She took off her raincoat and green scarf, spilling snow on the carpet, and, holding out her arms, touched his cheeks with her fingertips. She was a few months older than him, a student nurse at Walton Hospital, and sometimes she seemed older.

She said: "You'd better take off your coat; you look over-dressed."

She pressed his shoulders, digging at the slopes of muscle. The winking lights switched her smile on and off; her hair which was red but was gold now fell across her forehead, making a sanctified wanton of her.

She took off the amber beads at her throat, looking naked although she still wore a mist-grey dress. Previously, twice, they had made love, both times in the dark. Martin retreated into the hallway to undress; the union of lust and respect and, perhaps, love perplexing him. When he returned she was naked, except for a pair of high-heeled shoes. Her body was pale, stomach flat above the gold thatch of her pubis, breasts neat; a tall girl with sharp bones that made her vulnerable.

16

Her sensible fingernails clawed his back.

When they had dressed she straightened the cushions, and asked him if he would like a drink. "Whiskey? Irish with an e in it. There's always plenty of that around." She poured a glass of Paddy and water and dropped a cube of ice in it; the ice cracked and frosted; she poured herself a lemon squash. They took the drinks into the kitchen where the plates were still piled in the sink.

"Perhaps we should wash them," she said.

"I'll dry," feeling the future tighten around him.

His mother had said: "Whatever you do, don't wed too soon; there's time enough for kids and the tallyman. Enjoy your youth, lad, while you still own it." And he had wondered whether she was thinking of her spent years and he tried to think how many happy marriages he could count. Not many. But perhaps you only heard about warring couples; the rows of houses in Dingle looked content enough.

"You don't have to," Joanne said.

He picked up an Irish-linen cloth bearing a print of the Post Office in O'Connell Street, Dublin, and began to dry a dinner-plate twinkling with suds.

After a few minutes of domesticity he broke a Duralux plate and, apologising, said: "I've been thinking of leaving."

She squirted green liquid into a basin. "I thought we'd decided that," she said.

"There aren't the opportunities here."

"There are 10,000 studying full- or part-time at the Poly. Seven and a half thousand at the university. Night schools . . ."

"And 100,000 out of work."

"Liverpool's always been tough," she said. "Even in the good years. While the liners took the rich to Bermuda the poor starved."

"Or went south. It's another country down there. Sophisticated, computerised . . . The factories and docks here are finished."

"Since when did you want to work in a factory or a dock? I thought you wanted to study architecture at the Poly."

"And keep my da and mam?"

"Running away won't help them," she said.

"You have to leave sometime or you're doomed. In any case

17

I'll send them money."

"The Pool's a challenge," she said.

"So's London."

"Too English," she said.

"The Sinn Fein in you?" He flicked a morsel of turkey from a plate. "Isn't Liverpool English?"

"It's Irish," she said. "And Scotch and Welsh and black and brown . . . It's Scouse," she said.

"I love it too."

"What would you do in London that you can't do here?"

"There's work down there," he said. "And opportunity. And money . . ."

"Tell me one thing." She handed him a serving dish that rang when he tapped it with his knuckle. "Why didn't you tell me all this before we made love?"

"I should have."

"You thought I wouldn't let you? You can't think much of me, Martin."

"I haven't said I am leaving. I wanted to discuss it."

"You're going," she said.

"It seems a good time. Nineteen, my parents leaving the house for a while."

"Opportunism. You should do well in London."

Why didn't she protest more? He wanted debate not acceptance. Perhaps she was waiting for him to ask her to join him. Should he? When he was settled, perhaps . . .

She said: "I'll never leave Liverpool. Not while I'm young anyway. When I'm old maybe I'll retire to the Wicklow Mountains and nurse sheep."

He had been dismissed from her calculations, erased, as though the sex had meant nothing to her. He turned sharply, knocking his elbow on a cupboard. The serving dish shattered on the tiles.

They stared at the fragments, then she said: "I'll drive you home."

He found her present in the pocket of his overcoat. He handed it to her. "Sorry, I forgot." It was perfume, Opium, expensive.

"You had other things on your mind," she said.

As the Fiesta moved away from the familiar street he waved

at the snowman. It reminded him of Prince, its pipe pointing south, and he almost expected it to wave back.

* * *

The photograph album came out from the cupboard under the stairs at 11.30 on Boxing Day morning presenting Martin with a reason – pretext? – for leaving.

His ancestors, becalmed in time, stared at him knowingly. Handsome matriarchs with coiled hair and regal bosoms; an old man, face weighted by a walrus moustache, graspng a sporting rifle; soldiers from two world wars grinning toothily beneath tin hats, an officer smiling at death; slim girls in long dresses on Blackpool seafront after the second war; his parents, studio-lit and self-conscious, on their wedding day; a GI bride; urchins playing in a fountain.

Martin, sitting beside his mother on the sofa, turned a page while his father, dabbing with one finger at his postage-stamp moustache, lit his third and last Hamlet of the holiday and gazed at them ruminatively through the smoke. What struck Martin most forcibly about the photographs was the disparity of life-styles. Of course the Liverpudlian branch of the family had been poorer – his grandfather a driver on the Dockers' Umbrella, the Overhead Railway that had once traversed the docks from Dingle to Seaforth. But why were his London uncles so much more affluent than his father, even when he'd owned the shop?

There was Harry Renshaw, smiling plumply beside a white Porsche outside his mansion in The Bishops Avenue, Hampstead. There was Jack Renshaw – "bold and bad", according to his mother – drinking champagne at the Derby. And there was Walter Renshaw, much given to Christian endeavour and shrewd investment on the stock market, opening a church fête in Middlesex.

His mother pointed at a small boy wearing too-long shorts staring at the camera as though it were a machine-gun. "Your first day at your new school," she said. "When you got home you were sick."

Martin said: "Why have the London uncles been so lucky?"

19

"God's little acres these were. Used to be red deer here and you could see the Welsh hills."

"Uncle Harry, for instance . . ."

"Your father's an honest man."

"And his brothers aren't?"

"I didn't say that."

"Happiness," his father said, words wrapped in small billows of smoke, "isn't necessarily material. I don't envy my brothers. And as for Jack . . ."

"He's got a wonderful sense of humour," his mother said.

"The police don't find him very funny."

"Shush, Jim."

"Well," Martin said, "it seems odd to me."

"Yours not to reason why," his father said.

His mother turned a page of the album. Martin again, standing on the lanny at the pier-head watching one of the red, white and blue ferries butting across the Mersey.

"Why don't we see them more often?" Martin asked.

"They're not Scouse," said his mother which didn't seem much of a reason.

"Perhaps they don't want to go slumming," his father said. He stood up and pointed the smoking butt of his small cigar at the album. "Why don't you put that thing away? It causes trouble every Christmas."

Not before as far as Martin could remember. He gazed thoughtfully at the album. The uncles seemed to provoke more anger in his father than mere envy merited.

His mother closed the album.

Ducking his head, his father climbed the creaking stairs.

His mother said softly: "He's been a good father to you, lad."

And he had, he supposed. Games of ollies, and holidays at Morecambe and, once, Scarborough, and Saturday afternoons watching Everton and helping in the shop and his schooling before the shut-down. And security and belonging.

"Why is he so uptight about his brothers?"

His mother stared across a layer of cigar-smoke without replying. Was she thinking about his sister who had died aged eight months, of a virus, the doctors' designation for any ailment beyond their comprehension?

"He's right," Martin said, "happiness isn't material."

"Aye, he's right there."

"Then why is he so . . . jealous?"

"Proud," his mother said.

"I don't understand."

"No reason you should."

"I think I should find out," he said. "I think I have the right."

"Right?" Her gaze had lost direction and she answered from the past. "What right do you have? It was done before you were born."

"What was done?"

Her gaze refocussed. "Done? Nothing was done, pet. You know how sentimental I get at Christmas. Muddled." She dabbed at her eyes with a handkerchief that smelled of lavender water. Then she said: "Best you don't concern yourself with what happened long ago."

Sly with a cause, an ancient injustice, Martin told her that he was leaving home. When? Why not tomorrow? The end of Christmas, the beginning of his twentieth year. "I'll write, I'll send splosh," he said.

"Aye, you do that."

Surprised at her lack of surprise, he said: "I have to go."

"There's nothing for you here."

But there was. Everything.

"I'm sorry," he said.

"Don't be."

F/340342

He heard the click of her knitting needles when he was a boy, rhythmic and comforting, and he heard her shouting from upstairs while she made the beds that she could see whatever he was doing, if it was bad that was. He had been in this toy house for ever.

"We have to move on," he said. "Whether we want to or not."

"I know," she said. "I've always known," and he wished that his sister was here with them, fifteen years old now if she had lived.

"I'll be back."

"I know it."

"I don't want to go."

"You go, lad."

"All right then."

"You know what I'd like to do now?"

He shook his head.

"Go to the Gaumont. See a good film. *How Green Was My Valley*, something like that."

"Let's go," he said. "You and me."

But they didn't move and somewhere knitting needles clicked.

CHAPTER 2

The Pullman, cream with an orange streak on its flanks, left Lime Street at 7.05 am, burrowed into a tunnel and emerged among scattered yellow lights, LITTLEWOODS in red neon to the left. In the back rooms of terrace houses overlooking the track lives were lighting up, suburbs, dark and snow-fresh, yawning. The train began to pick up the rhythms of speed, unravelling a mooring rope in Martin's skull; the rope tightened, held for a moment, then snapped and he was adrift. Where was Prince?

Martin left his corner of the carriage and walked down the swaying aisle. Faces looked up at him incuriously. *They don't care in London.* How many times had he heard that? A tired-looking young woman with a baby ... two West Indians in leather jackets hunched in dawn meditation ... businessmen entrenched behind copies of the *Post* ... a lawyer with a pink-ribboned brief ... No Prince.

He returned to his corner and sat beneath his punished suitcase, secured with a belt, on the rack. He should have caught the 00.15, used on Sunday nights by moonlighters working in London and drawing benefits in Liverpool; it was cheaper than the Pullman. He should never have trusted Prince: Prince had been a Christmas apparition like Marley's Ghost. He stared out of the window; snow-covered fields fled behind the train in the strengthening light. One day, when he was very young, he had got lost among the looming buildings of William Brown Street; as the Pullman approached Stafford the same panic re-visited him. He took his lunch packet from the pocket of his reefer jacket, untied the string and began to eat a turkey sandwich.

23

Stafford was awake, the platform crowded. The new arrivals brought gusts of fresh air into the carriage with them. Martin helped a woman in her sixties with a patient face and rheumatic knuckles to put her case on the rack. She sat opposite him and he offered her a turkey sandwich but she refused.

"London bound?" she asked.

He nodded.

"Returning home?"

"Leaving home."

"I did that once." She smiled, remembering. "Never regretted it. I was considered to be rather wicked."

"And were you?"

"I suppose I was. It all ended very soon. He was killed. A war you've probably never heard of in Korea."

"I studied it," Martin said, "in history."

"History? I suppose it is." She fell silent, massaging the deformed joints of one hand with the ball of her thumb.

"Sorry I'm late, cully," Prince said. "Otherwise engaged." He winked at the old lady and took one of Martin's sandwiches. "How about a cuppa?"

The old lady took a Thermos from her basket. "You're very welcome . . ."

"Wouldn't deprive you. Britain's life-blood." Prince led Martin towards the buffet, stopping before they reached the counter. "Got to talk. Enemy on the warpath. But I've got ammunition." He took a sliver of soap from his pocket.

"The ticket-collector?"

"Who else. Record at stake. Sit opposite each other. You look one way, I'll look the other. There's a doctor in the next carriage," he added mysteriously.

"Got it," said Martin, not sure what he had got.

"Now listen carefully," Prince said, glass bead in his ear sparkling. "Just in case the enemy pulls a flanker. Ninety-one Dean Street. Four o'clock. Don't be late."

They returned to the old lady who smiled gently at them.

"Lot of work ahead on behalf of my clients," Prince said. "Means tests, that sort of thing." He stretched out his hand, nails savagely bitten, and took another sandwich. Chewing vigorously, he said: "Few sidelines too. Tell you about them one day."

"Where do you live in London?" Martin asked.

24

"Where I lay my head," Prince said.

The old lady asked: "What work do you do, young man? You have an interesting face."

"Scheme, ma'am, scheme."

"My husband was clever. Bit of a barrack-room lawyer in the army."

"Got to be a corporal, ma'am. Halfway between discipline and obedience. That's where the schemes are, ma'am."

"I suppose you're right. Where were you born?"

"England," Prince said.

"My husband came from Streatham."

"Where did your family come from?" Martin asked Prince.

Prince's response was alarming. One hand to his heart, he threw himself sideways and began to groan.

The old lady said: "Perhaps we should pull the communication cord," but a man with raw-shaved cheeks sitting in the opposite corner said: "No point, we're pulling into Nuneaton."

Bubbles dripped from Prince's mouth as the ticket collector, a plump-cheeked Pakistani, materialised.

The man in the opposite corner said: "Guide his tongue so he doesn't bite it. It's the only thing to do with epilepsy. He probably heard a warning, bells, something like that," he added without moving.

Martin spoke as though hypnotised: "There's a doctor in the next carriage."

The ticket collector said: "How do you know?" and then: "Which carriage?"

Martin pointed ahead. "At the end. Wearing glasses."

Snapping his clippers, the ticket-collector hurried away, his departure exciting a miraculously curative effect on Prince who stood up, winked elaborately at the old lady, saying to Martin: "You're learning, cully, you're learning," and was gone, to be seen seconds later striding briskly along the platform.

"Well," said the old lady.

"Wicked," said Martin.

They smiled conspiratorially.

The ticket collector pointed his clippers at Martin. "Aiding and abetting," he said. "That is what you are doing."

"He wasn't a doctor?"

"Lord, yes, he was a doctor all right. Of theology." The collector snipped his clippers near Martin's nose. "I'll remem-

25

ber you, sir," he said. "Oh yes, I'll remember you."

When he had gone Martin kicked the sliver of soap under the seat. The old lady closed her eyes. While she dozed she continued to massage her misshapen knuckles, first with one thumb, then the other.

Rugby.

Still a long way from Watford, the frontier town between north and south. The fields were greener now, fallen snow scattered in wings and small drifts as the train approached the more prosperous reaches of the British Isles.

Four o'clock. Dean Street. Where was that? Take a taxi, he supposed, break into his savings, £64 – £50 of it sewn inside the lining of his reefer jacket – already depleted by the Pullman fare. And then what? Department of Health and Social Services and a Job Centre? When he was earning he would investigate the uncles. He imagined their wives reclining at the hairdressers while his mother applied an ancient curler to her grey hair, and became angry.

Snug towns inched past the window, accelerated and were gone. He saw warm-bricked mansions inviolate among lawns and beech trees and Jaguars and Rovers nosing through gentle swells of countryside, and streams in no hurry to find their rivers.

Soon the stretches of countryside became shorter, interruptions more measured, greenery divided into parks and recreation grounds and winter-nipped gardens. A terrace of grand houses with cream porches, windows like lorgnettes, and a hibernating cricket ground glided past. The houses shrank, streets narrowed. Kensal Green which wasn't green at all, a tunnel, a factory, a scrapyard, a maze of thin terraces revolving on a pivot.

The old lady awoke and offered him a boiled sweet. "London can be a lonely place," she said. "This is where I live." She rummaged in her handbag and handed him a card. *Richmond Hill, Richmond*. "Bring your friend," she added. "He's very enterprising. Just like my husband," as though he were still alive.

A voice issued from loudspeakers. "We are now approaching London Euston. Thank you for travelling British Rail and we hope to see you again soon."

Gleaming railway lines crossing paths, predatory trains.

Martin lifted down the old lady's case, then his own.

The train stopped and sighed.

Martin's case burst as he alighted, distributing his worldly possessions across the platform.

It was 9.34.

*   *   *

London assaulted him.

The indifference of the purposeful pedestrians in Euston Road; the inexorable traffic; a street-corner harridan brandishing an empty bottle; policemen talking into their handsets and staring at him; turbaned Sikhs and back-packed Germans and blacks insulated by Walkman music.

London marched around him, isolating him.

He crossed the street in front of a bus. The driver, braking, thrust a fist at him. What if the suitcase, which he had since deposited at Euston, had burst here? The accident on the platform would stay with him forever; the pert girl picking up the bottle of vitamin tablets which his mother had slipped inside, toothpaste squashed beneath a heel, the balding hair-brush . . .

Opposite the Gothic ramparts of King's Cross and St. Pancras he turned into an area of small streets terraced with boarding houses, coats of fresh paint drawing attention to their age. Should he book into one, establish a base? No, Prince first – if he reached London on his journey into the record books. He emerged into a long, dull street, Gray's Inn Road. A young man with a shaven skull wearing motor-cycle boots and a flying jacket detached himself from a girl with muddy legs and spiked purple and yellow hair. "Got a ciggie?"

Martin said: "Sorry, I don't smoke."

"There are worse vices." He nodded at a poster behind Martin. AIDS – DON'T DIE OF IGNORANCE. "Watch it." He returned to the girl shaking his bullet head.

Martin was tempted to hurry back to Euston, pick up his treacherous suitcase and catch the next train back to Liverpool. A taxi approached, black and square like the Liverpool cabs. He stuck out a hand.

"Where to, guv?" The driver, flabby with a monk's fringe of grey hair, chewed gum energetically.

"Dean Street." Martin climbed into the back of the cab.

27

"Which one, guv? Forest Gate or Soho?"

"Soho," Martin said. It sounded right.

"Watch out for the clip-joints," as the taxi weaved through the traffic. "Picked up a punter the other day who was charged £100 for two near-beers. Thought he was going to get his leg over." He swung the taxi into a U-turn. "Scouse?"

"And proud of it."

"Got a few bob then. Building site, casual labour, two hundred quid a week undeclared, then back to Scouseland to pick up your benefits? The black economy. Nothing like it, is there, guv?"

Martin glanced at his digital watch. "I wouldn't know," he said. "I've only been in London for twenty-eight minutes."

The driver drove on in silence.

Martin watched the digits on the meter flickering. If he got out now he could walk.

"Is it much further?"

"A few bob. Greedy buggers these meters. You skint?"

"I've got enough," Martin said.

"You're lucky. Here," leaning forward and extracting a card from behind a photograph of a woman with a sad face, "take this if you ever want a good night's kip. B and B down Vauxhall Bridge Road. My brother's drum. He won't rip you off."

Martin slid the card into his wallet next to the old lady's and thanked the driver.

"You won't be the first to find the streets aren't paved with gold. Watch out for the rogues. Which end of Dean Street?"

"Here," Martin said. He climbed out.

"Two quid, guv."

"It's more." Martin pointed at the meter.

"Two quid. You watch out for the villains now. Thick on the ground in Soho. Know why it's called that?"

Martin shook his head.

"An old hunting cry — we cabbies know our London. Know who lived in Dean Street?"

"Dixie Dean?" Martin smiled for the first time since he had left home. "Used to nod them in for the Toffees. Everton," he explained.

"Karl Marx," the driver told him. He took the two £1 coins. "Take care, I've got a son your age," and drove away chewing.

He had a long time to kill. He walked past sex shops, touts

beckoning from stale doorways – at this hour? – restaurants, Italians and Greeks debating on the pavement . . .

Memorising landmarks, he made his way to Piccadilly. So now he had arrived. The centre of the world. He sat beneath Eros beside a huddle of Australians drinking beer from cans. The cold, no longer blunted by snow, slipped inside his reefer jacket.

He wandered past a dreamy young man with poet's hair strumming a guitar beside a beret containing a few coins, to the cinemas of Leicester Square. He passed Charlie Chaplin in bronze and, at the corner of Charing Cross Road, Sir Henry Irving.

The National Gallery in Trafalgar Square reminded him of the museum and art gallery in William Brown Street where he had once been lost, Nelson's Column reminded him of Wellington's Column.

He passed the time with the tourists and pigeons.

*   *   *

The premises at 91/92 Dean Street are a monument to politicians who care. Not that they have necessarily been present when guests take a compulsory shower or when their clothing is searched for bugs, not that they have smelled the medicated shampoo and leaked urine, not that they have slept in the dormitories beneath ceiling tiles broken to admit bottles of prohibited liquor, but it is, nevertheless, a relief to know that such establishments as the West End House Resettlement Unit do exist in London to offer the homeless an alternative to the cardboard shanties under Hungerford Bridge, a night's kip in a cruising homosexual's home or a tenure in a squat. This is the Welfare State at its best and one day something will have to be done to create a society where such expedients are not necessary. But not too recklessly: the scourge of unemployment is universal.

To be allocated one of the ninety beds you should be "without a settled way of life" as defined by the Department of Health and Social Services. To get it free you should be without funds. When Prince materialised in Diadem Court at the rear of the premises, once a hospital for nervous diseases, he was therefore agitated.

29

Joining Martin in the queue he said urgently: "Bread, bonce, boodle — give it to me. Once you're accepted come out here again and I'll hand it back. Then I can go in skint myself."

"I've only got a few pounds."

"Hand them over," Prince said, glancing round like a fugitive.

Martin hesitated; but he was an alien and this was Prince's city.

The queue — blacks and whites and Asians, the street-wise and the dazed — inched forward. Martin fingered his reefer jacket near the hem where the £50 was hidden.

"That too," Prince hissed. "First place they look."

"I can't . . ."

"Slit it, cully. Use your loaf." He handed Martin a razor-blade and screened him with a copy of the *Evening Standard*.

The queue moved forward again; only four ahead of Martin.

"But . . ."

"Slit it!"

Martin severed the stitching and eased out the five £10 notes.

Prince snatched them. "And the rest." He handed Martin back a 50p coin. "Keep that. Don't overplay your hand," and was gone.

Behind Martin a big man with a creased face sang softly and repetitively to himself.

Inside the building a brisk receptionist with knowing eyes questioned Martin.

"Name?"

"Martin James Renshaw."

"Age?"

"Nineteen."

"Just?"

"Christmas Day," Martin said.

"Bad luck. Where did you spend last night?"

"Liverpool."

"Address?"

Martin gave it.

"So you've come to find fame and fortune?"

"Something like that."

"And you're broke?"

Grey eyes searched Martin's face, humour creased at their corners.

"Fifty p."

"Not much of an investment for fame and fortune."

"My train fare, a meal, a taxi . . ."

"Taxi?" Even this decent man who had heard every evasion was surprised.

"I didn't know how to find Dean Street."

"You could have asked, son. There are buses, tubes."

"I panicked," Martin said.

"And blew your money?"

Martin nodded.

I don't believe you, the man's eyes said, but what the hell.

"Who sent you here?"

"I read about it."

"We try," the receptionist said. "We even get some regulars. That must prove something. You'll get a two-course dinner. Not half bad. And there's a TV lounge. Lights out at 10.30. A bit of cleaning tomorrow morning. Some of the punters go AWOL before we can put a broom in their hands. You won't be one of those, will you, Martin?"

Martin said he wouldn't.

"Sign here then." A statement of his circumstances. "And make sure no one pinches your money."

Martin said he would. Idiot!

He showered; his clothes were inspected and he was given a bed in a dormitory with graffiti-resistant walls. He emerged into the cold. Of Prince there was no sign. And this time he's got my money. Martin fingered the 50p coin in his pocket; not even enough to reclaim his luggage.

Prince rounded the corner of Diadem Court. With him was a young black with a shy smile and an athlete's walk. He wore running shoes and jeans patched at the knees and a mauve, V-necked sweater.

"This is Charlie," Prince said. "Just caught him making a run for it. Been on the Jack again, Charlie?"

"Had a few," Charlie said, "to keep the cold out." His speech was jumbled, as though he thought ahead of his words.

"Keep off the Jack," Prince said to Martin. "Cider, milk and meths. Devil's brew. Here." He gave Martin the money. "And my pickings." He handed over a thick wad of notes and winked. "There's always a wheeze, cully." He tapped the side of his nose. "Now make yourself scarce. They're not stupid in

31

there."

Martin wandered into Dean Street. It was dusk and touts were calling boldly from topless bars. One establishment offered THREE IN A BED – LIVE SHOW. A policeman whispered into his handset. A girl stared at Martin and ran her tongue from one corner of the mouth to the other. What would Karl Marx have made of that?

Flakes of snow peeled from the darkening sky. Martin circled Soho Square before returning to 91/92. The courtyard was empty and he went inside.

He ate chicken and chips and tinned apricots and custard, and watched television, an inane quiz, and the news which was concerned mostly with snow in Yorkshire and death in Beirut. Then he adjourned to the dormitory. Prince and Charlie were in beds on one side of him, a belligerent, bright-eyed Scotsman on the other.

Prince, whispering, asked for the money. "Safer with me, cully."

"I can look after it," Martin said. "I can look after myself."

"Don't bank on it."

"I'm not daft."

In the dark Martin found a hole in the mattress and slipped the money inside.

Conversations lingered, whispers, furtive movement. If his mother could see him now!

Prince was talking about Charlie. "The black hope. Jesse Owens ..." Martin gathered that Charlie hoped to compete later that year in the 800 metres in the Special Olympics for the mentally handicapped. "Been training, Charlie?" Prince asked.

A sleepy jumble of words.

Prince who appeared to understand him said: "Been on the lam? Not good enough, Charlie. Not good enough by a long chalk. Jogging in the morning, okay?"

"Okay," Charlie said.

From the other side of the dormitory a growling voice: "Fucking shut up and go to sleep."

Martin closed his eyes. He saw tall ships. Heard the creak of the stairs. Heard his mother's voice: "Time to get up, lad."

He shivered.

He closed his eyes. He was on a train and it was taking him home.

When he awoke his money had gone.

CHAPTER 3

————— ◆ —————

The girl walked angrily, shoes breaking webs of ice and brushing aside nests of snow on the suburban pastures of Hampstead Heath.

She was seventeen — nearly eighteen as she preferred it — and as she approached the high ground near Jack Straw's Castle she tried to analyse the cause of the anger.

Nothing disagreeable had occurred that morning. She had fed the squirrels in the garden, breakfasted on Muesli and orange juice, spoken perfunctorily with her mother, and her step-father behind the pink pages of the *Financial Times*, telephoned Katherine about the meeting that evening and walked to the heath to think.

Breath smoking on the iced air, she stopped, unaware that a young man was following her, and gazed across the dormitories of London, a resolute girl with fine dark hair and discerning eyes set beneath an embryonic frown that would one day settle permanently unless its questions were answered.

Perhaps it was the fact that nothing untoward had happened that had generated the inchoate anger. London was full of pockets of unrest and here she was eating Muesli and walking across the Elysian fields of North London. She recalled that, in 1780, the Gordon Rioters had attempted mayhem on the heath, then remembered that they had been defeated by drink in the Spaniards hostelry.

Was her outrage to be so ignominiously quelled? It certainly wasn't being injected with adrenalin by the nuclear disarmament meetings she and Katherine attended. They were predictable. What she wanted to protest about was complacency. And those who, practising it, converted souls into statistics.

Her step-father folding his Financial Times *with plump fingers, finishing his coffee and, yawning, making his way to the hall, heels tapping crisply on the parquet flooring. The Porsche in which he drove to the City, firing and, with a blue-smoked cough, moving down the drive. Her mother, dieting, biting the flesh from the slice of lemon in her tea and smiling vaguely across the table.*

But was privilege an adequate reason for outrage? Her step-father had worked hard for his life-style — he frequently expanded on this theme and there was no reason to doubt him — and by helping to maintain a "buoyant economy" he created employment.

An encouraging drop in the unemployed in the past year. Only two million, five hundred thousand, give or take 100,000 still out of work.

Statistics the currency of complacency.

She kicked a beer can.

A hundred yards away the young man watched.

The cold coaxed petals of snow from the sky. Even in winter the heath had a contented air about it. Such names — Kenwood, Parliament Hill, Judge's Walk, King's Bench Avenue ... Establishment.

She passed a copse abandoned for winter. A page of newspaper skipped past carrying news of a fledgling riot in Brixton. She had watched it on television. What had remained obscure was the reason for it. Like the reason for my shapeless wrath.

She plunged her hands into the pockets of her jeans jacket and, red scarf flowing behind her like a banner, tramped on, shoes crunching on the frozen grass.

The young man gained fifty yards.

What also aggravated her was not merely the indulgence of older generations but their platitudes. They surely realised that the middle-aged had always patronised the young so why perpetuate a cliché? They bracketed rebellion with measles.

The young man said: "Are you Jenny Renshaw?"

She said she was and examined the intruder into her thoughts. He was tall with black curls unfashionably cut and he looked like a seaman who had returned from oceans he had never wanted to visit.

35

"I was outside your house this morning."

"There is a bell," Jenny Renshaw said. "You could have rung. What do you want?"

"To talk. You've no idea how long it took me to find the courage to speak . . ."

"Forty-five minutes," she said, glancing at her watch. "The time I left the house. What do you want to talk about?" How did he know her name?

She turned and began to walk back towards The Bishops Avenue. Not just Bishops, *The*.

"It's a long story."

"Are you trying to pick me up?"

"God, no."

"No need to be quite so emphatic."

"Please don't be smart," he said. "It really did take courage."

"I'm sorry."

"The house," he said, "it was so big."

"But comfortable. Not remote."

"Intimidating," he said. "We live in a wendy house."

"You're from the north. Manchester?"

"You're not smart with accents."

"I know. The common touch. I haven't got it."

"Liverpool," Martin Renshaw said. "Scouse."

She frowned.

"Scouse," he said. "Lobscouse, an old Scandinavian dish that Liverpool adopted because it was good and cheap. Meat, vegetables and potatoes . . ."

"This is ridiculous," she said. "Who are you?"

"Martin. Your cousin. Although we're not really related because you're Harry Renshaw's step-daughter."

"The son of . . ."

"Jim Renshaw."

"I know Walter," she said. "And Jack, of course – but Jim . . . Harry hardly ever speaks about him."

"I'm not surprised. He's poor, you see."

"You can't hate Harry already. You haven't met him. Have you?"

"Not yet."

"Walter's very noble. But Jack's fun. You'd like him." She found it easy to speak to him: they anticipated each other. "He's a thief."

36

"That's his profession?"

"According to Harry."

"And what's my father, according to Harry?"

"Nothing," she admitted. "I'm sorry."

She paused and looked around. Distracted, she had wandered from her normal route home. The snow-patched grass ahead sloped down to the gypsies who had pitched camp again. According to the newspapers they were to be dispersed at the end of the week after the festive spirit of goodwill had finally spent itself.

Police watched wearily as a group of chanting demonstrators waved a banner in their faces. It was a tattered sheet and its message in black aerosol read: ROMANIES ROAM NO MORE. But the protestors weren't gypsies and the subjects of their protest appeared indifferent to their champions. Inside the semi-circle of dilapidated caravans and sagging, single-decker buses they went about their business as though they were alone; the men split wood and built fires and the women hung out laundry and suckled babies and the smell of cooking meat flavoured the air. In two days' time they would be lifted in the hands of the law and deposited elsewhere: they accepted this: it was written.

Jenny Renshaw stood still, mittened hands clasped, and let her anger flow but it still foundered: it was not meant for these particular outcasts. Were they true gypsies? Whatever they were their plight was woeful. So why didn't they arouse her sympathies? Perhaps because their adversity was historical and owed nothing to the injustices of today.

"Where are you living?" she asked Martin Renshaw.

"In a doss-house."

"Why did you come to Hampstead?"

"To make a start."

To beg? "You're not very forthcoming."

"Another time." He looked at her sharply. "You think I came to borrow money?"

She didn't reply: she boasted to herself that she never lied but suspected that evasion was probably dishonest.

"I don't beg," he said. "I came to London to work."

"For my step-father?"

"For Sainsbury's," he said. "Or Finefare or the Pizza Hut or the Bank of England or maybe in the summer picking hops."

"But why . . ."

"Forget it," he said.

"Could you come to dinner? One day next week?"

"And bring a doggy bag with me?"

"You're too sensitive," she said.

A boy with gypsy-black hair burst from the group of protestors and, head low, elbows pumping, ran towards them and she could see the fear in his eyes.

From the demonstrators a cry: "Stop him."

A policeman raised his hand but the boy, fourteen or fifteen, curved his run. The policeman dived, losing his peaked cap; his shoulder caught the boy knee-high and brought him down. The boy struggled and the policeman hit him on the side of the head and blood flowed onto his fist and Jenny was at the policeman, pulling at the collar of his tunic, shouting, "Leave him alone," anger at last finding direction. "What's he done, run? Is that a crime?"

And then the boy was free and running again and the policeman was standing up and speaking into his handset. Then, retrieving his cap with the chequered pattern above the peak, he said: "Why?" And there was weariness on his young, flushed face.

"Because he hadn't done anything."

"Victimisation?" He brushed the pattern with the tips of his fingers.

Martin said: "It's as good a word as any," and the policeman, turning on him with deliberation, said: "Keep out of this, son," and Jenny Renshaw said to Martin: "I don't need your help, this is my fight," but the anger was losing direction again.

The policeman said: "I should arrest you."

"Arrest me then." He was making her into a suffragette.

"Give me one good reason why I shouldn't."

Martin said: "Because she thought she was helping an innocent boy."

"You want to be nicked, son?"

"On what charge?"

"Don't make me cry." The policeman stood in front of Jenny, hands on his hips. "I'll give you one good reason. Because stupidity isn't a crime. Have you got a kid brother?"

She shook her head.

"Someone you're fond of? Parents, dog, terrapin?"

"My mother, I suppose."

"You suppose? Jesus!" The policeman put on his cap and looked older. "Well, supposing that young innocent," pointing in the direction the boy had taken, "had slipped this between the ribs of the mother you suppose you love one dark night."

He pulled a handkerchief from his pocket, bent down and picked up a metal handle lying in the grass. He pushed a button and a blade leaped out.

"How did you know?" she asked.

"He isn't a gypsy: he's a pikey — a fake. He's also a thief. After he'd slipped the knife between the ribs of your mother he would probably have cut the pearls from her throat. You come from a good family? Lots of jewellery?"

"Why don't you just arrest me," Jenny said.

The policeman picked up a wallet. "Not his, of course. Probably belongs to one of the good guys protesting on behalf of the gypsies. Ironic, isn't it."

A man with soft hair tied in a bun ran up and pointed at the wallet and said: "Hey, that's mine," as though the policeman had appropriated it.

"Just a minute, sir. All in good time." The policeman addressed Jenny. "Just remember in future, miss, that we're here to protect you. Although sometimes I wonder why, I really do." And: "Hey, what have we here?" as another policeman, emerging from behind a cluster of trees, frog-marched the boy across the grass.

As the boy went past, held in a half-nelson, he spat.

As they began to re-climb the slope Martin said: "You weren't to know."

"Please," she said, "go away," and there were tears on her cheeks and he went because he understood.

*   *   *

On the bus he considered the last five confusing days of his life.

Prince handing over the money in a caff in Tottenham Court Road saying: "Another lesson, cully, never sleep with it."

"You took it?"

"Charlie didn't, did you?"

Charlie, munching a bacon sandwich, washed it down with tea stiff with sugar and shook his head.

"Was it that easy?"

"Mattresses, first place to look. Saved someone else the trouble. What's the plot now? Sign on? A few words in your ear first. No charge."

He delved into the pocket of his black overcoat, produced a sheaf of greasy papers and laid them on the table. "First accommodation. Six pounds ninety a night, maximum eight weeks."

The proprietor of the café, thin with a pitted face, said: "Leave it out, Prince, this isn't an office."

Prince, tapping the side of his nose, said: "Don't forget your old man's war pension. Special pamphlet on the way. And get us another cuppa while you're there."

"What about me?" Charlie asked.

"You? You're laughing. What don't you qualify for? Except Leaflet 17A."

"What's that?" Charlie asked.

"Maternity grant. Lump sum. Well it would be, wouldn't it." Charlie laughed hugely.

Prince sipped his fresh mug of tea and ran one long-nailed finger down his lists. "Attendance, child benefit, child's special allowance, constant attendance, death grant . . ."

He licked the point of a yellow pencil busily.

From time to time regular customers who came to relax and study form greeted Prince warmly and thanked him for services rendered; Prince, immersed in his calculations, acknowledged them with the wave of an entrepreneur. "Laundry," he said, scribbling, "always good for a few bob. Never forget your dirty washing, Martin." Martin tried to isolate Prince's accent; but it was non-regional, classless. And he never swore. "Housing benefit supplement, notorious for foul-ups," talking to himself. "Means-tested, too. Lot of means-testing these days, Martin. Upsets the senior citizens. They talk about Jarrow. It's the indignity . . . Know why some old codgers sleep in cardboard shanties? The indignity, that's why. Fight for king and country and end up in a carton of Heinz 57 varieties. Is that the way to run a country? War tomorrow, you and me fighting. Fifty years on and we're sleeping in crates of Brand X soap powder. Do you know what really aggravates me, Martin?"

"Injustice?"

"The fact that so many people don't know what's going on in their own country. Privilege. What is it? A suit of armour. There's a shanty town at night next to the Royal Festival Hall.

40

Out they come into the rain, up with their umbrellas, into a taxi ... What shanty town? Jobs for everyone if they want to work ...”

“Some people care,” Martin said. “The people at Dean Street.”

“They care,” Prince said, “because they know. Pity you haven’t got a war wound,” he said scribbling.

Charlie stood up suddenly, knocking the table and slopping tea from the mugs. He said he was going jogging.

“Going back to your school?”

Charlie shook his head. “Dean Street,” he said.

“You be there,” Prince said. As Charlie loped out of the caff he told Martin: “He’s supposed to be running a hundred miles a week.”

“Does he stand a chance in the race?”

“Depends on his coach.”

“You?”

“He was being coached at a centre for the mentally handicapped but he ran away. Want the job?”

“In Dean Street?”

“We’ll be getting a house soon.”

“We?”

“A few of us.”

“What sort of a house?”

“A squat. Want to join us?”

“Let me get settled in first,” Martin said.

“Suit yourself. Sign on first. Don’t let on that you’ve got any bread. Lucky you have, eh, cully?”

They strode out of the caff without paying and navigated their way through the tourists studying the bookshops of Charing Cross Road. Americans in determined clothes, Australians snubbing the cold, map-reading Germans and Italians, Dutch and French and Scandinavians.

“I’ve written down where you should go,” Prince said, pointing at his scribble. “Good luck and don’t end up in a cardboard box.”

Martin went first to the Department of Employment in Chadwick Street, SW1, near the Horticultural Hall where he registered and was given a Form B1 to enable him to claim supplementary benefits. To stake the claims he went to the DHSS in Regency Street close-by. He was told that for two months he could draw £70 a week, inclusive of meals, plus £10 personal allowance and a little extra for laundry.

Later he went to a Job Centre. An Asian girl with beautiful eyes shook her head sorrowfully when his lack of qualifications was bared. Did he drive? He shook his head; they stared sadly at each other. But there were jobs and the Government was now paying £20 a week to encourage applicants to take low-paid work instead of vegetating on the dole. New vistas opened for Martin: he discovered that he could become a petrol-pump attendant, a floor-sweeper at a burger joint, a washer-up in a staff canteen . . . He said he would call back. The girl's hands unclasped on the desk; like the petals of a flower, he thought.

He consulted Prince's list of agencies which helped the destitute, settling for the Piccadilly Advice Centre in Shaftesbury Avenue. It was staffed by two girls who cared, but there were messages of cynicism in their gaze: they cared for individuals, about Mankind they weren't so sure. One of them advised him to spend his £6.90 night accommodation benefit at a bed and breakfast establishment. They were better than the workhouse, she implied, but not much.

Martin bought a money-belt and spent another night at Dean Street with Prince. Of Charlie there was no sign. "Full of repentance," Prince said in the dormitory. "Back at the centre. Training. All very hopeful – until he goes on the Jack again."

"Can you buy meths easily?"

"As winking. Anything's better than crack though. Cocaine, baking powder and water. Poor old Charlie. If he got into that it would be his last race, all the way to the cemetery."

Martin closed his eyes, debating whether to tell Prince about uncles Harry, Jack and Walter, and his suspicions about them. He decided against it: Prince would have an answer: he wanted his own. Bed-springs creaked rhythmically close-by. Footsteps. His hand strayed to his money-belt. He decided to go first to Harry's house in Hampstead, and then find a B and B in the streets opposite King's Cross.

The footsteps retreated.

The following morning he caught a Northern Line underground from Tottenham Court Road to Golders Green and walked to The Bishops Avenue. The house intimidated him. A stone maiden aimed a lichen-covered arse at him from a moss-green pool. Tall trees stood stiff in the cold; tall chimneys smoked. A police car coasted past – Martin remembered reading about a murder here – and a green Harrods van pulled up at the kerb. He strolled down the affluent street as the girl, surely Jenny Renshaw, walked angrily down the drive and out of the gate.

*   *   *

After the incident on the heath Martin left Hampstead where Byron, Keats, Robert Louis Stevenson and Freud once lived and caught a bus to Euston Square which contained the head-quarters of the miners' and railwaymen's unions. Suitcase in hand, he crossed the now-familiar Euston Road in search of a new home.

CHAPTER 4

❖

Adversity is the father of philanthropy and nowhere was this more evident than in the bed-and-breakfast hostels of London.

The DHSS allowed homeless new arrivals £6.90 a night for accommodation, scarcely a realistic profit margin for even the most humanitarian b-and-b landlords. So what they did was strip the rooms so that they could sleep five or six or more.

In this way a landlord with a mere five rooms could make £140 a night, or £50,000 a year, and reflect on vacation in Florida how he had kept young vagrants off the pitiless streets.

There is a rash of b-and-bs just south of the Euston Road which is also a popular bedding ground for prostitutes, both male and female, and terrorists lying low.

It is popular, too, with the police.

Most of the b-and-bs are neat and inviting from the outside and with freshly painted bricks, glazed porches – some with a Spanish or French theme – and comforting names popular in Blackpool or Morecambe or Scarborough where many prospective tenants once spent holidays.

Larkman House was, from the outside, just such an establishment even if, like some of its neighbours, the interior did not quite live up to expectations. Come in and make yourself at home cajoled the mock-Georgian front-door with the brass knocker; and you could almost smell the geraniums in the sun-lounge, taste the brown Windsor soup, tap the barometer in the hall.

And, indeed, the Larkmans, Bruce and Brenda (*B and B for b-and-b*), were hospitable but, like other landlords providing a service at knock-down prices, they had to impose house rules and cut down on luxuries. A sign in the hall stated NO SITE BOOTS, NO LIAISONS, NO FOREIGN CURRENCY and sometimes the faint-hearted, suspecting that this also implied NO HOPE, fled elsewhere; but such are the laws of supply and demand that they were often forced to return and the Larkmans, saddened but forgiving, squeezed them in for an extra £1 a night.

Breakfasts were frugal – the Larkmans possessed their own cereal and grapefruit-slice mountains purchased at the cash-and-carry – but none the less healthy for it, the bedrooms necessarily cramped and lit by naked bulbs; and because many of the guests were one-night transients the bed-linen was often steam-pressed rather than laundered.

The walls of the bedrooms were bare, those in the hall and breakfast-room adorned with framed photographs of the Larkmans in their vaudeville days – she had been a soubrette specialising in risqué numbers, he had delivered humorous and patriotic monologues – and pictures of deceased stars autographed in ink that had turned the colour of dried blood.

Despite the domestic turn their lives had taken both Bruce and Brenda Larkman were still unmistakably theatrical. Brenda, conceding that she was now forty-five, had retained her coquetry, Bruce had become sonorous, projecting his voice beyond the footlights of the past. He spent his well-earned leisure writing letters of moral outrage to the unreceptive editors of newspapers; she liked to swap badinage with the Irish in the pub round the corner, suggesting from time to time that terms at Larkman House were negotiable; thus a strapping building-site worker could have bed, breakfast *and* Brenda for a mere £3.

Although the only meal served was breakfast the whole house smelled mysteriously of fish pie.

It was 4 pm when Martin knocked on the door; it was answered by Brenda Larkman, glass of cooking sherry in hand. Her red hair was disarrayed, make-up smudged as though she had been crying; she wore a mauve dressing-gown extravagantly open at the breast and pink mules. She led Martin into the kitchen where Bruce was putting the finishing touches to a letter to a local newspaper about sex on television; as he scanned the lines he combed his grey, poet's hair with his fingers.

Brenda pointed to a chair, poured herself more sherry and,

eyeing Martin speculatively, said: "Scouse?" And when Martin said he was: "One night stand?" and Bruce said: "Money up front, you understand," holding his letter as though it were a script.

"Is it cheaper weekly?" Martin asked.

"Cheaper?" Bruce signed his letter with a flourish. "Couldn't be much cheaper than £6.90 a night, could it? You youngsters . . ." With a shake of his head he mourned the iniquities of youth.

Brenda said: "I've always liked Scousers. We often played the Liverpool Empire."

"We played every city of any consequence," Bruce said, addressing an envelope. "I used to make people believe in their country again. Just like they did in the war. *There'll always be an England*, that sort of spirit."

"I used to make them laugh," Mrs. Larkman said.

Martin inspected the kitchen. Clearly it was where the Larkmans lived. Two pre-packed meals, chicken suprême, stood on the draining-board, newspapers and magazines leaned in piles on top of the fridge, a moulting canary skittered up and down its perch in a cage bouncing on the end of a spring, a television flickered soundlessly in the corner, quiz-master and contestants all with pink apoplectic faces.

Bruce read his letter for the last time; his lips moved; its content pleased him. He read a few words aloud. "How can we expect a reversion to the God-fearing morals of yesteryear when the sexual act is cheapened by indecent exposure on the small screen?"

"I always finished with a song," Brenda said. "A little saucy, perhaps, nothing crude."

Fearing that she was going to break into song, Martin said: "Could I see the room?"

"Let's see the colour of your money first, lad," Bruce said.

"If you did want to stay on a weekly basis," Brenda said, "we might be able to arrange a little reduction." She searched for the smudged lipstick with the tip of her tongue. "Say £6.50 a night?"

"She's soft," Bruce informed Martin. "Still if you want it weekly. Money up front, of course." He stuck an adhesive Larkman House address on the top of the letter, folded it, slipped it into a manilla envelope and sealed it expansively.

"I can only take it on a nightly basis at the moment," Martin said.

"Until your Giro arrives?"

"I'm a bit short at the moment," Martin confessed.

"Don't worry," Brenda said. "We'll make adjustments when the time comes."

The canary buried its head beneath its wing; a feather pirouetted to the sand. In the corner the face of the quiz-master turned carmine.

"That's very kind of you," Martin said.

Bruce stood up, shorter than Martin had supposed. He adjusted the hair above his ears and held out his hand. "Six pounds ninety until you take it on a long-term basis. You young people . . ."

Martin handed him the money, counting the coins exactly.

"You'll have to abide by the house rules," Bruce said. "First and foremost no visitors. You understand what I mean by visitors?"

"Girls?"

"This is a decent house," Bruce said.

"I don't know any girls," Martin said, reflecting that he did know Harry Renshaw's step-daughter; the prospect of her visiting Larkman House was unlikely.

"No girls?" Brenda looked astonished. "A good-looking lad like you?"

"I've got a girlfriend in Liverpool."

"No drinking," Bruce said. "No drugs. Lights out by 10.30." He looked at his watch. "I'm off to the post office."

Brenda led the way up the stairs. There were two photographs on the walls of the landing, one of Max Miller, the other of Brenda Larkman wearing a sparkling dress with a short, flouncy skirt and fishnet stockings. "The Pavilion, Torquay," she said. "I used to kick my legs a bit in those days. I've still got quite good legs. For an old hoofer like me, that is."

She opened a door. The first thing Martin saw was a notice NO SMOKING. The room smelled of stale cigarette smoke. There were five beds indecently close together.

Someone had scrawled on the wall: *Brenda goes.* Brenda didn't appear to notice it.

"Cheap and cheerful," she said. "You should have seen some of the digs we stayed in."

There were stains on the floral wallpaper where insects had been squashed; floorboards were visible where the linoleum had worn thin between the beds.

"The bathroom's at the end of the corridor," Brenda said. "Three so you can all get a shave. Most of the lads shave at night. You've got quite a beard." She touched his chin.

Martin walked to the door. "I'll get my suitcase," he said.

"How about a little drinky before the rush starts?"

"I'm not a sherry drinker," Martin said.

"Not much of a drinker at all, I shouldn't think. And you don't smoke, I can see that by your fingers. What do you do, Martin?"

"Shoot smack," he wanted to tell her; instead he said: "I didn't have much money in Liverpool."

"The welfare will look after you now," she said. "Got a job yet?" She led the way downstairs.

"Not yet," Martin said.

"I like to get to know *some* of my young men," said Brenda pouring Martin a beer in the kitchen. "You know, take an interest in them. Follow their careers. Do you want to tell me about yourself, Martin? It's a pity we haven't got more time, but they all seem to come at once. Perhaps in the morning . . ." She poured herself more sherry.

"There's not much to tell."

"Is she pretty?"

"Joanne? She's very attractive, Irish . . ."

"I hope you'll stay," Brenda said. "You're – different . . . Some of the young men are, you know, crude."

"Are there any regulars in my room?"

"A couple. Geordie and a Brummie. Nice boys, well-mannered . . ."

Martin wondered which one of them had scrawled *Brenda goes*.

The panel game was coming to an end, credits rolling across faces that had now deepened to crimson.

The front-door bell rang.

"Here we go," Brenda said.

Martin heard three sets of footsteps clumping up the stairs. Twenty pounds and 70 pence.

The door leading from the kitchen opened and Bruce came in. Mission accomplished, said his expression.

He sat down and leaned confidentially across the table. "In case you were wondering," he said, "we don't encourage blacks."

*   *   *

At night the city, in repose, breathes deeply.

In the vaulted seats of government emptied of acrimonious debate; in royal parks as last lovers depart; in Mammon's towers and mansions undisturbed by the computerised flutter of profit and loss; in churches – All Hallows-by-the-Tower, St. Andrew's-by-the-Wardrobe, St. Ethelburga-the-Virgin – where prayers hang murmuring in incense; in avenues and arcades of shops (not Burlington if the poltergeist is abroad); beneath great bridges as the Thames slows in the moonlight. In Buckingham Palace with the Queen; in the Tower with the ravens. In parades of terrace houses asleep on duty; in squats and stews and cardboard boxes.

Martin, listening, found comfort and as he coasted towards sleep he looked down upon the dormitory in Larkman House.

He saw the Brummie in the corner sharing a joint with the Geordie, smelled its herbal fumes. He heard about a mugging gang that hunted at Euston and the queers in the amusement arcades near Piccadilly and he spotted the flash of a knife strapped to the calf of a Devonian with cider apples for vowels.

He heard fuck adapted as noun, adjective and verb.

He heard Irish jokes, English when related by an Irishman.

He heard about sexual encounters on building sites and the backyards of pubs and one on top of a bus.

He heard North and South divided and sub-divided until only tribal stockades remained.

He felt the saw-edge of confused anger.

He felt camaraderie.

The breathing of the city deepened.

He was in a field of marguerites combed by a breeze and his hands were beneath Joanne's clothes and she was fighting with a gypsy and she wore fishnet stockings.

*   *   *

The following morning Martin, after breakfasting on grapefruit

49

segments, tinned tomatoes on toast, waxen bread, margarine and marmalade in which splinters of orange were sparsely suspended and pale tea, returned to the Job Centre where he learned of a vacancy in the packing department of a shampoo factory in Kentish Town.

Rejecting this he bought the *Evening Standard*, consulted the classified advertisements and, armed with 10p coins, found a telephone kiosk that hadn't been vandalised and applied for positions as a debt-collector, library assistant with the North-East Thames Regional Health Authority, mail room assistant, foreign exchange cashier, casino floor manager, store detective, coding officer, travel consultant, payroll clerk with a firm of brassware specialists, salesperson at a men's boutique ... He discovered that most of the jobs had been taken, that *small friendly firms* could be unaccountably hostile, that there was a shortage of bricklayers and carpenters, that if he didn't have a car and a telephone he could forget it, that computers ruled, that *some experience* was all your teenage years.

One pound and 80p poorer, he emerged into Eversholt Street. A hard-nosed wind was throwing fragments of snow along the road; an Indian sat on the kerb chewing his finger-tips above grey mittens.

Martin went into a caff, clinically clean and managed by Greek-Cypriots, and ordered a cup of tea. A plump woman with sacks of cheek beneath her eyes slipped a couple of digestive biscuits onto the saucer.

The caff was full of old people, refugees from homes heated by one-bar electric fires, ovens left open to warm the kitchens. Martin knew about old people and the cold from his welfare days in Liverpool. Many would die before the cold sheathed its blade.

He picked up his change and returned to the kiosk but it was over-fed and wouldn't take any more coins. He went into Euston station; the receiver had been ripped from the first kiosk; from the second he called an employment agency.

A bored female voice said there were a few vacancies "of a clerical nature". Licking stamps, her voice implied. The salaries were less than he would be drawing in benefits. The agency's fee: his first week's pay. He mingled with the homeward crowds and returned to Larkman House.

"We don't encourage guests to be here during the day,"

50

Bruce said. He put down a weekly newspaper on the kitchen table and said to his wife with grim satisfaction: "They haven't published a word."

"Your letters are too provocative," Brenda Larkman said. And, smiling at Martin: "We do make exceptions. It's the rough elements we don't encourage."

"They can go to the libraries," Bruce said. "Or churches." He tapped the newspaper and, aiming his voice at the first row of stalls, said: "They don't care for the truth."

Brenda, Martin noted, had been to the hairdresser — copper waves as mannered as they were in the photograph on the landing — and she was wearing a white blouse with frilly sleeves and a skirt split up the thigh. It was very hot in the kitchen and the flesh above her lips was lightly beaded with sweat.

Bruce stared at a blank sheet of Larkman House notepaper. He wrote: "Dear sir," and stared at the canary which was peevishly tossing husks of seed from its feeding bowl. The same panel game was soundlessly in progress on the television but today the participants were German field-grey.

Brenda poured Martin a cup of tea.

"So," she said, "what kind of day did we have?"

The *we* alarmed Martin. It kept him in the kitchen, made a Larkman out of him.

He told Brenda about his vicissitudes.

"Never mind." She patted his hand. "You'll be all right. You're presentable, that's what you are."

"Get onto the building sites," Bruce said. "That's where the money is."

"Building sites aren't for Martin," Brenda said firmly. "He's creative . . ."

The suggestion of shared creativity under the same roof spurred Bruce and he began to write with great fluency. Occasionally he murmured aloud: "The nation should reconsider its options . . . a blight that is threatening our very existence . . ."

"You should go to night school," Brenda said and Martin knew that she was right but first he had to earn enough money on which to survive — it was at least £50 a week for a part-share of a flat.

The canary began to shower water from its drinking bowl around its cage.

"I'll try again tomorrow," Martin said.

51

"Tomorrow's Saturday," Brenda said. "Nothing happens on Saturdays. Well, not much," patting his hand again. "And it's quiet here. A lot of the lads go home to pick up their benefits."

"Just what I'm writing about," Bruce said, riffling a wing of grey hair with the end of his ballpoint pen. "Disgraceful. The black economy."

"Where would we be without it?" Mrs. Larkman demanded.

Bruce stared despondently at his uncompleted letter.

Martin, finishing his tea, said he would go upstairs and write a letter to his parents.

"Letter?" Bruce began to write again.

Mrs. Larkman climbed the stairs behind Martin, pausing on the landing to rub dust from her photograph. She touched her red hair lightly with her fingertips and followed Martin into the room.

She sat on the edge of the bed and, hands planted beside her, tested its suspension.

"The other lads will be here any minute," she said.

"It's about time," Martin agreed.

"Pity. But things will be quieter tomorrow."

Martin stared at the wall. *Brenda goes.*

He pulled his suitcase from beneath the bed, undid the belt and took out writing pad and envelopes.

"Mr. Larkman often goes out on Saturdays," Brenda said. "What are you doing tomorrow, Martin?"

At that moment Martin knew. He said: "I'm going to see my uncle in the East End."

Bad, bold Jack.

CHAPTER 5

———◆———

Overnight it snowed with application and by daylight the East End of London where Jack the Ripper once lurked was a soft and reflective place. In Hackney and Hoxton, Stepney and Shadwell, Bethnal Green and Bow, the sharp angles of warehouses were chastened, needlepoint church spires blunted. The snow cosseted Spitalfields market where, underground, bananas lay ripening and Middlesex Street where, on Sundays, Petticoat Lane's stallholders sold their wares. It cooled the night fumes of boisterous pubs and dicey clubs, made igloos of Pakistani corner shops and invested blocks of council flats with gentleness.

Jack Renshaw, returning from work, was grateful for the snow because it muffled his footsteps and imparted an air of respectability to his approach. He was a square, middle-aged man with a coal-like glitter to his eyes, black hair beginning to frost and very white skin; scar-tissue shone on his throat and his smile was studded with gold. He dressed sharply, favouring formal suits with waistcoats looped with watch, chain and cigar-cutter and he kept himself trim at a gymnasium in Aldgate.

Jack Renshaw was, by profession, a thief.

He saw nothing dishonourable in this, arguing that there was little justice in a judicial system in which a City financier who misappropriated £2 million by insider trading received a two-year suspended gaol sentence whereas a tea-leaf who stole the day's takings from a Bangladesh clothes shop got two years.

In fact by the standards of his own closed society he was honourable. When an old woman in the block was mugged and

53

robbed of £8 he organised the hunt for the assailants who were subsequently beaten to pulp; when the daughter of a colleague had been raped in a parking lot in Plaistow he had put out the word and the rapists had been so severely kicked in the genitals that there was little chance of them ever again fulfilling any sexual activity, let alone rape.

Insult Jack Renshaw's mother (deceased) and watch out for your knee-caps.

On this night when the snow had been falling in lovely Christmas flakes he and two partners had broken into a house on the River Stour in Suffolk, Constable Country, blown the safe and departed with jewellery worth £150,000. The house was owned by a judge. Jack Renshaw had no particular quarrel with judges — someone had to sentence the villains — but he did question the ability of the privileged to understand the criminal inclinations of the underprivileged.

Jack Renshaw had only committed one act of which he was ashamed.

And that had been a long time ago.

*　　*　　*

Jack Renshaw could probably have afforded a judge's house; instead he lived with his common-law wife, Grace, in a council flat on the third floor of a block, one of a complex of five built in the '60s, off the Commercial Road. And apart from bank holidays at Southend or Epping Forest he left the East End only in the pursuit of business or to celebrate its successful conclusion in a West End night-club. He was, he conceded, old-fashioned: he didn't mess with drugs and he didn't own a villa on the Costa del Sol.

On the green-walled communal balcony he dusted the snow from the shoulders of his Crombie, substituted for his working clothes in a bungalow near Ongar, and went into the flat which was as neat and as clean as a retired seaman's. The kitchen was the showpiece — fridge that dispensed ice, dish-washer, expansive cooker, micro-wave oven, so much mod-tech equipment that there wasn't much room in which to manoeuvre.

He made himself coffee, washed and shaved, undressed and lay on the bed beside Grace who was deeply asleep, one ample breast overlapping the fold of the sheets. He contemplated waking her and, anticipating her drowsy and sensual response, making love to her.

No, she deserved her sleep.

He lay back, hands behind his neck.

Outside the snow fell thickly.

In the judge's house the empty safe would be grating loosely in its fittings.

Jack Renshaw smiled and slept.

*   *   *

Martin knocked on the yellow-painted door at 12.30. It was opened by a blonde woman with pink, scything fingernails and wary eyes.

Martin said: "Is Jack Renshaw in?"

"Who wants to know?"

"I'm his nephew," Martin said.

"Wally's boy? No." She slashed the air with her fingernails. "You're not Wally's boy."

"I'm Jim's son."

"Jim?" She frowned. "Jim in Liverpool?" She peered at Martin; her cornflower-blue eyes focussed on him with a steadfast, contact-lens gaze. "You look like a Renshaw . . . But Jim, we hardly ever speak about him."

"Well," Martin said, "I'm his son."

Jack Renshaw, hair tousled, wearing a black towelling robe, said: "So you're Martin." He beckoned him inside. "Family," Jack explained to Grace. "Family's everything," placing a heavy arm across Martin's shoulders. "Drop of Scotch?"

"Beer, please," Martin said, "if you've got one."

"We've got everything," Jack said. "You, girl?" to Grace.

Grace, settling for a white wine with soda, said: "Don't forget lunch, Jack."

"Martin's coming with us, aren't you . . . Mart, Marty, what do they call you?"

"Martin," Martin said.

"Funny things names. Derek, Del. Why? John, Jack. In fact I was christened Jack. Not like your old man. He was James. Names fit people. Grace. Could she be anything else?"

He poured light ale frothing into Martin's glass.

They sat in the living-room, leather chairs sighing as they

55

moved. Jack poured himself a Chivas Regal; the ice cracked as he added water. Snow fell steadily past the windows muffling the cries of children playing snow games in the courtyard.

"So," Jack said, "how's my brother? Old Jim . . ."

Old Jim? Familiarity strummed a question mark. Hadn't Grace said they hardly ever spoke about Jim?

Martin said: "My father's fine."

"Honest Jim, eh?"

Honesty, as though it were an offence.

"He had a lot of bad luck," Martin said.

"Don't we all. But you've got to know what to do with it. Good luck, too. Mould it, Martin, squeeze it, direct it . . ." He drank some whisky. "What brings you here?"

"Family," Martin said.

"Well said." Jack's voice was pointed with laughter.

Grace said: "I met Jim once. About ten years ago. He was different to Harry and Wally. And Jack, of course."

"Brothers are different," Jack said. "Why should they be the same? We go our separate ways."

"Why didn't you keep in contact?" Martin asked.

"Married a Scouse. Didn't want to know us."

Grace sat on the arm of Jack's chair. "What's your dad like?" she asked Martin.

"Like I said, he's had a rough time lately like a lot of people up north. The shop was doing well enough until the docks closed. Then the dockers went to the supermarkets which were cheaper and he had to close down."

"Poor old Jim," Jack said. "He was the bright one, you know. Always did well at school. Not like me or Harry or Wally. Rough justice, eh, Martin?"

"What does Wally do?" Martin asked.

Grace answered him. "Good works. He and God are like that." She crossed two fingers.

"An accountant," Jack said. "And me?" anticipating Martin. "I'm a Bill Hill, a bookie. I keep books while your Uncle Wally cooks them." His dark eyes glittered. "So this is just a family visit, eh, Martin? You know, I like to get things straight. Grace thought you were the law, didn't you, Grace."

"A bit young," Grace said.

"All the coppers are beginning to look young," Jack said, "at our age."

"Your age."

"Just a family visit," Martin said.

"Glad to hear it." Jack glanced at his wristwatch, a Rolex Oyster, hours pointed with diamonds. He stood up. "First a few bevvies at the Widow, then a good eat-up. I'll get dressed."

Grace disappeared and emerged wearing a mink coat and ankle-strapped shoes followed by Jack in a blue pin-stripe with elegantly rolled lapels.

"You look good, girl," Jack said.

She kissed him on the cheek.

It had stopped snowing but the air still sparkled with ice-dust. Jack led them across the courtyard, past sliding, snow-balling children and a group of youths, black and white, examining a motorcycle. An old woman wearing carpet slippers and eating bread from a paper-bag drifted past; Jack stopped her and slipped her a £10 note.

He opened the door of a black, snow-bonneted Jaguar parked at the kerb. It was old and immaculate and inside it smelled of leather. They turned into the Commercial Road.

How could Jack be so different from his brothers?

As far as Martin knew the family had lived in a modest and gloomy house in Muswell Hill in North London. There were photographs in the album of the four boys playing in the grounds of Alexandra Palace. Their father had been a buyer for Gamages, The People's Popular Emporium, in Holborn, a man of lugubrious mien judging by the photographs, but the family seemed to have been united, the boys' mother compensating regally for her husband's despondency. Martin recalled a photograph of her magnificently authoritative and compassion-ate as a Red Cross nurse in the Second World War. She had been killed during the Blitz when a beam had fallen on her while she cradled a child whose leg was trapped in a bombed semi-detached. The uncles' father had died when they were in their early twenties; they had split up immediately.

Jack, it seemed to Martin, had *become* a Cockney, grown into the part.

"How's your mother?" Jack asked, steering the Jaguar through Limehouse towards Bow.

"Worried," Martin told him.

"Beautiful girl. Jim met her at the Lyceum. But she wouldn't live in London, hated it. So off he went up north. We warned

57

him but he wouldn't listen. Stubborn was Jim. But north and south . . . do they ever mix?"

"You'll like the Widow," Grace said. "Widow's Son, to give it its full handle. Supposed to have been a cottage there 200 years ago. A widow lived there whose son was a sailor. He was due back one Easter and she baked hot cross buns for him. But he never turned up, did he. And every Easter until she snuffed it she cooked these buns; after she died the buns were hung up and every year a sailor added another bun. The cottage was known as the Bun House. Then they built the pub in 1850 and the mouldy old buns were hung up and every year another one is added."

"Very historical, Grace," Jack said.

"I read a lot."

"Without moving her lips," Jack said.

Grace laughed. The laugh was a revelation, loud and ribald, a music hall laugh.

The pub in Devons Road, Bow, reminded Martin of one of the hostelries in the centre of Liverpool, ornamental mirrors and pictures of ships; buns hung from a wooden ceiling.

The Renshaws established themselves among a group at one end of the bar. Jack was greeted with good humour edged with respect. A whisky was thrust in his hand; he listened and he nodded and he smiled; he didn't speak often but when he did the others stopped.

Martin, sipping a beer, examined the group, four men and two girls. Their voices were sharp, like acid-drops; their humour was swift and their clothing expensive.

After a while Jack detached himself from the group with a plump man with wispy hair wearing a camel-hair coat; he looked affluent and furtive, glancing around for stealthy pursuers, smoking a cigarette as though it were a crime.

"That's Rabbit."

Martin turned. The speaker was compact with cropped hair as thick as fur and the face of a fighter who hadn't taken too much punishment. His hands were tattooed and from time to time he hunched his considerable shoulders beneath his blue coat.

"Why Rabbit?"

"Two theories. One that he looks like a rabbit caught in a car's headlights. Two that he once killed a bloke with a rabbit punch. Me, I favour the first." He hunched his shoulders. "So you're Jack's nephew?"

"We just met for the first time."

"So he told me." Had he been told to interrogate him? "Jack and me work together. Tough nut, Jack," the stranger said studying a gold signet ring on his finger. "No one messes with him. But he's dead straight is Jack." He smiled, sunlight on crags. "My name's Billy." He stuck out a hand.

Shaking it, feeling its strength, Martin said: "So what do you do, Billy."

"This and that. Mostly that. So what brings you to London, young Martin? Fame and fortune?"

"Something like that," Martin said.

"Well, you can find it all right. Don't let anyone tell you otherwise. Look at Rabbit. Even he makes a few bob flogging tickets. Wimbledon, Lord's, the Hammers ... Old Rabbit can get you anywhere – for a price." He nodded at the wispy-haired ticket tout. "Jack's having a bit of aggro with him at the moment: he sold a business acquaintance a stack of duff tickets. Jack wants his bread back. Wouldn't you?"

Martin said he would.

"So how are you going to earn all this money, Martin?"

"Get a job." It sounded pathetic.

"Hoping Jack can help you?"

He hadn't been but it was an idea.

"Or did you have something else in mind?"

"Something else?"

"You know, you being Jack's nephew."

"Nothing else," Martin said.

"That's good then." Billy twisted the ring on his finger and its diamond winked. "I wouldn't want anyone to upset Jack."

"Upset him? I'm his nephew, for Christ's sake. Family." His anger spurted like acid.

"Got spirit, too. Has your old man got spirit, Jack's brother?"

"He's a good man."

"Wasn't what I asked, Martin."

"That's what I'm telling you."

"Loyal, too." He squeezed Martin's bicep beneath his jacket. "I like that. Here, have another sherbet." He ordered a beer for Martin and a gin and tonic for himself. "Know something?

59

You're all right. And I can usually suss people."

The ticket tout eased his way past them.

"Take care, Rabbit," Bill said. "It may never happen. Then again it might."

The ticket tout stared at hm. Patches of red burned on his cheeks. He started to speak, shook his head and made for the door.

Jack Renshaw nodded at Billy from the other side of the group and Billy said: "Okay, time to go. To my gaff," he told Martin.

Billy drove a chocolate-coloured Thunderbird; Jack followed in the Jaguar. They stopped outside a terrace house in Cheapside; the snow had stopped falling and the street rasped with the scrape of shovels.

Like Jack's flat, Billy's house was luxuriously appointed. Custom-built kitchen panelled in walnut, 25-inch television with video, a flight-deck of stereo. Gold and silver Christmas decorations moved in imperceptible currents of air.

A girl was cooking in the kitchen. She had fine blonde hair and a model's face and Martin could see her nipples through her white shirt. She spoke exquisitely although, when she swallowed her words, her voice reminded Martin of squashed strawberries.

Billy smacked her bottom, tight-moulded beneath blue jeans, and introduced her as Flora. "Works for the Beeb."

"At Bush House," Flora said. "And no, I don't sodding well broadcast." And to Billy: "You're bleeding late again."

"My fault," said Jack.

Grace steered Martin away from hostilities and pointed out of the window. "St. Mary-le-Bow. That's where Bow Bells used to peal until they were destroyed in the Blitz. You were only a Cockney if you were born within their sound."

"Were you a Cockney?"

"Me? I wasn't born then."

"Sod the lot of you," Flora said. She began to cry. "And who's he?" pointing at Martin.

"My nephew," Jack said and Billy said: "Knock it off, Flora, there's a good girl," and, taking Martin aside, said: "She's all right, really. Likes a bit of rough, that's all."

Martin, turning away, said to the girl: "I'm sorry."

60

"You're the only one who is." She dabbed at her eye with the corner of a tea-towel.

"I'm sorry," Billy said, hunching his shoulders and smiling at her.

"No, you're not: you're a bastard."

"That as well."

"You don't understand," Flora said. "This is the first roast I've cooked. I wish I'd never come here."

"I'll call you a cab," Billy said.

"Bastard."

"I've bought you a present."

He fished a gold chain with a pearl in a pendant from his jacket pocket and swung it like a pendulum in front of her.

"Where did you nick that from?"

"Now, now."

"It's beautiful . . ."

"It's the thought that counts . . ."

"Bastard," but she wasn't crying any more.

She opened the oven and peered at her baptismal roast; it sizzled back at her.

Avocado pears to start, soft and nutritious, slopping gently with vinaigrette, washed down with white wine, Sancerre, poured from a bottle beaded with dew, followed by The Roast, beef, baby-pink and tender, accompanied by parsnips, carrots and jacket potatoes washed down this time with a rich Rioja.

"Cooked to a turn," Grace said.

"Really?" Flora looked at Billy.

He put his fingers to his lips and kissed them.

Martin said: "It's beautiful."

Flora's pleasure suffused the table. She ate ravenously. "It was all in a book," she said. "Anyone could have done it."

"No," Grace said, "it was up here," touching her brow with pink talons.

"I didn't think I could do it," Flora said.

"You can do anything," Billy said.

The knock came on the door after the cheese while Billy was pouring Courvoisier into balloon glasses.

The knock froze everyone except Flora.

Jack opened the door of the kitchen leading to a small back-

61

yard. Billy went into the living-room; Martin heard a drawer open and shut.

Flora, puzzled, said: "It's probably a tradesman."

"We don't have tradesmen in Cheapside," Billy said. "Only debt-collectors." He peered through a judas eye. He said: "Shit, it's Rabbit."

"What's he doing here?" a blade in Jack Renshaw's voice.

"I told him not to come here," Billy said.

"Let him in."

The ticket tout brought the cold in with him. He seemed to have shrunk since Martin had seen him in the pub. His wispy hair was tufted outwards, his hands trembled.

Jack said: "Well?"

The Rabbit shook his head. "Sorry, Jack."

"You cheated."

"If I'd known . . ."

"They were my friends. I paid your debts."

Martin sipped his brandy. Their words were emerging in capsules. He stared into the balloon glass and saw his face pulled into the shape of a lemon. He felt sick.

"Another week," Rabbit said.

"You've had time enough. And what the hell are you doing here?"

"Billy said . . ."

"No, I didn't," Billy said.

"You know the rules," Jack said. He tapped his right temple with one finger. "Show him the garden, Billy."

Rabbit followed hopelessly. Martin heard thuds. In slow motion he saw Flora's hand rise to her mouth, heard her intake of breath, returned her bright smile, counted Jack's fingers as he drummed them on the table.

Grace slotted a tape into the stereo. Frank Sinatra. "Strangers in the Night". "Our song," she said. "Everyone's song."

Billy came back. He cupped one hand to his ear. "Old blue eyes," he said. "Only time he made No 1."

He poured brandy into his glass. The bottle hovered over Martin's glass. "No, thanks," he said, hearing his voice boom round the room, "I've had enough."

Five minutes later he said: "Excuse me," and walked majestically through the kitchen into the backyard. Before vomiting he

62

noticed spots of blood as bright as poppy petals on the clean snow beside a crippled, three-legged chair.

*　　*　　*

He walked through darkening streets, vaguely westward, aware that he was drunk for the second time in two weeks, hoping that the cold was sobering him, ashamed that he had walked out of Billy's house like that, straight through the backyard into an alleyway, into another terrace and another, vowing that he would telephone, or write to Jack, apologising for his behaviour.

He walked with unerring determination, smiling at the East Enders who, shaking their heads, got out of his way. He rounded a corner sharply, bumped into brickwork and swore: "I'll never drink again." The lowering sky tilted, the clouds that had ceased to shed snow converged darkly on warehouse shells; the fallen snow froze and crunched like broken glass beneath his feet; groups of youths sneered; the streets were hostile.

He had no idea how long he had been walking, only that the vistas were narrowing, squeezing him. Shops shut their eyes, betting shops, DIYs, liquor stores; televisions flickered remotely in parlours. He smelled mud.

The young black broke from the Pakistani newsagents as Martin paused outside, debating whether to ask where he was. He had one hand to his head and he was screaming and there were three white youths in pursuit. They carried cudgels with string-bound handles and their hair was shaved and their faces were brutish beneath the scalping.

"Shit, man," the young black shouted to Martin. "Help me."

Martin stared at the white youths gravely. They came at him ferociously but their vision was focussed beyond him at the fleeing black figure. Martin lunged but they evaded him, scarcely bothered. One raised a cudgel and threw it; the black fell, curled in pain.

"Okay, coon," they bayed. "This is it, you black bastard," and they were almost upon him but just as suddenly they were dispersing and Martin, rising from the cobblestones where he had fallen, saw in the dusk black faces, four, five, six of them, one helping the fallen black to his feet, and shouting: "There's one of the bastards."

And then the boots were coming in and there was spit on his face and pain in his chest, in his groin. And then they were gone and he was making his way on bending legs to the smell of mud and the last thing he saw was the Thames, as grey as a snake, on its way to the sea.

CHAPTER 6

———◆◆◆———

Anarchy is the child of poverty. It is therefore difficult, as Jenny Renshaw was discovering, to follow even its blandest doctrines if you live in an affluent household. "So what do *you* care?" ask shaggy rebels and that most perfidious accusation which the young and rich have to endure hovers accusingly: *slumming*.

Jenny had, in fact, always lived in bourgeois circumstances. She had been born in a roomy ground-floor flat in a substantial terrace house with an area and white portico in a street in West London leading from Earl's Court, once the site of the court-house of the Earls of Warwick and Holland, more recently the home of visitors from Australia, hence Kangaroo Valley. When asked where they lived her mother said: "Near the Old Brompton Road," adding for the benefit of foreigners: "Where Jenny Lind and Beatrix Potter lived."

Her mother, who was embarrassingly elegant, owned a gown shop in Putney and aspired to similar premises in Chelsea, but her plans were constantly undermined by her husband's lack of business acumen. During the week he was a clerk with a furrier's; on Saturday afternoons he entertained children, delighting scoffing audiences with fumbled conjuring tricks; on Saturday evening he was a libertine.

Jenny remembered him most vividly on Sundays when, stricken with remorse and smelling of toothpaste and whisky, he sought solace in his stamp collection. Beckoning her to his knee, he would introduce her through a magnifying glass to the Pitcairn Islands or Trinidad and Tobago or a mournful British monarch. She hated the feel of his bones through his thighs and she hated stamps.

In the spring of 1980 he took off with the singer in a travelling disco and moved to Nottingham, leaving Jenny's mother thankful but improvident. The improvidence came to an abrupt end when Harry Renshaw, divorced and seeking a gift for an anonymous friend, called at the gown shop in Putney and, that evening, took its owner to dinner at an Italian restaurant in Knightsbridge.

They were married ten months later and, although it went unrecognised at the time, Jenny's disquiet was conceived.

Not that Harry and Edith Renshaw were not kind parents. They sent Jenny to an expensive private school in Highgate where moral fibre was given precedence over mathematics, even games, and then to board at Benenden; they took her on holidays to the Bahamas and Bermuda; they exhibited marital affection in front of her — the kiss on the cheek, the remembrance of birthdays — thus instilling in her a sense of security; they funded her adequately and disciplined her sensibly. When they moved to The Bishops Avenue they gave her a room with a bathroom en suite. In the room she painted landscapes, mostly from colour slides; on the heath she questioned the accident of birth.

Her mother, tall and fine-boned, retained her elegance, features even more delicately honed, skin a little strained at the corners of her eyes; a parent to be proud of. Her step-father who sold ships and cargoes on the Baltic Exchange grew a little more pink and plump than was, perhaps, good for him but retained his benevolence.

It was left to the German au pair, Herta, to instruct Jenny comprehensively in sex but, approaching eighteen, she was still a virgin. This did not dismay her; she enjoyed physical contact with virile young men but surely consummation could not be such a big deal. What did dismay her was her lack of understanding of herself. What was the form of her discontent?

Not inequality. The haves and the have-nots would always exist. As she had said to Katherine: "Communism is the equal distribution of hardship." No, it was more subtle.

She settled for complacency.

But, as she was to all intents and purposes a child of complacency, she had difficulty in convincing other young dissidents of her sincerity.

On New Year's Eve she told her mother that she had no intention of going to university.

They had just been shopping at Fortnum and Mason and in the big kitchen hung rustically with herbs and garlic they were unpacking their purchases, cheese and pâté and translucent Serrano ham and game pie and orange blossom honey.

"Really?" her mother said. "And may I ask why?"

"It's a waste of time; I'm not a scholar."

"And when did you decide this?"

"Thirty seconds ago. But I've been thinking about it for some time."

"It's up to you," her mother said, nibbling a crumb of Cheshire cheese. "Your father will be disappointed."

"Step-father," Jenny said.

"Whatever. You couldn't have wished for a better guardian." She placed a jar of caviar in the ice-dispensing refrigerator. "Well, it's your choice, you're almost eighteen." Her indulgence irritated Jenny: she had wanted a fight.

She said: "I want to learn about life not about learning."

"Plenty of time for that," her mother said. She stood at the window gazing, it seemed to Jenny, at retreating youth in which a young and incompetent magician made children laugh. The light of the winter afternoon struck pale light in her ash-blonde hair.

"I'm sorry," Jenny said.

"No need to be."

"Do you think Harry will be angry?"

"He won't be pleased," her mother said. "Why should he be?" As though he had made an investment in her.

"I thought he might understand?" wanting to add: "And I thought you might."

"Harry's been good to you," her mother said. *Didn't have to be*, her voice implied.

"I don't have to go to Oxford," Jenny said. "Not if I don't want to. Harry will understand."

"Harry wanted to join the Diplomatic Corps," her mother said. The remark puzzled Jenny. "He's a good man." She touched the pale hair which clung to her thin neck.

"There's more to life than learning," Jenny said.

"Such as what?"

"Living it. Breathing it. Competing in it."

67

Convention, she thought. Why do we abide by it? BECAUSE NO ONE PAUSES TO QUESTION.

She thought in capital letters.

Her step-father's reactions were more infuriating because they were practical.

Arriving home early from the City, he stood in front of the fire in the beamed living-room that smelled faintly of cigar-smoke and said: "So what are you going to do instead?"

"Get a job, I suppose."

"Qualifications?"

"A language," she said. "French. All those O-levels. Benenden. A pleasing personality . . ." She smiled at him, massaging the incipient frown between her eyes.

"I can get you a job in Paris. Nanny, something like that."

Nanny! Had he no idea of the turmoil within her? She realised that he was treating her decision as a whim, a platitude of youth.

"I could go to Moscow," she said.

"Chilly at this time of the year."

"I'll think of something." She felt tears starting in her eyes.

"Good girl." With the toe of one shoe he adjusted a log on the fire.

Jenny went to her room. It was pink and undisturbed. Proust lay on the bedside table; an already-forgotten pop group stared cockily from a poster on the wall; the carpet was dove-grey and deep, muffling thought.

She switched on the radio and caught an afternoon newscast. There had been disturbances in Brixton and Tottenham and the miners were contemplating strike action.

Afterwards an analyst from the London School of Economics spoke of the unrest. What was intriguing, he said, faint note of commitment in his voice, was that the dissent coincided with the beginning of Britain's economic recovery.

Could it be, he asked, that during the age when monetary policies prevailed a new breed of citizen was born? A dormant rebel who, living by his wits, resented the cavalier fashion in which his destiny was manipulated?

That rebel, the analyst suggested, was emerging now in a computerised age in which he had no place. "His only fuel," the analyst said, an edge to his voice, "is bitterness. He believes that his birthright was squandered."

68

A link-man emphasised in measured tones that the analyst had been expressing purely personal opinions. Had he, fuelled by bitterness, departed from his script?

Jenny gazed through the window at the numbed garden. With whom could she share her confusion? Katherine had of late been a disappointment, preferring the company of her boyfriend, who worked for the Hong Kong and Shanghai Bank, to the polemics of the discussion group to which they belonged in Belsize Park.

She remembered Martin Renshaw and her humiliation on the heath. She remembered his features, indecision awaiting resolve. She had been uncharacteristically rude, running away with her stupidity in tow like a kite.

She went downstairs and asked her mother for Jim Renshaw's address in Liverpool.

"What on earth for?" Her mother was sorting magazines in the television room.

"I thought I'd write to Martin." She saw no reason to reveal that he was in London.

"But we scarcely know the Liverpool branch of the family."

"Isn't it about time we did?"

"You're acting very strangely today," her mother said. She shrugged. "Very well, I have it somewhere. Pringle, somewhere like that." She found her address-book and handed it to Jenny.

Jenny sat at the table in her room beside a blue, fluffy bear who regarded her cynically from a single black-button eye and tried to compose a letter. How did she address them? *Dear uncle and aunt* ... But they're not my family. Martin is no relative of mine.

She wrote swiftly and surely.

She glanced at her watch: there was just time to catch the post. She ran down the garden path, passing Herta, shiny-lipped and flaxen, who smiled at her conspiratorially.

*   *   *

Martin's mother telephoned two evenings later, transferring the charges.

Harry took the call and his anger surprised Jenny: it was, after all, his sister-in-law.

She made a note of Martin's address in London — he had

written home recently — cradled the receiver and awaited her step-father's wrath.

It had, by this time, cooled, reviving when she told him that Martin had been in Hampstead. She said she had no idea what he wanted. Was it so unnatural that he should visit his uncle?

Harry poured himself a whisky and paced the living-room. He didn't reply. His reaction puzzled Jenny.

The following morning she caught an underground train to Euston and made her way to Larkman House. The clouds had thinned luminously and the air was brisk, the rows of boarding houses martial.

The woman who answered the door was red-haired and sleepy. She said: "Sorry, men only," cigarette in the corner of her mouth beating time to her words.

"I don't want a room: I wondered if Martin Renshaw was here."

The woman removed the cigarette from her mouth, shedding ash on the WELCOME doormat. "He hasn't been back for four days," she said. "I was getting worried. Are you the girl from Liverpool?"

"No, family," Jenny told her.

"Is he all right? It's not like Martin to do a moonlight."

A man's voice issued down the fish-smelling corridor. "Have you come to pay his rent? Four nights, that's nearly £28." And to the woman: "You know he hasn't done a moonlight: his suitcase is still here."

"Might be empty for all we know."

"It isn't," the man said. "I looked."

Jenny said: "I'm sure Martin will pay."

"He was going to stay on a regular basis. You know, a little cheaper. We like to help young men trying to make a go of it; it's a hard place, the Smoke."

"Did he say where he was going?" Jenny asked.

"If he'd given us a little in advance we could have kept his bed for him."

"Was he going back to Liverpool?"

"He did say ... Now what was it?" The woman stuck the cigarette back in her mouth. "Somewhere in London ... A nice boy, Martin. Wish we could have kept his bed for him."

Jenny looked in her purse. Eight pounds and a few silver and copper coins. She handed the woman a £5 note.

Brenda Larkman folded it, creasing a sharp edge with her fingernails. "He mentioned his uncle," she said. Smoke dribbled from her nostrils. "Uncle Jack would it be?"

"Where?" Jenny asked.

"In the East End, I think he said. No actual address, I'm afraid, and now if you'll . . ." The door closed, snuffing out the sentence.

Jenny telephoned her mother and asked for Uncle Jack's address. It was given with mystification and reproach.

Jenny returned to the bowels of the underground and emerged in the East End at Shadwell.

She walked briskly along Cable Street where ropes and cables had once been manufactured. In between helpings of Proust, Jenny had been reading about the extremes of politics. It was in this street in 1936 that East Enders and left-wingers had determined to halt a march by Sir Oswald Mosley and his Fascists. Fighting had preceded the march and the Home Secretary had cancelled the march. A few days later the shop windows of all the Jewish shops in the Mile End Road were smashed.

But on whose side would I have fought? Certainly not the Communists, nor the Fascists for that matter. For justice — no, against injustice, there was a subtle difference — she decided lamely. It was sad but moderation sagged between the poles of extremism. The pre-war politicians she despised were Baldwin and Chamberlain: they had been complacent.

As she walked she noticed men staring at her. Did they sense that, even though she wore an old black coat, jeans and scuffed tennis shoes, she came from more privileged pastures? Even the breeze prowling the side-streets smelled alien, sometimes spiced, sometimes muddy, quite unlike the wind that blew grandly across Hampstead Heath. And now, scarcely realising it, she walked with the self-conscious arrogance affected by girls suddenly aware that they are sexually desirable.

Outside a Chinese fish-and-chip shop she stopped a man wearing a peaked cap and asked him the way. He was younger than she had thought; he wore Dr. Marten boots and when he took off his cap his hair sprang into curls.

He examined the piece of paper on which she had written the address. "The buildings," he said. "Up there," pointing along a side-street. "Mind how you go, there's some chancers up there."

"I can take care of myself," Jenny said.

"Want any help?" He grinned.

"You've been very helpful," she said.

"Suit yourself."

The tall buildings looked dour. Snow on the courtyards soiled, aerosol graffiti on peeling green balconies. Old women had been beaten up and robbed in just such a place as this.

She knocked on the door of No. 23. She was conscious she was being observed. The man who answered the door was square and contained with black hair and the pallor of a night-worker.

He said: "You're Harry's step-daughter."

Inside the flat, more luxuriously appointed than the house in Hampstead, she told him she was looking for Martin who hadn't returned to his lodgings since Saturday.

"Jim's boy." He ran one finger down a ridge of scar tissue on his neck. "He seems to be acting as a sort of go-between."

A curious remark; the relationship of the Renshaw brothers puzzled Jenny.

The watch in the waistcoat pocket of his suit chimed. He consulted it, made a decision. "We'll go and see Billy," he said.

From the front seat of the Jaguar she glanced back at the apartment blocks. A legacy from the last general election was still visible on one wall. FUCK THE TORIES.

She said: "Can I ask you a question?"

"Be my guest."

"What did you vote in the last election?"

"Tory," he said. "What else?"

A taxi stood throbbing outside the terrace house where Billy apparently lived. A blonde girl was climbing into it. She was crying.

Billy said to Jack: "Too much aggro, couldn't take it any more."

The girl said: "Bastard," and slammed the door. The cab took off.

Inside the house Jack told Billy about Martin.

Billy hunched his shoulders. "He was well pissed," he said.

"We should have gone after him. Find him, Billy."

"I'll make a few calls," Billy said.

72

"You do that."

When Billy had gone Jack Renshaw sat opposite Jenny, an inward man in control of his menace. He didn't frighten her.

"So," he said, "Harry's done all right then." An accusation rather than a compliment.

"He works hard," she said.

"I admire your loyalty. What's Martin doing in London?"

"Didn't he tell you?"

"He didn't seem too sure."

"Looking for work like everyone down from the north. Looking up his family."

Jack didn't look convinced. "And what are you looking for?" he asked.

"I wish I knew."

"Then I'll tell you — reasons."

"That sounds too simple."

"It says everything." He leaned forward, peering with dark eyes from inside his cage. "How old are you?"

"Nearly eighteen."

"Don't make a mistake now," he said. "If you do your whole life will be a mistake."

"Did you?"

Billy opened the front-door and said: "London Hospital. Admitted Saturday evening. Well drunk and kicked half to death. No ID," he added.

The silence thickened. Then Jack said: "Find out who did it, Billy. Attend to them."

*   *   *

There were dark bruises beneath his closed eyes and his lips were crusted with blood and his limbs were stiff beneath the sheets. His features were composed of the innocence before birth and the knowledge before death.

The West Indian nurse said: "We didn't know who he was and he wouldn't tell us. Ashamed, I think. He was very drunk," she said. "Such a pity, at his age."

Jenny sat beside his bed at one end of the ward. In the next bed an old man blew small bubbles in his dreams.

She sat quite still for a moment, then she touched Martin's

73

cheek. He opened his eyes immediately and looked at her without recognition.

Then he smiled, squeezing the bruises on his face.

She said: "I've come to ask you to dinner."

CHAPTER 7

———— ◆ ————

The atmosphere at Larkman House was solicitous.

Martin's experience prompted Bruce to write a stiff letter to a newspaper about violence on the streets and so optimistic was he about publication that he only charged Martin for three of the five days he had been missing and Brenda put fresh sheets, stained but steam-pressed that morning, on his bed.

The attack had strengthened Martin's resolve to stay in London. Funded by a Giro from the DHSS, he limped the streets looking for a job but his bruises preceded him. In wall-to-wall carpeted offices in Cannon Street in the City where there was a clerical vacancy a healthy young man wearing a tight-waisted suit with a waistcoat pulled at a shiny moustache, regarded Martin ruefully, spoke frequently on the telephone about a BMW 325i and sipped Perrier water. After the third BMW call he hurried from the office suggesting over his shoulder that Martin should see a doctor. The floor manager of a shampoo factory in West London said: "We don't want knuckle here. On your bike."

When he returned to Larkman House, limbs aching, fingers chapped, shoes rimed with street salt, he sat on the edge of the bed and, before the other inmates arrived, wrote letters of application including one inspired plea to the DHSS itself.

Brenda Larkman made her move one late afternoon when Bruce had taken a bus to the cash-and-carry to replenish stocks of tea-bags, grapefruit segments and pale marmalade.

She knocked on the door of the dormitory while 'he was applying for a job with a chain of freezer shops. She was wearing the same dressing-gown and high-heeled mules that she had

had on the day he arrived, and the foothills of her considerable bosom were riding high.

She sat on the edge of the bed opposite him, holding a magazine.

"All work and no play . . ." She crossed her legs. "How are the bruises?"

"Getting better," Martin said tentatively.

"Poor lamb." She stretched across the divide and touched his knee. "Did I ever tell you that I did a bit of modelling?" She stroked the cover of the magazine which specialised in photographs of the wives of readers. She wet one finger and began to turn the pages.

He glimpsed rounded pastures of breasts and buttocks and copses of pubic hair. Most of the women were smiling coyly at the lens as their husbands stared through their viewfinders at familiar terrain.

The magazine fell open at a page featuring Brenda Larkman in two Polaroid colour snaps. Her eyes had been lit leonine yellow by the flash and she was wearing fishnet stockings – surely not the same pair exhibited on the wall outside – suspender belt, black brassière with peepholes for her nipples, mules – Christ! not the ones she was wearing today! – and a red hat with a floppy brim. Martin remembered a phrase from his childhood: "Red hat no drawers." Manifestly Brenda was wearing none; to draw readers' attention to this omission she had opened her thighs at an alarming angle.

She sat beside Martin.

"You're making me shy," she said illogically.

Martin, unable to think of a reply, stared at the photographs on the opposite page of a woman with a weight-lifter's arms and thighs like tree-trunks. She was eating an apple and her name was Eve.

Brenda placed her hand on Martin's thigh close to his crotch and said: "You're a nice-looking boy, Martin," and, with a squeeze of her plump fingers: "Do you like mature women?"

Panic expanded in his skull. He said: "Please, Mrs. Larkman . . ."

"Now you're shy." Her hand moved up his thigh like a soft-shelled crab. "Don't forget, there's many a new tune played on an old fiddle."

"I don't think . . ."

76

"Mr. Larkman won't be back for another hour if that's what you're worried about."

"It's not that, Mrs. Larkman."

"Brenda," she said. "What is it then? Afraid of getting out of control?"

"I'm engaged," he said, inspired.

"To that bit in Liverpool? You weren't engaged the other day."

"I wrote to her and proposed," Martin said.

"Well," Brenda said, "she need never know. And perhaps I can teach you a few tricks."

"I've just written to her again," Martin said. "I've got to get to the post office," reasoning that she was accustomed to headlong flights to catch the post. "Perhaps another time."

Brenda slapped the magazine shut. Martin heard her thighs slapping inside the pages. "There won't be another time," she said.

Martin grabbed the letter to the chain of freezer shops, slipped it into a Basildon Bond envelope and made for the door.

The following morning Brenda stopped him on his way to breakfast. "Mr. Larkman would like a word with you, Mr. Renshaw."

Hell hath no fury . . . Perhaps Bruce was going to accuse him of rape.

Bruce appeared from the kitchen, Paisley scarf knotted at the neck of his white, ketchup-stained shirt, hair draping his ears.

"Mrs. Larkman and I have been thinking," he said. He paused, staring beyond the footlights. "What with you spending so much of your time in the house and what with you drawing so much benefit we thought it only right and proper that we increase your rent to £8 a day."

Martin saw Bruce peering through the viewfinder of a Polaroid camera. He closed his eyes. Then, forgoing breakfast, he went upstairs and packed his suitcase.

*   *   *

Back to Euston, pivot of his life in London. Suitcase in the left-luggage. No more b and b. Nearly £50 a week of benefit blown just for a roof over your head.

He ordered a coffee in a smart cafeteria in the station. A

building site? According to the occupants of Larkman House you could pick up £40 a day, no questions, and sleep on the site.

But that wasn't why he had come to London. He shook his head and an old man wearing galoshes over his shoes said: "You all right, son?"

Martin said he was fine and thought: What would Prince do now?

He missed Prince.

He went to the Job Centre. There were a few jobs available — trainee salespeople, porters, junior required by a music publishing company ... Nothing, for one reason or another, that was suitable.

Perhaps Uncle Jack could help. If I hadn't made such a fool of myself. Or Walter?

First he had to find somewhere to spend the night. At three in the afternoon he made his way to the night shelter in Dean Street.

He asked the bushy-haired man at reception if Prince had booked in. No, Prince hadn't been seen for nearly a week. Martin, showered and searched, felt more alone than he had since he arrived in London.

He wandered into the courtyard. Men were still queueing, staring at the ground; some moved thoughtfully from one foot to the other, others gazed at the walls and through them.

A black man at the end of the queue performed a shuffling dance, then held out his arms as a farmer might when it rains after a long drought.

Martin said: "Hallo, Charlie."

Charlie said: "Who you are?"

"Don't you remember me?"

"I might," Charlie said.

"How's the running?"

"You're Martin," Charlie said.

"Still going to win the 800 metres?"

"Oh sure," Charlie said. "I'm going to win that," voice jumbled.

"Have you seen Prince?"

Charlie frowned. "Who's he?"

"You must remember Prince," Martin said. Not even Charlie could forget Prince. "Tall, pale, helps you with your running."

"That Prince! Thought you meant one of them royals."
So Charlie made small jokes.
"Where is he?" Martin asked.
Charlie frowned. "I did know."
"Try and think."
"I'll think during the night," Charlie said. "I think a lot when I'm asleep."
"Think hard," Martin said.
"Not too hard. Can't sleep if I think too hard."
"If you remember," Martin said, "wake me."

*   *   *

Hands shaking him. Martin grabbed them.
"It's me, Charlie. I remembered."
"Tell me, Charlie."
"South London," Charlie said.
"Shut the fuck up," said a voice.
"The nick," Charlie said.
"Prison?"
"If you don't sodding well shut up . . ."
"Near it."
"Which one, Charlie?"
"I forget," Charlie said.
"Think."
"Not the Scrubs. Not Brixton."
Martin could feel him thinking.
Charlie said: "Wandsworth, that's it."
"Close to Wandsworth prison?"
"Close," Charlie said.
"You've been there?"
"Oh, I've been there all right," Charlie said.
"We'll go there tomorrow," Martin said. "We'll find it all right."
"We'll run," Charlie said.
"For the last time . . ."
"Go back to sleep, Charlie."
"Great to see old Prince again."
"Go to sleep."
Martin closed his eyes. The bead in the lobe of Prince's ear glittered.

PART TWO

CHAPTER 8

Home is a mansion.

Home is a sand-blasted mews with a yellow door and a Porsche instead of a horse.

Home is a detached house in Pinner.

Home is a segment of a terrace – placed end to end, the terraces of Britain would encompass the world – or a semi-detached built between the two world wars, with a small car pinned to it like a brooch. The terraces and semis are the heartland of London and under their roofs there is much decency.

Home is a three-bedroomed apartment in Clapham, £130 a week.

Home is a share of a flat or a bedsit or b and b, five in a room and no site boots.

Home is a squat.

Home is a cardboard box.

*   *   *

One aching January morning Cuff, arranged like a mollusc inside two cardboard cartons, had fingered his toes and, discovering that there was no feeling in them, decided to move up the residential scale once more and find a squat.

The services of Cuff, scout and scavenger, were much sought after by the itinerants of London looking for accommodation.

Cuff could nose out a squat like a dog snouting a truffle.

Hoardings advertising SITE AVAILABLE FOR REDEVELOPMENT and Cuff, map-reading intuitively, calculated the focal point to which the hoardings pointed and established rights in a derelict school or a dispirited chapel. THIS BUILD-ING IS DANGEROUS and Cuff was inside in a trice.

A furniture removal van, a creaking door, a broken window, an unkempt garden and Cuff approached stealthily from the wings.

He avoided up-market squats – comfortable homes left temporarily untended by the affluent but unwary – because they involved too much aggro. (One irate house-owner had thrown a gravestone through a window every night until the unnerved squatters had departed.)

Cuff was a small man, shaped apologetically, who wore dead men's suits. He acquired them from widows whose names he found in funeral reports in local newspapers and had acquired a considerable travelling wardrobe.

On this pitiless morning he was wearing a charcoal-grey double-breasted that smelled of hospitals. Its formality was an asset although the discerning might have wondered why the owner of such a suit was not wearing an overcoat. He did, however, carry a bent umbrella with which he tried to spear the occasional leaf left over from autumn.

Thus attired, he took a bus across the Thames to Wands-worth, where the Huguenots once made hats for the cardinals of Rome, now an amorphous, thirteen-square-mile inner suburb bounded by Putney, Wimbledon, Clapham and the river. It possesses a bridge, a common and a prison that once housed Oscar Wilde.

Cuff, so named because the cuffs of his older suits sprouted whiskers, made his way with elaborate nonchalance along street upon street of lean houses.

What he awaited was the hunter's premonition of quarry: the feel that a gaunt building was unloved.

Just such a feeling assailed him within a couple of hundred yards of the walls of the prison. A grey and substantial corner house that had once resounded to the laughter of children. He felt that Mary Poppins might once have visited this house.

He approached it circumspectly. GUARD DOGS PATROL-LING AT NIGHT. Encouraging. A privet hedge tall and tousled beneath a bonnet of grubby snow. Dog-shit on the steps undisturbed by skidding feet. Distinctly promising.

Red, imitation burglar alarm attached to the wall.

Decay, a petrified essence of summer and autumn and winter – no spring.

Cuff, umbrella a mine-detector, moved in, an apology on the tip of his tongue.

As the occupants of a squat are sometimes prosecuted for breaking and entering Cuff sought the means by which there could be entering without breaking. If the worst came to the worst he would have to break a window, repair it and claim that a door was open.

He walked up the front path. The garden was an unmade bed and the house, windows shut with boards, was asleep in it.

He went behind it. There were tracks on the snow, cats and birds and rats. The garden was small with a high wall but there was a shed in one corner, an annexe for one lodger.

He tried the kitchen door; it was nailed shut. The French windows looked more promising but they were boarded from within.

Cuff decided to call Prince.

He made two calls near the site of the former Friendless Boys' Home for lads who had "lost their characters or are in danger of doing so", telling the operator on each occasion that he had put money in the slot and lost it; the operators took the number, said they would report the fault and put him through. Cuff could just remember the old days when you could back-dial a number without even pretending you had paid.

He called Dean Street and a pub in Soho and left messages giving the address in Wandsworth. He then found an off-licence where they sold draught cooking sherry and took half a litre back with him to the shed in the garden.

Prince arrived at 2.30.

Cuff, waving the bottle, said: "Thought you might be interested."

"I might," Prince said.

He disappeared, returned with a builder's board stating that work was in progress, stuck it in the front garden and turned his attention to the French windows at the back.

They gave up without a fight: one pane eased from a soft-leaded frame, hand inside, bolt drawn. The boards offered more resistance but they finally surrendered under assault from a spade.

The interior of the house betrayed the respectable Victorian exterior. Wallpaper hung in frozen tongues; icicles bared their teeth in the bathrooms; ceilings sagged; moss grew brightly in the kitchen.

A house waiting to be demolished because this bit of Wandsworth was going up-market.

"It'll do," Prince said. He sat on a rattan rocking chair, the only article of furniture in the house, beside a fireplace containing long-dead cinders. "Now we've got to decide who."

"What we need is a caretaker, a plumber, a bouncer . . . and Charlie, of course."

Cuff held up the bottle; it was quite empty.

"And a provider," Prince said. The rocking chair creaked. "You," he said to Cuff.

*   *   *

The squat, named Willow House because of the tree weeping in the front garden, was renamed Buck House.

One of the first occupants Martin met was a junkie.

Prince apologised for him. "We don't normally allow skagheads. Smoking a joint, well, no one goes to war about that. But smack, that's different; Mad Bull gets rid of them."

Who, Martin asked, was Mad Bull?

"Bouncer, chucker-out. Used to be in the grunt-and-groan business until another wrestler whacked him on the ear and broke his ear-drum. You'll meet him," Prince said.

"Why do you allow this junkie to stay?" Martin asked.

"He sort of grew up with us. We saw it happen. Maybe we were to blame. He's our conscience."

"You can cure him?" Martin looked at Prince sceptically.

"Maybe, maybe not. He's not over the top. Chasing the dragon, but not jacking up. We've got a couple of schemes. You know, the communal thing. Despite what *they* say about us maybe we can achieve a few things *they* can't. Camaraderie," he said. "What do *they* know about that?"

"What sorts of things?" They climbed the stairs stepping carefully over missing steps.

"A couple of challenges. Hood, for instance."

"Who's Hood?"

"A liar," Prince said. "Compulsive. Can't help himself. So,

we've issued a challenge: tell the truth for twenty-four hours and you win a prize. What we haven't decided," Prince said. "But that doesn't matter. What matters is the skaggie. He's promised that if Hood lasts twenty-four hours without telling a lie he'll try and kick smack."

"And the other?"

Prince, gazing at a door, broken at the hinges, bearing the legend LUCY'S ROOM, said: "Charlie. If Hood fails then it's up to Charlie. If he wins his race then Danny says he'll really chuck the dope. How's Charlie been?" Prince asked.

"I only met him yesterday. He ran here from Soho."

"Blowing, was he?"

"I was. Not Charlie."

Prince opened the broken door. The pink, flaking walls of the room were still adorned with crayoned pictures of thin houses basking beneath grinning suns. On a mattress lay a slender young man with a wisp of a beard; he was staring at the ceiling.

"Danny," Prince said, "this is Martin."

"Hi, Martin." Danny traced patterns in the air with one finger.

"He's joining us," Prince said.

"Welcome," Danny said.

"He's on a low," Prince said.

"I'm on a low," Danny said.

"Talk to him," Prince said.

"Talk to me," Danny said.

Prince walked briskly down the corridor, footsteps thick on the rotting floorboards.

"Stay with us," Danny said, "till they bring the hammers in. And the bulldozers. Not a lot you can do about a bulldozer, Martin."

Martin sat on the floor.

Danny said: "You want to know what a nice guy like me is doing in a dump like this? Well, I'll tell you: I'm not a nice guy." His voice was what Martin's mother would have described as educated. "Got a smoke?"

"I don't smoke."

"Not a joint, just a smoke. A ciggie."

"Sorry," Martin said.

"Shit. Know what I'd really like? The dragon, that's what. Catch that spiky little reptile by his tail and inhale his breath. Stick a little skag on a strip of shiny tin foil and burn a match

87

under it and watch the skag turn into liquid giving off those beautiful, beautiful fumes and stick a tube into them and breathe deeply. Ahhhhhh."

Danny closed his eyes.

Martin stood up and stared through a gap in the boards covering the window; the evening was settling cruelly.

He said: "I want to taste dew on a summer morning." He stared at the mauve cold. "And smell a breeze coming in from the sea. And kiss a girl and feel the warmth of her lips. Who wants drugs?" he asked.

"You don't understand," Danny said. He raised himself on one elbow.

"I understand that it's all possible without smack."

"Oh no." Danny's thin sinews moved beneath his denim shirt. "You don't understand at all."

"Tell me," Martin said.

"Great script, Martin."

Martin turned away from the encroaching night and looked at a tilted house with a cartoon dog beside it.

He said: "Tell me why I don't understand: I want to know."

"My parents didn't care. How's that?"

"Didn't they?"

"I never knew. Maybe I never cared."

"Maybe you were too young to know how," Martin said.

"Or maybe they didn't know how to. Isn't that sad?" Danny traced a figure eight with one finger. "You see I haven't got any real reasons. And that's what gets to the people who care. They've got to have reasons. Parents split up, inadequacy, suppressed homosexuality . . . Give them a reason and they're as happy as pigs in shit. No reason and you're holding out, baiting them."

Danny stood up, shakily pulling at the silken wisps of his beard, and joined Martin at the window. It was dark now and there were stars in the sky.

"Don't you want reasons?" Danny asked.

"Who wants reasons?"

"There was a crowd of us in Ipswich. Some of us smoked a little pot, nothing more. We didn't even drink that much: we weren't pubby people. Then one of the girls went to London for the weekend and came back with some coke. It seemed exciting: some of us snorted it. Then we tried nitrate acid and speed.

Just for kicks, nothing more. *Kicks*. Now there's a reason . . . the most common of all . . . more than insecurity or mother complexes or chronic masturbation . . . do you have any problems, Martin?"

"Bed-wetting," Martin said.

"Then we moved on to smack. Chasing the dragon. And I was hooked." He began to shiver. "I haven't jacked yet, mainlined . . . When I do it's all over. People talk disgustedly about kids mugging old people because they want money to shoot junk. What they don't understand is that the real junkie just doesn't care: there's only one reality and that's the next fix. I almost know how they feel." He held up one trembling hand.

"I'll get you a cigarette," Martin said. "And a beer."

"But if Hood can last twenty-four hours without lying then anything's possible."

"And Charlie?"

"Hood first," Danny said.

Martin went downstairs, cadged a cigarette from Cuff and took a can of Tennent's from a six-pack. But when he got back to Lucy's room Danny was asleep on his mattress.

*   *   *

There was now a mildewed bottle-green chaise-longue in the living-room, bricks substituted for a missing leg; three tea-chests stamped TYPHOO; a papier-mâché peacock also missing a leg; a white sun-lounger nibbled by rust; a disembowelled television; a threadbare length of Wilton carpet; two sodden cushions covered with red and gold brocade; a pile of *National Geographic* magazines; a hand-winched gramophone; and a cracked chamber-pot decorated with cornflowers.

Cuff, penitent, smoothed the lapels of his dead-man's suit and said: "It was all I could get. But there's a tip at Clapham and they're moving house down the road so there'll be some gear left over – I've had a word with the van driver."

Martin sat on the edge of the lounger and stared into the fireplace where the builder's hoarding was burning brightly, tongues of flame wolfing the name of the company.

"You've done well," Prince said to Cuff. He rocked jerkily in the rattan chair. "Help yourself to a Tennent's."

A mountainous fat man sat on the chaise-longue. Mad Bull

who, according to Prince, had once been wrestling champion of the Home Counties. But the broken ear-drum had affected his reflexes and one Saturday afternoon, rapturously applauded by tear-stained housewives, he had retired, to watch his muscles turn to fat. But not before he had head-butted an indignant opponent into submission. But who could disqualify Mad Bull on a day such as this? Who could face the wrath of his orgasmic fans? When he shook Martin's hand his grip was gentle.

Prince said to Martin: "Don't fret. Grub's on the way. Gosling's gone down to the supermarket to get some out-of-date items. Might be chuck-outs too."

"My mam used to buy a pennyworth of fades when she was a girl," Martin said. "Bruised apples," he explained. "And six pennyworth of mixed – fish, chips and peas." And she used to make wet nelly, he remembered; stale bread with currants and sultanas baked in the oven, also known as dockers' wedding cake.

His mouth watered.

"Gosling's clerical," Prince said. "Writs, summons, threats, that sort of thing."

"I think in words," Gosling said, taking food stamped with yesterday's date from a plastic bag. "My punishment, I suppose."

"For what?" Martin asked.

"Martin . . . backwards that's Nitram. I like it. A rare element, a celestial leader. You can often tell a bit about people by inverting their names. Star backwards – rats. Pop star, pop rats . . ."

Gosling who had pushed his rimless spectacles high on his slightly bulging forehead produced banana yoghurt, a sliced loaf of pallid bread, frozen fish fingers, a packet of Eccles cakes, a can of dog-food, kippers, streaky bacon and a jar of pineapple juice with a rusty lid.

"Has it ever occurred to you," he said, "how some words contradict themselves? Take butterfly. Could there be a more beautiful creature? Now analyse the word. Butter . . . fly . . . ugh! On the other hand there's primrose. Prim rose. Perfect."

"What are we going to cook in?" Prince asked.

Cuff went into the kitchen, returning with a scoured pan.

"The tip?" Prince asked.

Cuff apologised. "Fry the bacon first," he said to Gosling.

90

"That gives you fat. Then the bread. Then a yoghurt each washed down with a can of Tennent's."

The smell of frying bacon pushed the odour of mildew and distemper from the room. Martin's stomach whined.

They ate heartily, all except Mad Bull who, being a vegetarian, contented himself with a yoghurt, a couple of slices of bread and a beer.

The fire, spitting with bacon fat, burned brightly. A snug sense of achievement settled on the room.

But no one had asked Martin to stay.

Mad Bull picked up a metal rod, straightened it and poked the fire.

Gosling's lips moved.

Cuff shook his head over some distant misdemeanour.

Prince wrote on a pad.

He said to Martin: "I've got a wheeze. Want to hear about it?"

Martin who had been hoping he was about to ask him to stay nodded.

"Not my patent but an earner. Queues. First day of the sales. Establish myself overnight outside a store. Sleeping bag, coffee laced with brandy. In the morning, sell my position to the highest bidder. Twenty-five quid bottom price."

Prince's eyes glittered in his pale face.

Silence except for the spluttering fire and the distant wail of a police car. Martin thought about the iced darkness outside; the walls of the squat were an embrace.

"By the way," Prince said, "you've got the camp-bed. Cuff borrowed it from another squat."

*   *   *

The camp-bed in a large bedroom where, perhaps, a man with mutton-chop whiskers had once made love, after lights-out, to the mother of his children, after she had shed her petticoats in a rustle of silk, was not comfortable; but Martin didn't care. He didn't even mind the dust from the old curtains, discovered in the attic, in which he was mummified for the night. A star peering through the skylight.

Tomorrow he would visit the third London uncle, Walter. He closed his eyes. The star chimed and moved on its way.

CHAPTER 9

———◆———

Walter Renshaw, a man of good intentions, and his wife Holly
– mispronounced by some as Holy – lived in Feltham, a suburb
to the far west of London.

Feltham possesses a high street with mandatory chain stores,
shining office blocks reaching for the jets lowering themselves
from the clouds towards Heathrow, the RAOC officers' mess
and a church with a cemetery containing the bones of an
engraver executed in 1783 for forgery.

It also possesses acres of bungalows and semi-detacheds with
pointed roofs whose occupants treacherously confound the
image of Britain today. Old people are pampered instead of
punched, whites, blacks and browns live harmoniously, aspirin
is preferred to heroin and each small residence pulses with
private endeavour.

To observe the occupants of these homes at their most
perverse one should accompany a team collecting for charity at
Christmas. As carols ring out joyously from a lorry-borne
amplifier the occupants respond with a generosity not always
apparent in richer outposts. And such is the infirmity of some
that it is difficult not to conclude that they should be receiving
rather than giving.

Crusaders championing minorities at the expense of the
majority would be well advised to by-pass Feltham and other
such unfashionable communities.

Walter and Holly Renshaw, it must be admitted, did labour
energetically and virtuously. In their semi-detached, bigger than
most with double garage and glazing, they orchestrated the
saving of souls and much perseverance was required when the

owners of the souls expressly forbade salvation.

Walter was a lay preacher at a church outside the parochial bounds of Feltham and a member of many committees channelling funds in the direction of causes which he considered deserving. His endeavours were commendable and only once, accidentally, did they become an endangered species when distracted, by some humanitarian consideration, he left a tape on his video which he had been studying for sociological reasons. The tape was called *Unbridled Lust* and was casually activated by the cleaning woman during her mid-morning tea-break. Walter, incurable philanthropist, immediately increased her earnings by £1 an hour.

*   *   *

Martin took a winter-grimed train from Clapham Junction and, while it nosed its way through the suburbs, considered his circumstances. Stripped of evasions, what was he? Jobless squatter, that's what.

The squatting didn't upset him – he enjoyed the camaraderie of Buck House – but the joblessness did, particularly when he recalled earlier aspirations. After reading Ayn Rand's *The Fountainhead*, he had known that he was destined to be an architect. He had caught the movie of the book at a fleapit and had spent hours studying the architectural marvels and monstrosities of Liverpool. From the Philharmonic Hall and its adjacent pub, a lantern-slide of Edwardian England (pink marble stalls in the Gentlemen's), the colonnaded portals of Gambier Terrace where John Lennon once lived and the pink Playhouse in Williamson Square to the martial horrors of the new hotels, Atlantic Tower, St. George's, Crest, Holiday Inn, barrack blocks looking for parade-grounds.

In his dreams Martin squashed the hotels and other monuments to insensitivity with a rub of his thumb, a gardener massacring greenfly, and re-designed Merseyside's skyline with a fine black nib. Spires and domes and spheres joining the Town Hall and the Royal Liver and the Cunard.

But the skyline had faded as the family income shrank around the bare bone of his father's pride. How could you suspend Hanging Gardens of Babylon above wasted docks, when the head of the family refused to draw all his benefits?

93

Better go out and shift furniture.

Martin, ignoring two black-leathered Hell's Angels, clumsy without their bikes, testing the blades of Swiss army knives, gazed out of the windows at the Sunday-quiet suburbs. One of the Hell's Angels pricked his thumb with the point of a blade and stared thoughtfully at Martin. He was broad with a yellowish beard and his belly pushed at his leathers.

What about character? What would I do if the fat angel put the knife to my throat and demanded my wallet? To understand bravery you must understand cowardice.

The trouble was that Martin didn't understand himself. Contradictions. An inarticulate poet. A realistic idealist. He had to make his move before indecision became a permanent fixture.

The angel with the beard stood up and advanced upon Martin. Blood oozed from his thumb. Martin decided to make a fight of it.

The angel said: "Got the time on you, mate?"

Martin, consulting his digital, said it was 11.20.

"Thanks, mate." Sucking his wounded thumb, he returned to his partner.

The two of them alighted at Richmond. Martin glimpsed cherished houses, comfortable pews beside the aisle of the Thames. He consulted a map. Richmond stood snug between the regal acres of Old Deer and Richmond Parks.

Martin, forgetting the squat, thought that one day he might live here.

The train crossed the river, another of Britain's divides.

Martin alighted at Feltham. The station was a decrepit place, a survivor of pea-soup fogs. Prince, contemplating organising a competition for the most depressing station in Britain, was convinced that Kendal in Cumbria would be a runaway winner but Feltham would be in there with a chance.

Martin emerged opposite a church with a spire that had been incorporated into an office block and a stagnant pond. He made his way down the somnolent high street, plunging right into the bungalows and semis where small cars were receiving their weekly wash.

Walter, whom Martin had telephoned from Clapham, was flicking invisible specks of dust from his white Sierra with a leather. He shook Martin's hand firmly and stared at him speculatively.

Martin studied his God-fearing uncle. The Renshaw mould was unmistakable, but whereas Jack's character owed much to his mother Walter was manifestly a father's boy. His expression was sculpted by piety but not grievously so: he understood weakness in others and his smile was ready and forgiving: he reminded Martin of some of the Catholic priests in Liverpool who, seeking knowledge outside the vestry, joined members of their congregations for a few jars in the city's pubs.

Walter, an accountant by profession, was taller than Martin's father, shorter than Harry. His pale hair was stretched across his scalp, his spectacles sparkled, he wore a Bible-black suit and a grey tie bearing a designer logo.

Breaking the handshake, through which, it seemed to Martin, he had been attempting to transmit goodness, he pointed at the house and said: "Welcome aboard."

On cue the door opened, revealing Holly Renshaw, her smile a stranger on features composed bravely in the face of adversity. She wore an apron printed with wild flowers, each named both botanically and familiarly. Her hair was brown and straight; her legs muscular, braced against life. "You must forgive me," she said. For what he didn't know.

The interior of the house was ascetic although Martin discerned traces of discreet opulence, gold threads in a threadbare vestment. Rainbows twinkling in cut-glass, silver candelabra on the rosewood piano, Staunton chess pieces on a leather board leafed at the edges with gold.

The living-room smelled of incense and roasting lamb.

Walter, priest seeking the common touch, offered Martin a beer. "You should have come earlier," he said. "I was preaching in Hounslow." He poured himself a glass of mineral water. "Do you go to church, Martin?"

Martin said, truthfully enough, that he did although not, he feared, as regularly as he should.

"C of E?"

"That's the way I was brought up," Martin said, sitting in an easy chair in front of an imitation coal fire. "But I've been to both cathedrals, C of E and RC."

Both on one day. Lingering in Liverpool Cathedral, bigger than St. Paul's and the largest Anglican church in the world, before walking down Hope Street to the Metropolitan Cathedral of Christ the King with its tower of coloured glass that cast lambent light inside.

"You see," Martin said, reacting perversely to this uncle, "I think one church is much the same as another. After all, we're all worshipping the same God." Walter was Methodist or Baptist; he couldn't remember which.

"True, true." Walter paced the room and smiled indulgently. "But we can choose our mode of worship. Pomp and circumstance or ordinary, down-to-earth devotion. Which do you think is the more sincere, Martin?"

Martin was saved by a summons from the kitchen to his uncle to carve the joint.

The slices of meat were almost transparent, potatoes hard in the centre, cabbage soggy. They drank water. "Adam's ale," Walter said, smiling thinly.

Holly said: "So, Martin, at last you've come to Feltham."

It was Holly who had sent the photographs to Liverpool that had attracted Martin's attention on Boxing Day; Holly believed in family unity.

Martin, unsure whether she meant since he had come to London or since he was born, nodded, biting on grit in the cabbage. He noticed that an extra place had been set at the table.

"About time," his uncle said, chewing with application. "What made you suddenly decide to come to London?"

Martin sensed the same wariness he had felt in the presence of Jack Renshaw. Or was he becoming over-sensitive?

He told him that he intended to visit all his uncles, aware that he wasn't answering the question.

"You've seen Harry?" Holly asked.

"Only Jack so far."

"Ah, Jack."

"The black sheep," Walter said. He put down his knife and fork and polished his spectacles with a napkin.

"Why is he so . . . different?"

"We all went our different ways."

No one, Martin thought, was really answering questions.

Holly said: "There but for the grace of God . . ."

"Is he so bad?" Martin asked.

"No one's all bad, Martin." Walter replaced his spectacles and gazed without enthusiasm at his food. "Did your father suggest you should come and see us?"

"No," answered Martin, surprised.

"A good man, your father."

"Did you ever think about coming to Liverpool to see him?"
Silence stretched across the table.

Holly said: "Eat up, Walter, don't forget I've got a class this afternoon."

"Holly teaches at Sunday school," Walter explained.

He reached across the table and touched her hand but she withdrew it abruptly.

"Do you see much of Harry?" Martin asked.

"He's done really well," Walter said.

Martin looked at a photograph of the four brothers on the mantelpiece. They were young men with glossy hair grinning into the future. They wore open-neck shirts and their arms were around each other's shoulders. The photograph was black and white but they looked tanned. And inseparable.

The photograph worried Martin but he wasn't sure why.

Holly, following his gaze, said: "Walter keeps putting it away but I like it. It's how families should be," she said.

"Our boys visit us quite often," Walter said.

"Harold and Leonard," Holly said. "They both share flats in London. Harold's thinking of emigrating to Australia."

"He's already asked us to visit him down under," Walter said.

The four brothers grinned at Martin from the mantelpiece. Jack was winking.

"That was taken on Bournemouth sea-front," Holly told Martin. "Before they split up."

"We didn't split," Walter said. "We merely went our separate ways."

"With varying degrees of success," Holly said.

She collected the empty plates, returning from the kitchen with trifle made from green and yellow jelly and stale cake.

Walter said: "Come unto me all ye that labour and are heavy laden, and I will give you rest."

His smile was tight.

Martin ate his trifle quickly; it tasted of jellyfish.

After lunch they drank tea in the living-room, Holly sitting on the sofa, sturdy legs crossed.

"So," Walter said, sipping his tea, "have you got a job yet?"

Martin told them about the squat and the shortage of good

97

jobs and found himself elaborating: Walter did this to him.

"The social workers are great. They understand. But they're frustrated: they know that the people at the top are out of touch. That's what's wrong with this country: the people running it just don't understand. And probably don't want to. They might just as well be on another planet. What we should do," Martin said, Scouse vowels sharpening, "is swop the social workers for the politicians. Except that the social workers wouldn't want to go to Westminster: they're too honest."

"What sort of job do you want?" Holly asked. She poured herself more tea and dropped a sweetener into it, watching the white tablet swirl in a brown vortex before disappearing. "Perhaps Walter could help you."

Walter said: "I only run a small ship. Full crew at the moment. But if something crops up . . ."

"If someone falls overboard?"

"I'm quite serious," Walter said but his smile forgave.

"I'm sure you'll find something," Holly said. "You Renshaws usually do."

"How is your father?" Walter asked.

"He's fine," Martin said.

"Lucky Jim we used to call him."

"Not so lucky these days."

"It's not luck that this world is all about, Martin."

The fading light cast a pale spectrum in a cut-glass decanter.

"Why was he called Lucky Jim?"

"He had a way with the ladies," Walter said.

"You mustn't judge us by our age," Holly said.

Martin tried to picture a younger Holly. Those legs . . . With an effort he saw her, brown and lithe, darting around a tennis court. Perhaps that was where she had met Walter, at a tennis club.

"Then we went our separate ways," Walter said. He consulted his watch elaborately.

"All right," Holly said, "I know when I'm not wanted."

"I have to drive her to Sunday school . . ." Walter spread his hands at Martin.

Martin watched them drive away in the Sierra, their ship, and set off past the freshly-polished cars for the station.

He sat on a bench beside a waiting-room so bleak that it made a friend of the cold outside.

What was it about the photograph on the mantelpiece?

An express train sprinted through the station, throwing cold air at him.

Arms around each other's shoulders, grinning, they were conspirators. That was it!

In the train another question presented itself.

Why had there been an extra table-setting at lunch?

Then he had that, too.

For God.

CHAPTER 10

The police came to the squat the following morning. Two of them, in plain clothes, Lewis a young terrier and Heald an old dog.

While Heald banged on the front door Lewis slipped round the back. Lewis, crisply barbered and sharply dressed, wasn't enthusiastic about the job – only scum lived in squats – but Heald had refused to listen to reason.

The first to leave by the kitchen door was a small man surprisingly well-dressed in a charcoal-grey suit. He looked as though he was hurrying for a train.

"Whoa there, Silver," Lewis said, grabbing his collar.

His companion was fat, bald and powerful. Shit, thought Lewis. He said: "Hold it, fatso," bracing himself for a hammer blow, but the big man shrugged and walked peaceably back into the kitchen.

Heald, a bulky man nearing forty who moved loosely, banged again on the front door knowing he would have to wait while rehearsed evasions took place inside.

No one had told him to visit the squat: he merely considered it part of a policeman's duty to call on prospective clients, villains or victims.

Heald was a descendant of those stout policemen who once kept peace on their manors with a cautionary word or a thrust with their considerable bellies. Today he grieved for his calling: the police, once only the enemy of criminals, were now held in contempt by multitudes. Particularly by the young.

He was aware of the scapegoats – unemployment, drugs,

100

bent coppers – but he also blamed a breed who would have been outraged at such an indictment: the middle-aged arbiters who, scared of ridicule, had sanctioned the erosion of morals. Violence on TV, promiscuous sex (precursor of AIDS), porn above the comics in the corner shops . . .

Heald also blamed judges. Yesterday one had sentenced a child molester to a suspended sentence. *Stay at large until you corrupt another kid.* How would that owl in a wig have reacted if it had been his seven-year-old daughter who had been robbed of her innocence in a warehouse?

Of course there *were* bad coppers, more than there had been in that unspecified age of decency lodged in Heald's reasoning. Really bad bastards some of them. Nevertheless Heald was proud of the force. Observe them battling a brick-throwing mob, spittle running down their riot shields; consider a constable staring down the twin barrels of a sawn-off shotgun, escorting a lost child home, being kicked to death in a no-go area.

Heald gave the door another couple of bangs.

The only occupants he knew personally were Prince who, miraculously, had no form, and Charlie who had squatted on his manor before and Danny the skaghead. Except that Heald, who had big hands and grey, thoughtful eyes, didn't call them skagheads or junkies anymore, not since his son had been sent down from Durham University for snorting coke.

Stephen was now being helped by the Community Drug Project in South London. In the early hours of the morning, when past and the present march together, Heald saw him walking home from school, small and bespectacled and alone.

Prince said: "Nothing today, thank you."

Heald pushed past him. "Just checking, son, just checking. Like to know who's living on my parish."

Prince said: "We haven't stolen any gas or electricity and we didn't break in. Turf us out and we'll be a burden to society."

"You did break in," Heald said. "Through the French windows. But I'm not chucking anyone out: haven't got the authority."

He sat in the rocking chair and helped himself to a Tennent's. The tab came off the lid with a hiss. Heald poured beer down his throat and looked around. "Not bad," he said. "Not bad at all. Reasonable rent, too."

101

"Mustn't grumble," Prince said, sitting on the green chaise-longue. "Care to join us?"

"When I draw my pension."

"You haven't nicked enough punters to retire."

"No time like the present," Heald said. "Where did you get that?" pointing at the chaise-longue.

"Fell off the back of a dustcart," Prince said.

Lewis, potentially a good copper if he didn't get greedy, came into the room with two *tenants*. He introduced them as Cuff and Mad Bull. He didn't smile. Cuff apologised for being alive.

Heald said to Mad Bull: "I know you. Seen you fight. You were good."

Mad Bull, hand cupped to his deaf ear, smiled gently.

Heald said: "Where and who are the others?"

Prince told him about Gosling the Brain, Hood the Liar and Martin the Scouse. "Enter from the left," Prince said as Martin came down the treacherous staircase.

Heald looked at him with resignation. Young, well set up, another of the army of Dick Whittingtons foraging in the streets of London. A newcomer by the look of him but already in a squat. Not that Heald found squats as disgusting as some, admired the inmates' initiative in fact, but they were on the downward spiral.

"So, Martin, how long have you been in the Smoke?"

"Three weeks."

"Got a job yet?"

"Not yet," Martin said.

"Plenty going." But, of course, he would initially be drawing enough from the DHSS not to make it worthwhile. "Earn some bread by day, Martin, and study at night."

Stephen had studied.

"That's what I hope to do," Martin said.

"Keep at it, son. Watch out for the villains: they come in many shapes and sizes. Some even look like saints."

To Prince he said: "Okay, where's Danny?"

"Upstairs," Prince said.

"Got rid of his dope?"

"If you say so."

Lewis said: "Want me to take a look?"

Heald shook his head. What was the point? It wouldn't be in the cistern, it wouldn't be behind a loose brick – Prince was too

102

smart. An enigma, Prince. Accent unremarkable, vocabulary embracing slang and erudition . . . I don't even know his first name, Heald realised.

"Let's go up and see him then," Heald said.

"He's asleep," Prince said.

"Then we'll wake him up," Lewis said, but Heald said: "No, you stay here, look after these jokers," indicating Mad Bull and Cuff and Martin.

Danny was lying on his mattress. He stared dreamily at Heald. His pathetic beard moved Heald strangely.

Heald said: "Started mainlining yet, Danny?"

"I haven't started anything yet, sergeant."

"Of course you haven't, Danny. But should you need help . . ." He took a notebook from his pocket and wrote the address and phone number of SCODA. "Or this . . ." He printed his own phone number.

In the corridor outside he asked Prince: "How far gone is he?"

"He'll be okay," Prince said. "We're looking after him."

"But you aren't therapists."

"We're friends," Prince said.

*   *   *

Overnight it thawed. Water sluiced down gutters and drains, trees shed old snow that fell with muted drumbeats, and birds sang. Ponds became lakes, lakes tipped into parks and plumbers were deified. Then it froze again and London was a trap, slippery and sharp-toothed with danger.

*   *   *

Charlie, jogging steadily, led Martin past the walls of the gaunt prison and crossed Trinity Road onto Wandsworth Common.

Ice crunched beneath their feet. Their breath steamed. Martin rested beside the tennis courts and bowling green while Charlie pounded along the pale grass beside the railway line. Two runs a day — six to ten miles in the morning, four miles in the evening. In February he would change his routine, mixing long runs with bursts of speed, the Fartlek method which Martin had studied.

103

Martin watched him critically. His action was ungainly but his concentration was total. It was when Charlie wasn't running that Martin worried.

A week ago Charlie had become his responsibility. His contribution to the commune. Thus Danny, too, had become his charge: if Charlie won the 800 metres then Danny would stop chasing the dragon.

"But what about Hood?" Martin had asked Prince.

"What about him?"

"Danny said he would stop if Hood went twenty-four hours without telling a lie."

"So Hood's your responsibility too."

A soiled blue and white train trundled past. Charlie waved; some passengers waved back. Martin smiled. I belong, he thought.

But was his commitment too much? His life was beginning to belong to the squat. To cleaning and foraging and acquiring; to the smell of coffee and sausages spitting in a pan scoured as bright as a new coin by Mad Bull; to Prince's schemes and Gosling's words; to planning over pints of beer in the small pub down the road where old men sat undisturbed in the past.

But this wasn't why I came to London. I came looking for opportunity not acceptance. And what have I become? A member of a new class of society, a self-sufficient vagrant. A scrounger, as his father would have put it.

According to Prince they could expect up to three months in Buck House before the bailiffs and the bulldozers moved in; it all depended on Gosling's legal ingenuity.

Meanwhile the location helped when he was looking for a job; it was respectable. Not like Skelmsdale, the showpiece of hopelessness fifteen miles from Liverpool. Mention Skem at an interview and forget it: you bring the smell of despair with you.

Martin decided to stay in the squat until they were thrown out. Then he would go his own way. Reassured, Martin searched for the lithe, slightly undisciplined figure of Charlie. There were a couple of white joggers with agonised faces trotting towards Emmanuel School and children sliding on a path but of Charlie there was no sign.

In what direction had he been running? Martin clenched his fist in the pockets of his reefer. He ran towards Emmanuel, struck back across the cricket ground, followed the footpath past the ponds to Trinity Road. There were many West Indians abroad, heads ducked into the cold but none wearing a powder-blue tracksuit with a Union Jack on the back.

Martin passed the prison, crossed the railway and plunged into a crossword puzzle of small streets, Cicada, Jessica, Eglantine, Wilna, Allfarthing . . .

He collided with a woman emerging from the library wearing a green woollen hat on which moths had feasted. She dropped two books. He picked them up, Catherine Cookson and Ed McBain, and handed them to her. She smiled hesitantly searching for one of the holes in her hat with one finger.

He banged on the door of Buck House. Cuff opened it. The blue tracksuit was draped over the rocking-chair.

*   *   *

The pub, known as the Codgers, stood unremarkably on a corner of the street a hundred yards from the squat. It possessed an off-licence, two bars, saloon and public, one barely distinguishable from the other, a ruined dartboard, a brooding alsatian and a landlord of such forbidding mien that he had achieved a notoriety not far removed from popularity. The ceiling was smoked by tobacco fumes, horsebrasses adorned the mustard walls, above the bar in the saloon was nailed a sign bearing an arrow and the legend THE WEE ROOM. *Ladies, please remain seated during the whole performance. Gentlemen – Please stand a little closer – it may be shorter than you think.* Both bars smelled of lions' cages.

One end of the public bar was Jesty's corner. Jesty, encouraged, perhaps, by his name, told jokes. He cleared the bar. Why hadn't the pub ever been gentrified? What was the point, the landlord argued, with Jesty in residence? Life for Jesty, sandy and eager, was a series of jokes and the most hilarious was the fact that he knew they isolated him. He was by trade a postman.

"Knock, knock," said Jesty as Martin and Prince came into the bar.

"Who's there?" asked Prince.

"Eugene."

"Eugene who?"

"Eugene, me Tarzan."

"Nice one, Jesty," Prince said.

"What are you having?" Jesty asked.

Only masochists and newcomers, of which there were very few, fell for this one.

"My round," Prince said. "Giro day."

He ordered a vodka and soda for himself, a pint of bitter for Martin and a Scotch for Jesty.

"Did you hear the one . . ." but Prince had turned his back.

The landlord raised his heavy head from the racing results in the stop press of the *Evening Standard* and set about the chore of pouring the drinks. He was tall with larded black hair and a twitch in one eye that was incongruous in his lugubrious features. His name was Harry.

Prince handed him a £10 note.

"Nothing smaller?"

"Nothing."

The landlord sighed as though he had just been told he was suffering from an incurable malady.

Prince, elbow on the bar, said: "Hood will be here soon. Some people call him Porky."

"He's fat?"

"He tells lies. Porky pies. But I'm going to make a celebrity of him."

The twenty-four-hour marathon, Prince said, in which Hood would endeavour not to deviate from the truth, would receive maximum exposure. First a leak to the local press. The national papers would pick it up followed by radio and television.

"Upwardly mobile, that's what Hood will be. Invent a Christian name for him – Robin. Did you ever read Saki?"

Martin hadn't.

"*'I believe I take precedence,' he said coldly; 'you are merely the club bore: I am the club liar.'*"

"We'll have a referee," Prince said. "An arbitrator. Stay with him the whole twenty-four hours. Press conference. Sell his story to one of the Sundays."

Where had Prince come from? Where was he going? Martin had fished for answers but all he had caught was an enigma. He imagined Prince as a boy sitting at an old school desk carved with initials writing his schemes in an exercise book, saw him walking home with a skull full of plots; he reached the top of a rise . . . fade-out. What were the circumstances of his home?

Concentrating, Martin fashioned a house like a vicarage with cobwebs at the windows and roses at the door and a melancholy garden in which mists collected. That was the poet's face. But what about the sharp angles of his mind? His parents ... university professor and droll married to a seamstress with a sharp-needled wit? Brothers or sisters? Perhaps Prince was an orphan.

He said warily: "Prince, can I ask you something?"

"Anything," Prince said. "But don't expect answers."

"What's your first name? I mean you must have got one."

"Prince," Prince said. "What do you want, a king?"

The door opened with a jangle of bells and a stranger with a friendly pugilist's face came in. He placed both fists on the counter and ordered a Guinness. The landlord sighed. Jesty looked at him speculatively.

Prince said: "We'll need an office and a phone. Style," Prince said, "is everything."

"Why does Hood lie?" Martin asked.

"Can't help it."

"Then how is he going to last twenty-four hours without telling one?"

"Training," Prince said, ordering himself another vodka from the aggrieved landlord.

The door opened again and two of the old men who sat at a table beside the gas-fire came in. They sat down, rolled their cigarettes, spread their dominoes and blinked beneath their caps like old cats.

"Have you heard the one about the two women outside the gorilla's cage?" Jesty asked the man drinking Guinness.

Prince prodded the cube of ice in his drink. "Fire questions at him. Penalise him every time he tells a porky. Or ..." – Prince snapped two bony fingers – "give him a shot of truth drug. Just before the marathon. No," shaking his head, "that's not the way. There's winning and winning ..."

"So what's your definition of honesty?" Martin was curious.

Prince said: "Dishonesty is cheating the honest; it's a very rare crime."

"... the gorilla suddenly tears open the bars of the cage, grabs one of the women and has his way with her ..."

"Life," Prince said, "is circumstance, the accident of birth. No one should be too proud: we're all products of a small

107

explosion in the loins. And how many of us are mistakes? Churchill, perhaps, Hitler, Roosevelt, Stalin ... Maybe there wouldn't have been a second world war if it hadn't been for a mistake ... Maybe," Prince said, "life is a mistake."

"... so the other woman visits her friend in hospital next day and says, 'You must be terrribly upset,' and her friend says, 'Upset? Of course I'm upset. He hasn't called, written or telephoned.'"

"Hood will be here soon," Prince said ordering his third vodka.

The bells jangled and another veteran joined the tableau in front of the gas-fire.

The alsatian sniffed Martin's ankle.

"Another Guinness?" Jesty asked.

His companion consulted his watch. Shaking his head, he made for the door leaving Jesty alone.

"Jesus!" said the landlord.

Jesty smiled brightly and winked at Martin.

The bells tolled rustily once more and a large man wearing a tweed sports jacket and a yellow waistcoat came in. He wore a pugnacious moustache on a timid face and he blinked frequently and with deliberation. His cheeks were polished and, in between blinks, his eyes watered.

"Good evening, Porky," Prince said.

*   *   *

Transients called frequently at Buck House. Rarely were they turned away but their length of residence depended on Prince. He knew the reputations of many on the itinerant circuit, he assessed others; thieves, junkies and drunks were permitted a night's shelter, others with more endearing qualities – Prince rated loneliness highly – were allowed to stay longer.

Hood, a regular, was allotted a half-share of a room with a middle-aged man named Nolan (no women so far but it was only a matter of time) who earned a sort of a living entering competitions. His half of the room was littered with prizes – canteen of bronze cutlery from Thailand, exercise bicycle, set of encyclopedias, collection of garden tools ... he had recently enjoyed a cruise to the West Indies and was awaiting the results of a competition for slogans for a brand-name soup. Nolan

108

firmly believed that either *The super soup* or *It's souperlatively good* would win him a flight on Concorde.

Martin showed Hood to his shared room.

Nolan's crumpled face was protruding from a sleeping bag that he had won in a competition organised by a company manufacturing camping equipment. He was trying to assess which of ten alternatives he would find most attractive about a package deal to the Greek Islands. "Sun-kissed beaches?" he asked Martin.

Martin shook Hood's hand, fancying he felt lies flow between them.

He went downstairs and drank a last Tennent's with Prince. Snores reached them from above. Charlie's, he decided. Charlie and Hood my responsibilities. But in three months, maybe less, he would go his own way. Wouldn't he?

CHAPTER 11

◆

Jenny Renshaw rebelled on a Monday.

She told her parents over breakfast that she had invited Martin to dinner the following Friday and when her step-father said from behind the *Financial Times*: "Sorry, can't be done," she said: "Well, he's coming anyway."

"Really?" Harry lowered his pink newspaper. "Supposing we're having other guests."

"All the better," Jenny said.

"The answer is no." He smoothed his pale hair with one plump hand.

"Well he's coming anyway."

"Really? And who's going to do the cooking?"

"I am," Jenny said.

She tied her hair in a pony-tail, put on jeans and boots and moulting fur jacket and, crossing Hampstead Lane, struck across the Kenwood reaches of Hampstead Heath where, when winter was broken, daffodils would bloom, and carried on south across the grassland where once highwaymen had plundered. Since she was a child she had taken to the heath to confer with herself.

Why, she asked herself, are you so perverse? You scarcely know Martin Renshaw. And you could at least have discussed the invitation with your mother.

Not, surely, that old cliché, the rebellion of youth. No, it was mature assessment. She rounded a clump of hibernating trees and breathed sharp air into her lungs.

What angered her was the way the privileged – her step-father – distanced themselves from reality. To him Martin was

110

a statistic – homeless, jobless, a layabout. He wasn't because everyone is entitled to their own perceptions: the wino owns his foggy visions as much as the captain of industry owns his ambition.

None of us, Jenny Renshaw thought, is responsible for our birthright. None of us has to accept patronage.

She skirted Highgate Ponds where dogs were taking their owners for walks. But what was she to do? She caught a bus to the West End. The streets narrowed and clung together. She saw an aerosol slogan MUG A YUPPIE TODAY.

She heard menace. It whispered from between the pages of newspapers. Protest concerting, finding escape hatches in racism.

She got off the bus near Oxford Street. And remembered that she couldn't cook.

She turned down Regent Street, rounded Piccadilly and made her way to the main thoroughfare of Chinatown, Gerrard Street.

She bought a wok, bamboo steamers, hot-pot, deep-frying strainer, casserole, whisk and (afterthought) chopsticks.

She bought bean curd, soya beans, and black beans, chili, dried shrimps and fish, crystal sugar, egg noodles, lotus nuts, hoisin sauce and crackling pork skin.

She bought Chinese cabbage, dried mushrooms, bamboo shoots, peppers, garlic, ginger, celery and spinach.

She bought 100-year-old eggs.

She bought pork and duck and minced beef.

She bought herbs of which she had never heard.

She listened to wind-chimes calling to another land.

She smiled at people who smiled through her.

She bought (as another afterthought) rice.

She bought powder of pearls for her mother's skin.

She bought a Chinese cookery book.

She went home to study it.

*   *   *

Topping and tailing the French beans to accompany the brown rice (Chinese! Impulsiveness would be her undoing), Jenny remembered her first meeting with Harry Renshaw. The then-sleek face proffered for a kiss ... Why did grown-ups do it?

111

Tufted-nostrils and snouting lips bearing down upon you from a distorting mirror. The flavour of his aftershave. The way he jogged one crossed leg and the incipient plumpness of his thigh beneath grey suiting and his shiny black socks and the instinctive, humourless smile and the little finger crooked outside his teacup when he took her to the terrace of his club near Berkeley Square. Would she hear a nightingale sing?

The impressions had been filed in the mind of the schoolgirl as had her mother's exhortations to be polite to Uncle Harry and not to speak out of turn because he could be the turning point in their lives, whatever that meant. Her mother had looked fragilely beautiful that day as they walked across Berkeley Square and the new dress she had borrowed from her gown shop in Putney had reminded Jenny of a butterfly's wing and she had wished she was more ordinary, like other girls' mothers.

Jenny began to wash the brown rice. What if the meal was a disaster? She could hear the tap of her step-father's fingers, nails freshly pared, on the mahogany dining table.

Not that she had ever truly disliked Harry; in fact, as her mother often reminded her, he had been good to her – an allowance and a presence which, if it wasn't exactly paternal, was indulgent. Of her father, who sent Christmas and, belatedly, birthday presents, she thought very little. The sharpest images were the bony leg – perhaps that was why she had noticed Harry's ample thigh – and the Sunday smell of Saturday's whisky; although in unguarded moments, when she awoke at night, she heard the cries of children, joyous and accusing, as he fumbled a conjuring trick.

She looked at the kitchen clock. Martin was due in ten minutes at 7.30. She poured the rice into a saucepan of water, lit the gas, and turned her attention to the tiny, crispy pork chops. Then she mixed beaten egg with cornflour. What worried her was the bean curd with ragout.

Her mother peered round the door. "Is everything all right, dear?" Nothing, Jenny assured her, could be progressing more smoothly. *Like the maiden voyage of the* Titanic. Her mother smiled uncertainly. "If there's anything I can do . . ."

"You could entertain Martin for a few minutes."

Her mother retreated.

Her step-father's capitulation had been complete. Obdurate

refusal followed by the cancellation of the other engagement which Jenny assumed to be fictitious. The abruptness of the surrender worried Jenny; but perhaps he merely wanted to get it over and done with. But why was he so hostile to a nephew?

She regarded the enemy, the ragout, belligerently. Courgettes, onions, aubergine, tomatoes, bean curd, hoisin sauce . . . She consulted the book. Already the enemy was on the attack: ragout cooking time was half an hour, brown rice only twenty-eight minutes, and she had already started to cook the damned rice. She switched off the gas and counter-attacked with knife and chopper.

The front-door bell rang. Voices. Could she leave the kitchen at this crucial time to welcome him? She heard Herta's flaxen voice: she could.

They all stood awkwardly in the living-room for a few moments, then Harry went into his drinks routine and Herta began to talk to Martin in her husky, practising-English voice, showing no inclination to retire to her room. She was wearing a white dress with Bavarian embroidery; her hair was Germanically braided and the foothills of her breasts were mysteriously tanned despite the English winter.

They discussed Herta's views on the British way of life and Herta's views on Englishmen. She thought they were very sophisticated, much more virile than she had imagined, misled, she supposed, by male prejudice on the Continent. Jenny found this surprising because Herta had recently been enthusing about the stamina of a lusty Swede. That evening Herta was part of the family. But not for dinner!

Jenny glanced at her watch: the enemy had been cooking for twelve minutes! She fluttered her fingers at Martin. Martin, studiously averting his gaze from Herta's breasts, smiled uncertainly.

Add stock and bring to the boil . . . But if the ragout had been cooking for twelve minutes that meant that the rice . . . Swearing, she lit the gas again under the rice.

Simmer gently for 20 minutes. So she should have been simmering rather than boiling the mess in the casserole. She lowered the heat and applied herself to the minute pork chops which only took five minutes to cook. First deep fry the little miseries for three minutes then add them to the peppers etcetera which should have been sizzling for half a minute in the wok.

113

At last the wok. But if she wasn't careful the crispy pork chops would be ready weeks before the enemy, not to mention the brown rice and beans which, in any case, she had forgotten to put on the boil again. Chinese cooking was inscrutable.

*   *   *

She had only run away once, when she was eleven and then not very far and not because of any deep resentment although it did occur to her, possibly with hindsight, that since her second marriage her mother had abandoned emotion. That, with the acquisition of Harry, she no longer had anyone to reproach. Some women, it subsequently occurred to Jenny, need a companion, others a target.

She had packed a lunch in the kitchen one autumn day and borrowed £4 from her mother's purse and taken a bus to Kensington Gardens because of Peter Pan and Wendy and the Darlings and Nana and had walked beside the Serpentine, where rowing-boats pushed aside shoals of sunlight, and had eaten her lunch at 10.30 am.

She had visited the statue of Peter Pan and watched the model boats on the Round Pond and had been joined as she walked down the Broad Walk by a kind man with a sad face wearing a greenish raincoat who had told her that he had a daughter about her age and he was taking home two puppies but she could only have one. "Would you like the other one?" he had asked. And because the puppies were only a few hundred yards away in his car she had agreed even though, as she was running away from home, she wouldn't be able to take one.

But as they approached Palace Gate two square-shouldered men wearing overcoats despite the warmth approached from different angles and the sad man ran away but not fast enough because one of the men caught him and forced his arm behind his back.

Later, while her step-father was on his way from Hampstead, a policewoman asked her curious questions that disturbed hidden knowledge. And later she overheard fragments of conversation between one of the policemen and Harry. "Very lucky . . . an old customer . . . no charges, no evidence . . ." Until, seeing her, they severed the conversation, the way adults did when they noticed children.

114

Deciding to give the brown rice an extra two minutes, Jenny thought: "That was the day Peter Pan flew out of the window." She remembered waiting in her room to be punished for running away. But they hadn't punished her: she wished they had.

*   *   *

What she always remembered – possibly because her memory balked at what followed – were the empty plates, white bone china gold-rimmed, and the reflections of their chins on them. Harry's pendulous, her mother's tucked in, Martin's razor-nicked beneath an incipient cleft.

They all sat at the far end of the table beyond her mother's flower arrangement. Martin wore a blue blazer with silver buttons, striped tie and white shirt with one errant wing to its collar; Harry, determinedly casual – to make Martin feel ill at ease? – wore a buttoned cardigan and an open-neck blue shirt. Her mother was, as always, delicately elegant, grey silk and pearls, blonde hair arranged in precise curls in some historic fashion that was making a comeback.

Herta had finally retired to her room.

Jenny placed the bowls of oriental delicacies between the three of them and stood back, artist admiring her work. "Help yourselves," she said, sitting opposite Martin.

"No, dear, I'll serve," her mother said.

"It smells good," Martin said.

Chopsticks, she thought, he won't know how to use them. He picked them up expertly and made a few trial forays at invisible food. "Chinatown in Liverpool," he explained. "We used to go there for treats."

The food steamed in front of them.

Now!

The rice was like buckshot.

*   *   *

Over brandy – the Chinese drank it by the gallon, according to Harry – the conversation turned to the state of the country.

Booming, said Harry. Economy expanding, unemployment falling, wages up by eight per cent, tax cuts on the way.

Face flushed by national endeavour and brandy, Harry

115

leaned back in his chair, hands clasped across his cardigan. "And how is life treating you?" he asked Martin.

"Well enough," said Martin.

"Got a job yet?"

"Not yet." He took a bird-sip of brandy from his balloon glass.

"No problems. No need for anyone to be out of work today."

Martin, twirling his glass, didn't reply.

"Except, of course, those who don't want to work. Benefits, that sort of thing," waving one hand vaguely.

"I don't think that's quite true," Jenny said.

"Then, of course, there are those who do work but don't tell anyone about it. The black economy. Thank God we're getting tougher, we've been soft for too long. Stopping dole for school-leavers who don't want to train for a decent job for a start."

"Do you think they should be flogged?" Jenny asked.

"Now, now, Jenny," her mother said.

"Well, do you?"

Harry regarded her indulgently. Rebellious youth, his expression said. *I was young once.* "I don't answer facetious questions. What do you want to be, young man?" turning to Martin.

"A politician," Martin told him.

The grandfather clock chimed in the silence.

"Well," Jenny's mother said, "that's very laudable. But you'll need a lot of experience, of course."

"I would have thought so," Martin said. "I don't any more." His fingers were tight around his glass, the wing of his collar sticking out.

"I don't understand," Harry said, cream in his voice curdling.

"I just made that up. You know, about being a politician. But when I hear some of the crap talked about unemployment I think I'd make a good one."

"Bit left, are you, Martin?"

"I'm not left and I'm not right. Not a Communist or a Socialist or a Tory. I just know that in this country today there's a complete break-down in communication. The have and have-nots if you like. But it's worse than that: the haves just don't care. Why should they? The Big Bang, all that. They've got it

116

made: they don't have to wait for the Giro. Do you know what I read the other day? The *in* pet with Stock Exchange yuppies is a cockatoo. In Liverpool we eat them."

Jenny, listening to the rasp of his voice, loved him.

Her mother said: "How about coffee, dear."

"Tea," Jenny said. "With Chinese it's tea." She didn't move.

Harry said: "Why don't you buy a soapbox and stand on it?"

Martin said: "I'm sorry, sir, but I have to say what I think. When were you last in Skelmsdale, Toxteth . . . When were you last in the East End of your own city? In other words – and I'm sorry about this," apologising to Jenny and her mother, "what do you really know about your own country?"

"You're drawing benefits, I suppose?"

"Is that so different from tax evasion?"

"Now, you look . . ."

"Sorry, avoidance. With respect there is a difference: you're avoiding what would keep most people drawing benefits in the necessities of life for ten years."

"You don't agree that a hell of a lot of people are defrauding the State?"

"There were spivs in the last war," Martin said. "All I'm trying to say is that the whole system is wrong. Does the jobless docker in Dingle really care about tax cuts in the next budget? Tax cuts in what? He isn't earning anything."

"He could be," Harry said. "Just as you could be."

"Oh no, he couldn't. Come south? How? Sell his back-to-back for £15,000 and buy the equivalent for £60,000? Do you know something, sir," the sirs emerging like lozenges now, "there's a whole generation abroad now which knows nothing else except scavenging. And that's what their kids are learning from them. Do they care about monetary policies?"

Jenny's mother said: "I'll get the tea," and to Martin: "You must be very thirsty, all that lecturing."

"I'm sorry," said Martin, patently not.

"The fact of the matter," Harry said, "is that Britain has been dragged back from the brink of economic disaster. We're set on a revival course now and there are opportunities for anyone who wants to grab them."

"Not for the old craftsmen who were sacked when their workshops closed down."

"Who closed down the docks? The trade unions, that's

117

who."

"I'm not saying who's to blame," Martin said. "I'm merely saying that human beings shouldn't be treated like trade figures."

"Where are you living?" Harry asked.

"In a squat," Martin told him.

Jenny's mother brought in tea. Jasmine.

Martin, fingering the cutting edge of his collar, said: "I don't think I will if you don't mind." He glanced at his watch. "Time to be going."

Harry said: "I wish you luck. That Great Divide, it's always been there, you know."

"But never quite so deep," Martin said. He thanked Jenny's mother and made for the door.

In the hall he said to Jenny: "I am sorry, I really am."

"I didn't think you had it in you."

"Nor did I."

"Where's this squat of yours?"

He gave her the address.

"If you ever need ammunition for a shotgun I can cook some rice . . ."

She opened the door. Cold breathed in.

"I just couldn't help myself," he said.

"Take care crossing the Great Divide," she said. She kissed him on the cheek and closed the door.

*   *   *

Unable to sleep, Jenny walked restlessly around the house. Outside, the moon sailed high in pools of darkness. At 1.30 am she crossed the landing opposite the room where Herta slept. She heard voices, the creaking of floorboards. As her step-father emerged, tying the belt of his dressing-gown, she shrank into a shadow beside a tall cupboard. Harry, breathing heavily but managing to hum at the same time, crossed the landing and went into the room he shared with his wife. No secrets, no shame. Jenny returned to her room to plan.

CHAPTER 12

———◆———

And still as the winter days softened and stretched Martin belonged. He searched for the right job conscientiously: he existed triumphantly.

Although his responsibilities at Buck House were Charlie and Hood and, luminously in the background, Danny he shared the labour of survival. When Mad Bull accidentally broke a bailiff's rib he made a statement to the police that he had merely hugged him affectionately; with Cuff he collected sachets of ketchup, mustard and brown sauce from hamburger joints; with Prince he schemed.

They had been in the squat for six weeks now; if Gosling's predictions were accurate they could expect another six weeks' tenure and a couple more assaults on their privacy.

Meanwhile assorted visitors sojourned briefly. A teenage snooker player, hopefully potting his way towards stardom, who had been beaten up for hustling in Willesden; he stayed until the blood left his eyes before departing, carrying his cues like fishing-rods, for Birmingham. An arm-wrestler with ropes of tendons in his wrists who made a living in exclusive London clubs. A deaf and dumb mute who lingered for two nights before drifting wordlessly to another silent corner of London.

And a girl arrived. And stayed, the unlikely guest of Gosling who adored her myopically through his spectacles, the bulge of his forehead an arbour for words of courtship. She was a fey creature fashioned in pale hues, grey eyes and long hair of no precise colour, who smiled secretly at private visions and rarely spoke. She smoked the occasional joint, cooked and cleaned with dreamy method and returned from forays to unidentified

119

realms with a bag of withered apples, a careworn broom, chestnuts and a Marconi radio circa 1939. She wore dresses from an Edwardian print and no one knew what she saw when at night she stared with Gosling into the caverns of a scavenger's fire.

Except perhaps Danny. She was good with him when, sweating and shivering, he talked about mainlining and she sat beside him on his mattress and they leaned back against the wall and, after a while, they closed their eyes and it seemed to Martin that, unlike couples who part when they sleep, they were meeting somewhere.

*　　　*　　　*

"Where were you born?" Martin asked.

Hood, blinking, said: "King's Lynn."

Sitting on cushions, they faced each other across a coffee table constructed from half a plate-glass window and four flower pots.

"Correct. When?"

"April the tenth, 1938."

"Good. And you served in the RAF?"

Hood, who like many liars, often perceived himself streaking across summer skies at the controls of a combative jet, said: "No, the army. In the cookhouse."

"Excellent. And what did you do when you left the army?"

"Sold encyclopedias."

"And then?"

"The Scrubs," Hood said, pulling at his terrible moustache.

"Sensational," said Prince from his rocking chair. "Another week and you'll be ready."

Prince returned to the red exercise book in which he was scheming a free holiday in Portugal as the guest of a development company specialising in Timeshare. An inspired concept, he claimed. You flew to the Algarve with a group at your own expense and stayed in a hotel at their expense. At the first get-together in which a bronzed and personable executive explained the advantage of paying £5,000 for a week's holiday every year – longer if you paid more – you stood up and asked a low-key but pertinent question such as: "Can you guarantee maintenance until 1998?"

120

After the meeting the executive took you aside and, over a drink at a bar overlooking the sparkling Atlantic, inquired about your intentions and you insisted that they were honourable which, of course, they were.

A few more days in the sun viewing as few Timeshare apartments as possible, but at the same time maintaining credibility, and then, on the eve of the communal signing, preceded as always by a considerable intake of Spanish sparkling wine, you showed the executive a list of questions you intended to ask him in public.

"Are you aware that for £5,000 you could live on the Costa Blanca for a year? Or splurge on ten package deals, five in Florida and five in Thailand? Could you, perhaps, elaborate on your profit margin which must be considerable if you multiply £5,000 by 52 and then again by the 97 apartments in the block? Do investors receive the deeds for an apartment they will occupy for only one or two weeks? Have you paid for the block or is it mortgaged? If it's mortgaged what guarantee can you provide that it won't be repossessed?"

Clumping him on the back, you suggest a final, flippant question. "Can anyone really be so stupid as to invest five grand for seven days' sunstroke?" Ho-ho.

"Your pay-off?" the executive asks.

"No pay-off, colonel. It's merely that I've decided not to invest, the market being what it is at the moment. So if you could see your way to recompensing me for my trouble, my return air fare that is . . ."

And there you are, five days' holiday gratis.

"Or," Mad Bull had observed at the time of Prince's inspiration, "ten weeks in hospital minus front teeth and knee-caps."

"Me a group leader. Be your age," Prince had said.

Martin asked Hood: "How long were you inside?"

"Nine months."

"Try again."

Hood's eyes watered. "With remission six months."

"Watch it," Prince said, from the Algarve.

"And then?"

"Double-glazing," Hood said.

"Any medals?"

"No *comprendez*."

"When you were in the RAF?"

121

"Army," Hood said. "Potatoes not medals."

"Good, good. What about the other branch of your family?"

"What other branch?"

"The Royal connection by a morganatic marriage," because that one had to be knocked on the head.

"Non-existent," Hood said, unbuttoning his yellow waistcoat. "Do you want blood?"

"How's that gold-mine in Peru?"

"Worked out."

"And what are you doing now?"

"Answering your stupid fucking questions."

"Professionally . . ."

"Drawing the dole."

"And?"

"I have this idea for a movie."

"Shit," said Martin.

*   *   *

Towards the end of February Martin changed Charlie's routine. Steady runs broken up by 200- and 300-metre bursts of speed. He taught Charlie to exercise before running and to warm *down* afterwards. On one occasion he started to talk to him about aerobics and anaerobics and lactic acid in the muscles but Charlie smiled and said: "Forget all that shit, Marty, I just run."

Charlie was, apparently, autistic, which explained his garbled speech. The autism was rooted in childhood – Charlie had no idea who his parents were, only that his mother had lived somewhere in Brixton – and could, so Martin read, be accompanied by obsessions, ritualistic behaviour and anti-social attitudes. Martin decided that Charlie was not abnormal: he was different.

Martin had once looked at a picture in the *City Magazine*, published by Liverpool Council, of a team of mentally disabled athletes from the north-west who had won sixteen medals and eight place ribbons at the National Special Olympic Games. Their faces had, by conventional standards, been garbled. But for one star-burst of a moment Martin glimpsed their visions. And a boy with curly hair, head tilted, had asked sadly: "Why?"

122

Charlie had been entered for the Olympics by the special school in North London where he was supposed to reside. They were to be held at the Withdean stadium in Brighton in six months but at the moment it was lies that occupied Martin's mind. Hood was on trial in two days' time.

*   *   *

In the living-room of Buck House Prince, entrepreneur, conducted himself importantly.

He had acquired an office for the day – the public bar of the Codgers complete with telephone for a fee of £75 on the understanding that Jesty be excluded at all times.

He had sold Hood's story to a Sunday newspaper, the account, that was, of the morale-boost to Danny the junkie whose existence had been kept secret from the rest of the media, payment only to be made if Hood triumphed.

He had orchestrated publicity. Hood's endurance test had been cut to twelve hours to facilitate coverage and was scheduled to start at 7 am at the request of the early morning television shows and to finish at 7 pm which would give the Press ample time to print the story for the following day.

Peering through a slit in a boarded window at the reporters and photographers massed outside in the rain-powdered glare of floodlights, Martin felt that Prince was entitled to swagger a little.

Hood was not swaggering. His broom-like moustache had been trimmed, his RAF tie replaced by a polka-dot, yellow waistcoat burned – "Buy you another when we collect," Prince had told him – but he still looked unwholesome. His eyes watered, his cheeks were blotched, his hands shook.

Five minutes before he was due to make his appearance he asked for a drink.

The referee, a once-bearded football commentator on television, said: "I don't think that would be a good idea."

Hood said to Prince: "Did I ever tell you about the time I walked across a frozen lake to rescue a boy who had fallen through the ice?"

Prince gave him a whisky.

Sharp at seven Hood emerged into the front garden. Cameras rolled, reporters surged forward.

123

A voice: "Are you being paid for this, Mr. Hood?"
A pause.
The fine rain hung in the white light.
Hood said: "I hope to be."
A girl: "Have you always been a liar?"
"Ever since I can remember."
Hood reminded Martin of a contestant in an old game in which you were not permitted to say yes or no. *You did say yes, didn't you? No!*
The girl again: "Whose idea was this?"
"Prince's."
"Mine," said Prince, bead in his ear sparkling.
No one was interested in Prince.
A Welshman's voice: "What was the last lie you told?"
"I can't repeat it, can I."
Laughter.
Hood, gaining confidence, smiled into the microphones.
Questions came from all angles.
"How old are you?"
"Fifty."
"Where were you born?"
"Why was I born?"
"No, where."
"King's Lynn if memory serves me right."
Prince tapped him on the shoulder. "Watch it, cully. You're a reformed liar not a comedian."
Rain beaded Hood's moustache like dew.
Prince in his entrepreneur's voice: "Ladies and gentlemen, shall we adjourn to the office?"
No one moved.
"Is it true you were in the RAF?"
"It isn't true."
"Didn't you once claim to have been a fighter pilot?"
"And a doctor. And a great criminal barrister. And a film producer."
"Were you in the Forces?"
"Army. Peeling spuds."
"What do you do now, Mr. Hood?"
"Not a lot," Hood said.
"Any plans?"
"Not beyond seven this evening."

"Are lies ever justified, Mr. Hood?"

A pause. "I think they are sometimes. To avoid hurting people's feelings."

Prince: "Nice one."

"Would you be prepared to undertake a lie detector test?"

Prince, arm round Hood's shoulders, said: "He would not."

"How do we know whether he's lying or not?" The girl appealed to the referee.

"I have his curriculum vitae," said the once-bearded commentator who in his time had analysed a netful of penalty decisions. "A lot of other material. Everything he says can be checked."

"We have arranged for a lie detector . . ."

"My decision is final."

"No action replay?"

Laughter.

"Time to move on," said the commentator.

Photographers ahead, kneeling, snapping and filming, Prince and Hood made their way along the street in the dawn-light to the Codgers. Behind them came Mad Bull, shaven scalp slippery with rain, Gosling seeing nebulous words through his misted spectacles, Cuff wearing a torn raincoat that had belonged to a motorist killed in a car crash, and Charlie, jogging.

Danny stayed at home on his mattress.

*   *   *

1 pm. Half-way mark. "But no half-time," the commentator said.

The public bar was packed with journalists scribbling, talking, drinking, questioning Hood; some even tried to eat the desiccated snacks provided by the landlord. The bells above the door rang, the bell on the old-fashioned cash-register rang as the landlord savagely punched the keys, the telephone rang incessantly.

The *Standard* arrived. Hood was there, second lead on the front page. THE WHOLE TRUTH AND NOTHING BUT THE TRUTH.

"The camera lied," Prince said, pointing at a photograph of Hood in the front garden of the squat — Hood looked almost dashing.

Hood, giving a live interview for television, was holding out

125

well although he seemed to falter once on radio.

"Can you truthfully say you went to Oxford?"

"I can."

The hand holding the microphone trembled.

"You actually went to Oxford?"

"Last month. I've got an aunt who lives there."

The referee said later: "Don't make things difficult for me."

2 pm. Five hours to go.

The rain had stopped and, while Gosling minded the telephone, they all walked on the common picking up spectators like golfers at St. Andrew's. The air was soft; spring was falsely promised. Trains whooshed past; mothers aired their babies.

It was opening-time when they got back to the Codgers. Regulars were being diverted to the saloon bar where, for the day, public bar prices prevailed; Jesty stood on the pavement outside. Seeing Prince and Martin he said: "This will make you laugh . . ."

"Not now," Prince told him.

"In the bar then. I heard it in the post office this morning."

"Not tonight," Prince said. "You'll have to use the saloon."

"I always use the public."

"I'm sorry," Prince said. "I am. But business is business."

"I'm part of the scene," Jesty said.

"You are that, old son, but not this evening."

"Journalists like stories. I remember . . ."

Prince handed him a £5 note. "Here, buy yourself a pint."

"I don't want your money," Jesty said, pushing Prince's hand away.

He walked quickly down the street where, as a postman, he delivered people's lives sealed in envelopes. Martin imagined him in uniform. He resolved: "Tomorrow I'll listen to some of Jesty's jokes."

By 6.30 it looked as though Hood was going to make it although the strain was telling. The blotches on his cheeks had spread and his hand-tremble made waves in his pint of beer. He stood at Jesty's end of the bar parrying and fending off questions, answering with terse affirmatives or negatives. The heat from the camera crews' lights made him sweat and he loosened the knot of his polka-dot tie.

Cameramen aimed their lenses at him waiting for the last-minute count-down.

6.55.

The last questions were being fired at Hood. The media, it seemed to Martin, wanted Hood to win but at the same time they had to try and break him.

The representative of the Sunday paper that had bought Hood's story approached Prince. "Looks like we've got a deal," he said.

The cameras began to roll.

Thirty seconds left.

The questions faltered, died.

Then the girl who had asked Hood if he had always been a liar spoke up.

She said: "Mr. Hood, have you told a lie since seven this morning?"

Hood regarded her steadily through watering eyes.

"Yes," he said.

CHAPTER 13

———◆◆◆———

They found Jesty's decapitated body on the railway line near Beehive Bridge in the south London suburb of Mitcham where lavender once grew.

There was no note on the body, nor in the barely-furnished room he rented in Wandsworth. Just a joke scrawled on a page from an exercise book on the pillow of his unmade bed. *Boring wine-taster: "I must be off, I'm going to Bordeaux." His companion: "Give my regards to Mr. Deaux."*

Oddly his presence after death was missed in the Codgers as it had never been missed during his lifetime. His corner stool reproved; the alsatian took to sitting beside it and whining.

Guiltily, Prince led his cohorts into the saloon bar leaving the old men in the past where Jesty had once dwelled.

Some of the shared remorse, however, was re-channelled by Danny whose condition had deteriorated since Hood's failure.

His defeat was debated for days. The final utterance that he had lied when he hadn't. That in itself a lie. The injustice — before the discovery of Jesty's body — obsessed the occupants of Buck House. Even the girl who had asked the question was, it was rumoured, devastated.

Danny told Martin that he no longer wanted to kick skag. In withdrawal — the stained silver foil on which he had heated heroin before inhaling it lay on the floor of his room — he said: "Hood couldn't make it; nor can I. Maybe the time to start mainlining has arrived."

They also talked in the back garden which Danny was cultivating. "You see," he said, tugging weeds with long tap roots from the wet soil, "none of the preachers has any idea what smack can do to you."

"Tell me," Martin said, picking up stones and throwing them in a heap in a corner of the garden.

"Light up your life. Bring peace. Why not? It's better than this existence." Danny gestured with one muddy hand. "When I chase the dragon all my values change. Sounds are colours and colours are sounds and they're all rich and vibrant. And you know something? I read about crime and death and people going crazy through skag or dikes or acid and I don't give a shit: I'm on another planet and it's a beautiful place."

"So is this planet."

"Don't jest," Danny said in his soft voice. A tap root snapped and he staggered backwards. He touched the sparse hairs of his beard as though seeking strength. "To be able to cure a skaghead," Danny said, "you've got to know what it's like to be one. You've got to know the other world he inhabits. He'll do anything. Drug-orientated crime . . . It isn't crime to a junkie: the only reality is his next crank and he'll mug, rob, maim, kill even, to get it. To cure a junkie," Danny said, "you've got to prove that this world is better than his private planet. Tough, huh?"

"You want to kick it, don't you?"

"Do I? I can feel that needle sliding in. Then, wham, my life is a luxury. Life is warm. Life is kind . . . Do you know what withdrawal really is?"

Martin shook his head.

"It's being scared of coming back to this place. The rest of it, the sweating and honking and cramps, are just symptoms. Withdrawal itself is fear. You know something else? Drugs come in many shapes. Hood's drugs are lies and he couldn't kick them, could he."

"He tried," Martin said.

"I tried."

"Charlie's trying," Martin said.

"Good old Charlie. Have you ever wanted to experiment, Martin? Maybe a little speed, a snort of coke?"

"You make it sound attractive."

"Then don't listen to me." Thin fingers gripped Martin's arm. "I got hooked because I was inadequate, the preachers' favourite word. Did you know that? Inadequate." He pronounced it in syllables, testing them. "You're not inadequate.

129

You even believe that this world we didn't ask to be born into is beautiful. Me? I think it's shitty."

"Supposing I can prove it isn't?"

"Better than mine?"

"This one lasts," Martin said.

"Then maybe I'll stop being inadequate. If Charlie wins," and the smile on his face was wise and sad.

*   *   *

So Martin took Danny with him on training sessions with Charlie and sometimes they explored together although mostly Charlie preferred to go back to the squat, frightened that distant voices would call to him if he wandered too far.

The two of them took a boat trip on the Thames from Charing Cross, past Cleopatra's Needle on the port and the Festival Hall on the starboard, under Waterloo Bridge, alongside the three old warships, *Wellington*, *President* and *Chrysanthemum*, under Blackfriars to the wide stretch where, to the left, they could see the dome of St. Paul's, under two bridges to the Tower whose turrets and ramparts still kept guard against the unbridled assaults of progress.

And London was beautiful, with galleons of cloud navigating her domes and spires and cubes and the sea beginning to call from the east.

They also went to Kew Gardens, ravaged by a storm, where Danny seemed to blossom, lingering among languid fronds in the Palm House and trailing, like a child, through woodland and rock gardens, staring one-by-one up the ten storeys of the Chinese Pagoda, pausing to touch leaves and crumble soil between his fingers.

And Martin hoped that Danny glimpsed a world that at least shaped up to his private refuge.

*   *   *

The enemy came one morning at eleven when Prince, seated in what had once been a music room – there was a rodent-nibbled score of *The Student Prince* in one corner – was advising two clients about changes in benefits and Danny was in the garden planting spinach seeds and Martin was in his room writing to

130

his parents and Mad Bull was in the kitchen sorting through his aids to good health — sea salt, Vitamin C, iron tonic, sunflower-seed oil . . .

Martin, hearing the knock on the front door, observed them from an upstairs room. They were in their late thirties, one wearing a long sheepskin coat, the other a black, belted raincoat.

Prince shouted: "Sighted?"

"The law?"

"I don't think so. Try them."

Prince turned the key in the big lock and opened the door on the chain. "Who goes there?"

"Friends," said a college voice.

"Prove it."

Cards came through the gap. Martin, standing beside Prince, studied them. A solicitor's named Sims — the black overcoat — and the project consultant for a development company named Kester.

Prince said: "If you're friends who needs enemies?"

"We've got a proposition to put to you," said the college voice.

"Who's that?"

"Sims."

Prince said to Martin: "Get Mad Bull," and opened the door.

They sat precisely on the edge of the chaise-longue. Beneath their outdoor clothes they wore neat suits and striped network ties.

"What we don't want," Kester said as Sims made notes, "is aggro. Who does?" He switched on a smile. "But we do want this site and we want it quickly. As you know," to Prince, "it's only a matter of time before you're evicted."

"Time is money, cully."

Sims, hair tightly-curled and streaked with grey at the temples, opened a briefcase watched patiently by Kester who was more muscular, more sheathed. Kester seemed to suffer the lawyer with stoicism.

Sims, riffling papers, said: "If you are prepared to sign these which in effect give us the right to dispossess you by the thirtieth of this month then we are prepared to make a financial settlement."

Kester took over while Sims made notes with a gold pencil.

131

Kester's words were smooth pebbles honed from granite. To put it more plainly, he told Prince, the company was prepared to pay the squatters to get out in two days.

How much? asked Prince. How many were there? asked Kester. Twelve, said Prince counting on his bony fingers and adding a few. Kester looked at Sims who drummed manicured fingertips on his briefcase. £250, Kester said.

"We earn more than that in a week, cully."

"Earn?" Kester was theatrically incredulous.

"Hard work to keep a squat."

"Three hundred," Kester offered, glancing at Sims. "There are plenty of other 'desirable premises' you can occupy."

Mad Bull, wearing a grey vest and tracksuit trousers, folded his arms so that his fists inflated the cushions of his biceps.

"We like it here," Prince said. "All mod cons, all original features, close to station, stone's throw from the boozer."

"We have applied for a court order and when the due processes of the law have been invoked we shall obtain an eviction order."

"Not according to Gosling."

"Who's Gosling," as though Prince had unearthed an obscure work of reference.

"Our lawyer."

"I don't think I've had the pleasure . . ."

"No pleasure, cully, he's an assassin in court."

Kester said: "Sims means that if you don't get out the bull-dozers will come in."

"When?"

"A week."

"And you'll pay £300 for a couple of days' grace?"

"Five hundred pounds," Kester said. "Our final offer."

"That's less than fifty quid each."

Sims said: "I have the required sum here." From his briefcase he extracted a wad of new £10 notes.

Gosling came in and Prince held up one finger. Silence, the finger said.

"A lot of bread," Kester said.

"Not enough."

"How much?"

"More than you can afford: there's no price on pride. But you wouldn't understand that."

"I understand you're a lunatic."

His words had cutting edges now.

"My friend here," Prince said, "is very affectionate. Why don't you give Mr. Kester a great big hug?" nodding at Mad Bull.

Mad Bull moved forward, arms outstretched. He smiled at Kester fondly.

"I have to warn you," Sims said, standing up and snapping shut his briefcase, "that the consequences of any assault could be very serious. Witnesses . . ."

"What witnesses?" Prince asked. And to Kester: "My friend really likes you."

"Okay," Kester said. "Call him off. No deal."

Prince opened the door for them. "By the way," he said, "if you're interested in drawing benefits I'd always be happy to oblige."

*   *   *

"What," asked Gosling, "was his name?"

"Whose name?" Prince asked.

They were sitting round the fire, Prince, Gosling, Mad Bull, Charlie and Martin.

"The one Mad Bull wanted to hug."

"Kester," Prince told him.

"A good name. Almost kestrel – a bird of prey, a small falcon that hovers against the wind." Gosling drank tea brewed from second-hand tea-bags. "People adapt themselves to their names, you know."

"Prince?"

"Exactly. What was your name?" to Mad Bull.

"I forget," Mad Bull said.

"I can always tell a Derek or a David."

"A Martin?" Martin asked.

"You're a Martin all right."

"Gosling?"

"That's me," Gosling said. "Have you ever thought about nationalities? There are words appropriate to countries. French kissing, French knickers, French letters."

They gazed into the butterfly flames of the fire.

"Dutch courage," Gosling said. "My old Dutch, going

133

Dutch, Dutch uncle, Dutch courage ... something friendly about the Dutch."

Cuff entered bearing food. Stale bread which they toasted and leftovers from a caff collected by a waiter in exchange for dead men's clothes. Cuff mashed potatoes, cabbage and carrots together and fried bubble-and-squeak.

"Fuck," Gosling said. "Now why should that be an oath? Sexual intercourse, procreation and pleasure. We've made an obscenity out of fuck whereas sod and bugger – silly old sod, stupid bugger – are merely considered to be vulgarisms. What do they mean? Sodomy and buggery, that's what."

Appetising smells reached them from the Calor-gas cooker that Cuff had found on a tip. Oil flames flared. Charlie sang softly to himself.

"I'm studying homophones," Gosling said.

"What are they?" Prince asked. "Gay switchboard operators?"

"Words pronounced the same but having different meanings. Dear meaning darling and dear meaning expensive. Peel from an orange and peal from church bells."

"Hair and *Herr*," Prince said. "What was Hitler's first name?"

"*Heil*," Martin said.

Cuff brought in the bubble-and-squeak and they washed it down with elderberry wine. Afterwards Gosling lit a pipe and Martin turned on the antique radio that Gosling's girl had brought; he half-expected ancient music to issue from it but it was a nine o'clock newscast. Disturbances in Tottenham, miners voting to strike. Martin found some music, as dignified as the radio.

He went to bed at 10.30. He had been reading for five minutes when Gosling's girl came in silently. She raised her nightdress over her shoulders and let it fall to the floor. Her breasts were small with adolescent nipples. The hair at her pubis was soft and fair. She lay beside him under the blanket and put her arms around him. He held her and looked into her eyes but they were focussed somewhere beyond him. She stayed awhile, arms around his waist, then departed as silently as she had come.

CHAPTER 14

———◆———

Gentle days followed. Inquiring breezes and the grass in London's parks salad green.

She folded her clothes neatly in two cases and sandwiched between them the one-eyed bear, *The House at Pooh Corner*, a photograph of Robert Redford who looked like an adult who had not forgotten what it was to be young, a pack of trick cards used maladroitly by her father, a Valentine card from an unknown admirer, a tambourine and her paints.

She left a note: *I have to make my way in this life and your values are different from mine . . .*

She didn't blame her step-father for coveting Herta. What male wouldn't? She did blame her mother for her complicity.

She waited until her mother had driven to Highgate Village to go shopping and left the note on the kitchen table.

She looked through the window; the stonemaiden returned her gaze. Crocuses speared the lawn. Her childhood was invested with a cosiness it had never possessed in its time; the future was as daunting as the winter that had just passed. A parting of the flesh.

She telephoned for a taxi to take her to the underground station. She picked up her two cases; they hunched her with their weight.

She told the driver to drive her round the heath. She stopped him near a grass slope and gazed across London. From here it always slumbered but in its sleep it called to her.

A middle-aged man wearing a deerstalker helped her with her cases at the tube station. She remembered the stranger who had offered to show her the puppies in Kensington Gardens. She

135

often imagined she saw him in crowds. As the train tunnelled its way beneath the suburbs unease pointed with fear visited her. A tall, handsome West Indian stared at her incuriously. Euston, Tottenham Court Road, Leicester Square ... Waterloo, Kennington, Oval ... outposts of a foreign land.

She staggered out of the train. The station smelled of warm rust. Passengers strode briskly along the platform, pursuing their own lives. No one helped her with her cases. On the street outside she was lost. She consulted the map she had drawn with the help of an A-Z and began to walk. Past shops, DIY, café, newsagents ... a grey energetic street in a different hemisphere from Hampstead and Highgate. Her shoulders ached. At last someone did help, an Irishman with a friendly, battered face. He made her laugh and she would remember him for that.

The door of the gaunt house was opened by a huge fat man with a shaven scalp.

*   *   *

She brought a sleeping-bag and laid it on the floor of a small room with yellow walls and unboarded windows thicketed with the webs of long-dead spiders. She cleaned and cooked with Gosling's girl. She shopped and bought food from a delicatessen and, occasionally, bottles of wine. She foraged with Cuff and played Scrabble with Gosling, losing extravagantly. She persuaded Mad Bull to recount famous victories from his grunting past. She listened to Hood who, since his brief reign as a celebrity, lied with swashbuckling ingenuity. She ran with Charlie and talked gently to Danny.

Belong she didn't.

She asked Martin why, one March day when the winds had blown Prince east to brief clients in Norfolk and Suffolk about new ploys to extract money from the DHSS and to add 300 to his target of 10,000 miles of ticketless travel.

"I am not one of you," she said.

Prince's empty rocking chair moved in a draught.

"Don't be ridiculous."

"It's true and you know it."

Even Martin had distanced himself from her. Where was the rebel whose protest had spilled across the dining-table in Hampstead?

136

"It's in your mind," Martin said, hammering nails into a broken chair that Cuff had found on a skip.

"That's pathetic," peeling a shrivelled potato over a plastic bowl.

"Do you really like it here?"

"It's a survival kit," she said.

"That wasn't what I asked."

"I'm surviving. So why aren't I one of you?"

He hammered a nail fiercely. "You are one of us."

"Don't be so bloody obstinate."

"All right, if you don't belong, and it's you who's saying it not me, perhaps it's because you don't have to survive."

She considered this carefully. Then: "I'm not the first girl who's dropped out and had to survive."

"But you can always go back."

"Do you want me to?"

"That's your decision."

"You ran away too," she said.

"From rather different circumstances."

"What can I do?" she asked.

"Stop going to the delicatessen for a start. The food doesn't taste half as good as the stuff Cuff scrounges from the caff. And the wine," he said. "We prefer elderberry or dandelion. And stop trying to cure Danny — we were doing all right before you came along. And stop resurrecting Mad Bull's past: you're forcing him to make it up."

She blinked. "Have I done anything right?"

"You're doing a good job peeling those potatoes."

The potato dropped into the bowl splashing brown water onto the scrubbed table.

Worse than patronising, she thought lying in her sleeping bag. Slumming: that's what they think I'm doing. Well, to hell with the lot of you: I will belong.

A knock on the door. Martin. "I'm sorry," he said. "Can I come in?"

"Go to bed," she said.

"I *am* sorry."

She didn't reply.

How? she asked herself before burrowing into sleep because her father had claimed that questions posed at night were often answered in the morning. But he had been right, that bonythighed libertine: the answers surfaced from dreams daubed with crayons and chalk, dreams in which marching feet traversed canvasses made of stone.

She dressed in jeans and jersey, breakfasted off toast and peanut butter and tea, and strode across Wandsworth Bridge to the boutiques and trendy shops of King's Road, Chelsea. In an art shop near a branch of Hatchards she bought two boxes of coloured chalks and a slim volume about Leonardo da Vinci. Then she recrossed the fast and divisive waters of the Thames.

In Wandsworth she bought a cushion and, kneeling on it outside a supermarket, she opened her book and began to chalk the Mona Lisa.

Shoes passed by, brown and black, spike-heeled, polished and cracked, a predominance of trainers. Voices reached her. "What happens if it rains?" "Did Leonardo oversleep this morning?" A few coins dropped into the black felt hat beside the cushion as she searched with her chalks for that smile. For a while it eluded her, eyes staring expressionlessly at the grey sky. Then suddenly the mouth smiled mysteriously at the clouds and Jenny leaned against the wall, hands clasped round her knees, to divine its cause.

The young policeman said: "Sorry, young lady, you can't stay here: you're causing an obstruction."

Jenny looked around. The shoppers of Wandsworth were walking round the portrait; there were no snarl-ups. "What obstruction?" she asked.

"I don't want any trouble, miss. Just pack up your chalks and move on. I'm sorry but the law's the law."

A woman of about thirty with shining black hair and a beautiful voice and legs said: "What law, officer?"

The policeman turned. "Oh, it's you," he said. "You know as well as I do what law."

"I want to hear it from you."

"I'm not giving evidence," the policeman said.

A crowd began to gather. A big woman with small eyes perched on bunched cheeks said: "Leave her alone. She isn't doing any harm," and a West Indian said: "Move on, fuzz, you're causing an obstruction."

The policeman looked around uncertainly. Jenny began to feel sorry for him; but she couldn't pack up and move on – that was defeat.

The policeman said: "I'm not arresting her, just asking her to move on." Mona Lisa smiled at him.

The woman with the beautiful legs said: "There was no obstruction until you came along and I'm quite willing to testify to that effect."

The policeman's handset called him. He listened and, with relief, spoke into it. "There's been an accident," he said. He turned to Jenny. "Just don't cause any more trouble."

He walked briskly away. Coins showered into the felt hat.

The woman tossed a £1 into it and handed Jenny a card. "If you're ever in any trouble . . ." Her name was Lubin and she was a lawyer.

Half an hour later it began to rain and the smile on the face on the pavement turned to tears.

*   *   *

Martin was inventive. This surprised her as much as the distance he had put between the two of them — reduced since the Mona Lisa episode witnessed and recounted by Cuff. Why should it surprise her? Because, she thought guiltily, he comes from the North and my vision of those distant realms is girls working in mills that have long been stilled and miners with glistening shoulders trapped in the shafts of pits that have long been closed.

It was in the West End that he displayed his inventiveness. Not the National Gallery, not the Monument nor Westminster Abbey nor the Bank of England. Instead, guide book in hand, he took her to hushed corners where the past took diaphanous shape and forgotten rivers flowed deep beneath their feet. To Burlington Arcade, still patrolled by a uniformed beadle. To Tavistock Square in Bloomsbury where in a corner of the gardens, once known as the Field of Forty Footsteps, the footsteps of two seventeenth-century duellists who killed each other could allegedly still be seen. To the mummified remains of Jeremy Bentham, philosopher, in University College which he helped to found in Gower Street.

Together, and sometimes with Danny, they also trod the rarefied thoroughfares of London. Pall Mall and The Mall with the other Buck House at the end of its telescope; and Bond Street and Bruton Place and Berkeley Square to hear a

139

nightingale singing in the 200-year-old plane trees but hearing only the chirp of sparrows at their feet.

And once when Martin was going for an interview for a job he didn't want they visited the new seat of the affluent, Dockland, the eight square miles east of Tower Bridge where, amid neglected wharfs, glass towers probing the clouds contain one-room flats selling for £160,000 and gaunt warehouses have been transformed into cloistered retreats.

At Butler's Wharf where once tea and spice were unloaded they gazed into the trapped waters of the river – they were forever bumping into the Thames – and compared the life-style being hammered into shape around them with conditions in the squat.

From there Martin navigated the conversation towards the uncles. He told her about a photograph of the brothers he had seen on the mantelpiece at Walter Renshaw's house, a conspiracy of four. Or was it three? His father, believing that he was a partner in some youthful caprice, excluded from some more devious enterprise?

"Excluded?" She held his arm. "I don't understand."

"None of them wants to know me. Not really. Each in his own way has made it quite clear that I mustn't stick my nose into what doesn't concern me. They were all jumpy, too."

"You're being over-sensitive," Jenny said.

"Did your father invite me to dinner?"

"I did."

"Did he want me?"

"Not at first."

"There you are."

"Then he sort of surrendered."

"Surrendered! You make me sound like a formidable enemy. Don't you think he over-reacted to a visit from a nephew?"

"Perhaps."

His arm pressed against her hand. "Know what I think? I think Uncles Jack, Walter and Harry ganged up on my father. That photograph was taken just about the time their father died. Probably just before otherwise they wouldn't have been grinning. Would they? Anyway immediately afterwards my father went north with my mother and set up a little shop. And went broke while his brothers prospered."

"Jack prospered?"

"Lives like a lord," Martin said.

"Perhaps they ..." she was going to say "worked harder" but changed it to "... were more money-minded."

"Or perhaps they had more money to set themselves up."

"I really don't know what you're getting at," Jenny said, feeling his warmth through the blue serge of his jacket.

"The death of my grandfather ... the parting of the ways ... their different life-styles ... I think the three of them forged their father's will without my father knowing. Hasn't it ever seemed strange to you the way the three of them stay apart? As though they share some guilt which they don't want to resurrect?"

"Have you ever asked your father about it?"

"You don't know him: he's made a sin out of pride. Let's assume he doesn't know what happened ..."

"If it happened."

"... he'd never admit that his father preferred his three brothers. Then let's assume that he does know what happened. Would a man like that admit that he was so unpopular that his three brothers turned on him, a pariah?"

"I would," Jenny said.

"You don't know my old man. In any case he couldn't prove it, could he? Three against one."

"Nor could you," Jenny said. She watched a plank hesitate on the water before escaping from the mainstream into the dock. "And it's all rather wild, isn't it?"

"It figures."

"Because you've made it."

"I can't think of any other explanation," Martin said.

"And you'll never rest ..." A cold breeze left over from winter slid across the water. "Well, maybe I can help. Harry and my mother are going on holiday soon. Maybe I could have a look around. I know where the safe is ..."

Again he surprised her. "Maybe I could come too," he said.

*　　　*　　　*

When they got back to the squat Prince was buzzing, recounting his exploits in staccato bursts.

Most importantly, it seemed, he had completed another 328 miles of free travel. Had enlisted an accomplice who had lurked

141

in the toilet. When the ticket collector approached Prince had joined him. A rap on the lavatory door. Groans from inside. "Just a minute, inspector," from Prince. One ticket slid under the door – the accomplice's. Slid back, punched. Ticket collector proceeds down carriage.

Good business in East Anglia. Surprising how many people didn't know they didn't have to pay for chemists' prescriptions if they were drawing benefits. "Got one couple £70 for a bedding allowance. Incontinent," Prince explained. "Advised one old dear – no charge – to send her worn-out shoes which she couldn't afford to replace to the Prime Minister. But mostly accommodation. One family with umpteen children into a hotel costing the State £860 a week. But no fiddles. Everything legal and general. One con artist wanted me to set up the old lodger wheeze. Phantom lodgers at her b and b. Live with friends, draw the allowance for staying in the boarding house. Split the difference with her. Sorry, ma'am. And a young bird wanted a partnership. Worked for the DHSS. Wanted to invent phoney claimants, process them and award them benefits. Claim books sent to post offices. Prince armed with identification – building society accounts in the false names – goes and collects. Some people," Prince said, shaking his head, "are very dishonest."

On the homeward journey he had indulged in a minor wheeze he had been contemplating for some time. Buy a newspaper with a tricky crossword, *The Times*, *Telegraph*, *Guardian*, *Independent* ... Remove the crossword page and substitute for the same page in the following day's issue. Memorise the answers to the clues on the discarded page. Find section of carriage in which learned gentlemen are contemplating today's crossword. Brandish newspaper so that learned gentlemen can identify it. Fold said newspaper so that they cannot see pattern of crossword. Complete the crossword at a rate of knots, sigh deeply at the naivety of the crossword compiler, return newspaper to briefcase and observe effect upon learned gentlemen still struggling.

"Why not just fill it in with any old words?" Charlie asked.

"That," Prince said, "would be cheating."

He stood up leaving the rocking chair in motion and patrolled the living-room, pulling at a lock of dank hair. He had acquired a torn flying-jacket that further endowed him with restless authority. "Fortifications," he said. "We've got to start

142

arming because they'll be coming for us any day now. Not the bailiffs, not those scalliwags. No, Messrs Sims and Kester and their muscle. Came with hammers and pick-axe handles last time I heard of them."

"Ah, the kestrel," Gosling murmured.

"You," to Cuff, "get a dog. Curled lip, yellow fangs, that sort of pooch. You," to Charlie, "keep watch. Early in the mornings. That's when they come. Just like the fuzz. Catch you asleep with your bird. You," to Danny, "get ready to do a runner when they do come. You," to Mad Bull, "prepare yourself for a bit of cuddling. You," to Gosling, "get a mug shot of friend Sims and compose a WANTED poster. You," to Jenny, "design it. And you," stabbing his own chest with his thumb, "get wheezing."

"And me?" Gosling's girl asked.

"Creature comforts," Prince said. "Sausages and bubble, mugs of tea . . ."

"And me?" Martin asked.

"Strategist."

"There's a trap-door into the cellar. If we put thin boards over it. Coax them that way."

"Pure genius," Prince told him. "The stairs, too. Saw halfway through some of them. Water cannon," he said to himself. "And you," to Hood, "phone the media. Tell them there's a battle raging."

"They'll think I'm lying."

"Say you're Prince," Prince said.

He paced the room with feverish intent.

Martin said doubtfully: "Tear gas?"

"Or," said Prince, never at ease with the obvious, "what about changing names? Buck House next door. Hoods with hammers come to the wrong house."

"There are kids next door," Martin pointed out.

"Right, right. Forget I spoke." The bead in his ear glittered. "Pirate radio? Family of Barbadians being evicted by honkies?"

He stopped in front of Jenny. Touching her shoulder he said: "Heard about the Mona Lisa. Good girl."

Jenny glowed.

CHAPTER 15

———◆◆◆———

And then it really was spring. Window-boxes bloomed with hyacinth and tulip and in Epping Forest the black fallow deer gambolled prettily and in London Zoo two big cats mated and in the parks young couples kissed and occasionally the dark corners of the city were visited by hope born on questing breezes.

Danny, still resisting the needle, took himself to Kew Gardens to help repair the damage wreaked by the storm; Gosling won a further reprieve for the squatters; Cuff found a Monday Club where perishable food from the supermarkets was distributed free; Mad Bull discovered Royal Jelly and wheat germ; Nolan's *souperlatively good* won him a soup spoon; Charlie, sprinting exuberantly, chested invisible tapes on Wandsworth Common; Jenny, trying not to think about the daffodils that would be nodding outside Kenwood House, brought Degas and Rembrandt to the pavements of South London and visited Eleanor Lubin, the dark and lustrous lawyer who proved to her chagrin that not all the privileged were complacent.

Eleanor lived alone in a two-bedroom apartment in Holland Park. She earned buckets of money from City financiers striving to navigate charges of insider trading and defended the penniless and persecuted for nothing. She was not popular with all policemen.

"They need me," she told Jenny as they drank tea in her apartment. "Even though they don't always realise it. Lawyers like me maintain the status quo between the practice and malpractice of law enforcement. There's nothing I detest more than a bent copper and, Christ, how they hate being torn apart by a woman."

"Do you actually enjoy it?" Jenny asked.

Eleanor's hand went to her black hair as though she were adjusting a barrister's wig. "I enjoy justice," she said. "There are a lot of good coppers, the majority in fact, but the bad bastards, boy are they ever bad. That's what you've got to realise," she said, pouring more tea, "this country isn't just yuppies and yobbos. And you've got to realise it before you become committed."

"What's wrong with being committed?" Jenny glanced round the apartment, at the polished green plants and niches where silver and glass winked lazily.

"Total commitment is a kind of bigotry. Adopt it when you're too young and your vision is distorted for ever. People in this country keep talking about the divides, north and south, have and have-nots. The trick, surely, is to visit both and see for yourself."

"I've done just that," Jenny said indignantly.

"You've come from one extreme to another. Your perception is polarised. You've got to explore, otherwise you'll stay in an outpost, one or the other. You know the greatest divide?"

Jenny, gazing through the window at a bed of red tulips with pointed petals in the park where the privileged had once promenaded, said she didn't. She suspected she was being patronised but she didn't resent it: everyone has a mentor: this green and silver room was a study and this glossy woman was her professor and this was a tutorial.

". . . the greatest divide," Eleanor Lubin was saying, "is young and old. 'But he's an old man.' 'But he's just a kid.' Wrong, we are one. You see once upon a time a young person was committed to the notion that old people are another race. He spread the gospel and then when he became old he looked back and saw the young as a separate breed. Wouldn't it be gratifying just once to see an old man and a young man talking together without leaning on a barrier?"

"And black and white," Jenny said.

"At least they're trying. Some of them."

Warm scents breathed through the window.

Eleanor said: "You're in grave danger, Jenny."

"I am?"

"Of making a virtue out of poverty."

"Is wealth a virtue then?"

"Neither is," Eleanor told her. "They're merely different suits of clothes. Wear both."

And Jenny returned to the squat where the spring had mustered a parade of seedlings in Danny's black earth in the back garden. Mustard and cress grew on blotting-paper in the kitchen; Hood took to writing fiction – stories for Mills and Boon which he submitted under a female pseudonym; a bodger named Frank turned up, bodging the cistern, the lock on the front door and the gas-fuelled refrigerator in one day; and Cuff produced a dog.

It was a pink-eyed bull terrier so scarred that Cuff, apologising for its condition, suggested that it might have been trained to fight professionally. The suggestion was dubious because Hoover, as they named him for reasons no one could remember, was manifestly not pugnacious; what he was was clumsy; when food was placed in his bowl in the kitchen he knocked over a three-legged coffee table, acquired by Cuff from a skip, to reach it, when a cat peered round the back-door he ran into the wall. Only the incurably optimistic could envisage Hoover sinking his fangs into a bailiff's calf: realists conjectured that, aiming his moth-eaten muzzle at one intruder, he might conceivably incapacitate another. He settled enthusiastically into the Buck House life-style, peeing in moments of unco-ordinated excitement on the WELCOME doormat and accompanying Martin and Charlie onto the common where he chased non-existent fugitives and frightened babies.

The spring also winkled out the three uncles.

First, Walter who thought he would drop by as he was in the area having previously taken the precaution of obtaining the exact address from Martin's mother. His mission was vague but he asked a lot of questions. What had Martin been up to? Had he got a job?

Accompanied by God, he wandered round the living-room, stepping over Hoover twitching in clumsy dreams, understanding the plight of the underprivileged. He wore his Bible-black suit and Martin feared he might pray.

Had Martin been up to anything else? Such as what? You know, visiting the old homestead, tracing your ancestry, finding out what makes you tick . . . that sort of thing.

146

He accepted tea. He recommended a church in Wimbledon near the All England Tennis Club. Martin feared he might offer him a job.

How was Jim?

As far as Martin knew Jim was fine.

Did Jim ever discuss his brothers?

Not as far as Martin could remember.

Walter departed leaving a slipstream that smelled of incense but was probably mothballs.

The second uncle to visit the squat was Jack, as pale as Prince and exuding jovial menace. His approach was as buoyant as Walter's had been holy. Easter was early this year, next weekend in fact, and would Martin and Jenny – word had it that he was keeping company with Harry's step-daughter – care to accompany him and Grace to Southend on the Monday?

The black Jaguar called for them at 7.30 am. Two hours later they were beside an armada of small boats abandoned by the tide on the sun-silvered mud of the Thames's wide mouth. The longest pleasure pier in the world, one and a half miles of it, looked for the sea; trippers parading the esplanade with its decomposed shelters and a rotting wharf or two sampled cockles and whelks and candy-floss and rides in Dizzyworld whose mock-medieval walls contained Ye Olde Rock Shop, Ye Olde Chippy, Castle Kebab, Burger Master and a tattooist; and boarded a replica of the *Golden Hind* and waited for pubs such as the Foresters – "Night and day we are the one. The Foresters for Strippers Drag and all that" – to open their doors. A few wandered into the shopping precincts where, on trading days, chain stores elbowed each other for your custom, and some even reached the rarefied pastures of Thorpe Bay and Westcliff.

Grace shepherded her party into the Embassy Café opposite a children's playground on the esplanade and ordered four cups of tea, 18p each, while Jack regarded his nephew over ketchup, HP Sauce and vinegar and the steam from his tea.

"So," he said, feeling the scar tissue at his neck, "got a job yet?"

Martin confessed that he hadn't.

"Don't worry," Grace said. "Something will come up." For her age, she was magnificent, limbs Benidorm-brown after a solo holiday, bright blonde hair finger-combed.

"Maybe we can help," Jack said.

147

Martin tried to appear enthusiastic. But how could he train Charlie and care for Danny if he was otherwise occupied from nine till five?

"Can't promise anything," Jack said, sipping tea. "It all depends . . ."

On what? The answers dissolved in the steam. Outside a handful of airborne seagulls quarrelled over a fish.

Grace said to Jenny: "So what's it like living in a squat?"

"How did you know?"

"Brother Harry of course."

"I'd like to have a pound less than him," Jack said.

"You do all right," Grace said. "You're not exactly boracic." She returned to Jenny. "Rum to think of you in a squat after your education."

"They care in the squat," Jenny said and Martin was proud of her.

"Harry contacted us," Jack said.

"Why?" Martin asked.

"Wally contacted us too. Been doing the rounds, haven't you, Martin?"

"I wanted to see my uncles. Natural, isn't it?"

"Of course it is. Family." Jack watched a triumphant gull fly past the window with the fish in its beak. "But, you know, it's almost as though you were on a mission. Know something, Martin? Better not to get too involved with family. Same with neighbours." He shook his head wisely.

Beside them a Cockney, with a beer belly spilling over the leather belt of his trousers, was ordering pork chop, chips, peas and tomatoes for £1.95; on the other side two middle-aged women were deep into angina.

"No offence," Jack said.

"None taken."

"That's all right then. How about a stroll?"

"Till the pubs open," Grace said.

The tide was returning, refloating the tilted boats, and the sandy beach beside the mud was occupied with families taking the sun when it showed itself between scudding clouds. Young men with strong white bodies played ball; children swept the shallows with shrimping nets; determined men in shirtsleeves knotted handkerchiefs over their heads; pale girls massaged themselves with oil that smelled of jasmine and washing-up

148

liquid.

They sauntered past promenade hotels emerging from hibernation – Hope, Coney Island, Monte Carlo, Carousel, Ivy House – and went into a hostelry, the Minerva, where a Great Dane vetted customers. Jack ordered whisky, Grace white wine with soda, Martin a pint of bitter, Jenny a shandy. The tipplers jostled them. Big women with dimpled arms and small husbands, girls with shiny lips exchanging amorous secrets, bruisers with tattoos writhing on bare forearms. The knitting-needle click of yellow and orange pool balls, arm-wrestling on the bar, voices with the flints of the East End in them . . . bank holiday and pub inseparable this burgeoning Monday.

"Like a bet, do you?" Jack asked Martin abruptly.

"Occasionally," Martin said.

"You?" to Jenny.

"Just the Derby."

"People like you would make a geezer like me bankrupt. Here, girl," handing Grace a £10 note, "get another one in."

It struck Martin that Jack's Cockney wasn't quite genuine. As if it had been sharpened from the soapstone vowels of North London.

"So you think it's a mug's game?" Jack said to Martin.

"Not if you're a bookmaker."

"That's not easy," Jack said. "Laying off, all that. One race could break a stupid bookie. And, of course, you've got to look out for the fiddles. Always watch the punter with a wad of notes in his pocket: he's usually skint. Know the first job a bookie learns?"

Martin shook his head.

"Chalking up. Runners and prices."

Grace returned with the drinks. Conversation rampaged around them. The police, Martin gathered, had stopped two rival gangs of Hell's Angels on the approaches to Southend and sent them back.

"Fancy it, Martin?"

"Chalking up?"

"Just bought an old shop near Mitcham."

Where Jesty had killed himself. Since his death sackfuls of junk mail had arrived at his digs. Catalogues for seeds and household requisites, brochures for exotic holidays that he could never have afforded, application forms to join book clubs, lists of available properties in Andorra and the Costa Blanca, invitations to buy window-glazing, wigs and memory aids. "Used to fill in forms," his landlady had said. "Just so that he could get mail. And him a postman, poor sod."

"I hadn't thought about it," Martin said to Jack.

"Think. Eighty quid a week for starters."

Martin thought about Charlie sprinting through light rain, his face, in which innocence was sometimes disturbed by guile, fierce with trying. He saw Danny's palsied hand reaching for a hypodermic. How could he leave them?

"Can I think it over?"

Grace was on the verge of discovery. "So the rumours are true: the kids of today don't want work: easier to draw the dole and supplementary. Well I'll be ... Why did you come to London, Martin?"

"To find work," Martin admitted.

"So Jack's offering you some."

"I haven't turned it down."

"Haven't embraced it neither."

"I'm grateful. It's just that I've got a couple of interviews tomorrow."

Jack tossed whisky down his throat. "Eighty quid, not to be sneezed at. Hard graft though. Keep your mind off family matters, eh Martin?"

"Let me buy a round," Jenny said.

"My turn," Martin said.

"Might as well have one on the DHSS," Grace said.

Jenny tried to slip Martin a £10 note but he flat-handed it away.

"No more for me," Jenny said.

Martin felt momentarily that he had known her for a long time. That they anticipated each other.

One more drink and they walked out of the pub onto the esplanade. The clouds had chased each other away and the saline air was warm and water from the estuary sucked at the strips of sand. A little girl ran past pulling a dummy bird that trilled and flapped its wings; a small boy buried his face in candy-floss.

The attack came when they were on the opposite side of the road, from behind a derelict shelter in which old people were eating sandwiches and drinking tea from Thermos flasks.

150

Jack had walked ahead oblivious to other pedestrians. Oblivious to the two burly men approaching him, hands dug into the pockets of their windcheaters, one gingery, one balding.

They walked straight at him, hands suddenly glinting with metal. Then the action blurred with speed and brutal deliberation. One of Jack's arms fending them off, the other striking back. And the crowds, eyes on destinations that had suddenly materialised, skirting them as though they were beggars. And Grace screaming and brandishing her handbag. And Billy appearing from nowhere with a ten-pin bowling skittle which he wielded savagely, no match for the knuckle-dusters that later lay on the pavement like giants' jewellery. You could feel the thuds as the blows struck home and now Jack was standing back, an observer, and there was blood spraying, like sweat in stopped photographs of boxers' punches.

And now the assailants were victims, moving jerkily on the pavement. They reminded Martin of gasping fish. And Billy, skittle raised, was staring at the eggshell head of the bald man but, thank God, was thinking better of it and Jack was saying: "Okay, that's it, let's do a runner before the Old Bill gets here," and they were legging it down a side-street in the direction of the parked Jaguar which seemed remarkably adjacent to the violence. Or am I becoming fanciful? Martin taxed himself as the Jaguar sped through the lowlands of Essex towards the sanctuary of the East End. But why should we be fugitives? We weren't the assailants. Martin squeezed Jenny's hand and she pressed herself warmly against him.

*   *   *

The third uncle, Harry, came by taxi and told the driver to wait. He stood on the doorstep and asked for Jenny and when she came, accompanied by Martin, said: "Time to be going home, young lady."

"I'm staying." She was wearing a paint-smeared jean suit; her hair was brushed straight and shiny and her expression encompassed resolution which was a little beyond her years.

"Your mother's very upset."

"Then why didn't she come to get me?"

"She didn't know what to expect." Justifiably, his tightening

151

mouth implied.

"I've written to her. Told her I'm happy. Isn't that what she wants?"

"She wants the best for you. So do I."

Prince said over her shoulder: "Come in, cully. Make yourself at home."

Harry, standing in the centre of the living-room, looked like a vegetarian in an abattoir. He circulated, touching furniture with the tip of his finger and inspecting it for dust.

Prince, gesturing towards the chaise-longue, said: "Take a pew, squire." He retired to the music room.

"I'll stand," Harry said, taking up his customary stance in front of the empty grate. "For the last time, are you going to pack?"

"I'm sorry," Jenny said, "but you're wasting your time."

Gosling picked up a thesaurus and, with his girl, disappeared up the stairs.

In the kitchen Mad Bull made sandwiches with wholemeal bread and cottage cheese.

Harry turned to Martin. "This is your doing. You came to meddle, didn't you. To punish the successful members of the family for your own father's failure. Well, I'll give you a piece of advice. I suggest you go back to Liverpool where you belong because London isn't just a wicked city, it's dangerous."

Martin envisaged him staring down a boardroom table at some unsuspecting director who was about to be offered the opportunity to resign.

"Are you threatening me?" he asked.

"Advising you, Martin. Both Jack and Walter think it's good advice."

"I didn't realise I was so important." Had the fight in Southend been staged as a warning? Where had Billy suddenly appeared from? Jack had claimed that the two toughs had been sent by a bookmaking conglomerate to persuade him to sell his betting shops. A halftruth, perhaps: he could have been tipped off and employed Billy to illustrate what happens to cowboys who threatened him and what could happen to inquisitive nephews.

"Of course you're important. But your place is with your parents. They need you, Martin."

"They're in a hostel," Martin said, "while the builders are in the house."

"They'll be back. Nice if you were there to greet them."

"There comes a time," Martin said, "when chickens have to leave the roost. I'm staying here," he said. "And Jenny's staying with me." He reached for her hand.

"I admire your spirit," Harry said. "But not your instincts. Self-preservation doesn't seem to rank very high."

He moved closer to them. Martin could smell whisky on his breath and pick out the surfacing capillaries on his cheeks. "Jenny comes back before the end of the week. Before I get back from Jersey."

"Jenny stays," Jenny said.

"I won't come to get you by myself."

"We won't be alone either," Martin said. He called Mad Bull in the kitchen. "This gentleman," he said, "is my uncle. I'm very fond of him. Why don't you show him some affection?"

Sandwich in hand, arms hanging loosely, Mad Bull advanced. He wore tracksuit trousers and training shoes and a blue vest and his retired muscles moved reflectively. He raised his eyes, pushing a creased smile onto his shaven scalp, and looked amiably upon Harry Renshaw.

Full credit to Harry, Martin reflected later. Without losing authority he moved unhurriedly to the door, opened it and stepped into the garden, leaving his threats behind him.

CHAPTER 16

———◆◆◆———

The crash on Wall Street – a 500-point fall on the Dow Jones index – devastated the City of London. The *Financial Times* index closed 250 points down and financiers and investors lost billions.

The occupants of Britain's council estates where single mothers were bringing up two children on £30 a week and youths were shooting alley cats to be sold as rabbits grieved.

Miners surveying the stilled pit-heads of moribund collieries mourned.

Families peering from the shattered windows of vandalised apartment blocks stripped of metal fittings to be sold as scrap offered condolences.

The crash was all the buzz in Job Centres where the commodity in short supply was decent jobs.

Vagrants curled in cardboard cartons offered prayers for the victims before retreating into jumbled dreams.

The latest arrival at Buck House, an anarchist with wild ginger hair and beard, sympathised passionately and at great length.

Only Martin and Jenny listened to him, Jenny because she hoped he would provide signposts for the anger on the streets of London and discipline the rabble of her own rebellion, Martin because he wanted to share with her.

The anarchist was at his most voluble in the saloon bar of the Codgers – since Jesty's death the public had been left to the old men – indignation fuelled by bottles of Guinness.

"Why obey laws?" he demanded one evening while the landlord polished glasses with furious intent. "You were born into this world with your own soul. This means that the world is yours, perceived through your own vision. If you didn't exist then that world wouldn't exist. So give me one good reason why we should conform to other people's concepts?"

"To preserve civilisation?" Martin suggested.

This amused the anarchist. "Civilisation? Oh dear, oh dear. Preserve humiliation, starvation, the enmities of race and creed, the suffering of the underprivileged ... Is that what you mean?"

"You can't dismiss Mankind like that," Martin said.

The smile on the anarchist's face became fiercer; he combed his ginger beard energetically and wiped Guinness spume from his lips. "I can't dismiss civilisation? You are speaking on my behalf? I, sir, can dismiss it and I do. Everyone, *everyone*, is governed by regulations imposed by the privileged for their protection. Walk down the street and you are a puppet on a string. You can't spit, you can't swear, you can't cross the street against the lights, you can't urinate, you can't beg ... Why shouldn't you beg? If you're starving why shouldn't you ask the gentleman stepping out of his Rolls for the price of a meal?"

"Perhaps he can't afford it," the landlord suggested.

"The crash? Is that what we're talking about, the stock market lying in ruins? God, yes, I'd forgotten. Slipped my memory for a moment." The anarchist smoothed his beard into mourning. "That gentleman might not be able to replace his Rolls with this year's model. He might have to put the cook on short time. He might have to fly first-class instead of Concorde. Poor sod." He placed his hand on his heart. "I weep for him."

Jenny, seeking direction, said impatiently: "You seem very negative."

"Ah, so we must all be positive, must we? Even those born without the prerequisite initiative?"

"Just what is anarchism? Positively, that is."

"To quote Warren it is the belief that 'every man should be his own government, his own law, his own church'."

"Which leads to anarchy."

"Exactly. A much misused term. Given his own head the individual will gravitate to people of his own kind. Together they can co-exist outside central or local government."

"Squatters are anarchists?" Martin asked"

"Close. As Proudhon said: 'Property is theft.'"

Jenny said: "You want a classless society? Like Communism?"

"Communism!" The anarchist drained his Guinness as though it were poison. "Communism is the equal distribution of the commonplace. Anarchism is freedom."

Prince and Cuff came into the saloon and, observing the anarchist in full spate, positioned themselves at the far end of the bar.

Martin bought a second round; the landlord served him wearily. A wino came in and asked for a snakebite, a mixture of lager and cider; the landlord, brightening, refused to serve him and the wino, wet-eyed and ruminative, shuffled into the street.

Jenny sipped her shandy. Why had she sought discipline from an anarchist of all people? It was a contradiction in terms.

She said: "So you're dedicated to the overthrow of the State?"

"Passively."

"Passively or violently, you don't want any truck with it?"

"That, madam, goes without saying."

"So you don't draw any benefits?"

The anarchist drew deeply on his drink. Then he said: "A man has to live, madam, a man has to live."

*   *   *

By this time Charlie was averaging a hundred miles a week. Accompanied by Martin or Danny, or Hoover competing enthusiastically with canine ghosts, he was a popular fixture in the streets of Wandsworth and Clapham and, because of its proximity, Brixton was beginning to adopt him. West Indians and Nigerians spurred him on as he mixed distances and sprints and his perseverance spread to their pirate radio stations; although the games for the mentally handicapped were still five months away the DJs had begun to broadcast good-luck messages from listeners.

What warmed Martin during this period was his burgeoning understanding of Charlie. No longer did he have to ask him to repeat himself; no longer did he have to anticipate; Charlie in his own way made as much sense as anyone; it was merely that occasionally his words overtook his thoughts or his thoughts outdistanced his speech.

And, as the sentences fell into place, so did his features: cast aside convention and Charlie was handsomely carved. Forehead flat-boned, ears prim, jaw hard-muscled; a face that defended secrets no one understood. Only his eyes sometimes lacked focus, looking round the corners of vistas leading to remote horizons.

Also striding forward with Charlie was Danny. He chased the dragon twice a week at the most; his hypodermic and needles remained sterile in their wrappings. He began to take an interest in Charlie's running times, he supervised his warm-downs, he ran and he talked about a future without drugs if Charlie won the race in Brighton and the wisps of his beard grew stronger.

"I owe it to him," Charlie said as he and Martin loped past the old windmill on the middle of Wimbledon Common. "And, man, he owes it to me if I win."

"No ifs," Martin said breathlessly.

"Hey, how come you understand me and no one else except Danny and maybe Prince does?"

"Because we listen," Martin told him. "You make us listen. Maybe you don't care with other people."

Hoover, overtaking on the right, ran into an old man who struck him with his walking stick.

"I used to care," Charlie said. "Then I found people thought I was crazy. No point, was there?" He put in a burst, then waited. "Do you think I'm crazy?"

"No more than the next man. Who knows what anyone thinks?"

"Are you crazy?"

"Daft as a brush."

"Maybe that's what we've got in common."

"Except that you're not crazy."

"Maybe, maybe not." His breath steamed. "Who knows what anyone thinks? Hey, I like that. Do you know what I'm thinking right now?"

"That it's time to stop?"

"That you're crazy," Charlie said. "Bothering with me. Bothering with Danny."

"Prince bothers," Martin said. "So does Gosling, Cuff . . . all of them."

"You really think so?"

"No," Martin said. "They all think you're crazy."

Charlie whooped. "And they're right, man! A hundred miles a week for some old skaghead," pointing at Danny who was sitting beneath a silver birch arranging bread and cheese and pickled onions and bottles of beer on the rough grass. "Hell, he'd better kick that old skag if I win."

Watched with pink-eyed intensity by Hoover, they tore off hunks of bread, cut the cheddar into thick slices, bit into the vinegar-spurting onions and drank light ale straight from the bottle.

"Know something?" Danny tossed a piece of bread to Hoover who snapped his jaws like a rat-trap and missed. "I don't even want a smoke after this."

"Me neither," Charlie said.

"You aren't allowed to. You stick to your training, right? You stick to your training," he repeated softly.

"Tell me something," Charlie said, "isn't there any way you can kick dope without me?"

"What did he say?" Danny appealed to Martin.

"Just listen. And you," to Charlie, "make him listen. It's Danny you're talking to."

"Jesus," Danny said when Charlie had repeated himself. "I understood. And no, you're the only way. Blow it and I mainline."

"Sounds like a threat."

"Statement of fact."

"Bullshit," Charlie said. "You could kick it."

"Maybe I don't want to. I'm inadequate you see," in his educated voice.

"You inadequate? What about me?"

"You are me," Danny said. "That's the point. If you win I win."

"That sounds pretty pathetic."

"I told you. I'm inadequate."

"If Hood had gone the distance would you have quit?"

"Hood didn't go the distance."

Martin said: "But Charlie's going to."

"Sure I am," Charlie said. "Sure I am."

*　　　*　　　*

158

They came, as Prince had predicted, at dawn. They carried sledgehammers and pick-axe handles and axes and they moved sturdily and inexorably through the ground-mist. They wore rough clothes and kicking boots and some wore shame which they tried to wipe from their faces with the palms of their hands.

At their head stood Kester in his sheepskin, employed by many developers, so Gosling had discovered, to remove obstacles to the development of new buildings. A worthy representative of that breed of philanthropists who help the deprived in hard times — liquidators who sell a bankrupt's stock bought with his life's savings at knock-down prices; owners of sweat-shops in the East End who provide employment for Asians for understandably modest wages; estate agents who arrange mortgages for the homeless who, even if they can't meet the payments and are eventually evicted, live temporarily beneath their own roof; owners of boarding houses who enable young and bewildered newcomers to London to enjoy the camaraderie of sharing a room with five other itinerants for a mere £7 a night.

Kester, half young blood, half pugilist, jagged voice issuing through a bullhorn, informed the occupants of Buck House that the game was up.

Prince, preceded by a white handkerchief tied to a broomstick, opened the front door while Hood, composing lies, slipped out of the back door and made for a phone kiosk.

"So," Kester boomed, "you've seen the light."

"Dawn, isn't it?" Prince said.

"Don't be fucking funny with me," Kester said, lowering the bullhorn. "All out. Now."

"Financial settlement, cully?"

"You blew that."

"Five hundred pounds," Prince said.

Silence.

"Two-fifty," said Kester.

"Four hundred."

"Three-fifty."

"Get stuffed," white handkerchief dipping, door closing. And to Charlie who had raised the alarm: "Well done, my son."

159

Each to his post. Martin — Jenny had gone ahead to the empty house in Hampstead — laying fragile planks across the trap-door over the cellar. Cuff chalking the steps on the staircase that have not been sabotaged. Mad Bull flexing his biceps. Danny beside his window with sacks of wet sawdust. The anarchist, ginger hair alert, thrusting garden hose onto a kitchen tap. Gosling tightening trip-wires, his girl brewing tea. Prince scheming.

A thundering on the front door. Kester: "Your last chance."

Prince: "That means they're coming round the back."

Danny opening a window. Sighting a group of three wielding sledgehammers and axes beneath him. The first crash of a sledgehammer against the flimsy back door. Wet sawdust from a timber merchants in a sack from a skip dropping heavily. A thud and a groan.

Prince, in charge of the Alamo: "One down. Five left."

Another blow against the door. A shout from Kester. Another sack bursting, sawdust spilling thickly across the concrete path. And another blow. A splintering of wood. Another sack, the last. Danny, breathing quickly, glances at his hypodermic and his needles and his tin-foil and his Eucryl toothpowder tin that contains white powder unrelated to teeth and hides them inside his mattress.

The blade of an axe pierces the door. Green-painted panels splinter. A sledgehammer blow at the lock. The door, groaning, swings inwards. A barricade of timber nailed across the frame. Beyond the timber the besieged can see the attack force, hard-muscled and tattooed and spattered with sawdust. A jet of water from the hose grasped by the anarchist fighting the mercenaries of class warfare. Thumb partially blocking the jet, giving it strength, he aims it well. A puny weapon but water has always been the enemy of violence. Momentarily non-plussed the mercenaries pause, wiping their streaming faces. They are ridiculous and this upsets the logic of their assault.

They attack the barricade with undisciplined force.

The planks fracture snappily and three men, fierce and wet, grab pick-axe handles and advance warily into the unknown. Into the nylon thread from an angler's reel stretched as taut as a guitar string between a metal filing cabinet transported from a ruined office and the pillar at the foot of the staircase.

One sprawls, a second tangled in his legs. A noose round

160

thrashing limbs. The second escapes but the rope tightens round the first. The big body is dragged across the living-room, the end of the rope tied high on the balustrade of the staircase so that this stormtrooper cannot reach the knot.

Prince: "Four to go." Red spots burn on his flour-pale cheeks. The anarchist's beard thrusts forward, an orange banner proclaiming the freedom of the individual. Martin waits beside his trap-door. Hoover, over-excited, indiscriminately bites legs. Where is Hood?

The kitchen is now occupied, Gosling's girl who has been throwing teacups is held by one mercenary. She bites his hand and draws blood.

Kester stays in the garden exhorting his troops to further endeavour. The three who are not disabled spread out. One towards Martin, two in the direction of the staircase.

Tyres screeching to a halt outside.

Holding a pick-axe handle two-fisted, a middle-aged man with a single white streak in his long black hair advances upon Martin.

"Okay, shit-head," he says, "you're going to get yours."

The thin planks above the trap-door break and he is rolling down stone steps into the cellar and Martin and Gosling are shifting the filing cabinet so that it covers the escape hatch.

And, led by Hood, there are reporters and photographers and camera crews in the garden. Buck House is news.

From the top of the staircase Cuff taunts the survivors of the assault force. Prince opens the front door to admit the media.

Sirens crow and two police cars skid to a halt. Uniformed police pile out. Buck House is not unknown to the law either.

They shoulder their way through the assembling crowd. Hoover barks frenziedly and pees on the mat.

Police and media enter the premises as a young man with soft fair hair and a weightlifter's muscles charges the staircase. He is bathed in the camera crews' white light. Cuff, swallowing an apology, shouts abuse that is so bland that it infuriates this predator more than familiar obscenity. One foot smashes through a sabotaged step, the other searches for a hold, finds it, breaks it. The blonde warrior plunges to the floor where he is surrounded by cameramen.

Kester walks briskly to his car.

Reporters and photographers work busily while the attack

force remusters.

Mad Bull who has not been used – for Prince the obvious is a last resort – smiles benignly.

A policeman points at Hoover and says to no one in particular: "Got a licence for that thing?"

CHAPTER 17

———— ◆◆◆ ————

It was her birthday. Eighteen. A woman.

Martin came downstairs from his room in The Bishops Avenue at 8 am but she was still in bed.

Leaving her present, a brooch that sparkled with rainbows, on the kitchen table he wandered through the rooms, footsteps furtive on the fitted carpets. The Renshaws, accompanied by Herta, were in Jersey but their presence lingered. Harry's cigar butt like a brown bullet in an ashtray in his study, pollen dusting the mahogany table beneath the wilting daffodils that his wife had arranged.

He trailed his fingers across a coffee-table inlaid with mother-of-pearl, dipped his fingers into a rosebowl filled with books of matches from illustrious hotels.

He was a burglar stealing privacy.

An over-fed black cat observed him through leaded windows. Chandeliers tinkled. A grandfather clock chimed beside him.

Jenny came down the stairs wearing an old-fashioned dressing-gown printed with flowers of the field. He wished her a happy birthday and kissed her. She smelled of lemons. He gave her the brooch and she held it to her breast and suddenly it was a cheap trinket but she said it was beautiful.

They drank coffee and ate Muesli in the kitchen, beneath the old-fashioned, beamed ceiling. The kitchen in the Dingle would have fitted neatly into one corner; the whole house would barely have filled the living-room.

Facing each other across the table, they were newly-weds on the morning after the honeymoon. Except that all that had passed between them was kisses. Martin noticed the swell of her breasts at the V of her robe; he wanted to reach across the table and slip his hand beneath the flowers of the field. He concentrated on his coffee. The black cat stared at him through the window with slitted eyes.

The letter box zapped. She ran to the front door and returned clutching a sheaf of envelopes. She opened them excitedly, brooch at her breast tawdry in the sunlight.

What was restraining him? The violation of another man's house? Bullshit. He was scared of rejection, as simple as that. He imagined the look of incredulity on her face as he made a clumsy pass.

And he saw Joanne naked on the couch in Liverpool.

She said: "Look at that," showing him a mildly vulgar card that had rugby club stamped all over it.

"You've got a lot of friends," he said.

"Acquaintances. Only one or two real friends. Have you got many in Liverpool?" She slit an envelope with the bread-knife.

"A few."

"Would I like them?"

"Do you like football?"

"Rugby," she said.

"Then you wouldn't."

"Isn't that rather a sweeping assumption?"

He shrugged.

"I get on well enough with your friends in the squat."

"Any reason why you shouldn't?"

"If they like football, according to you." She held up a card, a field of bluebells and a mystified fawn. "You're very class-conscious, Martin." She turned the fawn upside down and a cheque fluttered onto the table. "From my father," she said. "On time for once."

"Aren't you class conscious?"

"I'm aware of inequality. Not class so much. It will probably bounce," she said, examining the cheque.

"It's the thought that counts."

"You should meet Eleanor," Jenny said.

"Who's she?"

"An enlightened lady."

"Rich?"

"There you go." She opened another funny card; Martin saw three Xs beside a flamboyant signature. "She's living proof that

164

the rich aren't necessarily like Harry."

Instead of drawing closer they were distancing themselves from each other. Sexual anticipation withered. In any case it should be consummated at the end of a birthday, after dinner and a bottle of red wine.

Jenny leaned across the table. She said: "You and I, no distinctions. Our crusade."

The V of her robe parted and he could see all of her breasts between the flowers of the field.

He stretched out his hand and found their warmth.

It was surely far too early for red wine.

Outside the windows the black cat blinked.

*   *   *

Now they were conspirators and the day was vibrant with their intimacy. Behind them sex, clumsy but still shared hours later; ahead felonious intent – the intrusion into the secrets locked in Harry Renshaw's safe.

And as she took him on a pilgrimage round Hampstead and its heath they held hands. Keats's home, the Admiral's House from which cannons once signalled naval victories, the Spaniards' Inn and Jack Straw's Castle, Dr. Johnson's summer house, Parliament Hill.

Were they justified in opening the safe?

"Why not?" Jenny asked. They had bought French bread and Cheshire cheese and a bottle of white plonk and they were sitting on a rise looking across the drowsing domes and turrets of London. "If there's been an injustice, why not?"

"Why not?" he agreed aware that she was now more committed than he was.

"We're investigating, not stealing."

"When?"

"This evening. After dark."

"How did you get the combination?"

"When he was in the shower. He left his wallet on the bedside table. He's probably reversed the last two digits. He does that with phone numbers so that my mother can't check them."

"How do you know that?" He poured wine into plastic cups.

"Agatha Christie," she said.

"You're very devious," he said.

165

"He's very obvious."

She tasted the wine, nodded wisely. Martin remembered Danny, beer bottle to his mouth, on Wimbledon Common. He touched her face, sketching a smile. The spring was theirs.

"Do you know what I think?" she asked. "I think that when you and I look into the night sky we see the same star." She brushed flakes of crust from her lips; her resolute face had a serenity about it today that he hadn't noticed before and her fine dark hair stirred in an imperceptible breeze; she pulled at the lobe of one ear as she did when she was painting. "And I laugh with you," she said. "That's good, isn't it? Humour and sex. Isn't that what every couple should have? Not necessarily in that order." She laughed.

"And not at the same time," Martin said.

"Are you very experienced, Martin?"

She must know perfectly well from this morning's perform-ance that he wasn't. He lay on his back, hands behind his head, and stared at the invisible stars in the soaring blue sky. "I've been around," he said.

She punched him. "Sod."

"And I'm an accomplished liar."

She leaned over him, breasts that had begun it all tight against the yellow material of her blouse, and stroked his chest beneath his open-neck shirt. A pulse throbbed in her neck.

He raised his head and kissed the pulse.

"Let's go home," she said, brown eyes searching his.

He rolled clear, stood up and offered her his hand. "Race you to those trees, Joanne!"

"Close," she said. "One J, two Ns and an E. There the similarity ends."

She walked briskly ahead of him.

*   *   *

On the telephone Charlie was reasonably articulate, as though he was measuring his words. He asked if he could visit them.

"Why, Charlie?" asked Martin who had left the number at the squat. "Anything wrong?"

"Nothing wrong. It's just this training. Isn't the same without you."

Warmed, Martin said: "Okay, I'll pick you up tomorrow at

166

Buck House and we'll run on the heath. Danny too?"

"Danny's helping Prince."

"But he's all right?"

"Just a little puff last night."

"Gos?"

"Playing with words. Hoover tried to bite Cuff."

"What happened?"

"Cuff apologised," Charlie said.

"Mad Bull?"

"Healthy."

"Hood?"

"Got a letter of encouragement from Bills and Moon. No stopping him now. And that Frank. Reckon he's here to stay. Mended your trap-door, fell through it and hurt his leg."

"Take care, Charlie."

Charlie said he would.

*   *   *

The safe was embedded in the floor of the cellar underneath a strip of worn red carpet. The cellar, cold and smelling of mould, was cluttered with the discarded past — old-fashioned dresses hanging from a pipe, dinner jacket with verdigris spots on the lapels, pile of Sunday newspaper colour magazines, exercise bicycle rusting from lack of exercise, box of fossils, deflated basketball, a conjuring set containing a bloodied plastic finger, one-armed doll staring wide-eyed at the ceiling ... "That's Beatrice," Jenny said. "I couldn't pronounce her name." He was a body snatcher and the final dissection, the heart, was the safe. He wanted to climb the steps back to the present but he couldn't retreat in front of Jenny; that was cowardice. Or was the greater cowardice not retreating? The cold found the bones in his fingers.

Jenny, kneeling, manipulated the combination. "Eight", a pause, "three", a stifled cough, "nine", clearing her throat. The knock on the front door reached them in muffled drum-beats. They froze. Police? Perhaps the safe was linked with the police station. Martin opened his mouth to speak but Jenny put her finger to her lips. Another knock reverberating with impatience. Jenny slid the carpet over the safe and spread the colour magazines as though they had been searching for an article.

167

Then the visitors found the front-door bell. Three short buzzes followed by the audible beating of his heart. She stood up spreading her hands. One more buzz, despairing. Martin imagined he heard retreating footsteps. He remained motionless, the beat of his heart fading. "Probably friends," she said at last. "Bridge maybe." She knelt and drew back the carpet.

"Another nine", biting her lower lip, "seven", brushing a lock of hair from her forehead, "two and", pulling the handle on the combat-green door, "Eureka!" The door remained obdurate. "I'll re-phrase that," she said.

Halfway through the second attempt the telephone rang upstairs. "Probably the same people," Jenny said. "Checking."

The phone stopped ringing, leaving behind thick silence.

She tried the combination again without reversing the final digits. Nothing. She sat on the carpet. "He's cleverer than I thought," she said. "As if he anticipated us." Martin said: "Try reversing the first two digits." Two minutes later the safe was open.

Bundles of faded documents tied with pink and blue ribbon. Deeds of the house. Birth certificates for Harry and Jenny's mother. Bank documents from Switzerland and the Cayman Islands. Copies of share certificates. Statement of probate "in the matter of the estate of William Herbert Renshaw deceased". Harry had received £10,321, a lot of money thirty-five years ago. Probate of his will granted to William Grey. Martin made a note of the name and the dates and told Jenny to close the safe. Before climbing the steps he closed Beatrice's eyes. As the door-bell rang.

The police had stepped out of a TV series. They stood at the doorway, cap-bands chequered blue and white, models of deference. "Excuse me, miss, we had a phone call."

Jenny: "Won't you come in?"

"Thank you, miss," removing their caps and holding them under their arms.

"Might I ask who you are, sir?"

"Martin Renshaw. The householder's nephew."

"And you, miss?"

"His step-daughter," Jenny said.

"Would you mind proving your identities," as apologetically as Cuff.

"Not at all," Martin said. "I'll have to go upstairs."

168

"Mind if I come with you?" His policeman had cropped black hair and he blinked a lot.

"What are you doing here, son?" he asked as Martin took a Post Office savings book containing £1.58 from his suitcase in the spare room.

"Just staying here."

"At the owner's invitation?"

"At Miss Renshaw's invitation."

"And how old is she?"

"Eighteen," Martin said. "Today."

"Why didn't you answer the door when Mr. Renshaw's friends knocked?"

Because we were robbing Mr. Renshaw's safe.

"We did but they had gone."

"Don't insult my intelligence, son." He pointed at the unmade bed. "Otherwise engaged?"

"None of your business."

"You're probably right. I sometimes wonder what is our business." He blinked, then knelt and searched Martin's suitcase. Martin was ashamed of its impoverished contents. The policeman stood up.

"Working?"

"I've been offered a job."

"Take it. And take my advice – stay out of trouble. You kids ..." He didn't finish the sentence.

Downstairs the other policeman, fresh and fair with a chipped tooth, tapped the handset into which he had been talking. "No form," he said. And to Jenny: "Sorry to have bothered you, miss. All in your own interests, you understand."

"But answer the door next time," Martin's policeman said. "Here, you'd better put the Hibberts out of their misery." He handed Martin a telephone number.

On the porch the fair-haired policeman saluted. "Thanks for your co-operation," he said.

Together they walked down the path into the next instalment of the TV series.

"Whew," said Martin.

"So what do we do now?"

"Trace Mr. William Grey."

"He's probably dead."

"Probably a solicitor. There'll be partners. Mind if I have a

169

drink?"

Martin poured himself a whisky. Added ice from the dispenser in the kitchen. Tasted it. Grimaced. Added ginger ale and listened to the ice cracking.

Jenny switched on the television. A documentary, the growing unrest in the country, a civil rights spokesman comparing London to a time-bomb.

"And we're not doing anything," Jenny said.

To foment protest or silence it? Martin wondered.

"I'm going to bed," Jenny said.

"And I'm coming with you."

And this time, although they would always remember the first, it was much better.

* * *

When they got back to the squat with Charlie who had spent the day with them in Hampstead, things had changed.

Frank the Bodger, raspberry-cheeked and unshaven, had invaded Martin's room which now smelled of old-fashioned glue and wood shavings.

Danny had decorated the living-room with leopard-spotted blooms that had survived the storm at Kew.

Hood had received more encouragement from his publishers. "Plotting and characterisation good but heroine has exceeded the bounds of propriety which our readers expect. Nothing that can't be fixed."

Cuff had departed temporarily to visit a wife that no one knew he possessed.

Gosling was peering through a fog of words for a sighting of his girl who had vanished as quietly as she had arrived.

Mad Bull, glossy with pills, was contemplating a come-back in the ring.

Nolan had won a trip round the cheese-producing districts of Holland. *Don't say cheese, say Dutch – then smile.*

Prince, anticipating lawful eviction after the illegal attempt by Kester and his storm-troopers, was confined to his room, scheming.

Martin considered asking Jenny if he could move in with her; instead he told the Bodger to shift his wood shavings.

CHAPTER 18

———◆◆———

Joanne heard about the Battle of Buck House on Radio City news. Martin had written to his parents four times, to her once; what he hadn't written was that he was living in a squat.

She worried about it as she drove her mother to Mass at the Metropolitan Cathedral of Christ and the King, leaving her father clumsily asleep in a bedroom that smelled like a four-ale bar.

His departure she understood: the South, a siren, beckoned the workless. Not her though. This gritty city, trying to pick itself up after the Siberian winds of recession, was hers. Especially today when starving streets were redolent of Sunday roast and the city centre bloomed optimistically with Spring Festival flowers.

She drove past the docks along the inner city ring road, turning up Parliament Street to the cathedral with its modern cone crowned with thorns designed by a non-Catholic. Its Anglican sister, the sandstone edifice at the other end of Hope Street, was designed by a Catholic! That was Liverpool for you.

Kneeling, she peered into the chapel of her hands and prayed for the city and its people and saw Martin lying on a verminous bed in a ruin occupied by degenerates and rats. Observing his vulnerability and youth – she always felt older than him – she experienced the affection she had felt for him before he struck south. Should she go to him?

She asked her mother as they walked briskly down Hope Street in search of lunch, her mother having abandoned the Sunday ritual which had become increasingly blighted by a drunken husband who spent his DHSS at the pub.

171

Her mother pointed at a group of middle-aged men turning into a public house. "From the pews to the pubs," she said without rancour. In fact she was remarkably philosophical about her husband; she understood despair. And she had retained her curiosity about life so that she remained one of those people whom you could still see when they were young; she walked with angular grace and the greyness in her hair was a refinement not a pension. She dressed like a wealthy countrywoman, without the brogues, and Joanne could not believe that she had ever been sexually attractive. Like me? But that doesn't mean that we don't lack sexuality. That last time with Martin, Catholic guilt an aphrodisiac, a wild heretical abandonment.

"I asked you a question," Joanne said.

"Don't force him into anything: he'll accuse you later."

"I couldn't force him if I tried."

"You could persuade him."

Did she know they had slept together? Slept! Surely a contradiction. She suspected that she did. Just as she had once done with the handsome young shipping clerk she had married. But you could never picture your parents making love even if you were the result. And me a fledgling nurse fully conversant with bodily functions. "Fancy a drink?" she said and, to her surprise, her mother said yes, a Guinness would be nice.

They passed the Everyman Theatre and the Casablanca and on the corner of Hardman Street turned into the crystal and copper depths of the Philharmonic Hotel, the bottle of Guinness for her mother, a half of Tetley's for herself. Beer was at its best at Sunday lunchtime.

"You still haven't answered the question," Joanne said. "Not really." She stood with her foot against the rail, bracing herself against the thirst building up behind them.

"It's your decision. And let's sit down."

"He's living in a slum," Joanne said. "Did you know they interviewed him?" They sat down.

"Was he repentant?"

"He was not."

"Don't save him," her mother said. "He'll never forgive you."

"You're still at Mass," Joanne said.

"You asked me."

"No harm in visiting him surely."

"Don't be surprised at what you find. It could be like reading someone's diary and getting upset at what you shouldn't have read."

"You think he's got another girl?"

"He's a healthy young man."

"Your faith in Mankind is amazing."

Her mother, sipping her Guinness, shrugged. "I'm realistic. I wouldn't want you to marry too soon." She didn't say "like me" and Joanne respected her for it. "Martin's only nineteen. Irishmen don't marry till they're thirty."

"He's not Irish," Joanne said.

"You are."

"Hanging around until himself'd made up his mind?"

"I wouldn't want you to have a routine marriage," her mother said. "It's worse than an arranged one. Everything predestined from the first mucky joke at the reception. The first child, the mortgage, the job which he can't leave because of the mortgage, a little philandering, recriminations interpreted as nagging, kiss and make up . . . all copies from some handbook handed down by their parents."

"But your marriage wasn't – isn't," she corrected herself, "like that."

"He's a good man," her mother said. "But some people haven't got the resistance. I haven't sometimes when I wake in the early hours but in the morning it passes; but with your father it lingers . . ."

They had lunch in Chinatown at the Yuet Ben which neither of them could afford. Pausing, sweet and sour half-way to her mouth, her mother said: "My advice is not to see him. But why ask for advice? People only want to hear what they've already decided to do."

"You're very wise, mother," Joanne said. "That wasn't what I wanted to hear."

*   *   *

The newcomer to the squat was named Jack Daniels, like the whiskey. A quiet man with suspicious eyes and a razored voice who claimed to have owned an antique shop in Newcastle. He despised the police for reasons which he never revealed; he disappeared by day to destinations that he never divulged; he walked with a limp and he dealt in coins. "Other people's", according to Prince.

"If you think he's a villain why not kick him out?" Martin asked Prince over supper.

"Innocent until proved guilty, cully." Prince scraped mould from a chunk of cheddar. "What's so wrong with mould?" he demanded. "People eat blue cheese, don't they?"

Mad Bull spread orange blossom honey on a slice of wholemeal bread; Hood scribbled while he ate; the anarchist, brooding on some heinous injustice, munched furiously; Gosling stared sadly through the kitchen window into the garden where birds had gathered for evensong.

A knock on the front door and Cuff, who had been away for three days, entered bearing bruised peaches and sprouting potatoes. He apologised for his absence but there was an unfamiliar exuberance in his voice.

"We didn't know you had a wife," Martin accused.

"No reason why we should," Prince said, reaching for the peanut butter.

"She wants a divorce," Cuff told them. "She wants to get married again. To someone not so humble as me, she said." There was no stopping Cuff. "That's what she always said, I didn't make enough of myself. Well, I had a decent job. At a funeral parlour. Did you know that?" No one did. "And I used to give her all my wages and the flowers that got left behind but it was no good. Do you know what she said? She said I lacked violence." He drank some tea. "A nice little house we had in Kilburn. Near the Gaumont. Lacked violence, I ask you. Well, maybe she's got it now: this fellow's done time for GBH. But I wouldn't want anything to happen to her . . ." His words lost direction. "I'm sorry," he said.

"Were you ever spliced, Gos?" Prince asked. It was confession time.

"Wed. Dew backwards. That's nice, isn't it. No, I was courting once but a spell in a house of correction put paid to that."

Hood, glancing up from the course of true love in his exercise book, said: "What did you go down for, Gos?"

"Forgery." Gosling didn't elaborate and no one pressed him because secrets were valid currency in the squat. No one asked him why his girl had left either.

174

"I'm composing crosswords," Gosling said.

"You've got a Scouser to thank for that," Martin said, peeling an over-ripe peach. "Arthur Wynne. Compiled the first one in 1913."

"Ever thought of going on *Mastermind*?" Prince asked.

"Were you ever married?" Martin asked Mad Bull.

"Once," Mad Bull said. He didn't elaborate.

"I wrestled once," Hood said. "Back in '62. Took on a big bruiser called the Terrible Turk . . ."

"Do us a favour," Prince said. "Get back to the marriage guidance counsellor sharing cucumber sandwiches with the girl next-door at the tennis club. What are you calling it, *Love All*?"

Charlie came in accompanied by Danny. They smelled healthily of sweat. They sat down and ate hungrily.

"Some black guys came and interviewed Charlie," Danny said.

"I should have been there," Martin said.

"No, it was okay. They understood."

The anarchist, rolling a cigarette with tobacco as black as liquorice, said: "Whatever happens it will be a triumph even if he isn't first past the post."

"Tape," Charlie said.

"What about the other competitors?" Danny asked. "Aren't they individuals?"

"Every race is a triumph for the individual. Every race is an analogy of what life should be."

"Supposing it's a dead heat?"

The anarchist ignored him.

Charlie said to Mad Bull: "Hear you're going to make a come-back," and when Mad Bull, smiling with his forehead, nodded, Prince said: "No one ever does. Take my tip, leave it out."

Still smiling, Mad Bull flexed a bicep at him.

"Think the women will still be mad for you?"

"Wild," Mad Bull said.

"Even if you're told to lose?"

"If I'm really evil," Mad Bull explained patiently. "You see it's the bad guys who make them frisky."

Cuff nodded wisely.

Another knock on the door. Jack Daniels limped into the

kitchen in a gust of night air. He halted the conversation, placed a bottle of Smirnoff vodka on the table. "My contribution," he said. He sat down and began to eat methodically, washing his food down with vodka and water. He didn't speak and one by one the others departed until he was alone.

"He frightens me," Jenny said later.

"He's just a loner." Martin sat on the edge of her bed.

"He's more than that. He's . . . deliberate. An iceberg."

Martin kissed her. Unlike the other occupants she had made the room hers. The pictures which she had brought from Hampstead – poppies in a field, a little girl with freckles and pigtails – on the pink walls, her clothes hanging in the cupboards, the bear staring with one-eyed intensity at a damp patch on the wall. Who had slept here before? Two demure girls in Edwardian clothes, he decided, who shed their modesty when the door closed behind them to discuss their swains.

"I think he carries a gun," Jenny said.

"Nonsense."

"Or a knife. Have you noticed how his hand keeps reaching inside his jacket?"

"Making sure his wallet's still there."

"A woman has more intuition than a man."

"That's sexism for you."

"But it's true. Why don't you check his room? During the day when he's out."

"That would be . . . immoral."

"So was breaking into Harry's safe."

*   *   *

The room was as contained as the man. Camp-bed neatly made, suitcase geometrically aligned beneath it. The wash-basin was scoured, mottled mirror above it polished, brushes, comb, toothpaste, laid out like exhibits. Wasn't over-cleanliness a symptom of guilt? Martin touched the suitcase with the toe of his shoe. Two felonies within a week! He was scared but he was excited too. What if Daniels breaks his routine and returns during the day? And what am I looking for? A Magnum, a butterfly knife, a lock of blood-stained hair? A pigeon, throat-pulsing, perched on the window-sill. I am prying into a man's

176

soul as neatly arranged as ... a prison cell? What right do I have? The safety of the other occupants, he assured himself, edging the suitcase from beneath the bed. It was old and green, bore the letters JD in faded gold and was fastened with a leather strap. It opened easily. Shirts and underclothes that smelled of washing powder, two silk ties, an address book which he didn't open, a photograph in a silver frame, recently shined, of a young woman, studio lights in her hair, smiling with love and trust, a Swiss army knife – even kids had those – two pullovers from Marks and, snug beneath them, a black Bible.

He closed the case, buckled the strap and slid it beneath the bed.

He was frisking the clothes hanging from two hooks on the wall when he heard a floorboard in the corridor creak. He stopped breathing and bit the inside of his mouth. *Sorry, Jack, mistook the room. Really? Yours is on the other side of the house.* He tasted blood. Another creak. Martin side-stepped towards the door. Composed a silly-mistake smile. The creaks receded methodically. Martin gave them a couple of minutes, then let himself out of the room. A figure at the end of the corridor.

"Sorry, Jack, mistook the room."

"I know the feeling," Frank the Bodger said.

*   *   *

Jack Daniels came home at 8 pm bearing fish and chips, one bag for each resident. He went upstairs, returning a couple of minutes later rinsing dry hands together. He sprinkled salt and vinegar on his meal and began to eat with controlled hunger. Half-way through his meal he said: "I don't know who broke into my room ..." glancing at each of them with his pale eyes "... but perhaps this was what he – or she – wanted." He placed the Swiss army knife on the kitchen table. "I was going to contribute it to the squat anyway. It's a useful tool – and weapon." Knives and forks scraped on plates. Then Frank the Bodger said: "As a matter of fact it was me, Jack. Mistook the room – I was going to mend Danny's window." His raspberry cheeks smiled across the table at Martin.

177

Joanne went to the little house in Dingle before catching the London Inter City from Lime Street. Martin's father was reading the *Daily Post*, his mother was in the kitchen opposite the new and despised lavatory; the old one in the yard had been an excursion – have a row and retire to the privy.

"Any messages for him?" she asked, accepting a mug of tea and sitting opposite Jim Renshaw.

"Tell him to come home and help his mam," Jim said.

"I don't need his help. He's doing all right. Let the lad make his way."

"Doing all right, is he? Has he got a job?"

"What if he's on benefit? He's got to get a start."

"Begging?"

"If someone in this house accepted he was on the parish more often we wouldn't be eating jam butties midday." Her cheeks had lost their polish, her grey curls their spring.

"You know what I think about charity."

"Begins at home, that's where." She handed Joanne a letter. "Here, read this, luv. He's doing fine . . ."

Joanne read the letter.

Dear mum and dad,

> *Just to let you know that the opportunities down here are terrific. So good, in fact, that I haven't made up my mind what to do yet. That doesn't matter because I'm on benefit but the sooner I get a job the better. Meanwhile I'm sharing a house with some other lads – you'd like them. One of them is a writer. How are you both keeping and have you got your new privy yet? I won't recognise the old place. Must rush now – interview coming up. Love to Joanne and tell her I'll write soon.*
>
> *Lots of love,*
> *Martin*
> *XXX*

"Just like our Martin," said Mrs. Renshaw who couldn't have heard about the squat.

"Martin's going places," Joanne said. The half-truths in the letter, she thought, sprang out like winkles on a pin.

"Give him our love."

178

"Tell him no one ever died of hard work," Jim said.

"Oh, dad," his wife said. "Put a zipper in it."

The carriage was half-full, mostly young men foraging south in search of work. Rain bowled across the fields hitting the windows of the train and sliding down in rivulets. She ate her sandwiches and drank coffee from a flask.

Supposing Martin did have another girl? The possibility lurched inside her. She had no illusions about herself. She was a tall, big-boned girl with reddish hair who carried herself with authority that was sometimes not far removed from grace and was confused by the conflicts of faith and passion. Nothing sensational there. She even had freckles. Hadn't anyone ever realised that they were a multitude of beauty spots?

The train paused at towns in the Midlands and then hurried south.

"So why you going south?" The West Indian sitting opposite her was middle-aged, with wise eyes and sparse hair.

"Haven't you heard? There's only one way to go these days."

"Hope you're right, sweet lady."

"And you?"

"To pavements of gold."

"They can be slippery," Joanne said.

"You're not staying?" pointing at her small bag on the rack.

"One night."

"True love?"

"Maybe."

"Let's drink to it."

He handed her a hip flask.

She swigged; she didn't know why. Rum.

He leaned forward. "Really want to know why I'm going to the Smoke?"

She shook her head.

"Know who's unemployed?"

"Lots of people," she said.

"Blacks is who."

"And whites."

"Highest percentage is blacks. So there's a big gathering of the clans in the Smoke and I'm going along. You read about the unrest on the streets?"

Of course she had.

"Analyse it, lady. It's the oldest conflict manufactured by

179

God. Black versus White. Why did that Man create two colours? If he hadn't we wouldn't have to look down upon you long-suffering whites."

"I'm Irish," Joanne said.

"Know what they call Indians in Liverpool? Smoked Irishmen."

"Laugh about it," she said. "For God's sake laugh."

London suburbs flitted past.

"I've got two kids," he said. "Late teens. Both on the dole." He leaned further forward so that their knees touched and took a swig of rum. "Even if there were jobs my kids wouldn't take 'em. Work? They don't know what it is. Why should they?" He offered Joanne the flask but she refused. "And the politicians yak about the economy. Why should my boys care about that old economy? Far as they're concerned it's as remote as justice. But I tell you something, those politicians, those economists, are going to pay for it. Boy, are they ever going to pay. While they were playing with figures kids were growing up."

The train braked. Terraces and backyards crowded the line.

The West Indian stood up. "Sorry to lecture you. But remember what I said. *They* created this, not us."

The train shuddered, inched forward and drew into Euston.

CHAPTER 19

———— ◦•◦ ————

Charlie disappeared the following day.

He had been training with Danny on Wandsworth Common and they had been sheltering beneath a golfing umbrella acquired by Cuff and, when thunder crashed, he had taken off as if he'd heard a starting pistol and Danny had tried to follow but it was no good, not with Charlie running like that.

"Which way did he go?" Prince asked.

"He was heading in this direction. But when he reached the edge of the common he vanished."

One of Danny's arms shook with a life of its own.

"Right or left?"

"I'm not sure," Danny said. "Why did he have to do that? Why?" His face was wet with rain.

"If it was right he was probably heading for Brixton," Prince said.

"Why Brixton?" Martin asked.

"He saw it last night on telly in the Codgers. Reckons he was born there. Reckons his mother might still be there somewhere."

"He could have told me," Danny said.

"He was ahead of his words. He probably wants to tell you now." Prince spread a map, torn at the creases, on a tea-chest in front of the empty grate. To Cuff: "Can you borrow a motor-bike?" and when Cuff nodded: "Can you ride one?" and when Cuff said he could: "Got a licence?" and when Cuff said he hadn't: "Off you go, then, shouldn't be too difficult to spot near Brixton, tracksuit with a Union Jack on the back, running like the clappers." He traced a triangle on the map with one finger. "Battersea Rise, Clapham Common, Acre Lane ... But he might have gone the other way. Nightingale Lane, Clapham Common South ..."

To Gosling: "You get a cab." He handed him a £5 note. "Stake out Wandsworth Bridge on the other side of the river in case he turned left."

To Danny: "You stay here. If he comes back you're the one he'll want to see." He squeezed Danny's arm with his bony fingers. Danny went upstairs.

To Jenny, softly: "Take care of Danny."

To Mad Bull, the anarchist and Frank the Bodger: "All of you stay here in case Kester and his mob come back. You," to the anarchist, "call the media if they do."

"What are you going to do?" the anarchist asked.

"Check out Dean Street with Martin."

Prince went upstairs to fetch his scuffed flying-jacket, and Martin went to his room to collect his mail-order raincoat.

He saw Danny through the half-open door of his room. The hypodermic was on the bed. In his hand a naked needle.

"Don't," Martin said from the doorway.

"You don't understand."

"Inadequate?"

"I never did anything well," Danny said. "Not even growing this." He tugged his sparse beard.

"I was lousy at studies, lousy at sport. What's the point?"

"Charlie's the point," Martin said.

"Charlie's gone. He ran away – from me."

"He'll come back."

"You're beginning to sound like the family doctor."

"Charlie depends on you."

"So why did he bugger off?"

"You know Charlie."

"I thought I knew Charlie. I thought I knew a lot of things when I was a kid. I thought my parents loved me." Muscles quivered in his jaw. "Do you know what I'd tell my kids? Never be afraid of crying. Why should anyone be ashamed of it? Because it's not manly? Clint Eastwood never cries? If kids were taught to cry there would be some better grown-up kids around."

182

Tears trickled down his cheeks.

He pricked his thumb with the needle drawing a pin-head of blood.

"Do you really want to know why kids become skagheads?" Danny asked. "Even when they know it's going to make them lie, cheat, rob? Even when they know it's going to kill them? Because the life in there," pointing at the Eucryl tin of heroin, "is better than this one. Get inside that tin and you're someone. It's your world and you count and you can cry and no one gives a shit and you can be inadequate and no one gives a shit. And it's so peaceful, Martin, so peaceful."

"Okay," Martin said, "shoot yourself full of dreams. But how long do they last?"

"It doesn't matter," Danny said. "At the time it just doesn't matter. Do you know what it would feel like if I injected now. Heaven would shoot up my arm and fill my skull."

"And you'd end up a corpse."

Danny picked up the syringe in its wrapping and studied it. "At least I'd be an adequate corpse."

"Wait till Charlie gets back," Martin said.

Danny licked the blood from his thumb. "What's it like to be one of the good guys, Martin? Gung ho, all that."

"Just wait."

"Waiting is what I do really well."

He sat on the edge of the bed. He placed the needle beside the hypodermic. He folded his arms. "I'm waiting," he said.

*　　　*　　　*

Ludicrously, the top deck of the bus felt precarious. When rain hit the windows like buckshot as it turned a corner it threatened to overturn. In front of Martin and Prince sat a young couple engrossed in their future and a Sikh in a turban and an old man suffering from Parkinson's Disease and a housewife counting a paucity of money.

"What do you know about Danny?" Martin asked Prince.

"Not a lot. Father's a professor at Oxford so they say. More interested in Mankind than his own son. Nothing unusual in that. Never trust a Holy Joe."

"Are we going to pull him through?"

"Depends on Charlie, doesn't it?"

183

"Was your father a professor?"

"Prince of Darkness," Prince said. "I'm working on a scheme by the way."

"Are you ever doing anything else?"

"Friend of mine. In the nick. Victimised by a screw. A really nastian Sebastian. You know, he's in for life whereas my mate will be out in nine months. So he puts the boot in."

"So what's the scheme?" Martin asked as the bus nosed through Chelsea.

"My mate hints there's some boodle outside for the screw if he can put in a good word for him. Get him remission. Screw delighted to co-operate. So out comes my mate and arranges a meet with the screw on some God-forsaken stretch of countryside. Dartmoor maybe. Hey, how about that, Dartmoor?" Prince rubbed his hands together. "Anyway they meet and my old pal takes him to a house where one room has been done up as a cell. Accomplices there — other prisoners from the nick. Put the screw through what he put my old buddy through. In front of the governor, short rations, a little bit of solitary . . ."

"Does he get remission?" Martin asked.

"Course he does. What do you think my mate is, a sadist?"

"And then?"

"They hand him his suitcase stuffed with boodle and tip off the Old Bill to knock him off at the station."

"Haven't they done enough already?"

"Right, cully." Prince's words accelerated. "Why sink to the screw's level? So, you see, my mate has a girl. Waited for him while he was inside. He tells her what he's going to do. She's disappointed. Pretty poxy stroke to pull, right? So when the fuzz finger the screw at the station the case's empty."

"And your friend and his girl go off with the full suitcase?"

"End. Fade. Lights."

They alighted from the bus near Piccadilly and walked towards Dean Street.

*   *   *

Charlie ran north but before reaching York Road and Wandsworth Bridge he turned west through small streets, Dighton Road, Tonsley Place, Fairfield Street, and then the broader

184

reaches of Putney Bridge Road. He had no idea why he was running in this direction; why he was running at all; but it was like this sometimes — he was searching for a beginnng and the pistons in his legs were taking him there. Sometimes he saw an avenue of trees, beeches or oaks, ahead of him, a green telescope with an ever-diminishing castle at one end. While he ran he observed acutely. Squatting houses with bright doorways beckoning. A thrush pecking in a garden, pausing, head tilted, to urge him on his way. The Thames as he crossed Putney Bridge making its run for the sea. Faces staring, unaware that he could hear their thoughts. A thirsty pub, the Queen's Elm; he had run past here with Danny who had told him that Queen Elizabeth I had sheltered beneath an elm tree there. He liked Danny; he wanted to dress his wounded thoughts. And he liked Martin whose thoughts reached out to him. Together the three of them formed a triangle. The wind blew a swarm of raindrops down Fulham Road; Charlie opened his mouth and felt them cold on his tongue. Still he ran easily. Why not? It was more natural than walking. Past a hospital which he perceived without walls, patients on their backs searching the clouds for cures. Lightning stuttered behind the hospital, thunder grumbled. Brompton Road with stationary taxis pulsing and shops where you bought and paid with plastic money and Harrods where, according to Danny, you could buy an elephant, and the pavement so crowded with thoughts that they collided. He crossed a broad street fending off the braying cars with the flat of his hand and ran into a park where the rain had printed blossom on the footpaths and across the grass to the Serpentine. Faced by the rain-plucked water, Charlie lost impetus. He became aware of an ache in his chest. He looked for Martin and Danny but heard nothing.

*   *   *

Gosling who had returned from Wandsworth Bridge without sighting Charlie was spelling names backwards for the benefit of Danny.

"Frank, Knarf,"

"Thanks," Frank the Bodger said.

"Mad Bull, Dam Llub, a bit Welsh that."

"What about Cuff?" Mad Bull asked.

"Oh dear," Gosling said.

They were sitting in Danny's room trying to distract his attention from the hypodermic and its accomplice, the needle.

Rain assaulted the window, veins of lightning quivered in the sky, thunder rolled.

"Charlie's gone," Danny said. He held one hand with the other to stop it shaking. "Do you think he knew?"

"Knew what?" Jenny asked.

"That I couldn't make it."

"You'll make it. Hood's made it."

"Oh to be published by Sllim and Noob," Gosling said.

"He knew," Danny said. "He hears me. Even when I'm not talking."

"These days I think in crossword clues," Gosling said. "Hood – an American bonnet. Danny – a mixed conjunction joins New York. Jenny – girl in a spin. Prince – half a negative in the cost."

Danny went to the window and pressed his face against it. "He knew," he said.

*　　　*　　　*

Charlie had not booked into the night shelter in Dean Street. Prince and Martin walked to Old Compton Street and entered a café opposite a peep show where, for 50p, you could briefly view a naked girl lying on a bed. An Italian with a flamboyant accent was dispensing espresso from a gleaming coffee machine, a captain on the bridge of his ship.

"Not looking good," Prince said, warming his hands on his cup. "Charlie should have been there by now."

Lightning parted the darkening sky and thunder cracked. Raindrops bounced high on the pavement outside. Inside various orphans of the storm steamed behind their cups of coffee.

Martin said: "Maybe he did go to Brixton. Maybe Gos picked him up on Wandsworth Bridge."

Prince shook his head, decisively scattering raindrops from his dank hair. "Just precautions. He's done this before. Always ends up at his last home."

A thin girl with chipped teeth and streaked hair wearing a simulated fur coat ran across the street from the peep show.

"How isa the business?" the owner inquired.

"Bleeding awful. The punters' glasses keep steaming up."

Martin said: "Shall we go back and see if he's turned up?"

"We'll give it another half-hour," Prince said, squeezing water from his flying-jacket.

*   *   *

He was barely running now. Crouching, peering through bead-curtains of rain. Big stores — Selfridges, John Lewis, Peter Robinson, Bourne and Hollingsworth. He had visited a couple of them with Martin and Danny; they smelled of scent, he remembered. The street was a canal with reflections pulled across its waters; taxis and cars made wings of spray in it. The water had drowned thoughts. Rusted the pistons in his legs — he smiled into the rain. But he was getting closer to the castle at the end of the avenue of trees; except that now it was a terrace house with corrugated iron across the downstairs windows and there were other children there, a boy and a girl, and a man was shouting and a woman was saying, "Hush, you'll wake the kids," as if they weren't awake already and then there was the sound of a blow and a stifled sob and they shut their eyes tight even though they were awake and then the police were hammering at the door and their cocoon was opened and cold air streamed into it ... Right past bookshops crammed with thoughts, tracksuit cold against his chest, heart beating hard against it, diving down a small and frowning street, the tree-lined avenue narrowing with it, obscuring the dwelling at the end of the telescope. And now he was in a courtyard.

"Hallo, cully," Prince said. "What kept you?"

*   *   *

The knock on the front door came as Jenny went downstairs to prepare supper. Cuff? Martin and Prince? Charlie? Kester?

"Who is it?"

A girl's voice: "Can I come in a minute?"

"Are you alone?" in case it was a trick to gain entry.

Gosling called down from Danny's bedroom: "She's alone."

Jenny opened the door. The girl who was wearing a shiny yellow sou'wester was tall with rain-wet reddish hair curling

187

from the hood.

She said: "I'm sorry to bother you but could I speak to Martin Renshaw?"

The accent was Liverpudlian.

Jenny said: "I know who you are. A J and two N's and an E but there the similarity ends."

CHAPTER 20

———◆———

On Sundays the City of London with its forty-eight miles of streets belongs to cats and tourists assembling at the haunches of St. Paul's.

The avenues and alleys are as tranquil as the graves of Nelson and Wellington inside the cathedral; the rustle of money is stilled in the Bank of England and the 350 foreign banks nudging each other with fiscal intimacy; the eyes of computers in the Stock Exchange and Lloyds and the gold and metal and fur markets are blind.

On a sunlit Sunday such as the one when Martin escorted Joanne round the financial square mile, when the air had been rinsed by rain, the tall cubes built on sites excavated by Hitler's bombs and the baronial mansions that were spared, and the needle-point spires and the bronze statue of Justice on the dome of the Old Bailey joined in communion. And the buttons on the uniforms of the policemen – gold unlike the silver sported by their Metropolitan neighbours – were as bright as altar crosses.

Martin took Joanne there because of the peace but was immediately guilty because, guide book in hand, he had recently been Jenny's courier. He waited for recriminations as they walked along Cheapside – the principal market of medieval London, he would have told Jenny, hence its appendages, Bread Street and Milk Street and Poultry . . . but he kept his counsel.

"I like your friends," Joanne said. She was wearing a green, spring coat and there were gleams of copper in her hair. "Not what I expected. You know, being a squat." He savoured her accent, final g's discarded, u's treated in cavalier style, and he felt easy with her and worried that it was so.

"A squat is just a place to stay. It doesn't make you a criminal."

"Doesn't make you a young hopeful either."

"Getting-on isn't everything."

"It's better than sitting in a park with a bottle of cider."

Martin said: "Who knows, they may be as happy as politicians."

"What makes you think they're happy?"

"They must be," Martin said, "they spend so much time making everyone else unhappy."

"All right," Joanne said, "sitting in a park with a bottle is fine. If that's what you want. But I don't think that is what you want."

"And what do I want?"

"A future," Joanne said. "It gets cold and wet in parks."

"I don't need buckets of money. I don't want to be an Uncle Harry."

"Or Jack?"

"He's too bold," Martin said.

"Or Uncle . . . What's his name?"

"Walter. Wally. He gives good works a bad name."

"There's nothing wrong with earning good money. Creating a decent life for yourself."

"I reckon seventy-five per cent of the population are doing jobs they don't like. What sort of future is that?"

"They might not like their jobs but there are com-pensations."

"Home life?"

"Anything wrong with that?"

"Nothing. As long as it's near Goodison Park."

"Or Anfield." Her hand reached for his arm, hesitated, clenched the air. "But what about the other twenty-five per cent? Become one of them."

"Architect?"

"Why not? Earn enough splosh" – he heard a ship lonely on the Mersey – "to keep you and go to night school at the Poly in Byrom Street."

"But that's Liverpool."

"I know where Byrom Street is," she said.

They reached the junction where the Bank with its sand-coloured windowless walls and the Royal Exchange presided. A middle-aged American couple climbed out of a taxi and stared at the bronze statue of the Duke of Wellington made from captured French guns. They held hands in the sunlight.

Martin and Joanne walked down Princes Street and turned into Gresham Street. Pigeons on the look-out for cats pecked warily among yesterday's puddles.

Joanne, smiling at a policeman on patrol above vaults stuffed with wealth, said: "You seem to know more about London than Liverpool."

"Why not? I came here to find work."

"And have you?"

"As a matter of fact," Martin said, tongue quick with the deceit of omission, "I have been offered a good job."

She glanced at him suspiciously. "What kind of a job?"

Martin, head down, quickened his pace. Every day had its own trappings ... cold meat on Mondays ... Friday, POETS Day – Piss Off Early Tomorrow's Saturday ... the football roar of Saturday ... Sunday wasn't meant for confessions that you had been offered a job in a betting shop.

"I'll tell you if I take it."

"Does it have prospects?"

"Glittering," Martin said.

"Know what I think?"

"Liverpool?"

"It's your home," Joanne said.

"Ta, wack. So much for the spirit of adventure that made Britain what it is today."

"Give your chin a rest," Joanne said.

"Let's go to church," Martin said, smiling.

"Which church?"

By which, she meant Catholic or C of E. Religion, class, north or south, country, county ... The British erect distinctions like garden fences, he thought.

He said: "The next church, whatever."

"I've only been in the Anglican Cathedral in Liverpool once," she said. "Do you know why?"

"Search me," spotting a small church.

"To see the monument to William Huskisson who was killed by Stephenson's Rocket."

"This will do," Martin said, pointing at the church. "After

all, whatever the faith there's only one God, isn't there?"

They entered St. Anne and St. Agnes. It was Lutheran.

*   *   *

Lying in bed across the corridor from Jenny, Martin's thoughts returned to Joanne who was sleeping downstairs. To a day's outing to Knowsley Safari Park – kissing in the back of a friend's car observed incuriously by a couple of lions – and a walk through Eastham Woods, chasing autumn leaves and falling in drifts of them. Guilt accompanied him into his dreams as he tried to re-direct himself to Hampstead and Jenny's bedroom where childhood still lingered. The dreams broke into islands containing one girl or the other. And as he made stepping stones of the islands his lips began to tremble as they had when he was younger, aborting any defiance he had wanted to express.

In the middle of the night there was an oasis of wakefulness. He listened to the busy hush of nocturnal London, to the wail of a motor-horn dying in the darkness, and peered determinedly into the future. In Liverpool it was a timetable: in London a blank canvas to be filled by a surrealist's brush.

By dawn his subconscious had taken a carnal turn. And then Jenny was beside him, naked and warm and smelling of sleep.

*   *   *

Gosling, polishing his spectacles, said: "Time's running out."

Prince, eating toast and peanut butter, asked: "How long?"

"A week, ten days. I've tried every delaying tactic in the book."

Joanne, sipping a mug of tea, half-listened to the breakfast conversation in the kitchen. She was sitting opposite Jenny and Martin. They were lovers, she knew that; what she wasn't sure about were her own feelings. Sorrow certainly, but sorrow tempered by a nurse's common sense – Martin was too young to settle. She wished sometimes that she wasn't so bloody realistic.

She said: "What will you all do when you have to leave?"

"Ask Cuff," Prince said.

"I've been scouting," Cuff said. He tossed a piece of bacon-

192

rind to Hoover who snapped his jaws decisively and missed it.
"Nothing so far," he apologised. "But one or two possibilities.
A nice little terrace property in Lewisham. Boarded up like the
Scrubs. Two minutes to the station. Three beds, one bath,
secluded garden."

"Too small," Prince said.

"How about Hampstead?" Joanne asked. She smiled help-
fully at Jenny.

"And another," Cuff said, "in Acton. Big but iffy. Could be
knocked down any day."

Gosling said: "Funny how few people know anything about
the names of their parishes. I made a study of it once. Acton —
Actun, old English for camp in the oak trees. Camberwell —
Cam meaning crooked, a well for the crippled."

"Leave it out, Gos," Prince said. "Keep trying," to Cuff.
"Summer's coming. What we want is a nice bit of garden for
Danny."

Jack Daniels came into the kitchen, poured himself a cup of
tea, drank it and left without speaking.

"He's creepy," Jenny said.

"Can't throw him out," Prince said. "We've got a democracy
here."

"Democracy shit," the anarchist said, finger-combing his
beard. "You all conform but you don't realise it."

"Who's talking about anarchy?"

"I am. There's only one truth and that's absolute freedom.
Who needs government? What we need to do is work voluntarily together."

"Isn't that what we're doing?" Martin asked.

"It's what you think you're doing," the anarchist told him.
"In fact you're imprisoned. Free? Hang around a street corner
and you can be done for loitering with intent. You didn't make
that law. Why should you obey it? You were born an
individual, you were born free."

"Feel free to leave," Prince said. "See you at Hyde Park
Corner."

Charlie, tracksuited, already jogging, ran through the kitchen
followed by Danny who had put away his syringe and needle.

Mad Bull came down and spread cottage cheese on bread as
dark as treacle.

Joanne said to Martin: "Can you see me to the station?"

"Of course." He stood up saying to Jenny: "Excuse me."

"When will you be back?" Jenny asked.

"Soon," he said.

The bus was crowded. Joanne surveyed the passengers. What would the anarchist have said about such headlong conformity? Personally she understood it perfectly: she saw each passenger in a capsule of ambition. Surely it is just as ambitious to model a life with two, maybe three, children in a suburban nest as it is to aspire to a penthouse? After all, what is ambition? Joanne asked herself. Who is to determine who has the greater sense of fulfilment: the tycoon in his Rolls or the man sitting in front of her having an extra-marital lech at the pert breasts on Page 3?

Joanne was fully aware why she thought this way. She remembered the security before her father had gone bankrupt. Tea on Sundays with sandwiches filled with tinned salmon or beetroot, homework in her room where Paul, John, George and Ringo still reigned and an hour's television, no more, unless it was Liverpool FC on the box, and holidays in the Lake District – squeezed into a carriage on the miniature steam railway at Ravenglass – and Blackpool illuminations and one Christmas, sky heavy with snow that never fell, when they had skated in Sefton Park and her mother waiting for her outside school dressed in autumn-coloured clothes, as reliable as the seasons. Togetherness logged in a family album.

Sitting on top of a red London bus she hoped all her fellow-passengers would return to their albums that evening. Sentimentality curbed by common-sense, disciplined by Catholicism; no wonder she had become a nurse. She was eager now to get back to the hospital, to its methodical remedies, its anaesthetised odours and its rigid compassion disguised by a no-nonsense attitude to mortality.

"Nearly there," Martin said.

She looked out of the window. The streets teemed with last-minute crowds and the sky over the rooftops of commerce was tiled with slates of grey cloud.

"What will you do when you're evicted?" she asked.

"Find another squat."

"Another person's property? Isn't that stealing?"

"Trespassing," he said. "Why not if no one else is living there?"

194

"It's a substitute life," she said, wishing that just this once she could keep her mouth shut.

"Helping each other? I don't think so."

"Helping each other to do what?"

"Live," Martin said.

In the great concourse of Euston Station they faced each other. Arrivals and departures milled around them.

"So what shall I tell your mam and da?"

"Tell them I'm well. Making out."

"Proper Dick Whittington," she said.

"Give them my love."

"Liverpool's not that far away you know."

"I know where Liverpool is," he said. "I know where Byrom Street is."

She touched his face with the tips of her fingers. It was thinner than she had remembered.

"Where are you going now?"

He smiled. "To work," he said.

He kissed her, turned and was gone.

CHAPTER 21

——— ◆◆◆ ———

Suddenly Britain's betting shops were becoming up-market —
satellite TV beaming races, computers checking tortuous bets,
drinking-vending machines, 3-D window displays, lawn-style
carpeting . . .

Jack Renshaw's betting shop near Mitcham had resisted such
innovations. The window was covered with a painting of a
moulting horse and a jockey whose colours had been confused
by woodworm; the runners and odds were still chalked on
blackboards; punters scrawled their bets on scraps of paper
beneath copies of the *Sporting Life* pinned to the wall; on wet
afternoons old men dozed in receptive corners.

Nor was the gambling spectacular. A 5p Each Way Yankee
was one of the most popular bets — one accumulator, six
doubles and four trebles costing £1.21 including tax.

But Martin, who suspected that Jack Renshaw's gambling
operations were a front for more nefarious activities, did not
despair. The mornings when he journeyed to work by bus were
soft and expectant; the days sharp and intimidating as he
chalked the ever-changing prices and, on the instructions of the
manager, kept watch for crooked punters.

The manager was named Doberman, son of a German POW
who had stayed in Britain after the war, and was therefore
known as Pincher. He was a vigilant man with sharp yellow
teeth and a pepper-and-salt moustache gnawed ragged in the
centre; he used out-of-date slang and equated many of life's
vagaries with betting prices.

As soon as Martin had mastered odds broadcast over a radio
receiver Pincher initiated him into the schemes perpetrated by

196

punters not prepared to trust their chances to fate. "Thieving bastards," he said, surveying his clientele from his office. "Five to four there isn't an honest John among the lot of them."

Pincher was currently on the look-out for slow counters who laid big bets at the last moment and counted out the money slowly while listening to the race, dogs usually, but scooped up the money and departed if their choice wasn't well placed.

"You look pretty useful," he said, studying Martin.

"Useful?"

"With your mitts."

Martin who had never thought about it said: "I doubt it."

"A Scouser not useful with his mitts? John Conteh, Tarleton, Ernie Roderick, Alan Rudkin . . . I'd give odds against that."

"Does it matter?"

"It matters if you're going to catch villains."

"I'm a bouncer too?"

"You're security," Pincher said. "Haven't got any form, have you?"

"Would I tell you?"

"I can soon check it out," Pincher said.

"No convictions," Martin said.

"You've got to suss out the staff as well. Cashiers working with punters or under-ringing bets and pocketing the difference." He gazed moodily at two employees sitting at the desk behind the grille. "And check the bog before we close: villains hide there to get at the loot."

Martin got to know the regulars. Kenny, a handsome bricklayer with streaked hair who specialised in exotic bets — Round Robins, Union Jacks, Goliaths — who claimed to have won £12,000 on a TV 6 bet and been robbed of £2,000 because the bet wasn't tax-paid and his stake was short by 12p; Eric, a small, rain-coated man with a stutter who crossed the road from his boarding house to spend all day in the shop; a septuagenarian named Winifred, allegedly related distantly to Royalty, who nipped brandy from a silver, monogrammed hip-flask while she made her selections; McDonald, a voluble Scot, who claimed to have been banned from Monte Carlo and had sailed twenty-three times round the world as a steward on the liners before casting his anchor in Tooting because Sir Harry Lauder had once lived there.

Martin arrived at the shop early. Swept up cigarette ends and

197

discarded betting slips – his predecessor had found a winning slip, persuaded his girlfriend to cash it and been fined £150 for fraud – pinned up the *Sporting Life* and chalked up the runners for the first races. After a snatched pub lunch and a pint of bitter he took up his position, standing on a chair, by the blackboards.

He was perched there when he spotted his first slow counter, a young man with permed curls counting out a £50 bet in £5 and £1 notes while the race was being broadcast. His choice falling back and suddenly the money was back in his hand and he was making for the door and Martin, without hesitation, was after him although, God knows, there was no reason why he should risk his life – it wasn't unknown for betting-shop shysters to carry knives – for the sake of Uncle Jack and Pincher Doberman.

The young man, curls bobbing, ran swiftly between startled pedestrians in the street of small shops. But Martin hadn't trained with Charlie for nothing. He was gaining and he was strangely exhilarated. The curls veered left into the mouth of a tube station. Martin followed. What did you do? Shout, "Stop thief"? People would turn the other way, and who could blame them?

The young man vaulted the ticket barrier and ran for the escalator. He was a quarter-way down when Martin reached the brink. Down, overtaking the moving steps. Faces staring from the ascending staircase. Advertisements – London theatres and bras. And I'm gaining. Sweet Jesus, anyone would think he had assaulted my mam.

The young man turned. Grinned. Waved! And launched himself from the foot of the escalator.

Martin followed towards the northbound platform past a youth playing a guitar. There were a dozen or so passengers on the platform, no permed curls. In the distance the rumble of an approaching train. The passengers moved towards the edge of the platform. And there he was, using a big man wearing green overalls as a shield. And whoosh the train was there and the doors were opening and the curls were bobbing towards them and Martin who had never played rugby in his life was in mid-air in a flying tackle and the curls were on the ground and the £5 and £1 notes were fluttering down the platform, falling onto the line, and a knife was spinning in the air like a flying fish and the voice beneath the curls was saying: "Shit, man, what is it to you?"

Martin received a £5 bonus for the capture.

Handing it to him, Pincher, biting at his moustache with his bottom teeth, said: "This wasn't some kind of set-up, was it?"

"What the hell is that supposed to mean?"

"You know, trying to establish yourself. Gain trust for the big heist."

"Big heist? Are Brink's-Mat taking over the betting shop?"

"Sorry, Martin, there are some right villains around."

In the evenings Martin trained with Charlie and sometimes Danny, before, tired and ravenous, sitting down to a meal with the other residents of Buck House swelled recently by two newcomers, a Pakistani teenager and a Mancunian named Ousby who had gained Prince's respect by living for five days in a department store.

Every evening Ousby, crouching and bird-bright, had secreted himself inside the store before closing and emerged, when the staff had gone home, to eat a cold supper washed down with a bottle of Chablis in the food and wine department, watched television in electrical appliances, bathed in a pink-tiled bathroom available on easy terms and slept in one of several model bedrooms. His spring-break had come to an end when he had awoken in a honeymoon double bed to find an absorbed crowd looking at him from the pavement outside.

The Pakistani had fled from a housing estate in North London, where he had lived with his parents, because of racist abuse. He had put up with it for two years until he had been stoned on his way back from a disco. Two of his front teeth were missing and when he spoke his words whistled faintly.

Although it wasn't the life Martin had envisaged it had its compensations. Too good to last, he feared, and it was.

* * *

Jenny, too, was content, frequently reminding herself of her good fortune. She was happy in the squat even though the rust stains in the bath were ineradicable and rain dripped through her bedroom ceiling and spring, quivering outside, never made it through the boarded windows of the living-room; she enjoyed the company of the occupants despite the fact that Jack

Daniels scared her and Cuff smelled of death; she found fulfilment chalking pictures on the pavement and only rarely experienced a desire to grab philistine legs as they crossed a Degas or a Rubens.

If she ever questioned her role, as all young people must do, recalling, perhaps, her restless lack of direction in the Elysian fields of Hampstead, she invoked Charlie and Danny – they, surely, personified a worthy cause – and relived her escape, hugging the camaraderie of her new life to her like a warm garment so that, when she closed her eyes in the early hours of the morning, when shark-fins of doubt cruise through the darkness, she saw the squat as a commune in a revolution and heard the cries of peasants repelling the cavalry.

More constructively she set about tracing William Grey, executor of the estate of her step-father's father.

The firm of solicitors in which Grey had been a partner had ceased to exist and there was a daunting number of William Greys in the London telephone directory. Here Prince played his part. Cuff had acquired a cordless telephone from a second-hand shop in Clapham and there was a telephone in the house next-door which was temporarily unoccupied. Prince instructed Cuff to gain entry and attach the cradle for the portable receiver to the connection for the conventional phone. This enabled the residents of Buck House to make calls from their home without the inconvenience of paying a bill and all that had to be done was to return the cordless instrument to its bed every night to be recharged.

William Greys, it seemed, had diversified interests. Jenny called an accountant, a builder, a violinist, a publican, a meteorologist . . . Occasionally hope flickered.

William Grey somewhere in South London: "Speaking. Who's that?"

A refined, parchment voice.

"Are you a solicitor, Mr. Grey?"

"Could you identify yourself, please."

Legal wariness?

"Smith," she said. "Maggie Smith," remembering the actress.

"Why do you think I'm a solicitor?"

"Aren't you, Mr. Grey?"

"I'm afraid you've got the wrong Grey; it's not an uncommon name, you know."

"What is your profession, Mr. Grey?"

"That's entirely my business, Miss Smith."

"I didn't mean to be . . ."

"Goodbye, Miss Smith."

Click. Such finality from such an innocuous sound. A severance of life. But why had he been so evasive? She wrote his address on her list of possibilities to be investigated in the future.

Then she spread her net to the Outer London directories. Hosts of William Greys. Not that there was any evidence to suggest that he lived anywhere near London. He was probably retired, dead even.

She consulted Eleanor Lubin at her home in Holland Park. It was early evening. Eleanor poured herself a Chivas Regal. She was still glossily elegant but she looked tired, drained. She gave Jenny a beer.

She told her that she had been defending a white youth – "You can get into trouble these days if you differentiate between pigmentation" – accused of carrying an offensive weapon, a Stanley knife, during an affray between young whites and blacks on Clapham Common. The youth, who called witnesses to testify that he was of a peaceable disposition and never carried a weapon, claimed that the police had planted the knife on him. "And I believed him. Until he called a witness 'a black bastard'. From then on the defence collapsed until he finally admitted carrying the knife and a length of bicycle chain. Do you know what a bicycle chain can do? Rip half your face away, that's what."

She slumped into a chair and sipped her whisky.

"What made you become a lawyer?" Jenny asked.

"All the old clichés. Justice for the underdog, the rights of the individual . . . Sometimes it all seems worth it. But this case won't have done me any good. *Perversely anti-police* . . . I can hear the opposition now. But it's not true: it's merely that someone has to sort out those policemen who are economical with the truth. In a way I'm glad when I'm proved wrong."

"Are you often?"

"There are more good coppers than bent ones. More good citizens than bad. Never forget that, Jenny Renshaw. And they're the ones who have to be protected." She crossed her shapely legs. "Have you ever thought of taking up law?"

201

Vaguely. But her step-father's views on lawyers had not been encouraging.

Eleanor said: "All lawyers are rebels in their way. Probing for the weaknesses in the legislature. If you ever want any guidance . . ."

Jenny sat opposite her. "I'm happy enough at the moment."

"The university of life?"

"There are worse universities," Jenny said, sipping beer. "Where did you go?"

"Oxford," Eleanor said. "But it's tempting to dream along with the spires."

"Have you ever regretted becoming a lawyer?"

Eleanor said: "Life is regrets; they're not always unpleasant." She tinkled the ice in her whisky. "Why do you want to find this man Grey?"

Jenny told her about Martin and his suspicions.

"I'll see what I can do," Eleanor said. She glanced at her watch. "Let's watch the News at Seven."

The pound, the dollar, AIDS and violence in south-east London.

Turning down the volume, Eleanor said: "If we're not careful we'll have a war on our hands."

"You're exaggerating," Jenny said. "Aren't you?"

"They should have seen it coming years ago."

"They?"

"The people who don't care," Eleanor said.

The following day she telephoned Jenny on the number of the neighbour next to the squat, thereby compounding a felony. Jenny answered on the cordless receiver.

Eleanor told her that she had checked William Grey on the Law List. "No joy but . . ." A barrister's theatrical pause.

"But what?" Jenny asked.

"I made other inquiries. A William Grey was disbarred from practising twenty-five years ago."

"For what?" Jenny asked.

Eleanor didn't know. "Something pretty serious though. I've got an old address for him," she said. "It's a long time ago but he might still live there."

The address was a stern Edwardian house in Crouch End in North London not far from the house where her step-father's father had once lived. It was as grey as the squat, brickwork

202

indelibly stained by the fogs of long ago. Starved plants grew hopelessly behind a privet hedge and black garbage bags were piled like great nuggets of coal in their midst.

There were four bells in the porch above cracked stone steps. Jenny rang three of them. Nothing. An Indian woman with greying hair wearing a red and orange sari answered the door when she rang the fourth. Jenny smelled curry.

The woman gave her the address of the landlord a mile away in Hornsey. Jenny walked. A Victorian house this time, also grey but well-groomed with mulched rose-bushes in the front garden and a burglar alarm stuck to the wall like a limpet mine. Three children, two cars and one dog, a Labrador, Jenny speculated.

The dog was a poodle. Its owners, Mr. and Mrs. Grafton, both in their sixties, were benignly colonial, still searching myopically for the lost Raj. Mr. Grafton reminded Jenny of the late Harold Macmillan.

They gave her tea and digestive biscuits in an undisturbed sitting-room with a gong in the fireplace, a cork sculpture in a glass case on the mantelpiece and an upright piano abandoned in one corner. The chairs on which the three of them sat were fragile and uncomfortable.

"So," Mr. Grafton said, feeding a biscuit to the poodle which was begging on a gazelle skin in front of the hearth, "you want to know about old Grey, do you?"

"Why did you say wanted to know?" Mrs. Grafton, distant eyes set in Pekinese features, asked a lot of questions but refrained from listening to the answers.

"I'm compiling a family history," Jenny told her. "A thesis," she said, "at college."

"We bought the house from him twenty years ago as an investment," Mr. Grafton said after a pause. He contrived not to answer questions at all, the result presumably of living with a woman who didn't listen to them. "For our old age." He favoured Jenny with a smile that just lacked Macmillan's aristocratic foxiness.

"Where did you say you were from?" Mrs. Grafton asked.

"Hampstead," Jenny told her.

"The old house has got a bit shabby lately," Mr. Grafton said. "People don't respect property any more. Heaven knows how many relatives they pack into the room when our backs are turned." He patted the poodle's coiffured head. "We were in Mauritius for many years. That's where the dodo was supposed to have lived. You know, dead as a dodo . . ."

"Do you know where Mr. Grey went after he sold you the house?"

"Think there was a bit of a stink about him. Don't know too much about it because we were only here on leave."

"Did he stay in London?"

"Somewhere to the south as I recall it."

"Do you have any correspondence?"

"Is it very important?" Mrs. Grafton asked.

"I think we do," Mr. Grafton said. "If we do it's in the attic."

Was he excessively wary? Jenny asked herself. Or am I over-reacting?

"What was he like?" Jenny said. "This Mr. Grey."

"Can barely remember him. A legal beadle. Got himself into a bit of a scrape."

"What sort of a scrape would that be, Mr. Grafton?"

"Some sort of legal hanky-panky. Never knew the details; didn't want to." He pursed mauvish lips. "Knew he was a bit short of the ready though: that's why he had to sell the house."

"It's full of coloureds now," Mrs. Grafton said.

"In Mauritius it was all Indians and Creoles," Mr. Grafton remarked. "Rain in the centre of the island, sunshine on the coast. Lots of rainbows but we never found a crock of gold."

"Why do they all want to come to London," Mrs. Grafton demanded.

"To find desirable residences like the one you let," Jenny said. And to Mr. Grafton: "You must have some idea where he went."

"South," Mr. Grafton repeated.

"South London?"

"Oh yes, I do think it was South London."

"Nothing more specific?"

Mr. Grafton concentrated, faded eyes narrowed; but he seemed to have returned to where the rainbows ended. He smiled apologetically.

"Who were the agents?"

"Who were the agents, dear?" Mr. Grafton asked his wife.

"Does it really matter?"

"It matters to me," Jenny said.

"There were so many," Mr. Grafton said.

"You must have acted through one."

"I suppose we must have. It's such a long time ago ... You weren't even born."

"Local?"

"I suppose so."

"Are you going to become a lawyer?" Mrs. Grafton asked. "I should think you'd be very good at it. Questioning witnesses, that sort of thing."

That was the second time in two days that someone had suggested she should take up law. She stood up abruptly, disturbing the poodle.

The Graftons saw her to the door. As she stepped into the hesitant sunlight Mrs. Grafton said: "Why did you say you wanted all this information?"

"I'm writing an article on unscrupulous landlords," Jenny said.

After lunch she checked out three estate agents operating in the area. The fourth, at least, kept records that went back twenty-five years *"mas o menos"* according to the junior partner who was studying Spanish at night school.

He was crisply-spoken, flushed and highly-sexed. On the way down to the vault where the records were stored he brushed his hand against her breast and, once below ground, propositioned her with a blunt lack of finesse that presumably drew the occasional dividend.

"Where did you say he moved to?" treating her rejection as a ploy not to be taken seriously.

"That's what I want to know."

"Right." He put his arm round her shoulders and led her to a metal cabinet beneath a naked bulb in a corner of the vault. "Grey, Grey, Grey ..." He riffled the indexed documents. "Why did you say you wanted to know?"

"I didn't. But I'm writing a family history."

"Quite." He brushed a lock of greying hair from his boyish forehead. "Nothing too legal, I hope?"

"Just family," Jenny said.

"Good, good."

His repetitions would have intrigued Gosling. *Good, good* but never *bad, bad*.

"Grey ... Sold his desirable property" – the junior partner

winked at Jenny — "to a Mr. Arthur Clement Grafton. Must have been a bit skint, let it go for a song."

"A quick sale," Jenny said. "Good business for you."

"I hope you don't think I was in business twenty years ago. I would have been . . . let's see . . . ten years old."

"Is there a forwarding address for him?" Jenny asked.

"Means a lot to you, doesn't it."

"Not all that much," she said.

"More to this than meets the eye, I suspect."

"You have a suspicious mind."

"Have to in this business. They say insurance teaches you more about human deceit than any other profession but real estate must run it a close second. How about dinner tonight?"

"I have a tremendous appetite," Jenny said. "He must have left some sort of address."

"I know a nice little restaurant in Finchley. Bit pretentious perhaps but adequate."

"Not tonight," she said. "I've got a date." In a squat. "Perhaps another night . . ."

"Wednesday?"

"That sounds good," she said.

"A date then."

"So where did our Mr. Grey move to?"

"Ah, Grey, Grey . . ." He consulted the file again. "South London," as though it were the other side of the Amazon.

"A little more exact?"

He looked at her shrewdly, whisking aside the insistent grey forelock with one finger. "Perhaps I should give it to you after dinner on Wednesday."

She almost admired him: lecherous intent was never so unambiguous.

"I need it now," she said.

"You're very cruel," he said hopefully.

"The address?"

"Dulwich," he said.

"Very fashionable. Don't statesmen — or is it stateswomen — buy houses there?"

"It depends," he said. "North, East, Village . . ." He gave her an address off East Dulwich Grove. "But that was a long time ago."

"Did he leave?"

"Not as far as I know. But he didn't keep in touch. Shall we go upstairs?"

"You first," she said.

"Right, right." His fingers strayed down her back towards her buttocks.

Upstairs, watched by two girls talking into telephones perched on shoulder-rests, he said: "So, here's to Wednesday."

"Wednesday?"

"Our date."

"Did we say Wednesday?"

"You know we did."

"My mistake," she said. "Night school."

"But surely . . ."

"Sorry," she said.

The girls smiled into their telephones while he wiped at the lock of hair. She almost felt sorry for him.

The following morning she went by bus to the address in Dulwich. A luminous morning, powdered rain falling from pale clouds.

She walked past a school, a church and a hospital. Youth, faith and death – or life, according to your mood. Youth handed to you in a file marked DON'T QUESTION. And, if you don't question, adulthood in another file marked ORDAINED. Panic stirred within her. What did she want? Certainly not the anarchist's discords; she doubted if even he believed them. Purpose, meaning, direction . . . Sometimes it seemed to her that everything we are taught is a substitute for an omnipotent and secret truth. The stars at night frightened her: they mocked: they knew. She wished she was in her bedroom in Hampstead and she wished she could draw the curtains and extinguish their knowledge.

She turned into a side-street. The address the estate agent had given her was a derelict plot of land. William Grey, you are elusive as truth.

*   *   *

Eleanor Lubin's brother was tall with his sister's glossy hair, a hawkish nose and a thoughtful brow which, when he was thinking deeply, he spanned between thumb and forefinger. He smiled infrequently but when he did it was a gift for you; he was dressed casually – white open-neck shirt beneath wind-cheater – and while Jenny and Eleanor conversed in the pizzeria in Oxford Street he played chess on a miniature computer.

When Eleanor went outside to make a phone call he reluctantly pushed aside the small board.

"Do you play?"

Manipulating elastic strands of cheese, she shook her head and said: "But please don't let me stop you."

"I was losing anyway." He glanced at the board as though he might still stand a chance.

"Are you a lawyer too?"

"Not quite. Another year and I will be."

"If you pass your exams."

"I'll pass them," he said without conceit.

"You're very sure of yourself."

He considered this; she couldn't imagine him committing a spontaneous act. He said: "Only in certain things."

"And the uncertainty?"

"Belief," he said.

"In yourself?"

"If you like. A contradiction? Not really." He cross-examined himself. "Assurance is a very different animal to belief. What do you believe in?"

"The stars," she said.

"*The fault, dear Brutus, is not in our stars, but in ourselves, that we are underlings.*"

"Why should we believe everything we are taught?"

"That's why I decided to take up law," he said. "Because it's the evolution of logic. A panacea for belief if you like."

"I thought the law was an ass."

"Not the law," he said. "Just some of the lawyers."

He moved a pawn abruptly. A red light gleamed beside CHECK. "Discovered," he told her.

"I don't understand."

"Chess is also an exercise in perfect logic. Two brains pitted equally against each other. Only one small element of luck – who has the white pieces."

"And who has the best brain."

"There are many sorts of brains," he said. "Could Dickens play chess?" Black, after pulsing its light, moved. "Jesus," Andrew Lubin exclaimed.

208

"You're white?"

"Correct."

"With the element of luck?"

"Against an electronic brain," he said.

"At what level?"

"I thought you didn't know anything about the game."

"You haven't answered the question," she said.

"Second level. You know what I think about the stars?"
She didn't.

"One of those stars up there is the earth. We're looking at ourselves. There's no beginning, no end. They're just words we've invented. I was looking at the sky this morning. Pools of blue and castles of white. That was just as mysterious once. Until we flew aeroplanes and looked down and saw pastures of mist. What we don't need is explanations."

"Beliefs?"

"We sure as hell need those," he said, moving a bishop and swearing as black swiftly answered. "I resign," he said.

She saw Eleanor coming back into the pizzeria. "Tell me one thing . . ."

"I lost."

"Do you play soccer or rugby?"

"M'lud, I object. My learned friend is trying to lead the witness."

"Which?"

"Soccer," he said.

CHAPTER 22

---◆---

While he trained for his come-back Mad Bull remembered.

Defending a boy at school named Tupper who was bullied –
ink over his genitals, text books mutilated – and his wet brown
eyes asking: "Why?" And then the pack is turning on me, the
protector, and there above me as the ink flows are Tupper's
eyes brown and bright with excitement.

And so he had journeyed from the flint-grey Cornish village
to Penzance to meet a man named Len who humped barrels for
a brewery, squat and smiling he was with a tight cap of greying
hair, who had taught him Cornish wrestling and then he was
back at school challenging the leader of the pack and wrestling
him until you could hear his muscles sighing, until he was
leader no more; and walking past Tupper and wishing it hadn't
been like that.

And then his father who had been a Welsh miner – that's
where I get the shoulders from – and was always talking about
a god named Nye Bevan was dead in an accident in a Cornish
tin mine which they had been trying to resurrect. And his
mother soon following him into their own green valley. Which
was when he joined the Navy to escape voices in empty rooms.

And wrestling on heaving ships and gymnasiums all over the
world that always smelled of liniment and disinfectant and old
sweat. A Japanese crouching, as resilient as a stone Buddha, an
Icelandic fisherman with muscles like leaping fish – and God the
girls there on that pumice-stone of an island – and a German
submariner with a blonde beard and a half-Nelson that seared
like flame.

And always the matelots cheering and the wets afterwards

210

and, in Germany, a girl named Elsbeth. Walking her home, the evening sky winter yellow behind the hills, grains of snow in the air. And the log fire spitting resin.

"You have a beautiful body," she said lying in front of the flames.

Embarrassed, I cover myself with the blanket we have brought from the bedroom.

Was it then that the great entertainer had been born?

Sitting on the edge of a sagging bed in a hotel in Cardiff. A civilian, married, jobless but with prospects.

A knock on the door. Enter a medium-sized man with pepper-and-salt hair and a sea dog's blazer and boozer's eyes and a mid-Atlantic accent.

We're following your career, he says. Great stuff. That Korean, wow! Champion of this, champion of that, you're a natural. Big bucks can be yours, my son.

Who's we?

"I'll tell you." And he does. An up-and-coming company to challenge the monopoly in wrestling in Britain. Good-looking boy like you . . . Girls knocking at your dressing room like flies round a honey-pot.

Good-looking? I suppose I was. A dark, singing Taffy on a Saturday-night hooley. But you're forty-seven now and youth is long ago and there is no singing.

The big bucks were £50 a fight or £100 a week which was good money, his wife agreed. Especially for doing what you do best and what you enjoy and how many workers can say that? But there were doubts even then in her voice; but he kissed them and laughed them away and soon he was on television on Saturday afternoons and he was winning.

Except that they weren't fights at all.

"Look at it this way," said his promoter twisting the buttons on his nautical blazer as though he were tuning a radio. "You're an entertainer," ordering two beers and a whisky for himself in the Angel in Cardiff. "Entertainers don't get hurt: fighters do. You dig?"

Nothing wrong with entertaining, he supposed. But where was the scent of victory? Still, nothing wrong, Taff, with an exhibition of athletic skill, is there?

"Pride?" asks his wife, comfortably pretty with a swell of life in her belly, as they lie in their double-bed in the new semi in

211

Eltham which £100 a week can buy with money to spare. "Doesn't pride come into it?"

"There's a good job going at a factory in Lewisham," he says. "Security. Forty pounds a week. Night work."

She pushes her belly into the small of his back. "I just want it to be good for you," she says. "And the baby," she says.

"Singers are entertainers," he says. "And skaters and actors. Is it so wrong?"

"Nothing's wrong now," she says, tightening her arms around him.

"Hey, that's some hold. Mind if I practise it?" And he turns to her.

Nothing wrong with it. Unless . . . But surely the punters *know*.

Mad Bull turned into the gymnasium in South London — gleaming weight machines, sauna, jacuzzi, like nothing he had seen before — and went into the changing rooms.

And he was in a dressing room, twelve years after he had left the Navy, with his promoter, hair all salt now, eyes rheumy, who was telling him: "Time to start losing a few now. Time marches on and you can still make big bucks, not so many maybe, but the public's got to have its villains so why not you? *Les girls*, they like the villains as much as the good guys. Well, some of them anyway. You know, the *real* talent," winking.

And that was when he had started to lose more fights than he won, when they had changed his name from Harry Welsh to Mad Bull, when he had gained a reputation for foul throws and butts and smashes and attacks on referees.

And it was about that time that he had begun to pay attention to the women, some of those not so young as those who had pestered Harry Welsh. And it was not long before his wife found out and moved out of the new detached house in Lewisham taking the boy with her.

Climbing into the ring to rehearse his come-back in a corner where, away from the piston movements of the weight machines, you could still smell sweat and liniment, he felt a twinge from his first serious injury. To the spine when he hadn't paid enough attention to his bridge.

But there had still been a lot of years left. A few more injuries. The divorce. The empty boarding house rooms. His son in the Navy, where else?

In the ring in the gleaming and clinical gym the younger man in the red tracksuit said: "Okay, grandpa, you take a count in the second, okay?"

"A submission for me in the first? Head butt, Flying Mare, Wheel, you name it."

"Okay, old man. You get one in the first. No more. Understand?" His name was Butcher and his blonde good looks were saved from effeminacy by a break in the line of his nose.

"I understand," Mad Bull said.

A forearm smash. Out through the ropes. Back on the count. How they had squealed. Loving it and me because I was so evil and in their minds I was knocking the shit out of indolent husbands and unfaithful lovers . . .

Until one day I didn't get up and I was in hospital and one ear was deaf and my skull was full of the past and I thought she was there, tucking her belly into me, and the boy was there wearing bell-bottoms, but she was a nurse and he was a doctor with a stethoscope and they were shaking their heads.

Overweight, drooping, cannon-ball head . . . Then the squat. And warmth. And friends.

"I said a *full*-nelson."

"Sorry," Mad Bull said.

"Get it right, for Christ's sake. Why are you doing this anyway?"

"Why do we do anything?"

"Skint?"

"Something like that."

"Yeah? Well, don't give me a hard time. See what some old bastard like you did to me?" stroking his ridged nose.

"Don't worry," Mad Bull assured him. "It'll be all right on the night." He smiled with his forehead and scalp.

"It had better be, old-timer. How old are you for Christ's sake?"

"Forty-eight," Mad Bull said.

"Jesus!"

"I never fought him," Mad Bull said, smiling again.

"I need a comedian?"

"Let's rehearse," Mad Bull said. "It's entertainment they want. Isn't it?"

Through the ropes. Climbing back. Hitting the padded corner post. Forearm smashes, a Flying Mare . . . Always remember the bridge. Without it you can be dead like my da,

213

crushed by a beam in a pit.

A pain in his chest. Like a piano string tightening.

But by the time he had got back to the squat it had loosened. He drank a mug of tea in the kitchen and listened to his friends through his good ear.

Prince: "If I was a fugitive . . ."

"You are," Gosling said.

"And I was on the run from the CIA or the Special Branch or whatever . . . Know what I'd do?"

"Enlighten us," Gosling said.

"Find an accomplice. Go to Heathrow. I book a ticket for Berlin, accomplice books a ticket for Paris. Inside the departure lounge we exchange boarding cards. Fuzz waiting for me in Berlin: I walk off free as a bird in Paris."

"I'd like to be a bird," Charlie said, words overtaking his thoughts.

"I wouldn't," Danny said. "They crap while they're asleep."

"Found us a place to live?" Frank the Bodger asked Cuff. He had been fixing the sink and water dripped steadily into the cupboard beneath it.

"A few more prospects," Cuff said.

"We can't live in a prospect: they're not hygienic."

"I found a DANGER FALLING MASONRY on an abandoned church."

"Sounds like an invitation," Prince said. "Air conditioning?"

"No windows," Cuff said. "Not much of a roof either," he added apologetically. "Not much masonry come to that."

Jenny came in with Martin. She deposited a pile of change on the table, sliding two £1 coins from it. "Eight pounds and forty-five p," she said. "You can't whack the Mona Lisa."

Mad Bull liked Jenny. She had pride. She could draw £51.74 assistance every fortnight plus £48.86 rent allowance but she chose to chalk her pictures on the pavements. His wife had understood about pride.

He thought about tomorrow and shivered. He drank some tea. One submission in the first round. Then the fury of Butcher's revenge. But it wasn't the main bout and they had been ordered to cut it short.

Entertainment?

In bed that night he was wrestling and a ship was heaving and he was Harry Welsh at Bellevue, Manchester, and he was winning, and the women were screaming for him but he was only wrestling for one girl and she was at home with the boy watching him on television.

But the television was blind and she was in another place and his room was crowded with echoes. He awoke sweating. He looked out of the window but the moon was cold in the sky. The sweat cooled on him. He turned and felt his heavy muscles turn with him. Why am I doing this thing? he asked himself. No one cares. Not even Danny, because he knows it's a non-contest. "Singers are entertainers. And skaters and actors. Is it so wrong?"

The contest was staged in a cavernous baths that smelled of chlorine in West London. Mad Bull and Butcher were third billing. From his corner Mad Bull surveyed the crowd. A full house. Prince, Martin and Gosling there in the second row. And the women of course. One empty seat in the front row.

He got his submission easily enough with an armlock and when he had finished groaning and pleading Butcher whispered: "Okay, grandpa, now it's my turn."

But now the seat was occupied.

And she was waving just as she had once waved to Harry Welsh.

He hit Butcher with a forearm smash.

"Hey, take it easy," Butcher said.

"Watch your bridge," Harry Welsh said.

They caterpulted from the ropes, missed each other; the second time Butcher was supposed to trick him into a fall and then a hold.

Harry Welsh caught him with a head butt.

And Butcher was retching and the referee was saying: "What's going on?"

Butcher stood up. They gripped hands.

"You bastard," Butcher whispered. "You stupid old bastard. What the hell do you think you're doing?"

"It's called wrestling," Harry Welsh said.

She was standing on her feet.

The piano string was taut in his chest.

"The bridge," Harry Welsh said. "Remember your bridge."

A hold, a lock, Butcher trying a wheel.

Spinning, spinning . . . But I can get my balance — the heave of the ship's deck helping — and into a Flying Mare. Pulling him

215

towards me, foot into his solar plexus and over he goes. Flying. The ring shudders.

Quiet now in the hall, all those who believe sensing that they are witnessing something beyond that belief.

Butcher hauling himself to his feet.

Referee trying to stop the fight. Thrust aside by both of them, bodies sweat-oiled for combat.

"Come here, you bastard," says Butcher.

"Here, take me."

"You're dead, shit-head."

"But I won't lie down."

A forearm smash from Butcher. Piano string tightening in his chest. On his back staring at the high ceiling. Jesus, do they dive into the pool from that height?

And he's jumping on my chest, boots coming in to splinter my ribs.

Heave to one side. Catching Butcher's ankle.

He's down sprawling.

Grandpa?

Knee on his back, twisting an arm. Screaming for real. Because this is the way limbs and tendons get snapped. Escaping.

Sharp chords in my chest.

A throw and now he's above my head, and I'm revolving with him – "Don't forget your bridge, butcher boy" – and now he's across my knee, spine threatened.

Out there she's still standing.

And the boy, where is he? On the High Seas?

A submission!

The referee waving his hands.

Butcher in a heap, gathering himself together. "You fucking bastard."

"Grandpa?"

"You're finished."

"I won," Harry Welsh says.

"They don't think so."

Outside the ring the women are booing and knuckling their fists.

All except one.

"I won," Harry Welsh says again.

And he raises two fists in triumph to the woman who isn't

216

booing and the piano string snaps inside his chest and he is on the canvas and Tupper's brown eyes are looking down upon him.

*   *   *

"How is he?" Martin asked the doctor.

"We're doing everything we can."

"From an agreed script?" Prince asked.

"I'm sorry, it's the truth."

"What happened?" Harry Welsh's wife asked.

"A massive coronary," the young doctor said in the corridor outside casualty.

"Is there any other kind?" Prince asked.

"He's strong," the doctor said. "There's no point in you staying."

"I'll stay," Harry Welsh's wife said.

"We'll go home," Martin said. "Tell him we're at home if he wants to know."

"I'll tell him," the doctor said and Martin realised that he hadn't been reciting: he was too young.

"I'm sorry," Prince said to the flushed, once-pretty woman. "About the way I spoke to the doctor."

"I understand," she said but you knew she didn't. "He won," she said, "but he lost a long time ago."

They stopped in the Codgers for a drink.

"I'll call the hospital later," Martin said.

"He thought a lot," Prince said sipping his vodka and soda. "Thought so much there was no time for words."

The alsatian moved restlessly.

Martin drank his beer. "We'll go home now," he said.

"Okay, home."

But when they got there the police were waiting for them.

CHAPTER 23

———◆◆◆———

Heald's day had begun badly. At the police station he had been rebuked by a superintendent for dealing too leniently with a bag-snatcher.

"You should have nicked him," said the superintendent, striking a Swan Vesta match in his spartan office.

"Not enough evidence." Standing in front of his desk, Heald watched smoke billowing from the superintendent's pipe; if he worked any harder at it smoke would come out of his ears.

"Got form, hasn't he?" He shuffled papers on the desk. "It's not the first handbag he's pinched, is it?" The pipe and its smoke invested the superintendent's bleak features with a misleading affability.

"He's got previous certainly. But you don't get convictions on a man's record."

"You could have had a word in his ear. He wouldn't be the first John to change his mind."

"He comes from a bad home." Awkwardness descended upon Heald; he was conscious of his bulk and the sleeves of his ready-made suit that were never long enough for his arms.

"And only nineteen. So?"

"He's not really a villain."

"So you did your stout custodian of the law bit? Smack him on the ear, don't-do-it-again-son . . . Did you pause to think about the victim? Mother of three, just cashed her Giro, ekeing out the cash to buy the Sunday joint. Did you consider her feelings?"

"She got her bag back," Heald said. "And her money."

"You almost sound as though you're aiding and abetting."

218

"One of six kids. Father sends them out thieving."

"A proper Fagin, eh? Black, of course."

"No," Heald said. "Just black."

"Touchy this morning, aren't we?" His pipe had gone out and he made a performance of relighting it. Smoke issued abundantly. "How's your son?"

"Better," he said.

"Still with the Community Drug Project?"

"They're doing a fine job."

"Caught him in time, eh? Pity about the university. He could have become Commissioner of Police."

"He doesn't want to join the force," Heald told him.

"Doesn't like the fuzz?" The superintendent aimed his pipe at Heald; smoke dribbled from the stem. "Sometimes I get the impression you're not over-fond of it."

"I believe in law and order and I believe in helping people." He wished he were more articulate. He had once told Mary: "Love is what you don't say," and she had held his hand tightly.

"Do you believe in shooting people? It's a different force from the one you joined, Heald. A lot of gun-slingers in our midst. I admire your ideals," in a voice that didn't, "but ideals don't help when you're looking down the wrong end of a sawn-off shotgun."

An ambulance brayed outside.

"It's a wicked world," the superintendent said. "And it's getting more wicked every minute. We've got to stay on top, Heald. You should have nicked your tea-leaf."

He struck another Swan Vesta and dismissed Heald with his eloquent pipe.

At the Central Criminal Court, the Old Bailey, Heald encountered the other pole of law enforcement, a forgiving judge. Sometimes it seemed to him that extremists and liberals were accomplices in a plot to sabotage society.

The Bailey always depressed him. The sonorous courtrooms beneath the green dome where passion, avarice and cunning became judicial platitudes. The corridors on the site of Newgate Prison echoing to the death march of the condemned on the way to the scaffold.

Justice could be smug, Heald decided, entering the court where his prisoner who had been convicted of attempted rape

219

and arson was to be sentenced. Invested with a divine arrogance. What right had judges and barristers, actors all, to manipulate lives? Life, after all, was what they knew so little about, only sampling it in the witness box and prison cell. Shouldn't a degree in jurisprudence be followed by six months' sojourn on the streets of Brixton?

Today's judge was a humanitarian. When he was sitting the bench was an altar, the jury a choir. He radiated a compassion that, in passing, lit a small flame of satisfaction within his own soul, and he reacted indulgently to the Press which deplored suspended sentences passed on a father who had sexually assaulted two of his daughters and on a youth who had savaged an old lady and robbed her of £3.55p. Did such protests not increase circulation and wasn't that their business, selling papers? When a mugger whom he had set free knocked a girl on the head on the eve of her wedding, damaging her brain, he reminded himself that the real culprit was the drug dealer who had made the assailant an addict who would rob, kill even, for a fix.

Heald believed in mercy. He also believed that some men and women were born evil.

Counsel for his prisoner had defended his client with such concentrated belief in human decency that the young man in the dock – "And he is only seventeen" – who had held a knife to a widow's throat, and would have raped her if he hadn't suddenly found himself impotent, was forced to wipe his eyes with a soiled handkerchief. His lamentable family circumstances, his sexual immaturity . . . The judge, taking into account that he had five previous convictions and had tried to burn down the widow's house, sentenced him to six months' youth custody which meant, Heald calculated, that with remission, he would be active in four months with his burgeoning lust and a box of matches.

From the Bailey, Heald crossed the street to the Magpie and Stump on the site of the hostelry where once you could hire a room to watch a hanging, breakfast thrown in. He ate a pub lunch, drank a pint of bitter and drove to Battersea on unofficial business.

The woman was in her late thirties. Separated from her husband. Mother of a teenage boy who was behaving irrationally.

220

Heald knocked firmly on the door of the small house where, in the front garden, marigolds bloomed.

She settled him on a sofa and made tea in the kitchen. A photograph framed in silver stood on the piano. The woman, full of laughter, and her husband and the boy, toothy and thin-legged, standing at the end of a pier somewhere; Heald looked closer – Felixstowe.

She poured his tea, a neat woman with bewildered blue eyes and fine blonde hair meticulously waved. What sort of woman had her husband preferred? An avaricious, sexually insatiable slut who would throw him out when she had drained him? Heald hoped so.

"In what way," Heald said, choosing his words with care, "is your son acting 'irrationally'?" It was her word.

"He used to be a happy kid. Now he's moody, bad-tempered."

"How old is he?"

"Sixteen," she said.

"A lot of teenagers get moody. It's a time of change: they're confused, a little frightened."

"He used to be fond of sport; he doesn't care anymore." She sipped her tea to give herself time to arrange her sentences; Heald knew about the habits of dialogue. "If I told you he'd done something bad you wouldn't arrest him, would you, Mr. Heald?"

"It depends how bad."

"Stealing?"

"From who?"

"Me," she said.

"No, I wouldn't arrest him. That's why you phoned me, isn't it, because you knew I wouldn't."

"They say you're a kind man."

He would never make inspector but he was kind; that was something, he supposed.

"I think you want to tell me something else, Mrs. Clarke."

"You're married aren't you, Mr. Heald?"

"Twenty years. To a good woman."

"I thought I was happily married," she said. She took a small bite out of a slice of fruitcake. "If only he'd left me when I was younger. What chance do I have now?"

Heald stared at his big hands protruding from the sleeves of

221

his jacket. Lego hands, he thought. Then because there was no answer he said: "Let me anticipate you, Mrs. Clarke. Yes, I do have a son."

"You know what I suspect?"

"I think I do." He hesitated. Then: "My boy has a drug problem."

He had pushed a button. Her tea grew cold as she talked. Outbreaks of violence, drowsiness, irritability, money missing from her purse. No father to help ... What could she do?

"First show him that you care."

"Don't you think I do that already?"

"About his problem? It's my guess you've never raised the subject."

"I'm frightened to. You know, he might leave home and then I'd have nobody. I thought perhaps you ..."

Heald shook his head. "I'm the law, the Old Bill, the fuzz, a pig according to the sort of people he's mixing with now. He'd never forgive you for telling me. So raise the subject gently. Not too many tales of horror. Then, together, try and find out why he started."

"I know the reason. His father ..."

Heald who had heard a broken home blamed for a whole catalogue of human frailties said: "Possibly, Mrs. Clarke. But you can't go on blaming your husband for the rest of your life; that way he'll damage you more than he already has."

What he didn't say was: "And by reviling him you've probably undermined any feeling of security the boy had left." The human capacity to abuse a child's trust always shocked him. So why had Stephen started snorting coke? Heald liked to think it was the emotional release of university life after an adolescence as a policeman's son. But most parents deluded themselves. More probably I was too busy being a kind cop to be kind to him.

Heald asked Mrs. Clarke: "Does he have any interests left?"

"Gardening," she told him. "Funnily enough he still likes gardening. His father never did."

"Encourage him. And at the same time find out what drugs he's into — amphetamines, cocaine, heroin, LSD ..." He gave her a pamphlet published by the DHSS, advising parents of children with a drug problem. "Do you mind if I take a look at your garden?"

222

Surprised, she led him through the kitchen onto a square of manicured grass surrounded by plants growing lushly on black soil.

Should he tell her? Not yet. Give her time to salvage some trust. Then, perhaps, they would laugh together at the fact that her son had been growing cannabis in the back garden.

*   *   *

The day so far had been shitty and Heald saw no prospect of it improving until, that was, he got home to Mary and they talked about Stephen whose prospects were now more optimistic, and perhaps ate scrambled eggs on toast cranked up with a little HP Sauce and drank half a bottle of a Sainsbury's red and played Scrabble and hopefully made love – he had known her now for twenty years and her familiar body still aroused him and he had never been unfaithful and no one except Mary believed him. His job projected him daily into the dark side of life; at least he understood that, not like some police officers who, retreating into the treacherous shadows, drank or shot smack or became as bent as the felons they apprehended. But sometimes, after the sort of day that was now spending itself, he needed to peer across the line of duty into the sunlight. To do this he wandered through streets of decent houses; he gazed into school playgrounds where whites and blacks and browns played together; he stepped stealthily into old churches to smell faith; he smiled at lovers in parks and he loitered in second-hand bookshops where young ideas were preserved like pressed flowers between bindings. He did this after leaving Mrs. Clarke's house and its garden sprouting with pot and the day was a phoenix rising from the ashes until he got back to the police station, picked up the telephone ringing on his desk, picked up the anonymous tip that stolen property had been secreted in the squat known as Buck House.

*   *   *

Heald felt betrayed. He didn't condone squatting but it was symptomatic of the age and he did admire the ingenuity of some of the squatters – and he had tacitly helped the occupants of Buck House to prolong their tenure. No police objections to the

223

occupants when the owners were seeking an eviction order in the courts, no interference with some of the more doubtful tenants. And he had left Danny alone: if the enigmatic Prince and his bandits could cure him then, Heald reasoned, there was hope for Mankind.

The informant, male, voice muffled, London or Home Counties by the sound of it, had asked for him specifically. No question of payment. A vindictive tip – a thief who had been shopped? – but, Heald sensed intuitively, a valid one.

The property, antiques, had allegedly been stolen from a house in Hampstead. 'Appy 'Ampstead – Heald remembered taking Mary and Stephen, when he was small, to the fair on the heath one late summer bank holiday. He picked up the old black telephone – no push-buttons here, no music from space in the background – asked for a line and dialled the number of the police at Hampstead.

A detective said yes, a burglary had been reported and two uniformed officers, Harrison and Ford – and yes, it had been noted that, jointly, they sounded like a certain film star – had just *remembered*, wearily intoned, that on a previous occasion they had called at the house in The Bishops Avenue – *The* emphasised – and found a young man and a girl there but, as the girl was the step-daughter of the owner and the young man was her boyfriend, no action had been taken.

"Name of the girl?"

"Jenny Renshaw."

It didn't mean anything to Heald. "Boyfriend?"

"Martin Renshaw. And, yes, it does sound incestuous but if you remember I said *step*-daughter so they're not blood relatives."

Martin Renshaw? The name of one of the occupants of the squat. He was disappointed.

The detective said: "You've had a tip?"

Heald guessed that he was middle-aged, balding, a little clumsy, disenchanted. Or am I looking into a mirror?

"The gear, some of it anyway, is supposed to be in a squat in Wandsworth."

"Okay," the detective said. "We'll get a warrant and come down tomorrow."

"The informant said they might be moving it tonight."

A sigh. "Can you handle it? We've got a full night. A girl's body on the heath. Strangled."

Heald remembered an old-fashioned roundabout there, horses with ravaged faces rising and falling.

Okay, he said, he would handle it.

"The gear's been treated for ultra-violet. And a black guy was apparently observed entering the premises the following day."

Heald called Mary and told her he would be late.

"I'm supposed to be surprised?"

"Scrambled eggs," he said. "And a bottle of Château Sainsbury best vintage. And then . . ."

"Supposing I'm not here?"

Shock lurched inside him. "What do you mean?"

"Supposing I've eloped with a felon? I was only joking . . ."

"I have to be looking at you for jokes like that."

"What time?" she asked.

"Nine with luck."

"Which means ten. Okay, I'll have the HP Sauce at the ready."

"What are you wearing?"

She sounded surprised. "Black stockings, suspenders, stiletto heels. Joking again. Why am I so jokey tonight?"

"So what are you wearing?"

"Jeans, trainers and a cashmere sweater."

"Change," he said and hung up, smiling at the old receiver.

Outside, the evening had a spring, Saturday flavour; dark and fresh, smelling of football pitches; a night for assignations. The sky above central London had a gingery glow to it and the streets beneath it were quick with life.

On nights such as this Heald liked to dwell on the stories unfolding in the metropolis. Millions of them. In one short and undistinguished street a dozen novels. Not girls strangled on heathland, not stolen property hidden in a squat. Stories with happy endings which were at a premium in police work. He liked to think about old couples still holding hands and kids trying to hit sixes over chestnut trees like their fathers. On nights such as this he became a voyeur, glancing into parlours where the citizenry he was employed to protect rested cosily in the flickering light of television sets.

He picked up Lewis at the pub on the corner and they drove to the magistrate's home, a square corner house with a per-

225

fumed garden, lights burning in too many rooms – the ploy burglars appreciated – and obtained the warrant. And indeed the magistrate, a lean and grey man whose humour had become sardonic over the courtroom years, was on his way out to dinner. Rob a magistrate and what chance of acquittal did you have?

Lewis took over the wheel of the police car and they drove in the direction of the squat. Lewis talked enthusiastically about the tip-off; as far as Lewis was concerned everyone was a potential villain, all guilty until proved otherwise. He was dressed sharply for Saturday night, close-shaved, and predatory and he made Heald feel avuncular.

"Stout custodian of the law", the superintendent's words. But he shouldn't be derisive. Stout or skinny, that's what we are. Heald wished devoutly that all kids realised this as they had done – well, most of them – in his youth. What had gone wrong? The country was a smouldering volcano of violence and, the superintendent was right, ideals didn't deflect bullets and so the police, combating violence with violence, had lost sympathy. But why had the violence erupted? The two popular scapegoats: drugs and unemployment. Well, maybe. But why had they been allowed to fester? Unerringly, Heald traced their origins to a stratum of society that, insulated against reality, had allowed morals to be sucked down the drain. Ah, those middle-aged trendies of the '60s.

Lewis, driving with verve, said: "What makes you so certain the gear's in the squat?"

Heald told him about the Renshaw connection.

"Any form, this Martin Renshaw?"

"I haven't checked him out yet."

Silent disapproval.

"Plenty of time," Heald said. "If he's got the gear then we nick him."

"What are we looking for?" Lewis asked.

"Couple of clocks, flintlock pistol, silver tea-set, scent bottles, miniatures . . ."

"Not exactly an Aladdin's Cave."

"Valued at £32,000 by Christie's."

"Chicken feed," Lewis said.

They drew up quietly outside the squat – Heald had always contended that the villains in TV serials escaped so easily

226

because the police cars squawked a warning – and walked up the path past the bowed silhouette of the weeping willow. Lewis went round the back to catch anyone who suddenly remembered that they had an urgent appointment.

"Who's there?" A man's voice from behind the door.

"Police. Open up."

"Got a warrant?"

"Yes," Heald shouted back, "we've got a warrant."

"Prove it," the voice said.

So they had one of those. Heald said: "Open the door and you can read it."

"Open the door and you'll bust your way in."

"Keep it shut and we'll bust our way in," Lewis shouted.

"Others have tried."

Lewis shouted: "Listen, prick, if you don't open that door we'll bust you in."

"Cool it," Heald said to Lewis. And to the voice: "You're obstructing the course of justice. Can be dodgy. Open up, take a look at the warrant and if it's okay which it is we'll come in and talk."

"What about?"

"Open up," Heald said. The rasp of a bolt, oil-snug turn of a key. They came face to face with a man with a wild ginger beard.

"So who are you, Rasputin?" Lewis asked.

"The warrant. Show it to me."

Heald showed him. A bull-terrier hurled himself at his legs and missed.

"Perhaps," Heald suggested, "you should buy that dog spectacles."

"Name?" Lewis said to the man with ginger hair.

"Hoover," the man said.

"First name?"

"He's only got one name," the man said, patting the dog.

Lewis gave him a small push in the chest with the flat of one hand. "Comedians don't make me laugh: they make me want to throw up."

"I know my rights."

"I know your rights, old son. I'll explain them down at the nick."

"Can you give me one good reason why I should even talk to you?"

227

"One," Lewis said, bunching his fist so that the knuckles shone white.

A man with a bulging forehead and Clark Kent spectacles appeared behind the ginger beard. "He's known as the anarchist," he said.

"You surprise me," Heald said, pushing past the two of them into the room.

It had multiplied since he had been here. A refined rubbish dump, a jumble-sale of discarded furniture, a showroom of inventiveness. Bookcases constructed from bricks, tea-chest covered with a holed damask table-cloth, more bricks supporting the broken leg of a coffee-table with a broken glass top, a super-glued china Siamese cat, a black-and-white television partially disembowelled; the chaise-longue and rocking chair he remembered. In the grate stood a vase of dried grasses.

"Sit down," Heald said. "We'll have a roll-call. Name?" to the man with the bulging forehead.

He said it was Gosling. No Christian name but it was an improvement on the anarchist.

"How many squatters?"

"A historical contradiction," Gosling observed. "Did you know that a squatter was a tenant of the Crown? I shall have to look into the etymology. Not to be confused with entomology," he added.

Lewis said: "Don't I know you, squire?"

"I once enjoyed the hospitality of Her Majesty."

"Fraud?"

"I assisted in the composition of legal documents."

"Fraud," Lewis said.

How could Lewis afford to dress so well, Heald wondered. Navy pin-stripe with beautifully rolled lapels, just the right amount of white cuff showing — not yards of hairy wrist.

"Who's the woman?" Heald said to Gosling.

"What woman?"

"The woman in the house." He pointed at the grasses in the hearth.

"Well done, Sherlock," the anarchist said.

"You'll be nicked before the night's out," Lewis said, shooting his cuffs.

"Jenny Renshaw," Gosling said. "Why?"

228

"It figures," Heald said.

"What figures?"

Lewis said: "Some more names, squire."

"You know about Danny."

"Yes," Heald said, "we know about Danny."

"And Hood?"

"We read about him," Lewis said. "Is he still telling porkies?"

"He's a literary giant. Writing romances. You know, handsome doctors, pilot, astronauts . . ."

"The characters are allowed to lust after each other now," Gosling observed.

"The doctors and the pilots?" the anarchist asked.

"Jesus," Lewis said.

"Who else?" Heald asked as Hood, eyes watering, came down the stairs. He had shaved off his terrible moustache and he looked naked but not without presence.

"What ho, Barbara Cartland," the anarchist said.

"Nesta Hood as a matter of fact," Hood said, eyeing the detectives. "Trouble is they've sent the cheque to Nesta Hood. Is Prince here? I thought he might be able to help."

"And then there's Prince," Heald said. "Where's he this fine evening?"

"Mad Bull's fighting," Gosling said. "He went with Martin to give him encouragement."

"And then there's Martin," Heald said. "Renshaw?"

Gosling, taking off his spectacles to polish them, nodded.

"And Charlie?"

"You've heard about Charlie?"

"The black hope of Brixton," Lewis said. "The pirate radios have taken him up."

"He's training," Gosling told him.

"At this time of night?"

"He likes the darkness," Gosling said. "He hears thoughts better. I can understand that. Words are better too. Set in velvet."

"Jesus wept!" exclaimed Lewis, writing in his notebook. "So that leaves . . ."

"My name's Cuff." He entered the room from the kitchen wearing a charcoal-grey suit two sizes too big for him.

229

"So what do you do?" Heald asked.

"Quartermaster," Cuff said, bending his slight body into an apology. "And chief scout."

"Very commendable. Found anywhere else to live?"

"Have you heard anything?" Gosling asked.

"Time's running out," Heald told him. "You know that." He admired Gosling's rearguard court actions based on the premise that possession is nine points of the law.

Lewis said: "Any more?"

Silence. Scrape of a match, reminding Heald of the superintendent, while Gosling lit his bulldog pipe.

Finally the anarchist said: "A few strolling mutineers. I see this place as the Battleship Potemkin," he explained.

"I see it as a thieves' kitchen," Lewis replied.

"There's Frank the Bodger," Cuff said.

"No surname, I presume," Heald said.

"Sorry," Cuff said. "He's mending the cistern," he added.

"If tenants don't want to give their names we don't ask them," the anarchist said.

"Tenants," Lewis said. "That's a laugh."

"We've forgotten Jack Daniels," Gosling said.

Lewis said: "So I was right."

Gosling said: "About what?"

"A thieves' kitchen. You don't know?"

Cuff said: "He's always been a mystery."

Hood said: "I was thinking of introducing a character like him in my next book."

Heald said: "He's a villain." He told Lewis to search Daniels' room.

"Is he wanted?" Cuff asked.

"He's always wanted," Heald said.

Lewis said from the top of the stairs: "He's done a runner; his room's empty."

230

CHAPTER 24

Sitting on a pile of cushions, hands clasped round his knees, Martin listened vaguely to the detectives' questions. A routine visit, he assumed; squats were fair game for police. But, with the probable exception of Jack Daniels, there was no one of criminal inclination in Buck House. What was it Prince had said about Daniels? "He dresses too well to be rich." Nevertheless he didn't have the stamp of poverty about him. Martin, drained by the exhilaration of Mad Bull's win and the anti-climax of his collapse, gave up.

He listened to Prince fencing with the detectives, listened to the creak of his rocking chair. In fact Prince was as much a conundrum as Daniels. Look at him now in his scuffed flying-jacket, white scarf at his neck, dark eyes and bead in the lobe of his ear glittering in the light from the naked bulb, cross between buccaneer and lugubrious clown. Martin suspected that he was an orphan, quicksilver cunning acquired at an orphanage.

However remote your parents, they were *there*. They had conceived you – that astounding revelation of adolescence – and you were theirs. Stairs creaking, muted movement in the bedroom next door, the absorbed sharing of the dining-table. From a distance his father's martyrdom became quite admirable. What bothered him was his mother's trust; like a child's. Convinced that I'm tramping the streets of London looking for a job, a worthwhile one that she can communicate to the neigh-bours, and that I'm living in some respectable hostel with packet soup for starters and a Gideon Bible on the bedside table. When was the last job interview he had attended? Try telling her that helping to cure a drug addict and training a

231

black runner to win a race in the Special Olympics was more important than obtaining gainful employment!

Does a mother question her child's future as she waves him to school? In his mother's case probably not: the thread between the tiny house and the shop was imperishable: he would become a grocer and open stores all over Merseyside. After the shop had shut Joanne had been his mother's anchor for his future. A nurse, sensible and caring, and it wasn't her fault that her father was a drunkard or that her mother was inclined to have airs and graces above her station.

Going to the theatre with Joanne. The Playhouse, Willy Russell's *Educating Rita*. In the days when my lips still trembled when I met strangers. (It was still a recurring dream, meeting a VIP who could exert a beneficial influence on his future but being unable to talk because his bottom lip was in shock.)

She had tucked her hand beneath his arm for the first time and he had felt proprietorial.

"I'm glad he's a Scouser," she said as they walked through rain-swept streets.

"Who?"

"Willy Russell. People don't realise how much talent comes from Liverpool. Everyone knows about George Harrison. Who knows that Rex Harrison was born here?"

"I didn't," Martin said.

"There you go."

"And Nicholas Monsarrat," he said.

"I sometimes think that anyone who's anyone is a Scouser."

"Tash Balmer," Martin said.

"Who's he when he's at home?"

"There you go — Liverpool, 1946, first player to score three League hat-tricks in a row."

And that night he had kissed her for the first time, in the rain, and his lips hadn't trembled at all.

Lewis: "Where the hell's this spade?"

Cuff: "You mean Charlie?"

Lewis: "Where is he?"

Cuff: "Running."

And what about the uncles, my pretext for coming to London? All three hiding behind different accomplices — God, Mammon and the Devil. And no closer to finding William Grey. If, that was, he was still alive.

The anarchist: "Don't forget Nolan."
Heald: "Who's Nolan?"
The anarchist: "He goes in for competitions."
Heald: "Where is he now?"
Prince: "In Dublin. 'Beginners Luck, BeGuinness Luck.'"
In his bed beneath the tall ships Martin had never anticipated anyone like Jenny. His early expectations — nothing more ambitious because of the trembling lip and a habit of listening to himself — had been confined to girls at college, before economic necessity had forced him to leave, and girls at work and girls in the same street. The Jennys of Liverpool were as unattainable as the girls who worked behind the perfumery counters at Lewis's. It was her spirit that attracted him, her quest for an unidentified truth, her refusal to accept her birthright. When she was away, as she was now, spending a weekend in the country with Eleanor Lubin, he saw her on Hampstead Heath wearing a white cotton dress (which she didn't possess) running, fine dark hair flowing behind her, a summer breeze dissipating the questions between her eyes. Just before she reached the picnicking heathland he caught her and they fell and kissed.

Danny came down the stairs pulling at his wispy beard and Heald said: "How are you doing, son?" Martin noticed a subtle change in his attitude.

"I'm okay. Where's Charlie?"

"Training," Gosling told him.

"When will he be back?"

"Any time now," Gosling told him.

"So," Prince said to Heald, "to what do we owe the honour?"

"All in good time," Heald said. "Why did you allow Jack Daniels to stay here?"

"I like whisky," Prince said.

"Another comedian," Lewis said. "Like I just told the beaver here," pointing at the anarchist, "funny men make me want to vomit."

Prince rocked a little quicker. "Why shouldn't he stay here?"

"We get all sorts," the anarchist said. "Even policemen."

"Because he's a villain," Heald said.

"Jack's a good name for a villain," Gosling said. "Nice sharp ring to it. Did you know that in Australia it means the pox?"

Heald said to Martin: "Where were you on the night of

233

March sixteen?"

"A Thursday," Lewis said.

Martin unclasped his hands from his knees. "I don't know. Why?" Unease visited him like the smell of approaching snow.

Heald: "You can't remember?"

Martin said he couldn't, wondering why he should.

All right, both detectives assured hm, it didn't matter; he became acutely aware that it did.

Heald said to Prince: "Mind if we take a look around?"

"Does it matter if I do? You've got a warrant. Or had you forgotten?"

Heald said: "Which is Charlie's room?" and Danny responded immediately: "You leave his room alone."

Lewis, nodding at Prince, said: "You heard the man – he's got a warrant," and the anarchist said: "You go into Charlie's room over my dead body. Ever heard of the rights of the individual?"

"Not recently," Lewis said. "Do you want me to take a look-see?" to Heald.

Heald, pulling one sleeve of his jacket towards his big knuckles, said: "I think you better had," and, abandoning the tug-o'-war with his sleeve, massaged one fist with the flat of the other hand. Then, apologetically, he spread his hands to Prince.

Danny waited till Lewis was half-way across the room before throwing himself at him shouting: "Bastard."

Lewis handed him off like a rugby three-quarter surging for the touchline. "Keep your distance, skaghead," he said.

As Danny spun on the floor Jesus Christ entered the squat.

He was tall, middle-aged, with a soft brown beard threaded with grey; his eyes were gentle and he wore a brown cassock, sandals and green socks.

Helping Danny to his feet, he said: "Peace be with you."

"And with you," Gosling said.

He was a familiar figure in the squat, an occasional visitor who stayed to meditate; he truly believed that he was Jesus and he wasn't perturbed that he couldn't work miracles because he believed that life was a miracle and Biblical miracles were figurative. He accepted persecution and waited patiently for his crucifixion and resurrection.

"All we need," Lewis remarked.

"Let me get at that supercilious bastard," Danny said, getting to his feet.

Jesus held him; he was very strong. He said: "Resist not evil: but whosoever shall smite thee on thy right cheek, turn to him the other also."

Shrugging, Lewis mounted the stairs.

Martin stood up. "I think we have a right to know what this is all about," he said to Heald.

Heald patrolled the room, picking up ornaments, mostly mended, and examining them. "It's very clean here," he said. "Is Jenny Renshaw a good housekeeper?"

"Clean as a whistle before she came," Prince said. "Why whistles?" he asked Gosling.

Heald stopped in front of Martin. "There's been a robbery in Hampstead. In The Bishops Avenue. A Mr. Harry Renshaw returned from holiday to find a lot of antiques missing from his house. But the house hadn't been broken into." A pause, Heald pulling at a sleeve of his jacket. "I believe you stayed in that house, Mr. Renshaw."

"That's right," Martin said. "With Jenny."

Danny stopped struggling and Jesus Christ let him go.

The anarchist said: "So why look in Charlie's room?"

Still addressing Martin, Heald said: "Police were called while you were at the house?"

"That's right," Martin said, worrying. "Just checking."

"A black man was seen to call at the house the following day."

"So?"

"He was with you."

"That's right: it was Charlie."

"So you see what we have here," Heald said slowly. "We have a robbery, right? The house hasn't been burglarised. You were staying there with Miss Renshaw. You are now both staying here – with a black man."

"So," the anarchist said, "you bust straight into Charlie's room. A bit racist, officer."

"Sergeant," Heald said.

"Obvious," Prince said. "Charlie's the only absentee. Less trouble. I'd have done the same. If I'd been a copper."

Lewis called out from the landing: "Does this Charlie own an antique clock?"

No one answered.

235

"A flintlock pistol?"

Martin's lip began to tremble.

Prince said: "A tip-off. That was what was missing. Right, sergeant?"

"We received certain information," Heald agreed.

"This is crazy," Martin said. "Charlie isn't a thief."

"What about you, Mr. Renshaw?"

"Would I be that stupid? To steal property from a house where I've been staying, where police have been called, and bring it here?"

"I don't know how stupid you are, Mr. Renshaw. I reserve judgement."

"Till when?"

"Until Lewis has finished searching your room."

"You've no right . . ."

"Every right in the world."

Jesus Christ intoned: "I was like a lamb or an ox that is brought to the slaughter."

Movement upstairs.

Martin thought: It can't be happening. Antiques in Charlie's room. In mine? Stupid! Could Charlie have stolen anything? Ridiculous. But what about the tip-off? Could the police have planted antiques in Charlie's room? Why should they? Why should anyone?

Heald said: "What were you doing in The Bishops Avenue?"

Prince said: "Private business, cully."

"So you're his brief?"

"His adviser."

Danny pulled at the wisps of his chin; Jesus Christ smoothed his beard with caressing, downward strokes, the anarchist combed urgently with his fingers.

Heald: "Where's Jack Daniels?"

Martin: "How the hell should I know?"

Prince: "I have to advise you, Mr. Renshaw, that you do not have to answer any of these questions."

Heald: "And I have to advise you, Prince" – didn't anyone ever say *Mr.* Prince? – "to mind your own business."

Prince: "Free country, cully."

Anarchist: "Since when?"

The sound of an object being dragged across the floor. A suitcase?

"I should like," Heald said to Martin, "to know how you came to live here, why you made a point of getting in touch with Harry Renshaw — your uncle, I believe — and at what point since your departure from Liverpool you struck up a liaison," voice apologetic, "with Jenny Renshaw."

"Watch it," Prince said.

"Why should he?" Heald asked.

Gosling cleared his throat. "Perhaps," he said "because you are experienced in the art of interrogation and Martin who has, as far as we know, committed no crime, is twenty, perhaps more, years younger than you and innocent in the ways of entrapment."

Lewis, triumphant, shouted: "Another clock . . . a silver tea-set . . . two miniatures . . ."

An elaborate practical joke, Martin thought.

"Okay, leave them there," Heald said and when Lewis came down the stairs: "Keep an eye on Renshaw."

He went outside, returning with an ultra-violet lamp, the type used for tanning. "You'd better come with me," he said to Martin.

They went upstairs. His room had been searched neatly and methodically. The battered suitcase that had burst open at Euston was on the bed open. Nestling among shirts and underwear were the antiques.

"I've never seen them before," Martin said.

"It's your suitcase, son."

"Someone's planted them there."

"I seem to have heard that before."

Heald plugged the lamp into a socket in the wall and placed it beside the suitcase. He turned the miniatures and the clock face-down. The words leaped at Martin. THE PROPERTY OF HARRY RENSHAW OF THE BISHOPS AVENUE, HAMPSTEAD. On each item.

"A lot of insurance companies advise the owners of valuable property to do this," Heald said. "It's a special solution that only shows up under ultra-violet: the thief never sees it — until it's too late, that is."

"I didn't steal them. Nor did Charlie."

"I'm not suggesting that you did. I warned you it's a wicked city." Heald sat on the edge of the bed.

"What are you suggesting then?"

"You would have been stupid to steal them after the police had called at the house, probably had it under observation."

"Just as stupid to keep the antiques here."

"According to my information you only received the property today; you were going to shift it tonight."

"I don't understand," Martin said.

"What I suggest happened is that you sussed out the house for a professional thief. Aiding and abetting they call it. How well do you know Jack Daniels?"

"Nobody knows him well," Martin said.

"The police do," Lewis said, entering the room. "Where is he?"

"I was talking to you, son."

"I don't know where Jack Daniels is." Just like the recurring dream in which he had to force his lip to speak.

Heald stood up. "You'd better get some things together," he said. "You'll have to come to the police station." He lifted Harry Renshaw's property from the suitcase and laid it on the bed.

Downstairs the anarchist said: "This is an outrage against human rights," and Lewis said: "Leave it out, son. Don't want to get nicked as well, do we?"

Prince, holding a snarling Hoover, said: "Don't worry, cully. Have you out in a trice."

Martin, one detective on either side of him, had reached the front door when Charlie, in his blue tracksuit, came in through the kitchen.

*   *   *

Heald explained the situation: they would like Charlie and Martin to accompany them to the police station to help them with their inquiries.

Charlie, understanding leaping ahead of his words, spoke agitatedly, chest heaving.

Lewis, notebook in hand, said: "What's he saying, for Christ's sake? Can't we just tell him he's nicked?"

Charlie stopped talking. His breathing filled the room. Martin placed a hand on his shoulder. "Don't worry, Charlie, you and me together. Just like any other day."

It was then that Danny, weeping, threw a punch at Lewis;

238

but Jesus caught it, held him.

"Right," Lewis said. "Assaulting a police officer . . ."

"He didn't assault you," Heald said. "I'll look after Charlie, you take Renshaw. Let's get your things together," he said to Charlie.

They went upstairs.

"You can't arrest him," Gosling said. "He's not fit to plead."

"That's for the magistrate to decide," Lewis said.

"He's not a thief."

"How would you know? You want to watch the company you keep."

"Then you'd better go," the anarchist said.

"Can I make a phone call?" Martin asked.

"If you had a phone. Want to call our lawyer, do we?"

The anarchist said to Prince: "Why don't you let the dog go? He likes natty suiting."

Heald came down the stairs with Charlie. Charlie was carrying a suitcase as bruised as Martin's. He was shaking his head slowly, blinking rapidly.

Heald slid the bolt on the front-door.

In the front garden, beside the willow, Martin turned and looked at the open door, at the tenants gathered there.

Hoover barked.

They reached the front gate. Lewis opened it.

Charlie made his break between the gate and the police car.

And he was away.

Running, running.

CHAPTER 25

———◆◆———

Detached and disbelieving, Martin watches the scene as he is bundled into the police car, Lewis pounding hopelessly after Charlie.

The car, Heald at the wheel, taking off, tyres squealing.

Lights and silhouettes blurring past the windows.

Lewis, panting disproportionately to the brevity of the chase: "No good, skip, he lost me."

Car nosing through the darkness, blind predator.

Inside the police station, in front of a burly uniformed sergeant listening to the charge.

". . . in possession of stolen property knowing it to have been stolen."

Alone in a cement-floored, green-tiled cell, sitting on the edge of a water-proofed, foam-rubber mattress staring at a lavatory in the corner.

"Here, lad, drink this."

Mug of tea, saccharine-sweet and steaming.

Two oiled clicks as the iron door closes.

He sips the tea.

Observes himself. Bottom lip beginning to tremble. Then his limbs.

Disciplining that errant bottom lip, he opens his mouth and screams soundlessly.

Then he is on the bunk. Striped pyjamas and grey blanket.

He closes his eyes.

And is on a tube train. It stops at a station, sighs and waits throbbing. He alights. At the other end of the empty platform stands a dwarf carrying a gun.

He runs. Hears a gunshot. He is in a white-tiled tunnel narrowing ahead of him. He listens to the thud of his heart, the rasp of his lungs.

He is wearing black boots and they weigh him to the ground. Tendrils of smoke at the end of the tunnel.

And now he is forcing himself up a *descending* escalator, inching past frozen passengers. He looks down. At the bottom of the *ascending* staircase stands the dwarf aiming the gun.

A thud. One of the frozen passengers falls, melts. The heat is intense, flames trickling down the moving steps of the escalator.

He runs through the inferno, butterflies of flame alighting on his clothes. Out through the mouth of the station into a wood.

Snow falling, butterflies of flame extinguished by selective flakes.

The wood is numb.

The cold and the quiet are childhood.

A robin nods urgently from a card on the mantelpiece.

He turns. The dwarf, a glittering bead in the lobe of one ear, is squeezing the trigger of his pistol.

A thud on the cell door and the voice of a guardian policeman: "Come on, lad, let's be having you."

*   *   *

For Sunday breakfast he ate eggs, sausages and fried bread. At 10.30 a policeman opened the metal door and said: "Sorry about your sister, lad."

"I haven't ..." and Prince's voice behind the policeman: "Happened very suddenly, Martin. Not unexpected, though ..."

"Five minutes," the police officer said.

Prince came in and sat on the end of the bed. "Sorry about Doris," he said, putting one finger to his lips.

Martin spread his hands.

"She didn't suffer. Decent of the law to let me in on compassionate grounds."

"Poor Doris," Martin said. "Still, we all knew it was coming," gesturing helplessly.

"Need to tell a few next-of-kin. Eleanor ..."

"Of course, Eleanor."

"Where is she? Need her. Circumstances like this."

"Spending the weekend in the country," Martin said.

241

"Big place, the country."

"On the Thames, I think."

"Long river, the Thames."

"Her brother?"

"I didn't know she had a brother," Martin said.

Silence. The smell of stale urine, despite the water-proofing on the bed, pervaded the cell.

Prince, softly: "We need a brief. Eleanor . . . Back tonight?"

"I don't even know where she lives. Phone book?"

Prince: "Brill, Martin. She's ex-directory."

Martin: "Sorry, you don't understand how I feel. Perhaps Jenny . . ."

Finger tapping one side of his nose: "Not stupid, Mart. Not totally stupid."

A voice from the other side of the door: "Time's up, lads. Sorry in the circumstances . . ."

Prince to Martin: "Sorry about Doris. But there's always a wheeze."

"Mad Bull?"

"As comfortable as can be expected."

"Danny?"

"Likewise. Upset about Charlie . . ."

"Time's up," said the sergeant.

"All right, squire," Prince said, "you've been very reasonable."

As the door opened Martin said: "Don't bother the uncles. Family reasons . . ."

"Understood," Prince said. "Not stupid."

The door shut behind him. Loneliness filled the cell.

*   *   *

The party this blossoming mid-May day was held in the grounds of a Tudor mansion on a grassy bank of the upper reaches of the Thames.

The tresses of a willow tree combed the water; birds sang and champagne corks popped; passengers on motor-cruisers waved at the young people languidly enjoying themselves.

For lunch: caviar, Beluga; salmon, Scottish; salad, avocado pears and chicory; sweet, precocious strawberries and cream; wine, Sancerre.

242

No one wore striped blazers or boaters: they were understood. Jenny wore jeans and a yellow blouse.

Eleanor's brother, Andrew, leaning on one elbow, features predatory beneath thumb and forefinger spanning his forehead, moved the white queen on the miniature computer.

"Bored?" Jenny asked.

"Have to keep the mind occupied." He smiled, abandoning a gambit. "Sorry."

"You needn't bother about me. I was merely wondering why you bother to come if you want to play chess."

"The party was Elly's idea," he said, which didn't seem to be any sort of an answer. "And she's disappeared indoors with our host."

"But you must know a lot of people here."

"One or two." He saluted a girl with Alice-in-Wonderland hair and a long lavender skirt.

"Are you always anti-social?"

"I can't see any point in mixing with people I neither like nor dislike." He refilled her glass with champagne. "Are you still painting and leading a communal life?"

"Don't be disparaging," she said.

"I didn't mean to be." He regarded her wisely through brown eyes; in middle-age his nose might become beaky. He patted the grass beside him as the girl in the lavender skirt walked over to them. "This is Lucy," he said. "The name fits, doesn't it?"

"Lucinda," the girl said. "I'm a witch. What's your name?"

"Jenny," Jenny said.

"Jenny wren . . ."

"Bright and inquisitive," Andrew said.

"What do you do, Jenny?"

"Paint," Jenny said.

"Houses?"

"Pavements."

They ate caviar glistening stickily in the sunlight and Andrew remarked how contradictory it was that Russia, fount of Communism, should provide capitalist countries with their luxuries – caviar, mink, ermine, diamonds. "But we all indulge double standards even if we don't recognise them," brown eyes searching Jenny's face.

The water made soft, muddy sounds against the river-bank. Laughter reached them from a passing yacht. On the other side

243

of the river children played on a pebble beach beside a field of cows. A blonde young man with elaborately dishevelled good looks put an old 78 on an antique gramophone and cranked the handle. The voice of Richard Tauber, scratched by the needle, issued from the cornucopian trumpet. "Vienna, City of My Dreams".

The young man sat beside Jenny. His features were vaguely familiar. Should she know him? she asked. A familiar question, it transpired: he was a model. Casual clothes and aftershave mostly; designer stubble, he reckoned, had been introduced by the competitors of agencies promoting men's toiletries. The public image of the male model had changed dramatically in the past decade, he informed her. Once upon a time it had been assumed that they were all gay. No longer, no, ma'am. He turned over the record – "Yours is My Heart Alone" – and brought her a plate of salmon and salad and a glass of Sancerre.

She half-listened to him, a little drunk with champagne and sunshine. From the other side of the picnic hampers a girl's voice: "Oh, fuck off, Jamie," What were they doing now in the squat? Brewing up, breaking open a pack of Tennent's, debating, plotting ... Charlie circling Wandsworth Common; Danny, pulling at the silks of his beard and biding his time; Mad Bull, victor or vanquished; Prince mapping his last thousand miles of free travel; Martin ...

"You should take up modelling," said the young man whose name was David.

"I haven't got the composure."

"You've got the looks."

Lucinda the witch brushed back a lock of glossy hair from Andrew Lubin's forehead.

Silver coins of light shimmered on the water. Sparrows approached the hampers.

... Martin. She missed him. But he would be uneasy here, suspecting condescension. She missed the squat too but it was pleasant enough here ... She scooped a spoonful of soft flesh from half an avocado. The squat was rebellion and she exulted in it but rebellion has to have a cause.

David brought her strawberries and cream.

"What were you thinking about just now?" he asked. "You certainly weren't listening to me."

244

"Injustice," she said. *But you can't take up arms against a generalisation.*

"Us and them?"

"Something like that."

"It was ever thus," he said.

"Doesn't it bother you?"

"What can I do about it?"

"Grow designer stubble," she said.

Lucinda popped a strawberry into Andrew's mouth. His jaws worked. A little juice escaped from the corner of his mouth.

He was in the act of swallowing when they heard a splash followed by a shout. Fifty yards away a boy was struggling in the water. Up went his arms, classically, before his head disappeared. The cabin cruiser from which he had fallen stopped.

The boy's head surfaced. Jenny stood up as Andrew Lubin sprinted past her. Was it really true that you went down for good the third time? Andrew was kicking off his training shoes on the edge of the bank. A life belt trailing rope sailed out from the boat, landed just out of the boy's reach and was borne rapidly away by the current. Andrew waded through shallow water, flung himself forward and swam with a powerful crawl towards the boy.

The boy's head disappeared again. When he resurfaced he was farther away from Andrew. Andrew went after him, arms flailing. An elderly man jumped from the boat, and surfaced disembodied, face in panic beneath plastered white hair.

Andrew grasped one of the boy's arms, then the other, and now he was swimming on his back towards the shore towing the boy behind him.

The boy, aged about ten with spiky ginger hair, sat on the grass beneath the willow gasping and shuddering. Andrew touched his ginger hair. "Not bad," he said, "for a first lesson. Next lesson – learn to float." The boy looked up at him, almost smiled, and Andrew, taking Jenny's hand, said: "Come on, no hearts and flowers," and, running, led her towards the house.

*   *   *

It was aristocratically disordered. Two wet labradors in front of a grate thick with cold ash; moth-eaten carpets, leather armchairs that sighed with the incumbent's weight; ancestors

245

peering gloomily from panelled walls; dried flowers from another decade in chipped vases; a billiard table with two ivory balls the colour of old teeth. A minstrel gallery and sonorously ticking clocks, none of them agreeing about the time.

Andrew wearing their host's clothes – flannel trousers, lumberjack shirt and Harris tweed jacket, all too small for him – took Jenny on a tour. Of Eleanor there was no sign and the host, middle-aged and as sleek as Eleanor was glossy, had made only one brief appearance. Jenny guessed that they had been making love. This surprised her. Why she couldn't imagine: Eleanor was a sensuous woman. Perhaps it was because she was a lawyer.

"He's a lawyer too," Andrew said. "In the City. Saved a few inside traders from leaving their stock for the dock. Pots of money. Elly's known him for donkey's years."

"It's a pity she's interested in that sort of law."

They stopped opposite an ancestor with a Duke of Wellington nose who regarded them belligerently.

"Well, don't forget the scales of justice have to be balanced . . . Have you noticed anything odd about that old josser up there," pointing at the ancestor. "He's got six fingers on one hand, one for the till."

He led her down a corridor into a cavernous kitchen. The floor was flag-stoned, the walls lined with old ceramics. "Cup of tea?"

"After champagne?"

"I drink gallons of the stuff while I'm swotting."

"No sugar," she said, sitting at a table scrubbed bone-white. "You seem to know your way around the kitchen."

"I'm almost old Wyndham's brother-in-law."

"They're getting married?"

"Not as far as I know," Andrew said, endangering the too-tight jacket as he stretched for a tea caddy.

She watched him brew the tea with pedantic accomplishment, two teaspoonfuls of Earl Grey plus one for the pot.

"I never saw you as a tea freak," she said.

"Don't you drink it in the squat?"

"Tea-bags, recycled."

"I had an aunt who used tea-bags. She used to open them and complain that it wasn't like it was in the old days, too dry and dusty."

She sipped her tea. "Well," she said, "if you fail your exams you can always get a job in Assam."

"I told you, I shan't fail them."

"Modest with it."

"It isn't conceit," he said. "It's fact."

"What sort of law will you take up?"

"Company, of course," but she couldn't tell whether he was laughing at her.

The garden was in better shape than the house. Walls and paths of mellow brick, miniature hedges, roses poised for summer, herbaceous border, greenhouses that smelled of geraniums and perspiration, lawns of clipped, sweet grass stretching to a yew hedge, separating the garden from the turf sweeping down to the river.

"You think this is unjust, don't you?" Andrew said. He sat on a wooden bench and she sat beside him and he rested his arm lightly on her shoulders.

"What makes you think that?"

"I was listening to your conversation with David."

Not Lucinda the witch; that was something.

"I wasn't really listening to David," she said. "Did you know that designer stubble was introduced by companies wanting to wipe aftershave off the market?"

"You should go to university, you know."

"A lecture in the offing?"

"You can't put the world to rights. Not one person; even Vanessa Redgrave realises that. All you can do is strike one blow for justice: that's all we're allowed."

"You should become an MP."

"One day perhaps. An independent not a party hack. And before I'm too old because there comes a time when originality becomes eccentricity." He stirred his tea and watched a single tea-leaf spinning in the vortex. "Let's find a cause for you. Greenpeace?"

"I admire them, true crusaders. But I'm more interested in people."

"Probationary work?"

She shook her head.

"Social services?"

"I don't think so."

"Politics?"

247

"Not for me."

He was making her feel immature.

"What do you detest most of all?"

"Smugness," she said promptly.

"Then you must become a courtroom lawyer."

"Aren't lawyers sometimes smug?"

"Often. Especially when they're on the side of RIGHT," spelling it out. "But they can also be passionate, incisive, enemies of injustice. And you can pick your cause; that's why Elly chose crooked cops. There aren't that many of them but she weeds them out. It's her vocation, the fight against corruption within the law. The trouble is she's getting a reputation as a criminals' lawyer."

"Does that bother her?"

"It doesn't deter her." He finished his tea. "Can you imagine the euphoria of making an eloquent closing speech that gets an innocent man acquitted?"

She could; but it wasn't the answer. Her enemies were arrogance and indifference. So why not prosecute them? How? Her step-father stepped into the dock. Both qualities personified. So why not campaign against corruption in the citadels of finance? It wasn't a campaign she had ever envisaged but it was surely striking at the pinnacles of privileged assumption. Jenny Renshaw for the prosecution, Eleanor Lubin's lover for the defence!

And I can live with Martin and study law at the same time.

Andrew stood up, pulling her to her feet. The sky was fading to apricot, pinned with a single star. They went indoors.

Their host, Henry Wyndham, was pouring drinks from a trolley; Eleanor sat in one of the sighing armchairs beside the two somnolent dogs. She looked . . . contented. Jenny glanced at Wyndham to see what sort of man had been responsible for such satisfaction. He didn't look like a great lover – slim with wings of greying hair dipping over his ears and the gaze of an interrogator – but who am I to judge? Eleanor had, in Jenny's eyes, changed abruptly. She saw her now as a voluptuary disciplined by her profession; and glimpsed her naked except for black barrister's gown, stockings and high-heeled shoes.

Wyndham offered drinks. Andrew asked for a beer. Jenny refused.

"Where's everyone?" Andrew asked.

248

"Gone on to someone else's place," Eleanor told him.

"They could have asked . . ."

"Apparently you were too preoccupied. But Lucy left a phone number."

Wyndham said: "We're going to Oxford for dinner. Want to come along?"

No, Jenny said, she had to go home. To find out if Mad Bull had won, to be with Martin.

Andrew's car, an old, souped-up Lancia, waited for them in the moonlight. Tyres spitting gravel, it took off down the drive.

At the gates Jenny glanced behind. Mist was rising from the river and the house, surfacing from it, was as benign as the monarchy.

*   *   *

A drunk was shovelled into the cell next to Martin's after supper. He beat the metal door with his fists and shouted obscenities. Then he began to cry, then to snore. Martin, lying beneath the grey blanket, glanced at his watch: in less than twelve hours he would be taken to the magistrates' court. He closed his eyes but the drunk's snores penetrated the wall and there were no tall ships on which to sail into sleep.

249

CHAPTER 26

---◆◆◆---

S. P. Holmes was a pear-shaped man whose clothes hung upon him sadly. His bland features were beginning to follow the cut of his suits; his eyes were canine brown and devotional: his scalp was fringed with soft, greying hair.

A casual observer might have supposed that S. P. Holmes had been frustrated in a desire to take monastic orders. They would have been wrong: ever since he could remember he had wanted to be a crook and his shame was that he had always lacked the courage of criminal intent.

At school – public, minor – he had frequently been accused of misdemeanours and caned. By the housemaster across tight-trousered buttocks, by prefects with a slipper across his bare arse.

All this he could have accepted if he had been guilty. What incensed him was his innocence: that he had never mustered the fortitude to perpetrate the crimes for which he had been punished.

How did he come to possess such nefarious instincts? In cold-breathed dormitories he had lain awake, sore and humiliated, seeking the answer, finally settling for the solution to hand. Useless at sport, no Einstein at studies ... How do you assert yourself? By villainy, that's how.

Holmes remembered clumsy boys who had tried to manufacture popularity through buffoonery. Sad. Sadder still to be an unrequited rogue.

In mid-adolescence he had determined to become a private detective, one of the seedy species who, feet on their desks beside a bottle of bourbon, swapped badinage with the criminal fraternity of which they were associate members. That aspiration had been laid to rest by nomenclature. A detective named Holmes? "Elementary, my dear Holmes", from a client named Watson.

So Holmes had decided to become a solicitor sympathising with miscreants, preferably those guilty as charged. But these sympathies had so often attracted the wrath of the Law Society that, one by one, his partners had departed to offices where the preference was for clients who were presumed to be innocent or, at worst, victims of circumstance.

Thus at the age of fifty-eight S. P. Holmes – initials, according to disappointed clients, standing for variable Starting Price for consultations – laboured alone in a confessional that smelled of snuff and yesterday's whisky, in a grey area of South London where boroughs merged unheeded, and lived by himself in a bachelor flat in Streatham equipped with three televisions which enabled him to catch the crime on the news, tape gangster movies and watch videos of old Raymond Chandler thrillers.

He had finished a TV supper and was watching Dick Powell as Philip Marlowe in *Farewell My Lovely* reach for his gun, when he was disturbed by a knock on the door. Police knuckles? He looked through the Judas eye and beheld, sinisterly distorted, two faces who, unless the police had become consummate masters of disguise, were patently not enforcers of the law. He asked them who they were and was told that they wished to consult him professionally and urgently. A consultation was £25, variable: Holmes opened the door.

One of the visitors was an angular young man with long dank hair who wore a punished flying-jacket and white silk scarf and sported a glass bead in the lobe of one ear; his companion whose head bulged with brains wore spectacles that twinkled as brightly as a cut-glass decanter. Holmes knew instinctively that their overriding preoccupation was not honesty and warmed to them.

"A wet, gentlemen?" He pointed at the bottle of bourbon and turned down the volume of the television, silencing Marlowe's gun. They accepted readily and Holmes, who tended to mix windy rhetoric with underworld jargon, said: "Before we go any further – and I tell this to all my clients – I must

251

inform you that time is money and that I shall charge a fee for whatever ensues."

"All right by me, squire," said the angular young man, settling himself in an armchair and crossing his leg.

"How much?" asked his companion, sitting at the table beside the residue of Holmes's TV supper.

Never address yourself to the client who queries fees. Holmes turned to the younger man who was swinging one leg with metronomic regularity. "Out of hours, at home, a modest £50."

"Twenty-five," said the spectacles.

"Then I'm afraid we shall only be wasting each other's time. I bid you good-evening, gentlemen."

They both stood up and Holmes said: "Thirty?"

They sat down again and the young man who claimed unconvincingly that his name was Prince — hadn't there been a notorious burglar of that name? — explained their mission with staccato diction that the solicitor found confusing. As far as he could make out a friend — for friend read accomplice — had been caught bang to rights with a haul of stolen antiques. He had spent the weekend at the police station and was due to appear at South Western Magistrates' Court in the morning.

"So you want him sprung, gentlemen? Remanded on bail? Shouldn't be too difficult provided we can prove that he's not likely to abscond and provided we can come up with the cash." Fingering his monk's fringe he looked at them speculatively.

"How much?" the man named Gosling inquired again.

"Two hundred, three hundred pounds."

"We can manage that," Gosling said.

But not a miserable £50 for a consultation! S. P. Holmes couldn't abide meanness in the criminal mind. "Who gave you my name?" he inquired.

"Does it matter, squire?" Prince asked.

"A satisfied client?"

"Not in the nick if that's what you mean."

"I told Prince about you," Gosling said.

"And where did you hear about me?"

"In Wormwood Scrubs," Gosling said. "Named after the plant that grows on waste land. They make absinthe from it," he added. "Banned in France. Sends you crazy."

Holmes, wondering if Gosling had been drinking it, asked:

"And why, pray, were you in the Scrubs?"

"Fraud," Gosling said and the solicitor regarded him with renewed respect.

"So where does your, ah, friend live?"

Prince named a street in Wandsworth.

"Near Heathfield Road?"

"Where's that, cully?" Prince asked.

"The address of Wandsworth Prison," the solicitor informed him.

"Not far," Gosling said.

"Let's hope he gets no closer," said the solicitor who, after the initial bargaining, liked to create an atmosphere of conviviality. "An apartment?"

"A squat," Prince told him.

Then the chances of a remand on bail were seriously jeopardised. But if I tell them that, the solicitor reasoned, my chances of collecting the £30 and the fee for the court appearance are also in jeopardy. He stared at the small screen where Dick Powell was exchanging silent wisecracks with Claire Trevor.

"Is he in regular employment?" he asked.

"In a betting shop," Gosling said.

Could anything be worse? Holmes said: "That will go in his favour. Anyone to testify on his behalf?"

"Me," Prince said. "And Gosling."

The solicitor said nothing.

"So there you are, squire," Prince said. "See you in court."

"There are one or two other matters," the solicitor said quickly. "First of all . . ."

Gosling handed over six £5 notes. "And then, of course, the fee for the court appearance."

"How much?" Gosling asked.

"Shall we say £50?"

"No harm in saying it," Prince said.

"But you're quite prepared to pay £300 bail." A titillating thought occurred to Holmes. "This allegedly stolen property . . . Has it all been recovered? If not perhaps you would be able to look more favourably on the question of remuneration . . ."

Gosling said: "He's innocent."

"Aren't they all?"

"Straight up," Prince said.

253

"If you say so."

"So what are his chances?"

"That depends on the police," Holmes said. "How strenuously they oppose bail. What is the value of the allegedly stolen property?"

"Considerable, I should imagine," Gosling said.

Another nail in the bail . . . "If he's an upright young fellow as you make out then we stand a fair chance. Rest assured that I shall do my best."

Thrusting the £5 notes into the inside pocket of his disgraceful jacket, Holmes stood up: any further discussion would only endanger reimbursement. "You'll have the courtroom fee with you tomorrow morning, gentlemen?"

"And the bail," Gosling said. "We'll have a whip-round."

After they had gone a disturbing thought occurred to Holmes. Perhaps this young man, Renshaw, was innocent. Well, there was always a first. He turned up the volume of the television.

*   *   *

The dawn sunlight the following morning was hesitant at first, finding pink feathers in the pigeon-grey sky, but it rapidly gained lustre, burnishing the capital with copper light.

A beam of this bold light found its way through the bars of Martin's cell and turned to rust.

Anger consumed Martin as he washed and dressed and ate his substantial breakfast. Why had he been set up? Had Jack Daniels off-loaded the antiques in case of a police-raid?

Find Daniels. Prince would see to that.

Hope spurted. Soured. The Renshaw connection between the house in Hampstead and the squat was only too evident, conclusions inescapable: he and Charlie had cased the premises and tipped off the thief.

The van stopped at other police stations on its way to the courthouse. Martin's fellow passengers were two guilt-ridden drunks, a homosexual with a clawed face, a pickpocket with fluttering fingers, an old man with rheumy eyes who had smashed a plate-glass window to get a roof over his head for the weekend, a young man with a saint's features who had taken a knife to his common-law wife, a thwarted rapist who had tried to assault a young woman returning home from a judo lesson, and two youths who had held up a newsagent with pistol replicas while a policeman in plain clothes happened to be buying his Sunday newspaper.

They were all locked up beneath the courtrooms.

What were his chances of being released on bail? Reasonable, surely. No previous convictions, a good home in Liverpool . . . He had to be released to prove his innocence.

Up the steps into the dock like a hand-puppet. In front of him the stipendiary magistrate, a silver-haired dispenser of justice whose daily encounters with human frailty had divested him of emotion and invested him with laconic efficiency.

Martin looked around. Jenny was there, blowing him a kiss, and Prince saluting and Gosling transmitting words and Cuff apologising for circumstances beyond his control.

The charge was read. Holmes whom he had met briefly got to his feet in the well of the court and applied for a remand on bail. It was opposed with alacrity by the police. No fixed abode – a squat, in fact; his co-defendant, Charles Stanley Sampson, had absconded and there was reason to believe that Renshaw would do likewise. In the face of such inexorable logic Holmes sat down.

Remanded in custody.

In prison! Innocent until proved guilty . . . How do you prove your innocence in a cell?

*   *   *

The council of war, observed dispassionately by the landlord and restlessly by the alsatian, was held at a table in the lounge bar of the Codgers.

Agenda: (1) Spring Martin;
        (2) Find Charlie;
        (3) Find Daniels.

It was dusk, and rain that had followed in the wake of the sunshine tapped on the windows; so inexorable was it that you could smell its wet-dust scent above the odour of stale beer in the bar.

Said Prince, in the chair: "So Martin was set up, right? Anyone disagree?"

No one did. Neither Jenny who had tried in vain to contact

255

Eleanor the previous evening nor Gosling nor Cuff nor Hood nor the anarchist.

"By whom? By Jack Daniels, natch. Agreed?"

No dissent.

"So you," to Cuff, "put out feelers to find him. Right?"

Cuff nodded meekly.

"Aided and abetted by Gosling and me. I'll take the East End. You," to Cuff, "sniff out the squats, b and bs etcetera. You," to Gosling, "look up some of your old acquaintances when you were a guest of Her Majesty."

Prince wagged one finger at the landlord who was polishing a glass with distaste. "Another round, squire. On Hood."

Hood, who had endorsed and cashed his cheque from Mills and Boon, nodded agreeably. On a pad in front of him he had written: *Lovers parted by cruel injustice. Hero in gaol.*

"It would help," continued Prince, "if we knew why he was framed. Why they were framed," he corrected himself. "Any theories?"

No one had.

Prince said: "His uncle Jack. Bit of a villain, Jenny?"

"Bit of a character, too."

"Martin must have been the prime target," Prince said. "Why would anyone want to nobble Charlie?"

"A victim of circumstance," said Hood, scribbling. "He was observed at the scene of the crime and therefore he had to be involved."

"So you," to Hood, "suss out Dean Street."

"The law will have sussed it out," the anarchist observed.

"So you do the job properly." Prince poured soda into the vodka the landlord had placed in front of him. "The problem is Brixton."

"Why Brixton?" Hood asked.

"Got a home there somewhere. But we'd all be suspect in the area where he must have lived. What we need is a black connection."

Silence. Tyres hissed on the road outside.

"You," Prince said turning to Jenny, "chat up your legal beagle. Holmes is useless. Should have sussed him out. Need her in court to spring Martin."

"Except," Jenny said, "that she has to be briefed by a solicitor."

"Holmes?" Cuff suggested. "Can't do any harm."

"Why not?" Prince said. "Elementary, my dear Cuff."

Cuff blinked happily.

"Any questions?"

"What about Mad Bull?" Jenny said.

"Tonight. Visiting hours. You," pointing at the anarchist. "But don't let Jesus Christ go: patients would think they were dead."

It was left to the anarchist, incited by the perversity that accompanied him even in his dreams, to voice the unspeakable.

"Haven't we ignored one possibility?" he asked.

"What's that, cully?" Prince asked.

"That they're guilty?"

CHAPTER 27

———◆◆———

He ran all night. Even when he was resting, sleeping even, or drinking from ponds and small rivers, he was running. South towards the sea and green hills like cushions that he had visited once when time began – played football on the brow of a steep hill with countryside unrolled beneath and diamonds of frost nesting in the grass and the twigs of trees sheathed in ice.

He ran through suburbs, Tooting and Norbury and Waddon. Past sealed shops and lives locked up in small houses. Then bigger houses where, in the bedrooms, thoughts were chasing each other into dreams. Some people found dreams bewildering: Charlie could never understand why: Man invented time and when the bonds were severed thoughts ran free. Charlie understood dreams.

Purley, Coulsdon ... bright stars sent messages and the moon looked on and the green cushions were closer.

He stopped beside a friendly house. He saw his breath smoking. A policeman said: "Where are you going at this time of night, son?"

"Training," Charlie said.

"This late?"

"Fewer people about," Charlie said, arranging his words with care.

"Suppose you're right. Why doesn't everyone jog at night?"

"Might bump into each other," Charlie said, concentrating.

The policeman laughed. "Bit of a wag, are we?"

"Have to go," Charlie said. He patted his chest with the flat of one hand. "Rhythm," he said, and was proud of the answer.

"Mind if I have your name, son?"

"Charlie," Charlie said.

"Chaplin?"

"Brown," Charlie said.

"You're joking, of course."

Shaking his head, patting his chest again, he set off. At the end of the road he turned. The policeman was watching him. He waved. The policeman waved back.

He could smell the countryside now. Blossom and grass pure in the night air.

Ahead the swooping lights of a motorway. He found a road that dived beneath it. A signpost pointing to East Grinstead.

There was an ache in his chest like a sharp stone, so he looked for shelter.

He noticed a big house, lights being snuffed out. He waited behind a hedge. Soon the house was full of liberated dreams.

He opened the gate, paused, and made his way through the moonlight to the garage. The back of a Land Rover and the nose of an old saloon protruded through the open door.

The garage smelled comfortably of petrol. Behind the saloon which reminded him of a duchess he found a heap of sacking.

Inside the house a clock chimed three.

He curled up on the sacking, closed his eyes and waited for his dreams to cut loose.

*   *   *

In his bedroom Danny stared solemnly at the hypodermic. Then with nail-bitten fingers he ripped off the transparent plastic wrapping. The syringe lay warm on the palm of his hand. With his free hand he picked up the phial of heroin dissolved in tap-water. A nerve leaped beneath one eye. Just thrust a needle direct into a vein and even though he had never tried shooting up, only inhaling, he could imagine the joyful peace as the smack coursed up his arm into his mind. And then the withdrawal as the experts who had never been inadequate liked to call it. But they didn't even understand it. Cold turkey, all that shit. Withdrawal was knowing that peace was being taken from you and until the adequates knocked that one on the head there would always be skagheads. Screaming and vomiting and dying . . . and they talked about loss of pride! Who gives a fuck about pride when all you want is a crank? Danny placed the phial on

259

the table scarred with cigarette burns beside the mattress. Then he picked up a needle packaged in toughened paper. Took it out and tested the point of the needle with his thumb. He remembered threading sewing needles for his mother. He fitted the needle onto the syringe, dipped the needle into the phial. He held the syringe up and gazed at it, movie doctor about to inject a patient. "Swab, nurse." Still holding the loaded syringe in one hand he pulled at the silk of his beard with the other. Tears stung his eyes. He blinked them away. There were in London many organisations who would help you in a crisis situation like this. But all I want is Charlie. He stuck the tip of the needle into the inky line of a vein.

*   *   *

"Who are you?"

The voice penetrated his eyelids; he allowed them to open.

She wore red tights, white, fur-lined boots, a blue denim skirt and a navy coat with a hood that rested on her shoulders. She was about five years old.

He said: "My name's Charlie," but he knew the words had emerged in disorder — it was too soon after sleep to try and discipline them and his dreams had not yet retired.

"You speak funnily," she said. Her eyes were brown and wide, dark hair as yet uncombed and she was missing a tooth.

"I know," Charlie said.

"And you're black."

"I know," Charlie said. He smiled at her. He looked around the garage. There was a cricket bat in the corner and, on a table, a tray of sprouting potatoes, and, on a ledge above his head, three decayed pumpkins.

"You've got very white teeth."

"Clean them," he managed.

From outside a woman's voice. "Kathy, where are you?"

"She's not angry," Kathy assured Charlie.

"That's good."

"Kathy!"

The woman was framed in the doorway. She saw Kathy first. "So there you are. What on earth . . ." Then Charlie. Hand to her mouth.

Charlie, standing up, concentrated. "Sorry," he said. "Cold,

260

tired . . ." He pointed at the heap of sacking. He hoped she wouldn't scream.

The woman's hand dropped from her mouth. She looked as though she were dressed for the allotment — green rubber boots and a coat like her daughter's — but she was still beautiful, tall with Kathy's eyes and fair hair that shone in the early light.

Her thoughts reached Charlie and there wasn't a scream in them.

She said: "You still look tired."

"I like him," Kathy said. "He's black."

"He's that all right," the woman said.

And she smiled.

Charlie opened his mouth to speak but no words came out; that sometimes happened.

Kathy said: "Would you like some Alpen?"

Her mother said: "You can even have a second Alpen. Sorry, family joke."

Kathy's father emerged from behind her mother; he was gingery with a rugby forward's face and a shot-gun loose in one hand.

He said: "You'd better tell us . . ." but Kathy's mother said: "Don't worry, Tom, he's okay. You must be cold," she said to Charlie.

"Okay," Charlie said.

"Come on then. Into the kitchen."

Kathy said: "You can have my Alpen."

Charlie, nodding, not sure about her father's thoughts, followed them into the house which was surrounded by a muddy garden and stables from which munching horses regarded them patiently. Behind the house in a chopped-up field stood a circle of show-jumps.

The kitchen was a mess but big enough to accommodate it. Bacon sizzled in a black frying pan.

Kathy's mother said: "I'm sure you would prefer that."

Hunger leaped in Charlie's stomach.

"Not . . . too . . . much . . . trouble?"

"Of course not. Where do you live, Charlie?" turning the rashers of bacon with a scoop with a charred handle.

Kathy said: "Charlie lives in Africa, don't you, Charlie?"

"Big place," Charlie said.

He was consumed with hunger.

261

Kathy's mother broke some eggs and spilled them into the pan. They spat at her.

"Coffee, Charlie?" she asked.

Tea, really, but coffee would do.

Abruptly he wondered: "Where is Martin having breakfast?" And: "How's Danny?"

The antiques . . . Where had they come from? "No justice," the man in the terrace house had said long ago. "Not if you're black."

What difference could that make?

Where had the antiques come from?

They sat at the kitchen table. There was a bowl of shrivelled apples and bruised bananas upon it. The smell of coffee joined the crispy scent of the bacon.

Charlie winked at Kathy who winked back elaborately.

He ate warm bread.

"So where have you come from?" Kathy's father asked.

"London," Charlie said.

"Where are you heading for?" His thoughts weren't unkind but they were dry with disbelief. Like autumn leaves that had lingered into winter.

Charlie said: "South."

Knives and forks scraping on plates.

"To Africa?" Kathy asked.

"South," Charlie told her.

"Where did you live," her father asked, "before you decided to run south?"

Too many questions. Charlie stuffed his mouth with food.

"He lived in a house," Kathy said. "Didn't you, Charlie?"

"A big house," he said.

"A big house?" her father asked. "Lots of corridors, big rooms with lots of beds in them?"

Charlie rolled some bread into a pellet.

Kathy's father said: "Excuse me a minute, I've got to call the vet."

Charlie followed his thoughts out of the kitchen into another room that had not yet awoken from the night.

Heard the dialling.

The whispered voice.

And he was on his feet, bowing, still eating, winking at Kathy, spreading his hands, thanking.

262

"Africa," he said to Kathy.

And he was running, running.

*   *   *

"Don't."

Danny, thumb resting on the plunger of the hypodermic, looked up. Jesus Christ stood in the doorway of the bedroom.

"I must," Danny said.

Jesus Christ stretched out his hand. "Pull the thorn out of your flesh and hand it to me."

"You don't understand."

"I understand," Jesus Christ said. He took a step forward.

Danny shook his head. The nerve leapt beneath his eye. "How can you?"

"Blessed is the man that endureth temptation: for when he is tried, he shall receive the crown of life."

"Do you think I'm inadequate?"

"We're all inadequate; we wouldn't be on this earth if we weren't."

"You?"

"I most of all." His voice was serene. He touched Danny's bared arm.

Danny pulled out the needle.

Jesus Christ pressed the plunger and a thin jet of poison sprang across the room.

He looked at the needle and said: "There was given to me a thorn in the flesh, the messenger of Satan to buffet me."

Dark blood trickled down Danny's arm.

CHAPTER 28

———— ◆◆ ————

Wednesday. Five days until Martin's next court appearance. The atmosphere in the squat was one of urgent endeavour and apprehension generated by the imminent expulsion of the occupants.

"Nothing more we can do?" Prince asked over breakfast two days after Martin had been taken to the remand wing of Brixton prison.

"Nothing," said Gosling, feeding Hoover a piece of fried bread. "We've had a good innings. Longer than I expected thanks to Hood."

Hood, plotting amours in an exercise book, eyes wet with vicarious ardour, looked up.

"You made Buck House famous," Gosling explained. "Without you we wouldn't have had the coverage when Kester and his toughs paid us a visit."

Hood permitted himself a wan, literary smile before returning to romantic liaisons.

"But now," Gosling elaborated, "they've got the law behind them. A court order, eviction backed by the police."

"Is there any point in telling the Press?" Prince asked.

"Not really. Not this time. It's legal and general."

Gosling spoke distractedly: his life in which words had increasingly replaced impressions, imparting a sense of detachment, had suddenly acquired complications outside lexical interpretation. The girl had been waiting for him on his return from the magistrates' court. Pregnant. Not that he minded that. She listened quietly to him, smiling gently, and he could imagine her with her hands crossed across her swollen belly

264

tasting his words as though they were medicinal lozenges. What agitated him – although Prince had enthused about maternity benefits – was the prospect of a nomadic pregnancy. This could be solved by an offer from a daily newspaper to join their crossword team on a trial basis. The pay wasn't spectacular but, augmented by the DHSS, it would be enough to rent a flat. But did he want one? To be tied once and for all to meters, gas and electricity, prowling landlords and tinned salmon on Saturday evenings? Does a gypsy truly want to leave his caravan?

Disturbed, words fluttering away from him, moths unnetted, unpinned, Gosling kissed the girl who smiled at him gently from her privacy, and left the squat to find old comrades, with whom he had shared Her Majesty's hospitality.

Benny Marks, fence. But he didn't creep round a second-hand jeweller's, loupe screwed in one eye, cheating thieves before shopping them to the police. Benny Marks was one of the new breed of crooks. Businessman – scrap-metal; office equipped with computers and Fax, honesty in his dishonesty which was handling stolen bullion. Savile Row suits, spectacles that changed hue in the sunlight, features shared by brutality and joviality.

In Marks's East End office Gosling, who before being moved to an open prison had shared a cell with him in Brixton, broached the subject of Jack Daniels.

"Small time tea-leaf," Marks said. "Why?"

"I might be able to put some business his way."

Marks clasped his big hands; two gold rings glowed from the church made by his fingers. "Do me a favour, Gos, no porkies, right?"

"I'm not lying," Gosling said.

"You was never a real villain, Gos. Why do you want Daniels."

"He's set up a friend of mine. A kid."

"Has he now. And why would he do a thing like that?"

"I wish I knew," Gosling said.

"How old's this kid?"

"Nineteen," Gosling said.

"Kid? They're granny-bashing at fourteen these days."

"And a black," Gosling told him. "Got problems."

"Problems?"

"Confused."

"A black nutter and a kid of nineteen stitched up by a Div. Four thief . . . You can do better than that, Gos."

"Just tell me where I can find him," Gosling said.

"Haven't taken to snitching, have we?"

"You know me better than that."

"Do I?" Marks considered the gold rings on his fingers. "What's the name of the kid?"

"Renshaw," Gosling said.

"Good name. Now there's a real tea-leaf for you, Jack Renshaw."

"His uncle," Gosling said.

"Stroll on! Why come to me if he's Jack Renshaw's nephew?"

"He doesn't want family involved."

"Doesn't want mummy and daddy to know he's in the nick?"

"That's right," Gosling said.

"My old man was in the nick the day I was born."

"So, can you help?"

"Doubtful, Gos. Don't want any aggro from Jack Renshaw. Put a lot of business my way, has Jack."

"Helping his nephew? He'd be grateful."

"Bad news, Gos, meddling in family affairs. And stop looking at me like that."

"Like what?"

"Straight in the eyes. Never trust anyone who looks you straight in the eyes. One of life's rules." He stood up. "Take my advice, Gos. Keep out of it. Now on your bike – I've got a golden opportunity to attend to."

The only other possibility was Rex Halliwell. The royal implication of the name had indelibly stamped Halliwell: he was tall and languid, invariably pink from a bath and he usually wore an Old Etonian tie although when confronted by an Old Etonian he would explain that black striped with blue was, in fact, the colours of the Thames Valley Harriers.

Gosling found him drinking a pink gin in the Grenadier, in Belgravia, a tavern perversely favoured by Halliwell because it is said to be haunted by the ghost of a Grenadier who had died following a flogging for cheating at cards, a pastime at which Halliwell excelled.

Gosling, observed without enthusiasm by Halliwell, ordered

himself a half-pint of bitter from a barman wearing a white mess jacket.

Halliwell beckoned him out of the barman's earshot. "What the hell are you doing here?" he asked. "I'm known here."

"You were known at Pentonville, too," Gosling said.

Halliwell had gained credence as a prison visitor and acted as a courier for those unable to follow their professions in jail.

"For God's sake!" Halliwell glanced around nervously but it was relatively early in the morning and there were few drinkers in the bar. "What do you want?"

"Brigade of Guards today?" Gosling said, pointing at the stripes on Halliwell's tie. "Left your wallet at home as well?"

"Whatever you want," Halliwell said, "get on with it – I've got a business appointment here in ten minutes."

"Rich widow?"

"A curate as a matter of fact."

"Not after the organ fund, are we?"

Halliwell sipped his gin. "Just tell me what you want."

"Jack Daniels," Gosling said.

"The thief?"

Gosling nodded.

"What do you want him for? He's a petty criminal."

"Not like a con-man?"

"For Christ's sake keep your voice down."

"All you need know," Gosling said, "is that I want to find him."

"No idea, old man," relaxing. "Not the type I mix with." Halliwell glanced ostentatiously at his wristwatch, adjusted his tie, smoothed his wavy hair that was greying artificially at the temples.

"You can find out. A silver-tongued rogue. Isn't that the platitude of the judiciary?"

"Jesus wept!" Halliwell exclaimed. "Do you want a drink?"

"A rare pleasure," Gosling said. "A pint please. Sure you've got your wallet with you?"

Halliwell produced a £10 note from his inside pocket like a card-sharp who had palmed a card.

Gosling drank deeply. "So," he said, "you'll do it?"

"Outside my line of duty, old man."

"When were you in the Guards?" Gosling asked loudly.

"For God's sake . . ."

267

The barman looked up.

"I expect the curate would like to know as well."

"You shit," Halliwell said.

"Possibly of Germanic origin. 'Scitan', to defecate."

"I'll make inquiries," Halliwell said. And, smiling, he said softly: "Now piss off."

"Nineteen seventy was it? My, how time flies." Gosling drained his beer and walked out of the pub.

In Buck House, Wandsworth, that evening progress reports were submitted.

Penitently Cuff confessed that he hadn't had any luck at the squats and b and bs. Neither had Prince in the East End, nor Hood at Dean Street. Jenny said she was seeing Eleanor Lubin the following day, Gosling said he would try and find a black thief to help them in Brixton.

They were interrupted by the anarchist who came in through the kitchen door. He looked uncharacteristically subdued.

"So," Prince said, "how's Mad Bull?"

The anarchist sat down at the table. "He's dead," he said.

Later Prince said to Jenny: "Maybe it was better that way. He was finished anyway."

"Why?" Jenny asked.

"He won," Prince said.

*   *   *

Thursday. Rising early, Jenny caught a bus to Clapham Junction and a train to Twickenham where Walter Renshaw's offices were situated.

Sitting in a corner of the carriage she watched the suburbs twirling past, small, embroidered gardens rain-fresh, flowering trees snowy with blossoms. She wanted to wander through modest streets that smelled of privet; knock on doors; pluck out injustices buried in acceptance and take them to court. Eleanor Lubin and Andrew had done that for her.

Walter Renshaw's accountancy offices, housed in a converted church hall, were near the rugby ground. Computers flickered where pens had once scratched but they did nothing to dispel the atmosphere of morose application.

Walter was sitting at his desk contemplating his first cup of weak tea when Jenny entered his office. He stood up, offered her a cold hand, and, sitting down again and regarding her speculatively through rimless spectacles, said: "So young Martin's in some sort of trouble, is he," in a voice that implied that he had expected no less.

Briskly, Jenny explained.

Walter listened intently, occasionally pursing his lips in disbelief but not — or so it seemed to Jenny — at the appropriate moments. On the wall behind him were the framed words FOR THE LORD IS FULL OF COMPASSION AND MERCY. A faint odour of mothballs reached Jenny from Walter's suit.

When she had finished he said: "Do you go to church, Jenny?"

"Sometimes," she said. "Why?"

Frowning, he unravelled a paper-clip. "That is where all answers lie," he said.

"Not if you're in a cell in Brixton prison."

"I advised Martin to worship more often."

"At the moment," Jenny said, "he needs more than spiritual help."

A timid girl came in with a cup of tea for Jenny.

When she had gone Walter, returning to secular considerations, said: "Financial?"

"Not entirely. Martin needs a permanent — and respectable — address if he's going to get bail."

Walter stood up and walked to the window where he stood in profile gazing at the blue sky hung with fragments of white cloud over the rugby ground stands.

Finally he said: "I only wish we had the room."

"He doesn't have to stay with you."

"But that," Walter said, "would be an untruth."

"He could sleep on a couch," Jenny said.

"What about Uncle Jack?"

"He's a crook," Jenny said.

"That's no way to talk . . ."

"Isn't he?"

"Black Jack and Lucky Jim," said Walter.

"And Harry?"

"Happy Harry. We always knew he'd go places."

"Martin reckons you've done all right. And Jack, of course. It's Martin's father who seems to have missed out."

Walter sat down and attacked another paper-clip. Staring at

269

it intently, he said: "I understand that you have been making some inquiries."

"About what?"

"A Mr. William Grey."

Who had told him. The Graftons? The estate agent? Or had she spoken on the telephone to the right Grey without realising it?

"R.I.P.," Walter said. "The past, it's hallowed ground. Leave it undisturbed."

The phone jarred the silence that had settled between them. Walter answered it curtly. "Not now. I told you, not in office hours." He replaced the receiver and joined the two mutilated paper-clips into a Christmas cracker puzzle.

"The past," Jenny said, "is the present."

He smiled forgivingly. "I have a suggestion to make."

What Walter proposed was a fixed abode for Martin in exchange for a pledge that he would drop his inquiries.

And I, Jenny thought, am now in the driving seat.

She considered the proposition. So Martin had been right: there was a skeleton in the cupboard and she had made it rattle.

"So what do you think?" he asked.

"Interesting," she told him.

"Is that all? I thought you wanted to get Martin out of prison."

"And I thought you hadn't got any room."

"That's irrelevant – he'll have an address."

"You'll have to come to court," said Jenny who had telephoned Eleanor for advice before setting out for Twickenham. "And take the oath. I swear by Almighty God . . ."

"If Martin's innocent then he should be given the opportunity to prove his innocence. But first he'll have to promise to abandon his investigation."

Jenny thought: But do I?

"You're absolutely sure he's innocent?"

"Absolutely." But why had anyone bothered to frame him? And why had Charlie wanted to come to Hampstead? Ashamed, she said: "No doubt about it."

"What was he doing in Harry's house?"

"I invited him there."

"While Harry was on holiday?"

"That was why I invited him."

"The case against Martin," Walter remarked, holding up the paper-clips, one dangling from the other, "doesn't appear too favourable. And what about the black man? Why did he run away?"

"Because he was frightened."

"If he was innocent?"

"Because he was innocent," Jenny said. "And confused . . ."

"Confused?"

"His thoughts overtake his words."

"Ah."

The "ah" irritated Jenny more than anything Walter had so far uttered. She said: "Supposing Jesus was black, would you still worship him?"

"I worship God," Walter said.

"Christianity . . . Doesn't that imply Christ?"

"We seem to be diverging from the point."

"We'll need bail money."

"We?"

"Martin's friends."

Prince reckoned that the occupants of the squat could get the money together. Maybe £300 or so. But why not squeeze Walter now that he wanted a deal?

"Can't they raise it?"

Jenny pointed at the framed words on the wall. "Compassion and Mercy?"

"Are you by any chance trying to blackmail me?"

"Yes," Jenny said.

"It's a good thing I've got a sense of humour." He tossed the mangled paper-clips into the wastepaper basket. "Supposing Martin absconds like the black?"

"Then you lose your money," Jenny said. "But he won't," she added. "And one other thing . . ."

Walter sighed.

"Martin doesn't want his parents to know. So you must promise not to tell them."

"I promise."

Jenny said: "We seem to understand each other better than when I came in."

Walter shrugged. "All in a good cause," he said.

"You'll be there on Monday, in court?"

"I'll be there."

"With your cheque-book?"

"Have you ever heard of over-kill, young lady?"

The phone rang. Walter picked up the receiver. A woman's voice. Walter: "I thought I told you . . ." He looked up. Waved his hand, a brush-stroke of his fingers, dismissing a fellow conspirator.

It was still only 10.30. Jenny caught a train to Waterloo and by midday was sitting beside the lake in St. James's Park feeding the ducks with Eleanor Lubin.

The scene reminded Jenny of the garden on the banks of the Thames. Picnickers and lovers entwined on the grass, pelicans and ducks and geese on the mossy waters.

Eleanor, sitting upright, hands clasped round green-skirted knees, told her there was a moderate-to-good chance that Martin might be released on bail. It all depended on the magistrate and the impression imparted by Uncle Walter. "Is he likely to renege?" she asked.

Jenny didn't think so.

"Then all we need is a solicitor to brief me."

Jenny told her about S. P. Holmes.

"He's a rogue," Eleanor said. "But I don't suppose it matters. He won't be performing. If he was Martin would be sent to the Tower."

She tore a corner off a corned-beef sandwich and threw it to a cruising duck. She looked highly professional today; spectacles – possibly plain glass – hair pinned in a bun.

She said: "He is innocent, isn't he?"

"Of course."

"But you don't really know . . . You see I have to believe in his innocence. If I don't and I enter a plea of not guilty then I am an enemy of our legislative system and an enemy of myself."

"I understand that," Jenny told her. Close-by a boy and a girl lay down and began to kiss.

"Have you seen him since he was arrested?"

"Only in court."

"Then how do you know he's innocent?"

"I know," Jenny said.

"But it is possible that he could have cased the joint?"

"It's possible."

"And offered to hide the stolen property?"

"My lord, I protest. Is my learned friend prosecuting or

272

defending?"

"Trying to ascertain the truth, m'lud."

The girl on the grass wiped her lips with a tissue and began to eat an apple with quick, snapping bites while the boy lit a cigarette and, lying on his back, blew wavering smoke-rings.

Eleanor, brushing crumbs from her skirt, said: "One last question. The truth and nothing but the truth."

"Shoot," Jenny said.

"Have you ever doubted Martin's innocence?"

"You've already asked me that."

"I asked you if he was innocent."

"You don't know Martin."

"Would the witness please answer the question."

Reluctantly, Jenny considered it. Of course there was always an element of doubt. She was immediately assailed by guilt. But I do *know* that he's innocent.

She said: "Of course I've doubted."

"Good," Eleanor said, standing up and throwing a last morsel of soggy bread to a duck, "then I'll take the case. Now let's see Mr. S. P. Holmes."

*　　*　　*

Friday. In Brixton prison a black named Eliezer Mundy shared his theories about the unrest in the country with his cell-mate, Martin Renshaw.

Mundy had been remanded in custody — wrongly, he insisted — on charges of forgery, to wit the manufacture at a small plastics factory of credit cards copied from discarded counterfoils. Mundy readily admitted an earler predilection for currency, specialising in the acquisition of foreign coins of the same weight and size as the £1 which, when inserted in certain machines, would yield more change than they were worth, but claimed that he had gone straight since opening a pirate radio station in a terrace house less than a mile from the jail.

He was a small and muscular man with a mournful moustache that belied his physical and verbal energy. Exercising in a corner of the cell he told Martin, who was lying on his bunk staring at the ceiling, that the unrest was inevitable.

"You see, man, it's really ironic. All of a sudden Britain is said to be on the road to recovery and what happens? The

273

beneficiaries of this great providence start making a fuss, that's what. *This royal throne of kings, this sceptre'd isle, This earth of majesty, this seat of Mars, This other Eden, demi-paradise* . . . Maybe," Munday said, "Shakespeare never saw Brixton on a wet Sunday afternoon."

"Why don't you go back to Guyana?"

"Good question. Because I was born here. Does that surprise you? Or do you think I escaped from a plantation and stowed away on a banana boat?"

Mundy, breathing hard, although whether through physical effort or indignation Martin couldn't tell, sprang to his feet and sat on the edge of his bunk, sweat streaming down his cheeks and lodging in his gloomy moustache.

Martin was grateful for Eliezer Mundy: he stoked the anger that had replaced fear. Why am I in prison when I'm innocent? Being treated as guilty until proved innocent? True there were privileges not enjoyed by convicted prisoners – he could wear his own clothes! – but he was still behind bars, still mixing with criminals.

Jenny's friend, Eleanor Lubin, thought he had a fifty-fifty chance of being released on bail. Evens! Just because I live in a squat in a city where thousands are homeless. Does that mean that anyone wrongly accused of a crime who has no permanent address goes to prison?

Listening to Mundy, whose nourishment was wrath, Martin planned his campaign, his revenge. The key was Jack Daniels. Find him but first find Charlie. Who else apart from Danny and myself understands him? We are a trinity and without us he is doomed.

Charlie believed that he had once lived in Brixton. But, according to Jenny when she had visited the prison, it was impossible for a white to make inquiries in a black ghetto. Martin gazed at Mundy towelling the sweat from his face.

What were his chances of being acquitted? Fair to middling, Mundy said. Would he continue broadcasting from his pirate station? "Bet your ass," Mundy said. And it was then that it occurred to Martin that this pirate might be able to find Charlie.

*　　　*　　　*

Sunday. The choice of day was deliberate, a brilliancy schemed

274

by Kester, project consultant and storm-trooper of the development company. Who would expect bailiffs on the morning of the Christian Sabbath when in church, bed or allotment working men paused from the travail of the weekday? Certainly not the depleted occupants of Buck House – Gosling dozing beside his girl, sensing with his finger-tips the life within her belly; Cuff in a waking dream in which it was he who died in a car accident and bequeathed his blood-stained suit to another; the anarchist, staring into a mottled mirror, speculating on the impact of a beardless revolutionary; Jesus Christ at prayer at the foot of his bed; Hood, already scribbling – for the Muse takes no heed of calendar days – and debating whether to consummate the liaison of a physician and a receptionist with heart-breaking legs; Frank the Bodger, staring through his window into childhood and damming a country stream and telling his father that one day he would build a dam across the Nile and hearing his laughter; Danny, limbs twitching in pursuit of the dragon, pacing Charlie in the last strides of the 800 metres; Prince, in the kitchen listening to birdsong, retreating briefly into the unscheming past into which no one but himself was admitted; Jenny addressing a jury.

The police appeared at 7.55, bored but implacable in the burgeoning sunlight. Hoover barked inside the house and Prince came to the door as the bailiffs arrived with the court order. He accepted it amiably and told them to wait while the *tenants* got their possessions together. Would the bailiffs care for some tea? They drank from chipped mugs in the kitchen while, one by one, carrying battered suitcases and sleeping bags, the occupants came down the stairs. Prince counted them and said to the bailiffs, middle-aged, self-effacing men in Sunday suits: "All present and correct." Danny, seeing the police through the open front door, retreated upstairs unseen by Prince.

Preceded by Hoover, barking excitedly and peeing with abandon, they filed past the weeping willow onto the road where they stood in a huddle like refugees of war. Kester was there, too, sitting at the wheel of a Land Rover. He leaned out and told them that the house would be demolished tomorrow. Pointing at a uniformed policeman who had taken up position outside the front door, he said: "So don't try and come back: find someone else's property to vandalise."

275

Prince, tossing one end of his white silk scarf round his neck, said: "Don't worry, cully, we have," and, taking a notebook from the pocket of his flying-jacket, he read out an address in The Drive, Banstead, Surrey, a rural outpost of London. He winked elaborately at the refugees, who knew it was Kester's home.

Then Prince stood to attention and saluted the old grey house, once a bastion of Victorian family virtues, ultimately a home for the homeless, and led his band down the street, past the Codgers, into the nomadic and uncertain future. And no one noticed that Danny was not among them.

CHAPTER 29

———◆◆◆———

The silver-haired magistrate greeted Eleanor Lubin like an old but respected adversary, a welcome diversion from the predictable litany that was his daily fare.

She for her part respected his professionalism by keeping her plea lucid and brief: Martin's age and innocence and his willingness to stay at a fixed abode with his uncle, a lay preacher, who was also willing to put up bail.

The magistrate, head cocked to one side, listened attentively but nevertheless managing to convey the impression that, although he was impressed by Eleanor's condensed eloquence, he was unimpressed by its substance.

When she had finished he said: "Isn't it a fact that Renshaw's co-defendant has absconded?"

Eleanor agreed – did not admit – that this was indeed so.

"So it wouldn't be wholly illogical to suppose that this young man might do the same?"

Eleanor submitted respectfully that, although it might not be wholly illogical, it would indisputably be unfair. "Why should one man be judged by the actions of another?"

"I think, Miss Lubin, that you are treading a thin divide between moral indignation and judicial interpretation."

"I think, your honour, that this court should create a precedent and erase that demarcation line from the statute book."

The magistrate almost smiled.

Five minutes later Martin was released on £250 bail.

*   *   *

As he walked into the sunlight accompanied by Walter Renshaw, illumined by benefaction, and reluctantly gave his word not to ask any more questions about the uncles, half a dozen men wearing orange hard hats began the destruction of Buck House. They came with a Hymac, Kango pneumatic drills for the foundations, pick-axes, sledge-hammers, steel cables and a bulldozer but, although their intent was brutal, they worked with the delicacy of masons, preserving the materials which the Victorian builders had so stolidly put together.

First the tall chimneys through which smoke had once climbed to compound the fogs; then the grey slates quarried from distant moorland; then, with reverence, the lead beneath which they rolled back like arthritic carpets.

In his room Danny lay at peace. Having seen the police, knowing that they recognised a skaghead when they saw one, believing that they might confiscate his dope and arrest him, he had retreated upstairs, placed heroin on a strip of aluminum foil and heated it with the stump of a candle. He had watched the powder melt into a shining globule of fluid and hungrily inhaled the fumes. His anxieties had dissolved in a languor of gently shifting dimensions. This morning he had repeated the process submerging into even deeper tranquillity.

Two floors above him the demolition squad prised away the slats and plaster of attic ceilings where maids, house-, kitchen-, pantry- and parlour-, had once lived, often beckoned to sleep by the ancestor of Danny's poison, opium mixed with alcohol and masquerading under the name laudanum which was believed to cure anything from colds to colic. Who would suspect that Battley's Sedative Solution contained sherry and opium?

Into the little rooms gawped the spoilers as long-preserved secrets of love and domestic ambition withered beneath them. Then, layer by layer, they stripped away the wallpaper – pink roses and sprigs of lavender and a stratum of cherubs – to reach with their picks the old bricks that would soon become the bulwarks of period cottages.

When they came upon some piece of construction that had no place in the materialistic future, either too ravaged or too obdurate, they fastened steel cable around it, attaching the free end to the bulldozer. The bulldozer backed away and down

278

came the useless appendage with a satisfying rumble and thump.

Hearing this sound faintly from the depths of his repose Danny fancied that he was having a wisdom tooth removed. But the extraction caused no pain and he smiled sweetly.

*   *   *

The former occupants of Buck House who had slept in various locations – Jenny in Eleanor Lubin's home – celebrated Martin's release in the Codgers while Cuff continued to forage for alternative accommodation. There was among the company a minority who fancied that they detected in the landlord's taciturn features relief that, although they had been evicted, they had returned to their old hostelry; the majority suggested that, if this were true, he might break the habit of a lifetime and buy a round of drinks; it was a telling point and the minority conceded defeat.

Jenny sat next to Martin, squeezing his arm, occasionally rubbing her cheek against his. Gosling and the anarchist and Hood, smiling at the course of true love, and Frank the Bodger sat on the opposite side of an unlit, tooth-stumped gas-fire; Prince sat between them beside Gosling's girl; Jesus Christ sat a little distance away in a corner gazing with infinite sadness in the direction of Calvary. The air smelled of Mansion Polish.

"So," Prince said, "we've still got to find Jack Daniels."

"First Charlie," Martin said, and he told them about Eliezer Mundy, also released that morning, who knew his ghetto.

In the distance they heard the crump of falling masonry.

"There goes my bedroom," Gosling said.

"Poor old Bull," Martin said, sipping his beer. "You become more aware of missing faces when you've been away. Charlie, Jack Daniels . . ."

"Christ!" Prince leaped to his feet, barged through the swing doors and, closely pursued by Hoover, ran towards the ever-diminishing pile of Buck House.

*   *   *

After the attics a nursery. The man known as Jellyhead because he suffered from headaches brought on by the excessive use of

279

gelignite stared down at it reflectively. He was in charge of the demolition team, big with tufty grey hair and a belligerent belly and he enjoyed destroying buildings, preferably with explosive – he had made videos of factory chimneys tottering and disintegrating – but in the absence of big game he was content with modest edifices such as the squat. But he was also a family man, eight children, five of them boys, all adroitly destructive, and he was strangely moved by this fledgling room with its defiant wallpaper: toy soldiers with black helmets and red jackets. How many generations of children – all boys, he felt – had grown up here and where were they now, the great-great-grandchildren and their progeny? He imagined them called to arms in two world wars, young officers leading sappers laden with explosive, and he saw them blown to pieces by enemy cannon. Shaking his head to dislodge such fancies, he dropped through the gaping space where the ceiling had been, lightly for a man of his girth, and landed beside a black, coal-burning grate. Scattered in one corner of the nursery were pages torn from a magazine. He picked up one. WIN A SUNSHINE HOLIDAY IN THE CARIBBEAN. He shrugged and let it flutter to the floor. With a hammer and chisel he removed layers of wallpaper and plaster; the bricks beneath were crumbling with damp – surprising what layered wallpaper could hold together. He tried two other walls but the brickwork was too eroded even to be advertised as "fine, weathered". He whistled down two members of the squad; they struck holes on either side of the chimney-breast, then looped steel cable around it, threading the cable through the doors of other rooms so that when the bulldozer backed away the chimney-breast would collapse, plunging through floorboards that were dangerously soggy, and take the three other walls with it into the room below.

In the room below Danny, lying on his mattress, listened to the noises above him. Rats. He felt sorry for rats, born to be exterminated.

*   *   *

The bulldozer stood in a lane behind the squat, invisible from the road, so that, when it pulled the steel cable, errant bricks and mortar would fall in the back garden.

Seeing the decapitated building shudder Prince shouted:

"There's a man in there," but there was no one in front of the house to pay any heed.

He ran desperately, bony knees flailing, white scarf streaming behind him, outstripping the rest of the pack. Hoover galloped beside him.

Through the gate, past the willow into the groaning interior of the house. Powder spilled finely from the ceiling, the walls moved gently. Up the stairs that had once helped to defeat the first onslaught of the spoilers, down the corridor to Danny's room.

The house swayed.

Prince kicked open the door of Danny's room. From the mattress Danny smiled at him angelically.

Prince grabbed his arm. "Run for it, cully, the house is falling down."

Danny's smile encompassed his face. "Don't worry, Prince," he said. "It's made of foam-rubber."

Above them the rasp and pluck of the house's bones being pulled from their sockets. The ceiling broke in the centre and bricks and plaster slid down the shards of splintered floor-boards onto Danny's bed.

Prince pulled Danny onto the floor.

"Don't fret," Danny said, as a chunk of brickwork punched another hole through the ceiling and fell onto the mattress.

Prince grasped Danny's hands and pulled him across the floor. A brick hit him on the shoulder, dust stung his eyes and grazed his throat.

As he reached the door there came from the nursery above the crack of fracturing masonry and the chimney-breast plunged through the ceiling.

Prince dragged Danny into the corridor. The walls bulged, the floor tilted, spurts of plaster fell from the ceiling.

He reached the stairs and descended them backwards. Danny's feet bounced on each step. A crump and a breath of distemper-smelling air as the corridor fell in upon itself.

The anarchist took one of Danny's legs, Martin the other.

Beneath them the foundations of a suburban dynasty shuddered and its portals, the lintel cracked, snapped behind them as they manhandled Danny, still smiling, into the garden and onto the road.

The house died in a roar of stricken masonry and a cloud of

281

dust rose towards the sky.

It wasn't what the purveyors of materials for the construction of period homes had wanted but it reminded the man known as Jellyhead, at the controls of the bulldozer, of a nuclear explosion in miniature and it gave him great pleasure.

CHAPTER 30

———◆◆◆———

Cuff, scout, called first at a newsagent's in Lambeth where the soft porn was just out of reach of small children and midgets. Ignoring the piles of morning papers, the height of each attesting to its circulation in the area, he bought a Mars Bar and two local papers and retired to a caff renowned for its bacon-and-egg sandwiches.

Sipping his tea and taking small bites from his chocolate bar, he studied the HOUSES FOR SALE columns, looking for the giveaway, "immediate occupation", indicating that the premises might be empty. There were three such ads but in each case the telephone number was familiar, all agents, none of them likely to believe that he was a serious purchaser.

Years ago he had foraged seriously for a house to buy and had settled finally for a small semi with a pattern of coloured glass above the door in Kilburn and had passed every living moment among the corpses in the funeral parlour where he worked, yearning to get home to his wife and his supper and decorating and love-making twice a week, certainly on Saturdays.

He now believed that, with some women, that old platitude of marriage, nagging, was a latent force awaiting release through their partners' humility. He had released that force although he still didn't accept that deference was weakness.

His wife had changed within the space of five years from an ardent but ambitious newly-wed to a creature not far removed from the shrew off which so many comedians fed. It seemed that, faced with his ready contrition, she could not refrain from criticism. His clothes ... his postage-stamp moustache, sub-

283

sequently removed, which *was* inclined to be wet . . . his midnight cough . . . most of all, his lack of initiative.

Paradoxically he had ultimately shown initiative: he had left home. And taken to the paths of vagrancy which some, like himself, followed to enjoy unfettered privacy, others because they perceived no alternative.

And now she was divorcing him. The prospect made him faintly uneasy, the ratchet that had permitted his freewheeling life-style removed.

Finishing his tea, he left the caff and headed for some of the rendezvous where, in fair weather, London's bedouins gathered to discuss where to pitch their tents.

He went first to Kennington Park across the A3 from the Oval cricket ground where, although it was only 10.30 am, a group of migrants were drinking cider and cooking sherry from bottles wrapped in brown-paper bags. They had becalmed faces and distant eyes and they sat on the turf where the gibbet had once stood in communal reverie.

A couple of them were very young, seventeen or so.

Cuff, apologising for the intrusion, asked if he could join them and an elderly man with the tufted eyebrows and button-blue eyes of a leader of men passed him a bottle of sherry. He wiped the neck of the bottle, took a swig and passed it back.

After a while he asked if anyone had heard of any available squats. It was possible: when one leader decided to spend the summer in the countryside his comrades sometimes followed, a self-sufficient unit often mistaken for gypsies.

One of the teenagers, a Scot with prematurely weathered features, said: "Would we be sitting here like bairns playing hooky if we did?"

And his companion, Welsh with thin white features curtained by long black hair, said: "'Ard to come by these days, boy. Tightening up, they are. Even Prince Charles evicted a couple."

The leader of men spoke sonorously. His name was Ralph; he was reputed to have been wounded in Korea and one of the fingers of his left hand was missing. "Go south to Elysian fields, young man. Strike where your presence is least expected." He massaged his depleted fingers.

Cuff thanked them and, skirting a ruminative policeman, left the park. Powdered rain was falling, as light as dew but enough to dispatch London's migrants to shelter.

284

He found three in the reference section of a public library, one asleep, the other two staring blankly at Debrett's and Pears Cyclopaedia. Cuff's whispered questions pierced the measured breathing of concentrated research.

A bespectacled librarian wearing a tweed jacket asked them to conduct their studies more quietly. He was a decent man, Cuff thought; perhaps books did that for you, preserved decency. But none of the venerable students knew of any vacant squats: Kennington and its environs was a popular area. "Up and coming," one of them confided.

Cuff, shrinking tortoise-like from the rain in his voluminous blue chalk-stripe, visited a bus terminus, a public lavatory where punished footwear could be seen beneath the doors of the cubicles, a suburban railway station where the ticket collector, thankful he was working, allowed the workless to sojourn in the decrepit, disinfectant-smelling waiting room, a wooden shelter overlooking tennis courts deserted in the sifted rain, a railway arch that smelled of fish, a patch of allotments with sheds en suite, and two churches where vagrants snored their prayers.

But no one could help; squats were jealously guarded, especially in the rain. Nor was the usual spoor – boarded windows, dangerous building warnings, SITE SCHEDULED FOR DEVELOPMENT bills – productive. So Cuff took the leader of men's advice and struck south to the richer realms of Cheam.

But house-owners had grown canny. Dogs barked, alarm-bells shrilled.

Disheartened, Cuff adjourned to the Harrow, a pub in Cheam Village – its parochial beginnings scarcely visible amid the comfortable houses of the late '30s – where he met a plasterer with powdery hands and bloodied knuckles who was staying in a boarding house in the neighbouring suburb of Sutton. Two streets away, the plasterer confided, plied with a second pint of bitter, there was a derelict school where the homeless occasionally slept.

Cuff telephoned Prince at 3 pm at the call-box 200 yards from Buck House. Prince answered and told him that Buck House was a heap of rubble. "So where are we going to reside? Number ten?" And when Cuff told him about the school he said: "Any port. Take a shufty, cully. Give me a bell in an hour."

The plasterer hadn't confided just how derelict the school was. Prefabricated, too. But any port . . . He telephoned Prince at four and at dusk the tenants of Buck House, deceased, went back to school.

*　　　*　　　*

It was raining *inside* the school, moisture in various measures falling inexorably through gaps in the roof, through broken and spouting pipes, through glassless windows. Water ran down the walls and dripped from hanging struts and bounced high in the darkness and the classrooms were wet with manufactured drizzle.

Oil lamps burned in some rooms where claims, smoky and conspiratorial, had already been staked and Prince, pursuing the beam of his flashlight, led his followers past these occupied retreats, driving the rats ahead of him.

Finally the beam of the torch found a platform where although water dripped it could be circumnavigated. Gosling and Cuff found a couple of broken chairs in the hall, broke them up and lit a fire in front of the platform. The flames lit streaming walls that had once encompassed ranks of children singing hymns or fidgeting, awaiting prizes and holidays. An old Japanese motorcycle stood in one corner.

Gosling produced the frying pan, Cuff the sausages and the bacon, only just beginning to moulder, and the stale sliced bread. While Hood slipped down the road for two packs of Tennent's, the others unrolled sleeping-bags from their sorry baggage, produced plates and assorted cutlery.

The firelight reached them softly. The sausages burst. The dripping water reminded them of their good fortune. Prince found four keys still intact in a piano in the corner and played a few discordant notes.

Jesus Christ said grace. They ate and they drank. Then, all except Martin and Jenny fell easily asleep.

Martin, taking the flashlight, walked across an asphalt playground. The drizzle had stopped and the night was quick with rain-fresh sound. He opened a protesting door and peered into a classroom. A sum remained unsolved on a blackboard; Christmas lingered on the walls – crayoned pictures of apoplectic Santas, opaque pine trees and reindeer with jig-saw horns.

He walked down a corridor. Cobwebbed endeavour and despair touched him. A door ajar. He followed the flashlight into the room, a study. A desk smashed as though someone had struck it with a sledge-hammer. A khaki filing cabinet, the top drawer bearing a label ABBOTT – CROSSWELL. What sort of man or woman had sat here with his cabinet of young lives? Had they thought: Will just one child whom I helped return one day?

Martin walked round the study. It was dry and in front of the desk was a rug worn in the middle by the shuffling feet of recalcitrant pupils. He returned to the platform and fetched Jenny.

The row started in the morning, beginning with the felicities with which the aggrieved often hide their true intent, even from themselves. Martin thanked Jenny for everything she had done to secure his release. He had, he confided, but one regret. And what was that? moving an infinitesimal distance from him in the double sleeping-bag.

"I asked Prince not to get my family involved."

"Who else apart from Walter was there to provide a fixed abode?"

"Eleanor Lubin?" Martin suggested.

"Wouldn't that be just a little suspect? Defending barrister giving her own address?"

"At least I wouldn't have had to promise to drop our inquiries. That's blackmail."

"You'd prefer to be in jail?"

"You know I'm grateful." He touched her breast. "But he made me swear not to ask any more questions."

"That doesn't mean other people can't ask them. Prince, for instance."

"What it means," Martin said, "is that the uncles have got something to hide."

"So why did Walter make it so obvious?"

"Because he's an amateur?"

"An amateur what?"

"I wish I knew," Martin said.

She raised herself on one elbow, surveyed the study in the daylight. He saw it through her eyes. The squalor of abandonment, decay not even blessed with longevity.

He said: "It's only temporary."

"I know," she said. "I'm not complaining." She brushed a

287

strand of hair from her forehead.

"I can't blame you for hating it."

In fact the principal must have been delighted to leave, installed now in a panelled study where he could comfort himself that his fulfilment was the moulding of young lives. Abbott or Crosswell for Prime Minister?

"I don't hate it. But no one can like it, can they?"

"Some do: they've been squatting here for weeks."

"Then they're masochists."

"They don't have any alternative."

"Of course they do," Jenny said abruptly. "Everyone has an alternative."

"It depends on your state of mind."

"Rebellion shouldn't be sordid."

"They're not rebelling: they're surviving."

"Is that what you're doing?"

"We have a cause. Charlie, Danny ..." He stared at the ceiling; a jagged length of pipe hung perilously above him. "Don't you care about them?"

"You know I do. I stayed at Buck House, didn't I?"

"You make it sound like a penance. What was it like in the country residence with Eleanor?"

Jenny reached for her brassière and fastened it behind her back. She struggled into a black jersey. She shivered. "Comfortable," she said.

"Sunken baths?"

"Hot baths. And my feet sank into deep carpets and my bed was soft and warm."

"They didn't run to that in the police cell."

"I told you, I didn't know you were there until it was too late."

"So where is this palace?"

"Near Sonning," she said, reaching for her jeans.

"Lawns reaching down to the Thames?"

"Eight bedrooms, stables and a billiard room."

"Servants?"

"More than likely."

He watched her pulling on her stone-washed jeans; the backs of her knees looked vulnerable.

He said: "There's a street in Wallasey built in the '30s. Semis, mostly. Shoulder to shoulder, two strides through the front garden and you're on the pavement. Proud little houses they

288

were once; you should see them now."

She brushed her hair so vigorously that it crackled.

"The paint's peeling, the fences are rotting, the pavement's cracked. But the residents have got work. Oh, they've got work all right. Know what they do?"

She shook her head, still brushing energetically.

"They sift the rubbish on a tip and flog the pickings to the scrap-merchants. And whatever's left over they keep to repair their homes with. Family of twelve live in one, father and elder lads all unemployed."

"Isn't there any work?"

"Oh, there are jobs all right. Part-time barman, thirty quid a week. The queue will stretch to the brewery for that one. Gardener, temp, one month only . . . double-glazing fitter, must have car . . ."

"I read," Jenny said, stowing her brush in her Levi bag, "that unemployment was down in the north-west."

"It's down in this street. Know why? Because they've formed a community association and they're paid £1 an hour to guard their own homes."

"Why don't they come south then?"

"The great divide? Good question. In the case of the family of twelve because there would be nowhere for them to live together. In the case of craftsmen who've lost their jobs, because their crafts don't exist down here. In the case of older people because Merseyside's all they've ever known. And as for householders . . . How can they afford to sell up and buy the same property down here for four times the price? Lastly, why the hell should they?"

"Why did you?"

"Because I'm young."

"You won't be much longer."

"What's that supposed to mean?"

"When did you last apply for a job?" Jenny asked.

"Shelf-filling at Sainsbury's? I forget."

"You could study at the same time."

"Law? Like Eleanor's brother?"

"Why not?"

"Because I wanted to be an architect."

"Then study architecture."

"After a night filling shelves with Heinz baked beans and

289

disposable nappies?" Martin heard his Scouse accent thickening. "Was Eleanor's brother at the house party?"

"As a matter of fact," Jenny said, "he drove me home."

"Nice car?"

"Lancia."

"Very nippy. Where are you going?" as she closed her bag, zipping up the argument.

"Into Sutton to get a decent breakfast."

"Before you go I've got an idea."

She stopped at the door.

"The family of twelve. Any chance of them getting jobs as servants with Eleanor's friend? They're very good with dogs and children."

The door slammed behind her dislodging the length of piping which fell on the rug beside the sleeping-bag.

*   *   *

Confused, Jenny faced Eleanor Lubin across the flickering beam of the television in her home.

She said: "Martin and I don't seem to get angry about the same things."

Eleanor, legs tucked beneath her, sipping a glass of white wine, said: "The poor become angry, the rich indignant."

"I'm not rich."

"You know what I mean: upbringing points protest in different directions. He's angry about realities: you're indignant that no one cares about them."

"I'm angry," Jenny said.

"Then sculpt your anger."

A buzz at the door. Eleanor pushed a button and Andrew's voice issued through the grille. She released the lock at the entrance.

Andrew poured himself a whisky, water and ice and flung his long frame into an easy chair. He pointed at the news on the TV. "Civil war, soon. Which side will you represent, sister?"

"The underdogs, of course. Haven't you got a home of your own?"

"Bad day. Need sympathy. Pipe and slippers."

"Why didn't you go and see Lucy?"

"Because you told me on the phone that Jenny would be

290

here." He smiled crookedly at Jenny across the top of his glass.

Jenny said: "You could have played chess."

"I'm tired of losing. A mock trial at college today. I was defending a rapist. He was convicted."

"Was he guilty?" Eleanor asked.

"As hell."

"Then you shouldn't have taken the case."

"If every lawyer who believed his client to be guilty refused to take the case the courts would be empty," Andrew said. "I hear you've moved," he said to Jenny.

"To Sutton."

"Know it well. One of the best public libraries in the land, good football team. Soccer," prodding a finger at Jenny. "Victorian houses preserved in respectability, a mile of shops and a pub called the Cricketers. Where are you living?"

"In a squat."

"Well-appointed?"

Jenny described the school, omitting the rats.

"Stay here tonight," Eleanor said.

The apartment had a contentment about it, like deep-polished furniture. Jenny visualised the squat. Heard the rodent scutter in the night.

She thanked her and said: "I must go home."

"Then I'll drive you," Andrew said.

"Just to the station."

In the silver Lancia he lectured her mildly. "Mustn't blow your life on aimless rebellion. If ever you want any help . . ." For once he seemed to be grasping for words.

Outside the station he kissed her on the cheek. Glancing back she saw him, one elbow on the wheel, finger and thumb spanning his forehead, watching her.

On the train she felt dizzy, snowflakes crowding her skull. Walking down Sutton High Street from the station sweat iced on her forehead. In panic she rested in a doorway.

"Anything wrong, miss?" the policeman asked.

She said she was all right but, just the same, he accompanied her to the bottom of the High Street.

"I'm fine," she told him. "Honest."

"Where do you live, miss?"

In a squat. "I'm meeting my boyfriend," she said.

"Lucky fellow." The smile spread beneath the helmet. "Now

you take care." He walked away at a measured pace.

When she got back to the school she kicked off her shoes and, still clothed, slid into the sleeping-bag in the study.

The following day Martin took her temperature. It was 103. Outside the morning was warm and gentle.

*   *   *

Not in Liverpool. It was bright enough but a breeze snapped in from the Irish Sea, just briskly enough to remind visitors from the South that the lungs of the North blow sturdily.

The breeze frisked through the street in Bootle rattling shutters and banging broken doors, forcing the plump woman with the drained features to hold onto her hat.

From time to time she paused to scrutinise the number of a house. Many of them had lost their numbers, and their names; they were divided and sub-divided into flats and faces suspended in the windows regarded this small but determined woman blown in from some other part of the city with suspicion.

She stopped outside No 14 and hesitated as the breeze unwound the tight grey curls outside the Sunday hat, an intruder on a mission that she would have preferred to forgo. Suddenly she straightened her back, pushed open the gate, strode up the path and knocked boldly on the door.

The appearance of Joanne's mother, incongruously elegant, further intimidated her: there were some women living in these wasted places who still behaved as though they were the wives of slave-traders.

"Why, Mrs. Renshaw," Joanne's mother said. "What a surprise. Please come in. Did you want to see Joanne?" Mrs. Renshaw nodded, angry with herself for being on the defensive but the rooms were so tall and there was about them a distinction that the little houses tumbling towards the Mersey in Dingle lacked. Then, remembering that Joanne's father drank, she rallied: the rooms in Dingle were warm and comfortable.

Joanne came down the stairs. She had been on night duty and she was wearing a pink dressing-gown and her red hair rested untidily on its collar.

As her mother left the room Joanne pointed at a sofa that looked as if it were preserved for wakes. "Please sit down."

292

Mrs. Renshaw sat down. She twisted her wedding ring. She patted the russet cushions beside her. She said: "It's our Martin; he's been in prison."

Joanne sat opposite her beside a standard lamp with a mottled brass stem. "What for?"

"Receiving stolen property. He was kept in custody because he had no fixed abode. Something like that. Then he was released."

"So he's not guilty?"

"Of course not," Mrs. Renshaw said. She had never quite made up her mind about Joanne: she mucked in well enough in Dingle and she ate jam butties and she called a swimsuit a cozzie but she was still more Dublin than Scouse.

"How did you know?"

"Letter from Uncle Walter," Mrs. Renshaw said. "Arrived this morning. First class an' all. Walter coughed up bail so it's not the last we'll be hearing about that."

"Where is Martin now?" Joanne asked.

"With Walter. In a fixed abode." She stared at the gold ring. "Can you go and see him, lass? See what he's at. You know like, he should never have gone south."

She could feel tears gathering and she searched in her worn bag for tissues, but there were none there, only a purse containing her bus fare home and a comb with broken teeth and a compact that Jim had given her when they were courting. "Will you go, lass?" she said, preparing to leave before the tears betrayed her.

"All right," Joanne said. "I'll go. But I can't promise anything."

She laid her arm lightly on Mrs. Renshaw's shoulder as she led her out of the tall room to the front-door. At the gate Mrs. Renshaw turned and waved; then the breeze blew the tears from her eyes.

*   *   *

Charlie ran from May into June.

He slept in barns and fields and the spare rooms of people for whom he did odd jobs; he foraged as Cuff had taught him; he eluded the good intentions of police and humanitarians who provide food and clothing for the destitute; he chopped down

293

trees and he dug ditches and he trimmed brambles for an old lady who had once lived in Africa; wherever he went, contrary to popular opinion, good thoughts swarmed around him like bees.

It was when he saw the sea, just a sliver of it, cupped between chalk hills where harebells grew in the short grass, that he stopped.

Messages reached him just as messages had once reached Mole. Or was it Ratty? He stared at the sea and the sea stared back, twinkling. Mole or Ratty. He heard a voice reading to him. He turned the telescope of the years away from the sea.

Turned it towards London and began to run.

CHAPTER 31

———◆◆———

Squatters, like sparring couples and harried robber bands, part abruptly. Sometimes it is merely that a predestined time for change has arrived. In the case of the former occupants of Buck House the catalyst was more specific: the abandoned school was the pits.

It breathed damply, its joints creaked, its frame was disfigured with graffiti, refuse rotted in its orifices. By night the sewer patter of rats was augmented by the rustle of autumn leaves stored by the wind and, outside, the orgasmic wail of mating cats; by day children pelted it with stones, and the long-term residents, bleak-faced and winter-seasoned, rose threateningly from their ravaged mattresses.

The first to leave was Jesus Christ who strode powerfully and benevolently across the playground towards a green hill far away and was gone. He was followed by the Bodger who, discovering that all the fixtures and fittings had disintegrated beyond his talents, packed his tool-box and went upon his destructive way. Nolan, casual visitor, won a holiday in Normandy with THERE ARE FERRIES AT THE END OF MY GARDEN and Hood, finding that the Muse was a grudging visitor, found lodgings in Herne Hill where Ruskin had lived before him.

Jenny, sweating and shivering in the sleeping bag, watched them go with a sense of desolation saw-toothed with desperation by her fever.

Martin, handing her aspirins and a glass of water, tried to comfort her. "Don't worry, they haven't gone for ever. The vagrants of London always meet again. As if they're all carried

295

on the same currents of survival."

What he didn't understand was that it was the circumstances they left behind them rather than their departure that upset her. What was she doing in this slum?

She closed her eyes. She was never sure when she was awake or asleep. Her heartbeat was a beating drum, her breathing waves on shingle.

From time to time Martin's voice inserted itself between sounds and images. The doctor wouldn't come to the school . . . in the morning they would take a taxi to his surgery.

"Tell Eleanor," she said.

More aspirins, dry and sour on the tongue. A pain in her chest. She touched the pain with the tips of her fingers: it was a blade sheathed in fur.

Gosling visited her, everything he said a crossword clue. And Cuff dripping blood. And Mad Bull with biceps like balloons.

She asked for the manager of the Codgers to pour her a shandy and he broke the glass on the counter and, gripping the handle, jabbed it towards her face.

Martin's hand, dry and warm, on her forehead.

Prince's voice, floating: "Can't keep her here, cully."

Martin: "Her fever's down a little."

"That's the way with fevers. Up and down like a starving bell-ringer. Give the brief a call."

"You're right, of course." Jenny heard his reluctance with great clarity.

Another drink; it tasted like the water in swimming pools and she was drowning in the shallow end and the fish-bubbles of her own breath were spiralling past her vision.

She awoke as she fell down the gaping filter.

"It's all right," Martin said. "Everything's going to be all right. A doctor soon . . . a warm bed." Grieving for him, she reached out and held his hand.

But he was the man in Kensington Gardens leading her towards his car and she was inside and his flaky hand was on her thigh. And the au pair, Herta, was looking through the window, running the tip of her tongue between her lips.

"Come on," Andrew Lubin said. "We'll soon get you out of here."

"Why," Martin's voice "couldn't Eleanor come?"

"In Birmingham on a court case. Have you called a doctor?"

"He wouldn't come."

"She should have been seen by a doctor."

"That's why we called Eleanor. She needs a decent place to stay . . ." voice trailing away.

Jenny, sad for him, said: "You've been very good, Martin."

Andrew: "Can you walk?"

"Of course I can walk."

"Put your arm round my shoulder."

"And the other one round mine," Martin said.

"Have you got a blanket?" Andrew asked.

Martin put his reefer jacket round her shoulders.

"It's only 'flu," Jenny told them.

Fresh air on her face as they walk across the playground. Cuff and company solemnly observing them as they make their way down the asphalt path to the Lancia.

Martin: "I'll come along too."

Pleasure expanding inside her.

Andrew: "Be my guest."

And she is in the back of the car and Andrew is at the wheel and Martin is beside her, arm around her shoulder, and Cuff and company are lined up on the pavement and the car is moving away and her eyes are closed and the darkness throbs gently.

From time to time it is pierced by antagonism.

Andrew: "When did the fever start?"

"Last night. After she'd been to your place."

"Not mine, Elly's. You should have brought her straight round."

"At that time of night? With a fever?"

"That place is a cemetery."

"It's only temporary."

"Until what? Another squat?"

"We can't all live in ancestral homes."

"I don't. Digs."

"Not all of us can afford them."

"Rubbish. A job, benefits, a grant . . ."

"Did you see some of my fellow tenants? Could Cuff – little fellow in a suit too big for him – afford digs?"

"I was talking about you."

Silence except for the sound of traffic. She opens her eyes and

297

watches traffic lights change from red to green. What do you do if you're colour blind?

The car is moving again. She sees its pistons riding snug in their oil. She closes her eyes again. And the pistons take her to Hampstead Heath and she is bounding in slow motion across Parliament Hill above the grave of Boadicea.

Martin: "I'll get a job. First there's something I have to do . . ."

"There always is. What does your father do, Martin?"

"Why?"

"A lot of people blame their parents for their own shortcomings."

"He was a grocer."

"So was Margaret Thatcher's father."

"What was your father?" Martin asks.

"A civil servant."

"So was Hitler's."

The car stops. Eleanor's voice. Jenny smiles at her; a stupid smile, she feels. The bed is warm and it smells of cleanliness.

The doctor is a woman. She has kind hands. She listens and peers. Jenny understands that she will not die. The doctor writes a prescription with a fine flourish.

Eleanor waits at the bedside while Martin or Andrew or both go to the chemist's. "Take this . . . and this . . . drink lots of water . . ."

And she is deep in the pillows burrowing towards childhood.

*   *   *

The pirate radio station was housed in a terrace in Brixton off the Stockwell Road. There Eliezer Mundy, pulling at his mournful moustache, broadcast rock, reggae, soul and exhortations to his black neighbours not to submit to white racism. He accepted that one day soon his studio would be raided and closed down and he knew with equal certainty that he would re-open with expediency in another terrace in another cramped street.

The Mundy Evening Show – broadcast every day except Sunday – was not the only pirate station operating in London but it was the most popular because, in addition to being articulate and fervent, Mundy possessed the common touch. He

298

broadcast local grievances and advice and maintained that the forgery charges were part of a conspiracy to gag him.

His equipment was rudimentary, his range limited, but other sections of the media often picked up a cause aired on the Mundy Evening Show.

Why not Charlie? Martin reasoned. So one peerless June morning when he had drawn his benefits – sorely depleted since he had resided in London for more than eight weeks – he caught a bus to Brixton, home of West Indians, Nigerians, Asians, Maltese, Chileans, Vietnamese, Cypriots and, at the time of the '81 riots, white British who made up sixty-two per cent of the population there.

But for a white man – policeman? – it was not easy to glean information from the West Indian concentrate. Martin tried the market at Atlantic Road where peppers, chillis, mangoes and melons were heaped in polished piles.

He was greeted without cordiality.

"Eliezer who? Never heard of that man."

"But he runs a radio show."

"Don't listen, man. You fuzz?"

"Friend. I shared a cell with him."

"Then you go back there."

Finally a stallholder selling herbs that could cure the nation's ills said: "You stay here and I'll see if there's any Eliezer wants to know you."

There was.

Martin was escorted to a council estate to the north-east of Brixton on the borders of Tulse Hill.

Eliezer greeted him in a small garden where cornflowers and marigolds grew. He held out his hand. "Received any stolen property lately?"

"Forged any plastic lately?"

Eliezer beckoned him into the semi-detached council house which was as neat as a sailor's cabin. It was 6 pm. Eliezer's two children, a boy and a girl, both with his luminous eyes, were studying for exams in their bedroom.

Eliezer's wife was in the kitchen cooking a meal that smelled of spices.

Eliezer produced a bottle of Scotch. "You dig?"

They touched glasses. The whisky burned in Martin's stomach.

299

He told Eliezer about Charlie and the Special Olympics.

"Sure I heard about him weeks ago on some other criminal transmission. Eight hundred metres. What's the matter with Charlie?"

"He's missing."

"My beam only stretches as far as Streatham."

"But he lived in Brixton once upon a time."

"Once upon a time there were innocent children, black, brown and white."

"You're not on the air," Martin said.

"Can't resist feeds like that. So what you want me to do?"

"Come home, Charlie."

"Where's home?"

"Just say Dean Street. We can always contact him there."

"*Home*. I wonder. You say he was born here?"

"Lived here."

"Could be that home came after that."

"Just broadcast," Martin said. "Get to him."

"Difficult if he's in another part of the country."

"Other channels could pick it up."

"So when are the Special Olympics?"

"July," Martin said. "Brighton."

"He stands a chance?"

"If he's still in training."

Eliezer poured more whisky. Chinked glasses again. "You eating here tonight?"

"Try and stop me."

"Okay, but you've got to let me do it my way. You might not like it but it'll work, believe me."

"I want Charlie to win, that's all."

And he told Eliezer about Danny.

*   *   *

This time Joanne travelled south on a coach filled with Scousers looking for a week's work in London. It was Sunday afternoon and the men were quiet. Some played cards on their suitcases, others read the tabloids, but mostly they slept, or stared out of the windows at the somnolent Midlands on either side of the motorway. From M6 to M1 and, with Birmingham behind them, the run-up to London past Northamptonshire, Bucks and

300

Herts, skirting Watford, border town of the Great Divide.

In the countryside men played cricket, their bowling and batting drowsily graceful from a distance; barges crawling with children idled on canals; families spread themselves in the corners of green fields or marched imperialistically between hedgerows behind a leader armed with a stick.

Beside Joanne a middle-aged man with big, bruised hands delicately tore paper napkins into ballet dancers and carnations and jumping frogs. "The kids like 'em," he explained. He handed Joanne a red carnation. "Know what I miss about working on Merseyside? Coming home. Kids doing their homework. Wife brewing up in the kitchen. Tea — bubble-and-squeak and corned beef and piccalilli. Reading *Echo*. Watching telly, moggy in front of fire. Going to bed with wife. Knowing it'll all be there in morning . . ."

He handed her a white carnation.

The coach cut through the suburbs of North London, Edgware, Mill Hill, Colindale, Hendon . . . From Waterloo, Joanne caught a train to Feltham and walked in the dusk from the station to Walter Renshaw's ambitious semi. There was a Porsche outside and a black Jaguar and from inside the house came the sound of altercation. She paused at the half-open door.

"You're a bloody fool, Walter. Why couldn't you leave well alone?" A Cockney voice. Martin's Uncle Jack?

"A self-righteous humbug. Does your faith permit blackmail?" Uncle Harry?

"He is my nephew. I couldn't let him rot in prison."

The Cockney voice: "A bit of bird never did anyone any harm."

Joanne rang the doorbell.

Walter, drained of piety, said: "And who might you be?" the light in the porch glinting on his censorious spectacles.

"Joanne," she said. "From Liverpool. I'm Martin's girlfriend."

"You'd better come in," he said without enthusiasm. "These gentlemen were just leaving."

"Jack and Harry?"

"You're very smart, young lady," Harry said, plumply elegant in yellow cashmere sweater and hound's-tooth trousers. "What are you doing here?"

"I came to find out why Martin had been in prison."

301

"Who told you he had been?"

"Holy Joe," Jack said, looking at Walter. "He must have told Jim." He stepped past Joanne. "I'll be in touch," he said to Walter and walked down the path to the Jaguar.

Walter led Joanne into the pristine living-room; she sat on an uncomfortable chair.

Harry, following, said: "Are you still Martin's girl-friend?"

"I know about your step-daughter," Joanne said.

"A young man must sow his wild oats. Do you think he'll go back to Liverpool?"

"To me, you mean? That's for him to decide." She turned to Walter. "Where is he?"

Walter spread his hands. "I wish I knew."

"I thought he was supposed to stay with you. At a fixed abode."

"He's broken his word," Walter said.

"If he breaks bail you'll be £250 short," Harry said with satisfaction.

"He wouldn't do that," Walter said. "Would he?"

Joanne gazed at the photograph on the mantelpiece of the four brothers bold with a shared secret.

"So he must be at the squat," Joanne said.

"Presumably." Walter glanced at his watch. "You've just got time . . ."

"I'll drive you to the station," Harry said.

She caught a train to Clapham Junction, a bus to Wandsworth. And in the moonlight gazed forlornly at the space where Buck House had been. A gap where a tooth had been drawn. She called at the Codgers but the landlord was unhelpful. She spent the night at a YWCA. The following morning she telephoned Walter. His wife said he was at the office. "Is it a personal call? My husband doesn't take personal calls at the office."

"Not even from you, Mrs. Renshaw?" Joanne laughed into the receiver to show that she was joking.

"Are you the young lady who called last night when I was on my way back from Sunday school?"

"This is strictly business."

"Well, I don't know . . ."

"I can put a lot of business your husband's way . . ."

Mrs. Renshaw gave her the number.

"As a matter of fact," Walter said, "Martin just telephoned."

"Is he going to stay with you?"

"Probably not a good idea. After all, what's an address?"

"You mean you didn't ask him?"

"He's promised me he'll answer to the bail. I told him you were here."

"Where can I see him?" Joanne asked.

"He told me to tell you Leicester Square," Walter told her. "Seven o'clock tonight. Charlie Chaplin's statue. And now . . ."

". . . you've got pressing business. Goodbye, Uncle Walter. I'm sorry there was no room at the inn."

Leicester Square was crowded, vibrant with the evening ahead. Joanne, approaching from the bookshops of Charing Cross Road, paused outside the Empire Cinema beside a group of French teenagers, an American wearing a stetson and two Italian women with flawless complexions weighted with jewellery. Behind them a blonde man begged with a flute on which he blew sad, tuneless notes.

Joanne knew this square with its cinemas and snack bars, because she had written a paper on John Hunter, the surgeon and anatomist, who had once lived here. So had Sir Joshua Reynolds and Hogarth. "Goodbye Piccadilly, Farewell Leicester Square . . ."

She rounded the unprepossessing garden in the centre and saw Martin waiting beside Charlie Chaplin in bronze. Martin looked thinner and tougher and older. Seeing her, he waved and walked towards her, smiling shyly as he had once smiled after they had made love.

They strolled along New Coventry Street, stopping in front of a young man, hair styled in Rastafarian dreadlocks, playing the guitar. Teenagers sat at his feet drinking beer from cans, beating time with the empties.

"Hogarth could have captured this," Joanne said. "Beer Street, Gin Lane . . ."

"Or me. Rake's Progress."

"Your parents know," Joanne said, slipping her hand under his arm.

"About what?"

"Prison," she said. "Walter told them."

"The bastard. But it absolves me. I don't have to keep my promise to stop asking questions."

"What you should do," Joanne said, "is get in touch with your mam."

"Tell her I'm working in a betting shop? Tell her I might get three years? Tell her I'm living in a slum?"

"Write to her then; I'll take the letter back. Tell her the charge was a mistake. Say you've got a good job but don't say what."

"Supposing I do go to jail?"

"Don't suppose," Joanne said. "Go out and prove you're innocent. And then . . ."

"Come back to Liverpool?"

"Why not? You can study there. I'll be earning decent money soon – the nurses got a rise." She was making a formula of the future; she couldn't help it; that was her way.

"Since when did nurses earn decent money? The system doesn't reward decency."

"You're beginning to sound like an anarchist. Negative."

"Your honesty does you credit. Do you ever lie to yourself?"

Three black youths wearing jeans and shirts without sleeves stood beside them. One carried a transistor radio on a shoulder-strap. Pop music poured from it but the guitarist didn't appear to mind.

Two skinheads ran through the sitting teenagers kicking the cans of beer. The teenagers picked up the cans and went on beating time with them.

Joanne moved closer to Martin.

"Introducing the Mundy Evening Show. And here is your host, me, Eliezer Mundy." The youth carrying the radio turned up the volume.

The guitarist said: "I dig him," and stopped playing.

"And what a tale I have to tell tonight," Eliezer said. "For discrimination and victimisation it has just about everything. Underprivileged guy – black, natch – framed for a crime he didn't commit. For why? Because he's a runner and he's good and the whiteys don't want him to win, that's why. And now he is on the run – from the fuzz – and you and I, dear listeners, are going to find him and see that he wins that race. More about that later . . ."

But Joanne didn't hear any more. Martin, hands clenched, led her away towards Eros, God of Love.

304

There were half a dozen race meetings the following day and
Martin got to work early. Pincher was waiting for him amid the
detritus of yesterday's bets. He was smoking nervously and
biting at his ragged moustache.

"Early today," he said. "Under starter's orders. But where
were you yesterday?" He walked behind the cashiers' counter
and faced Martin through the grille.

"Sick," Martin said. "I told you on the phone."

"Not too sick to go up West though."

Martin stared at him. How could he have known? Joanne
wouldn't have told him so, unless he had been spotted, it must
have been Walter who had told Jack who had told Doberman.
At least he didn't know that he had spent most of the day at
Jenny's bedside.

"Well?" Pincher sucked his moustache with his bottom lip.

"I had to keep an appointment."

"More important than chalking up the odds? What was she
like, tasty?"

"An old friend," Martin said. "From Liverpool."

"Cilla Black?" Pincher squashed his cigarette savagely in an
empty Rowntree's Fruit Gums tin. "Of course we all know
where you were last week. Much betting in the nick?"

"I was on remand," Martin said.

"Gives the shop a bad name."

"How can it? I haven't done anything."

"Can't have a breath of scandal in a betting shop, Marty.
They'd be at us, the buggers. Accusing us of short-changing
them. All that stuff. I can hear them now. You're accusing us
when he – pointing at you, Marty – has just come out of
Brixton? That's what they'd say, lay you odds."

"To hell with them," Martin said.

"Not the right attitude, Marty. Pity about yesterday." Pincher lit another cigarette, sucked the smoke into his lungs and
coughed a mortuary cough.

"One day? I told you I was sick."

"Doctor's certificate?"

"I didn't have pneumonia," which apparently was what
Jenny was suffering from.

"Always get a certificate, Marty."

Martin said: "Are you giving me the push?"

"Absenteeism," Pincher said, tapping at his cigarette with a yellow-stained finger. "Fully justified."

"You can't do it," Martin said. "Wrongful dismissal. I can appeal."

"Why not? Of course they'll have to take that little matter of the till being short into account."

"I don't touch the till," Martin said.

"You must have forgotten."

"Forgotten what?"

"Derby Day. You did some paying out. Ask the other two lads. Nothing personal but they reckon you'd had a few sherbets."

Pincher pushed a small manila envelope under the grill. "Here, take this. One week's money on the nose. Less deductions — got to be legal. No hard feelings?"

"Did Jack put you up to this?"

"Jack who?"

"You know Jack who."

"Can't say I do, Marty. Lots of Jacks around in this game. Now why don't you be a good boy and shove off? There's a good betting shop near Tooting underground. Have a wager on the 3.30 at Windsor. I've had the word on a nice little filly . . ."

"Get stuffed," Martin said.

"Any message for Jack?"

"Jack who?" Martin said.

*   *   *

By the time Martin got back to Sutton after visiting Jenny, the anarchist had left, the fire of his protest quenched by the school, and only Prince, Gosling and his girl, Cuff and Danny remained.

An evening mist had filled the hollows of the suburbs and settled on the school, drifting behind the fire that Gosling had built in front of the platform.

Abjectly, Cuff reported failure. Gosling said that, in view of his girl's condition, he would have to find alternative accommodation. Prince, only 753 miles short of his target, announced another sortie into British Rail's network.

306

Smoke from the fire rose steadily and mingled with the mist. From another part of the school came the sound of shouting and breaking glass.

Prince read from a newspaper: "Losses on the Underground through ticket evasion estimated at £12 millon a year. Interesting." He stared into the glowing caverns of the fire. "Always travel in the rush hour, that's the wheeze."

Gosling asked mildly: "Why are you so obsessed with dishonesty?"

"Dishonesty? Everything's relative, cully."

"Relative to what? Another monstrosity that slipped in before infrastructure and after confrontation."

Prince ignored him. "Expenses, biggest fiddle in the civilised world. Freebies, company cars, first-class travel, *Put it on the bill, barman.* All the best people do it. Does the Prime Minister pay for a winter break in Washington? Insider trading? Absolutely kosher in the City until you get caught. Everyone at it. Be a mug, wouldn't you, if you knew a good thing and ignored it? Insurance companies, fair game. Up the storm damage claim a few quid to cover the cost of a gutter that's been leaking for years. Dishonest? Never. Accepted practice. So what's so criminal about travelling to Torquay without paying the full fare? Nice little caper, by the way, from Wokingham to Waterloo. Early morning train, turn left for the Underground instead of carrying straight on and you don't go past a ticket collector."

"I didn't say it was criminal," Gosling remarked. "I said it was dishonest."

"There's a difference?"

"Call it a transgression."

"Call it what you like," Prince said, stirring the fire with a stick, "but in my book you can only be dishonest with yourself. And by the way the trick is to buy a ticket from Paddington to Reading, get off at Exeter, wait for a slow train and tell the ticket collector at Torquay that you got on at Newton Abbot."

Martin stretched. "I'm going to sleep," he said and walked across the mist-shrouded playground to the study where the double sleeping-bag lay unzipped and lonely. He slid the envelope containing his week's wages and the benefits accumulated before he had got a job underneath and zipped himself in.

307

But he couldn't sleep, his mind ached with problems. Jenny was recovering from pneumonia but he couldn't bring her back here. Where then? Charlie had been cynically projected by Mundy as the victim of racial prejudice. Unless Jack Daniels can be found I will go to prison . . .

He decided to get up and brew a cup of tea on the fire.

The original squatters loomed behind the fire as he reached the platform. Six of them carrying pick-handles and knives and chains. The knuckles of the leader gleamed with brass; his face was bleak and bunched, and he was fleshily powerful beneath a leather shirt and greasy jeans. There was about him an air of hopeless aggression.

He said: "All right, fuck off the lot of you." Accent Midlands. "We've been fair but this is our drum so on your bikes."

"Can't it wait till the morning, cully?" Prince stood up, gaunt in the firelight.

"Now." He stepped forward, bunching brass-bound knuckles. "Piss off." The other five took up positions around the fire, all in varying stages of drunkenness. One broke a bottle against the wall; meths and milk spilled onto Gosling's sleeping bag.

Gosling said: "You can't send her out." He put his arms round the girl's shoulders.

"Who said we were going to?" One of the drunks blew her a kiss. "Don't worry, darlin', we'll keep you warm."

Prince whispered to Martin: "The girl. Get her out. Across the playground. When I kick the fire. Right?"

Cuff, drained of apologies, said: "We've got as much right here as you."

"Tell that to Tiny Tim," the leader said, pointing at the drunk with the broken bottle who was muscled like a retired weight-lifter. "Now bugger off."

"All except the girl," Tiny Tim said, gouging the air with the broken bottle.

The knuckle-duster glowed warmly. Water in a pan on the fire bubbled. The smell of meths rose sharply in the heat.

Prince's kick lifted the pan high in the air. Boiling water fell on the leader. He screamed. Burning embers scattered across the platform. Small blue flames scuttered across the pools of meths and milk.

Martin grabbed the girl's arm. Pulled her to the back of the stage. Through a door. Onto the playground. Through the mist

308

to a gap in a wooden fence. Bundled her through.

When he got back to the hall bedding on the platform was blazing and flames were exploring the walls and the piano. Prince was lunging at the leader with a burning brand; Tiny Tim was threatening Cuff and Danny with the broken bottle. Gosling, armed only with words, had been pinioned against the wall by two drunks while a third hit him in the stomach.

Martin hit them with the leg of a chair, knocking one to the floor. The other two let go of Gosling and Martin, scything with the chair-leg, shouted: "Get on the platform."

Cuff, blood from a wound on his arm joining the second-hand blood on his jacket, dodged a second gouging blow from Tiny Tim and joined Gosling and Danny on the platform. Prince, backing, joined them.

The six faced them and began to advance slowly, chains swinging, knives wicked in the flaring light.

The flames found the curtains framing the stage and swarmed up them. The floorboards burned vigorously.

The six were now at the foot of the stage.

One end of the piano was burning fiercely; Martin stationed himself at the opposite end. He waited a moment, then heaved. The blazing piano trundled towards the six as they began to climb onto the stage.

It tipped gently over the edge and disintegrated, tossing burning brands of lacquered wood at them. The leader's leather shirt caught fire.

Tearing it off, he shouted: "I'll do for you."

He climbed onto the stage. Stepped onto the burning floorboards. And through them so that only his head and torso were visible. The flames lit his matted hair which burned crisply.

Two of his comrades dragged him clear and beat out the halo of flames.

As Martin, Prince, Gosling and Cuff retreated through the door behind the stage the tank on the motorcycle in the hall blew. A wall leaned outwards, the ceiling sagged.

The attackers, clothes winged with flames, ran back in the direction of their quarters dodging flaming struts and spars.

The mist was cool on Martin's face as he led the way to the gap in the fence; as, sirens braying, fire engines and police cars with flashing lights drew up at the kerb.

The fugitives from Buck House looked at each other. Then

309

Gosling found his girl and, arm round her shoulders, walked down the hill. And Cuff, blood pouring thickly from his arm, tottered to an ambulance. And Prince, pulling at the bead in his ear, strode long-legged into the night.

Martin lingered for a few minutes watching the flames engulf the ruins of the school. He thought of the lessons that had been learned and forgotten there. Then he, too, walked briskly away with Danny and it wasn't until much later that he remembered that he had left all his money in the sleeping bag in the study. Burned with Abbott – Crosswell.

Of Hoover there was no sign.

PART THREE

CHAPTER 32

———◆◆◆———

Martin and Danny slept rough for the rest of the night in a recreation ground in a sprawling council house estate at Morden.

They were awoken at 6.30 by a dog about its business with its owner, an old man with a road-map of mauve capillaries on his face.

The old man said: "Skint, son?"

Rising, shivering, Martin nodded.

"Know the feeling. Fancy a cuppa?"

They walked past small houses to routine shops around the underground station at the terminal of the Northern Line to a caff where a busy young man wearing steamed-up spectacles served tea and bacon sandwiches and rounds of toast.

A notice on the door proclaimed NO DOGS but the old man pushed the brown-nosed mongrel under a table and ordered three cups of tea.

"Can't sleep," he explained. "Can't when you're older, you know. Especially when you live by yourself. You wake wondering if you've died overnight."

Martin sipped his tea. It was very sweet. He felt energy pumping into his veins. "It's very kind of you," he said. He was hungry but he could hardly mention that.

"I was an old soldier," the old man said. "Funny, when I think about old soldiers I think about the Great War. The war to end all wars. I remember thinking when World War II broke out that it was a lifetime since the end of the last one. But it wasn't, you know. Just over twenty years. I suppose even the last war's history to you."

313

"It did finish twenty years before I was born," Martin said, looking wistfully at two truck drivers wolfing bacon sandwiches.

"Time ceases to exist when you get older. Trooping the Colour, second Saturday in June – that's how I count it." He peered at Danny. "You don't say much, son."

"Too early in the morning," Danny told him.

"Drugs?"

Danny didn't reply; he had to hold his mug of tea with two trembling hands to get it to his lips.

The proprietor with the steamed-up glasses placed two bacon sandwiches, doorstops of white bread with tongues of crispy bacon protruding from them, on the table.

The old man said: "Thought you both looked hungry. Don't get so hungry when you're older. Saw a youngster pointing at an old geezer sitting on a park bench the other day saying, 'He forgot to die.' Nice, wasn't it. But I know what he meant: some of us look as if the mortuary's on strike."

"You're not so old," Martin said, munching. Bacon fat dribbled down his chin.

"Scouser, aren't you? Thought as much. Knew some good Scousers in the war. Tough as old boots. Got on well with the Russians. I was on the Russian convoys," he explained. "Got frost-bite. Scars to prove it. Old women used to touch your cheek and point out where the frost had bitten. Kind they were . . ."

He ordered two more mugs of tea. They arrived steaming. The brown-nosed dog sat peering through the window at the swift legs of commuters.

"Lots of kindness in Russia. People don't realise it. They look after their old people. Here you get the OAP and the telly. Know something? Those soap operas . . . To a lot of old people – never call us folk – they're more real than life. Hardly surprising, is it? More happens in one episode than a whole year of their lives."

Martin, gazing through the steam at the old man, didn't know what to say. But suddenly he knew about loneliness.

He said: "I'll come back and buy you a bacon sandwich. And a cuppa."

"No, you won't, son. But it's a nice thought." He stretched one hand under the table and patted the dog's haunches. "He's

314

my mate," he said. "Aren't you, Ben." A tail thumped.

As they left the caff the old man brushed against Martin. "Over there," he said. "Get the tube up to the Smoke. And don't forget, ration your youth, it doesn't last that long." He patted Danny on the shoulder.

The dog tugged the lead.

Martin and Danny crossed the broad street to the Underground station. The Smoke? They hadn't got a penny between them.

He slipped his hand into his trouser pocket. His fingers touched four warm £1 coins.

He looked for the old man but he had disappeared. With his dog.

* * *

He went first to Holland Park.

Eleanor Lubin came to the door. "Jenny's fine," she said. "But she's asleep at the moment. I think it would be better to leave her. Why not call her this evening?"

Martin told her about the fire and the fight. "Danny's not feeling well," he said.

"I'll be all right," Danny said. "Not the first time."

"You must stay here," Eleanor said.

"And where are you going?" Eleanor asked Martin.

"To find Charlie."

"And Jack Daniels?"

"And Jack Daniels," Martin said.

He hesitated. She began to close the door. She smiled at him. The door closed gently leaving him alone.

On the corner of the street he noticed a silver Lancia.

* * *

He went next to Larkman House.

Brenda Larkman answered the door. Red hair disarrayed, glass of cooking sherry in one hand, much as he remembered her the first time he had seen her.

She stared at him, eyes not focussed. "No luggage?"

"It's me," he said. "Martin. Martin Renshaw."

"I remember you," she said. "Please accompany me to the

315

kitchen."

Bruce was sitting in front of the parrot writing a letter. He looked up and combed a wing of hair over his ear with the tips of his fingers. "Hallo, Martin," he said. "Long time no see."

"Still writing, Mr. Larkman?"

"Too much red blood in what I write. They're scared of it."

"What is it this time?" Martin asked.

"Graffiti," Bruce said. The parrot sprayed seed from his bowl with an indignant beak. "In the tube stations, on the walls – of Barclays Bank of all places – on the hoardings. Where has decency gone, I ask you. Where?"

Brenda sipped her sherry; her dressing-gown fell back at the thigh revealing generous lengths of black fishnet.

Bruce said: "Seem to remember you left rather abruptly, Martin. Why was that?"

"An opportunity I couldn't refuse."

"Excellent, excellent. You young people, too many of you afraid to work. But nice to see you back. Not everyone returns to express appreciation for past favours . . ."

Martin glanced at Brenda; she was refilling her glass.

There was another quiz show on the television – squares being filled with a bewildering display of flashing lights and letters.

Martin said: "I was wondering . . ."

"Weekly rates?" Bruce asked.

"I'm a bit short at the moment."

The parrot side-stepped along its perch.

"There was a fire last night," Martin said.

"Where?"

"In a squat," Martin said.

The parrot stopped in the middle of his perch.

Brenda said: "You should have stayed on. No vacancies I'm afraid."

She snapped her thighs together.

*   *   *

From King's Cross Martin walked along Gray's Inn Road where, a lifetime ago, he had boarded a taxi for the night shelter in Soho, and made his way along Holborn, down Kingsway and along the Strand turning left to the Victoria Embankment at

316

Charing Cross. It was a warm day and pleasure steamers and barges moved at a leisurely pace among the clouds reflected on the Thames. He passed Big Ben and the Houses of Parliament benign in the occasional sunlight and, from Millbank, turned into Vauxhall Bridge Road and then Regency Street where his branch of the DHSS was situated.

He needn't have bothered. He had lost his B1 form. Burned. He had lost his birth certificate. Burned. The girl regarded him cynically. He notified her of his change of address – Walter Renshaw's – and departed.

He thought about walking to the Job Centre. But what was the point? What he needed first was money and accommodation. He searched his pockets. His capital was 14p.

He sat in Victoria Tower Gardens in the shadow of the House of Lords. Sparrows pecked at his feet. Tourists, particularly women, paused to stare at Emily Pankhurst in bronze; he would have to bring Jenny to see her mentor. The river slid quietly past. Martin felt curiously tranquil.

Why? He stared across the river towards Lambeth Palace. He watched a flock of schoolgirls no doubt heading towards the Houses of Parliament. He watched a man with a beard knitted by neglect carrying a placard FLEE FROM THE WRATH TO COME.

A rosary of nuns strode past. They were supposed to smile gently. These looked bad-tempered as though they had been guided to Westminster Abbey instead of the Cathedral.

The sun warmed him.

If he hadn't been hungry again the tranquillity would have lingered.

An important young man wearing a bowler hat sat on the bench beside him, opened a briefcase made of soft black leather and produced sandwiches wrapped in cling-wrap. One salmon and cucumber between brown bread, one cheese and tomato, also between brown bread, one ham and mustard between white. And a yoghurt containing woodland fruits, and a flask of coffee.

He began to eat with obvious enjoyment.

Martin fingered his 14p. How much for one bite from the salmon and cucumber? Knock-down price for the ham and mustard?

The young man crossed his legs and tossed glutinous crumbs

317

to the sparrows. He poured coffee into a plastic cup and drank thirstily. A precocious peer? An MP? He licked his fingers before embarking upon the cheese and tomato.

"Beautiful day," he observed.

"Beautiful," Martin said, watching his jaw muscles work on the cheese and tomato.

"Flaming June. Well, almost. Are you going to Wimbledon?"

Martin, swallowing, said he hadn't thought about it.

"Those girls, steroids, you know."

"Let's hope we win the Test," Martin said.

"Not my game, cricket. Thinking of taking up squash. Get the old weight down." He patted his stomach and bit into a ham and mustard sandwich.

Martin gnawed the inside of his bottom lip.

He threw what was left of the sandwiches to the sparrows. Martin waited until he had disappeared then robbed the birds of their meal. They chirruped peevishly.

Martin was joined on the bench by a middle-aged woman in black with beautiful pale hands. She took a Cornish pasty from a paper bag, opened a library book, a Dick Francis thriller, and began to read. Each bite from the pasty dispatched savoury odours in Martin's direction.

"Are you hungry, young man?"

He averted his gaze from the half-eaten pasty. "A bit peckish."

"Here." The woman produced another pasty. "Let's share."

He took the pasty. The pasty tasted of meat and pepper and potatoes. He took small bites, chewing each one thoroughly.

"A drink?" She poured orange juice with vitamin C added into a cup and handed it to him.

He sipped carefully.

She placed a leather bookmark between the pages of the book and laid it on the bench. "Always take care of books," she said. "They're people's thoughts." She massaged her fingers, thumb and forefinger lingering on the wedding ring. "Out of work?"

Martin said he was and found to his disgust that he was wondering whether she would give him any money.

"You look as though you should be at university. I should have liked to have gone. To Oxford or Cambridge. To a college with doors that open like a book. I'm a historian," she told him.

"The Victorians. I'm writing a book, *The Age of Hypocrisy*."
She handed him a cherry tart cupped in silver foil.

If she did offer him money would he accept? He hoped not.

She said: "Things haven't changed much, have they, only the fashion of the hypocrisies. For the privileged Victorian the poor were non-existent: for the privileged Elizabethan of the twentieth century they're an irritant."

Big Ben boomed the half-hour, 1.30.

"Well," she said, "I must be off." She rolled the wrappings of her lunch into a tight ball and dropped it into a litter-bin.

Martin waited.

She stood up. "Well, young man, I wish you luck. How old are you?"

"Nineteen."

"Still young enough."

"For what?" He stood up.

"To learn," she said. She studied him for a moment and he knew she was aware of what he was anticipating and he knew she was debating what she should do. She shook her head slowly and walked briskly towards Parliament Square.

He was glad she hadn't offered him money. In any case he wouldn't have accepted it. He fingered the three coins in his pocket. Had he looked so hungry? And why had she categorised him as university material? The green sports jacket with the leather-patched elbows bought at a thrift shop? The embryonic beard that had only sprouted because he had been unable to shave at the school in Sutton? He touched his face, a hungry dog's. What he needed was a wash, a comb, a toothbrush.

He walked along Whitehall, past the bureaucratic blocks of government and the mounted troopers of the Household Cavalry, and down the Strand to the Strand Palace Hotel.

He hesitated in the foyer surrounded by American tourists. Then he headed for the toilets. He washed his hands and face in hot, soft water; he combed his hair with the comb provided.

Then he departed. He was learning.

* * *

Charlie washed more thoroughly. In an outhouse in the grounds of a white house with a green roof near a golf-course somewhere on the southern outskirts of London.

Hot water from a shower sprayed his shoulders and coursed down his body. He rubbed a bar of brick-coloured soap on his chest and arms and watched the suds, glazed with rainbow colours by the sunlight streaming through the window, run with the water.

He liked the rubbery feel of his muscles. The colour of his skin shining dark and wet. The smell of the soap, like hospitals. What he liked most was the freedom of his body in the slippery heat and he was happy that, running, he had found this place.

He had been here for a week. Spotted by the owner, tall with a quick face and a cap of black and grey hair, sitting on the lawn staring at the hedge that, at intervals, had been carved into figures – a cockerel, a cat, a teapot and a poodle.

He had been given accommodation in the outhouse which was furnished with a bed and a table and chair and divided into sleeping quarters and shower-room which was not much bigger than a cupboard.

And the following day he had been put to work. No pay, just accommodation and meals, but that suited Charlie because money had always worried him and, in any case, he enjoyed washing and polishing the Rolls-Royce, finding a deep shine in its maroon paintwork, smelling the leather inside, and lopping branches from overhanging trees and raking the gravel on the drive and chopping wood and fighting the brambles invading the vegetable garden even when they drew blood from his arms and feeling the needle-sprays of the shower relaxing his muscles and sinking into dark, cushioned sleep, being awoken at dawn by birds scattering dew from their beaks.

The reason for his flight had become blurred. He only knew with any certainty that a great injustice had been perpetrated against him, that he had to avoid anyone in uniform. The confusion did not bother him: everyone forgot and forgetfulness only mattered if you believed in time. Why should anyone believe in years, months, hours? Man had invented the ticking clock, its moving hands. Why believe in an invention? When such inventions went wrong the inventors changed the numbers of days in the months, or the number of days in the year – Leap Year – or daubed a date-line across the globe.

Ahead in the manufactured calendar he knew there was a contest. The details of that, too, were smudged. Except

320

that Danny depended on it.

Where was Danny?

And Martin?

The three of us in a park, wet grass beneath our feet, and the dog, pink-eyed and determined, running into the trunks of trees.

Unconsciously Charlie began to jog beneath the comforting needles of water.

A knock on the door. "Hey, Charlie, I've brought you a towel." *Her* voice.

He didn't mind the man's thoughts. They were like coins, but honest enough. Kind in their way. But he wasn't sure about the woman. She was blonde and rounded and, when her husband was in London, she sun-bathed topless beside the swimming pool and sometimes when he was working close-by she pressed her hands against her breasts and raised them. Her thoughts were mouth-wet.

The door opened.

"My," she said, "you've certainly got a body."

She reached across the confined space and turned off the shower. Drops of water stayed trembling on his chest. He turned away from her.

"Here," she said, "let me."

She reached out with the towel. Her breasts were free and swinging with her movements.

He took the towel. "No, it's all right," conscious that his thoughts were ahead of his words.

"Come on, don't be shy. No need to be shy with a body like that."

Like what? It was a body.

He wrapped the towel round his waist. He pushed past her into the room. She watched him, arms folded across her breasts.

He dressed quickly. Made for the door.

"Black bastard," she said.

And he was running, running.

*   *   *

The queue in the courtyard behind Dean Street was ominously long. Paddies, Jocks, Taffies, Cockneys, Geordies, Scousers, Brummies, West Indians, Asians . . . all waiting submissively for

321

a bed in the capital city of the United Kingdom and the Commonwealth.

Martin waited beside a giant with a foraging nose and a voice as rounded as cider apples. As they inched forward he observed: "Looks like we might be roughing it again tonight. Where did you kip last night?"

"In a park," Martin told him, proud of it.

"Skint?"

Martin held up his three coins.

"Might try the Fields."

"Which fields?"

"Newcomer aren't you, my handsome. Lincoln's Inn Fields. Sleep within the cradle of the law. But you have to wait till they've finished playing tennis."

Baffled, Martin plunged his hands deep in his trouser pockets, a new boy again.

There were three hopefuls ahead of Martin and the giant when the last bed was taken. The rest of the queue dipped their heads and drifted away.

Martin and the giant stared at each other. A grin broke below the magnificent nose. "Old sea-dog? Wrong, lad. Gentleman of the Road? Wrong again. So what's it to be? The Fields or Cardboard City?"

"Whatever you say."

"On a smiling evening like this?" He spread his arms and embraced it. "Got to be the Fields, hasn't it."

*   *   *

Martin. Charlie. Grey. Daniels.

In her waking moments Jenny sensed connections, the conclusions of fading dreams. Martin and Charlie. Obvious – both accused of the same crime. But Grey and Daniels . . . Had she become a sleuth in her fevered sleep? A nocturnal Miss Marple?

She opened her eyes. The window focussed immediately. She took her pulse; the beat was slow and measured.

Grey and Daniels . . . She swung her legs out of bed, put on Eleanor's dressing-gown with the gold dragon embroidered on the back. She walked to the door: her legs bent.

She went into the kitchen where Andrew, in jeans and white shirt, was poring over a chess problem in the morning

322

newspaper.

He said: "The doctor told you to stay in bed. Coffee?"

She drank it hot and sweet and black. "Where's Eleanor?"

"Old Bailey. Defending an arsonist."

"Why?" Jenny asked.

"Because she doesn't think he's guilty."

"Then he's an alleged arsonist."

"Back to bed," he said.

"Too much to do."

"Such as?"

"A problem. Like that," pointing at the newspaper.

She said: "I can't make out what black is up to."

"How many pieces?"

"Apart from the king two principals. A knight" – Daniels, dark and devious – "and a bishop" – Grey, old and lurking.

"A combination perhaps."

"What's that?" Jenny asked. A kitchen, she thought, could be almost as intimate as a bedroom.

"Let the master tell you." He reached for a book. "Botvinnik: A combination is a forced variation with sacrifice."

Forced! By Martin's determination to find Grey. Grey forced to enlist Daniels to frame him. Discredit him. Get him out of the way – in jail.

But where was the sacrifice? A payment to Daniels?

Jenny finished her coffee and went back to the bedroom followed by Andrew's voice: "Into bed and stay there . . ."

She dressed in boots, jeans, blue blouse and V-neck.

As she reached the front door Andrew, standing at the kitchen door, said: "Where the hell do you think you're going?"

"To crack a combination."

"The hell you are."

"The hell I am," she said, shutting the door behind her and running on rubber legs towards Bayswater Road.

CHAPTER 33

———◆◆◆———

To practise as a barrister in England one must be accepted by one of four inns of court. One of these, providing both education and food, is Lincoln's Inn which lies behind the Gothic spires of the Law Courts at the eastern extremity of the Strand and close to the Old Curiosity Shop said to have been the setting for Charles Dickens's novel.

Its Fields are its grounds comprising several acres of green seclusion surrounded by mellow buildings – one of them is the Royal College of Surgeons – whose residents have included Ramsay MacDonald and Nell Gwynne. Once a duelling ground and site for executions, it is laid out with tennis and netball courts and at lunchtime the bouncing girls are observed appreciatively by flocks of male spectators.

By night the Fields, close to Carey Street, site of the bankruptcy courts, is occupied by the homeless.

"Used to be full of old jossers," said the giant whose name was Ross. "But look at them now," gesturing at the vagrants assembling in the warm dusk. "Some of them are kids of fourteen. If they don't watch out they'll forget what it's like to sleep under a roof."

"Like you?" Martin sat on the grass beside Ross as the last game of tennis drew to a close.

"Aye, just like me, lad." He wiped the neck of a bottle of cider and handed it to Martin who swigged from it. "But I'm different to most of the vagrants."

Martin waited to discover why. Around him the night tenants of the Fields were arranging their quarters – cardboard crates, mostly, and tents made from plastic sheets. Others sat in

324

groups sharing packs of Tennent's and Special Brew and bottles of cider and blackcurrant cordial cocktails spiked with meths, aftershave or hair lacquer. One or two of the younger arrivals shot crack into their veins but they were the minority and not as convivial as their fellows.

"The kids," Ross said, rolling his vowels richly, "are mostly from up north. Runaways from homes broken up by unemployment. The veterans are proud old bastards who lost their jobs and couldn't beg – a lot of them won't draw benefits – and old soldiers fading away because they found they couldn't become civvies, and loners who don't fit anywhere because they were directed down the wrong paths when their minds were buds. *What do you want to be when you grow up?* people ask, and really they don't give a bugger. What are you going to do, my handsome?"

"I wanted to be an architect," Martin told him.

"Then start drawing before it's too late." He tilted the brown bottle and passed it to Martin.

Two policemen stopped on one side of the square and gazed benevolently at the street arabs pitching camp. A young man in a dinner jacket and a girl in a shimmering gown ran, laughing, towards the wine bar on one corner. Snores issued from a cardboard container on a bench near the netball courts.

"You said," Martin ventured, "that you were different."

"Aye, different because I haven't got an excuse. Different because I'm ordinary and there's a paradox for you. Old sea dog? Eccentric philosopher? Refugee from *The Archers*? None of those exotic creatures, lad: I was a men's outfitter in Norfolk. Nice fusty little shop that didn't take into account fads or fashions. Peaked caps and gloves and sports coats, all the colour of autumn, in the window. Nice pub opposite, Crown and Sceptre, and a sweet shop on one side where they made their own toffee – used to take the fillings out of your teeth faster than the dentist could put them in – and a chemist on the other, name of Balsam, funny that.

"Nice little house, too. White-washed with roses growing up a green trellis and a fair-to-middling garden – better if it hadn't been for the sycamore tree – and an ornamental pond with frogs in it and a garage for the old Austin Princess . . . Have you noticed that people only abbreviate expensive cars? Merc, Jag, Roller . . . You never hear about anyone climbing into an Aus

325

or a Vaux."

"So," Martin asked patiently, "what happened?"

Ross tapped his nose. "The sycamore tree happened," he said after a while. "For years my wife had been onto me to cut it down. 'You're always complaining about the garden,' she kept saying, 'so why not get rid of the villain of the piece?' Well, I'll tell you, lad, it was my garden, my sycamore tree and one day she said it once too often and I sat down and took stock and decided to leave the sycamore tree where it was. And the garden and the house and the shop and my wife."

"Did you have any children?"

"Just a dog. A mongrel. Bit like Jumble. Do you know who Jumble was?"

"William's dog? Richmal Crompton?"

"Aye. I was brought up on him. And Biggles."

"Did you ever go back?"

"Once. Viewed it from a distance. It was like looking at a tableau. The shop was still there, and Balsams, and the house. Only one thing was missing."

"The sycamore tree?"

"It died," Ross said.

Stars glittered in the sky but the turf was still warm from the spent day. Someone was playing a mouth-organ; two men with slurred voices fought without enthusiasm. An aircraft with a winking light joined the stars.

Martin wondered where they were going to sleep. Right here, curled up, beneath the high night sky?

Ross stretched luxuriously. "Time to kip, my handsome," he announced. "Come into the dormitory. Got any valuables with you?" And when Martin shook his head: "They'd take your balls off if they thought they could pawn them." So saying he led Martin beneath a yellow plastic sheet. Inside Martin could make out three blurred shapes on the grass.

Ross said: "Gentlemen, I want you to meet a newcomer, Martin Renshaw. Martin, this is the wing commander."

"Delighted to make your acquaintance." A raffish voice issued from one of the bundles. "Tangmere, Meteors, bit before your time."

"And Cliff," Ross said. "Just out of the Scrubs."

"Shoplifting," a young voice said. "No wonder I got pinched. Ever tried to lift a shop?"

"And Jones the Boat," Ross said. "Marine engineer."

"Degree from the University of Newcastle upon Tyne," a Welsh voice said. "Not much good to you, a degree, when they close down the shipbuilding yard. Anyway, welcome on board, Martin. Find yourself a berth."

"Here." Ross handed Martin a blanket from a corner of darkness. "The grass gets wet at night."

"What about you?"

"Never worry about old Ross; he always makes out."

"Here, Ross," the young voice said. "I swiped you a sleeping-bag from a Government surplus."

"Don't want to go back to the Scrubs again, do we?"

"Not a bad nick. Not in the winter when it's frosty in the Fields. Did you know it was built so that the sun shone in every cell? Believe that and you'll believe anything."

Martin lay down on one half of the blanket and folded the other across his body. Snores and coughs and jumbled words and cries of fear submerged by day filled the night.

"Goodnight, lad."

"Goodnight, Ross," Martin said.

*   *   *

Historians would always date the civil unrest that swept Britain that summer from the police raid on Eliezer Mundy's pirate radio station in Brixton.

It was Mundy's racist broadcasts concerning Charlie, accompanied by incitements to violence, that finally broke the tolerance of the authorities.

But what happened that morning in late June while the queues lengthened outside Lords' cricket ground and the courts of the All England Club in Wimbledon is open to debate depending whether you accept the accounts of the police or Eliezer Mundy and his cohorts.

According to the police the raid was orderly, almost respect-able. They were admitted by Mundy who, with two assistants, was preparing his evening broadcast. They took away "certain documents" and took "certain steps" to ensure that Mundy could not use the studio again.

According to Mundy, he and his two assistants were forcibly restrained while his broadcasting equipment was vandalised, then punched and kicked as a salutary lesson.

That evening the Mundy Evening Show went on the air as usual from another studio in another terrace that he had prepared for just such an eventuality.

"The fuzz didn't pull any punches and nor will I." And he went on to describe the unseemly violence perpetrated that morning and to broadcast appeals for a sighting of Charlie "prevented from competing in the Special Olympics by white prejudice".

By midnight a police car had been stoned and fighting had broken out between a gang of whites and a gang of blacks in Brixton near the market.

By morning the newspapers, television and radio had picked up the story. Why had riots re-occurred? Reporters' inquiries pointed them towards Eliezer Mundy. Eliezer Mundy pointed them towards Charlie, wherever he was.

The reports took different standpoints about the trouble but all linked the racial tension with the strikes. Had Britain reached a watershed in its history of tolerance?

And all the reports named Charlie as the innocent catalyst of the disturbances. The missing torch-bearer of black grievances.

The charge against him of receiving stolen property was widely publicised. The fame of Buck House where the property was (allegedly) discovered was recalled. Martin was named, so was Eleanor Lubin defending. On the question of Charlie's innocence there was, on the advice of fretting lawyers paid to protect the media from libel, contempt of court and other such irritants, considerable circumspection and Eliezer Mundy, granting uninhibited interviews outside the old studio, sentinel policeman in the background, had to be briefed, contained and edited.

But there was surprising uniformity in the editorial columns. First, find Charlie. Then establish the facts of the case. Then, *if certain truths are established*, let him run in the Special Olympics. *Charlie*, wrote one leader writer, *has become not only the personification of black aspirations but the symbol of all those who believe themselves to be the sacrificial lambs of privilege and prejudice. If he runs then that will be proof that in this country fair play still triumphs*. And the writer recalled the words of the American, Eunice Kennedy Shriver, founder of the Olympics for the mentally handicapped: "*In a world where poverty, war and oppression have often dimmed people's hopes, Special Olympians rekindle that hope with their spiritual strength, their excellence and their achievements. For as we hope for the best in them, hope is reborn in us."*

Should Charlie actually win the race, the writer concluded, *we shall have witnessed more than hope: we shall have perceived a symbolic victory over adversity which may be reflected in the maladies plaguing our land.*

Martin had mixed feelings and he aired them to Eliezer Mundy that afternoon while, between interviews, the celebrity was working out in his council house.

"Why did you do that?" he demanded angrily.

"Do what, man?" Mundy began his press-ups.

"Make out Charlie was a victim of racism."

"Switch on the radio, turn on the box, look at the papers — there's your answer."

"We didn't want that sort of publicity."

"We? Sure you don't mean you."

"We," Martin said. "Everyone who wants to find him."

"But he'll tug at the hearts of that old jury on *both* your behalves?"

The muscles in Mundy's wiry body moved rhythmically.

"It won't get that far," Martin said. "We'll prove our innocence before it gets to court."

"*We* again. Got to find Charlie first. And Eliezer Mundy's made that possible. Everyone from Caithness to Cornwall has heard of Charlie now."

"Heard that he's on the run from the police? Heard that the racists are gunning for him? You know that's bullshit."

"Is it?" Mundy asked. "I don't know, man. Why was he framed?"

"It's me they wanted to frame. He was seen at the house in Hampstead."

"Sure you were framed? Sure you didn't fancy some of those antique clocks?"

"You know better than that," Martin said.

"So, why were you set up?"

Mundy sat up. Sweat trickled down his chest.

"To get me out of the way."

"Of what?"

"It doesn't matter," Martin said. "I don't want the whole of

Britain to know about it."

Mundy grinned. "Could spread further, man. Europe, America, Australia . . . good human interest story."

Hands behind his head, he switched to sit-ups.

"If you hear anything let me know," Martin said.

"Since when was Cardboard City on the phone?"

Martin wrote down Eleanor Lubin's number.

"Where do you reckon he is now?" Mundy asked.

"Heading for Brixton," Martin said.

*   *   *

At 2.30 pm Charlie, running well, reached Bromley where H. G. Wells was born and W. G. Grace died. He stopped in the sunlit garden of a pub, ate the remains of several ploughman's lunches, drank dregs of beer and jogged on to the Central Library where he rested in the reading room. But now thoughts were reaching him as questions, barbed and probing. He noticed two elderly men consulting a newspaper and staring at him. He rose and made for the exit. Questions followed him. He turned to face them. The questions hesitated, stopped. He ran. But why was he running? Two policemen, one hostile, one kind . . . but both hunters. I am the fox and the hunters can see me in my tracksuit. He would have to buy new clothes with the money he had earned.

Beckenham. He went into a men's outfitters and bought a white shirt and black, baggy trousers from a dapper middle-aged assistant trailing a tape-measure from the pocket of his pin-stripe. In the mirrored cubicle he heard the click of a telephone. Thoughts magnified into whispers. "He's here . . . Of course it's him." Replacing the receiver abruptly as Charlie laid out his money in orderly fashion on the counter. The exact money. No one ever realised how good he was with addition and subtraction; even the teachers at the school in North London had been surprised. The assistant's thoughts weren't unkind, just helpful. Charlie shook him by the hand. Then he dodged out of the shop and ran.

Past shops and pubs, the Three Tuns and the George, past traffic lights and a gaggle of schoolchildren. He remembered Martin and Danny. The three of them. Together. Aiming for something they shared. What it was eluded him but he felt that

330

the answers lay ahead of his striding legs. Running at a steady pace, he struck north-west.

* * *

Jenny, too, was in South London. In Dulwich approaching the derelict plot where William Grey had once lived. It looked marginally less derelict in the sunshine, Queen Anne's lace and teasels and wild oats growing amongst the rubble, convolvulus climbing the wire mesh fence. A ginger cat blinked at her; a thrush sang in an elderberry tree. The suburb where a house had been built recently for the Prime Minister drowsed in a contented fashion.

Jenny searched for a house close to the site with an air of permanent possession. She rejected two buildings with multiple bells and homed in upon a residence across the street with a trim lawn and beds of old-fashioned flowers.

She rang the bell which startled an aggrieved silence. She was about to depart when a fragile old lady appeared from behind the house carrying a basket filled with weeds. She was wearing a pale blue dress, a picture hat to which artificial flowers clung forlornly and gardening gloves.

Jenny asked her about the plot across the street.

"Used to be two houses, my dear. One had a beautiful little garden. Hollyhocks, peonies, Canterbury bells, sweet Williams . . . The other was a jungle. The owners used to fight about it, you know."

"Literally?"

"Well, not quite but it got very nasty especially when one of them – the old one – had drunk too much which was quite often. Are you fond of gardening, my dear?"

"We had a nice garden in Hampstead," Jenny said evasively.

"Then you shall see mine."

The garden was Kew in miniature. An herbaceous border planted with columbine, Japanese anemones, geums, Christmas roses . . . rock garden cushioned with dwarf phlox, alyssum, candytuft . . . formal beds of snapdragons, salvia and cherry pie not yet in bloom. The lawn was as smooth as moss.

The garden next door was a wilderness.

"The same situation," the old lady said in her silvery voice. "Except that we don't fight."

331

They sat in a small conservatory adjoining the house. It was littered with seed catalogues and samples. Scents of late summer and autumn reached Jenny from a thick glass mortar in which dried rose petals had been crushed with a pestle.

On her second cup of tea and scone Jenny learned that she was gardening correspondent for a national newspaper. Her name was Willoughby.

Patiently, Jenny led her back to the plot across the street. "Which was the gardener?" she asked.

"Oh, Mr. Grey," Mrs. Willoughby said. "He was the one who drank, too. You would have thought it would have been the other way round, wouldn't you. And he was in his seventies, you know."

"Why do you think he drank?" Jenny asked.

"I'm afraid he lived in reduced circumstances. But a charming man when he was sober. We used to give each other cuttings."

"A professional man?"

"I think he had been a lawyer," Mrs. Willoughby said. "He didn't talk much about the past."

Jenny was elaborately casual about the crucial question. "I don't suppose," she said, nibbling a scone, "you have any idea where he lives now?"

"Oh, but I do, my dear. He writes regularly. You see the poor man hasn't got a garden any more — just a balcony — and he likes to hear about mine."

"Could you let me have his address, Mrs. Willoughby?" She stared into her cup of tea.

"He isn't in any trouble, is he?"

"Not as far as I know. I just want to get in touch with him. Something to do with a legacy."

"Has he come into money? I should be so happy for him."

Jenny didn't reply.

"Well, I suppose it can't do any harm," Mrs. Willoughby said.

She went into the house. Jenny crushed some dried petals with the pestle; the released scent was too strong, a concentrate. She felt dizzy, a legacy of her fever.

Mrs. Willoughby returned carrying a letter written in elaborate script. "He writes a beautiful letter," she said.

"The address, Mrs. Willoughby?"

"Here, my eyesight isn't as good as it used to be."

Jenny read the address. It was the same William Grey who on the telephone had been evasive about his profession and hung up on her.

Jenny stood up. "You've been very kind, Mrs. Willoughby."

"Tell Mr. Grey that my tiger lilies are early this year. Such a nice man. Not like my neighbour. She's an old bitch," Mrs. Willoughby said.

*   *   *

Martin and Ross collected cheese sandwiches from the Dripping Factory, a church where bread and dripping had once been provided for the hungry, and ate them in the gardens of Russell Square. Three winos sharing a bottle wrapped in a brown-paper bag sat at the other end of the bench.

With his last 10p Martin had telephoned Eleanor Lubin's home. Andrew answered. Jenny was certainly better: she had gone out! And no, there hadn't been any calls about Charlie.

"Is Jenny fit enough to go out?" Martin asked.

The money ran out half-way through the answer.

Perhaps she had got a lead on William Grey. And as there was nothing more he could do about Charlie that left Jack Daniels.

"So where's it to be tonight?" Ross asked. "Dean Street, the Fields, Cardboard City, the Embankment, Charing Cross . . . If it's raining we might try the trains. Waterloo's favourite; the ticket collectors and guards are decent enough and you can go round on the loop-line all night."

"Whatever you say, Ross."

Martin took what remained of his capital from his pocket. Two 2p pieces. Coins. Hadn't that been Daniels's front? He told Ross he'd meet him outside the night shelter at 5 pm and went to a post office to consult the yellow pages of the classified telephone directory.

He went to Portobello Road, where antiques, junk and old coins were sold in the market. But Saturday was the day when the market came into its own. He got back to Dean Street at five. Ross was there at the end of the queue. Again the last bed was taken before they reached the entrance; Martin was not displeased.

Ross said: "I fancy a steak. How about you?"

"What are we going to use for money?"

"Don't you bother about that, my handsome," Ross said. "Let's find a promising caff first. That jacket of yours will help – you look learned."

Ross chose a caff in Tottenham Court Road. Its windows ran with condensation; its kitchen rang with frantic endeavour.

A balding waiter greeted them briskly and offered two menus but Ross swept them aside. "Steak and chips for two. Egg on yours, lad?"

Martin nodded.

"Make my steak rare," Ross said as the waiter started to move away. "Yours?" to Martin.

"Well done."

"Okay," the waiter said. "One cooked, one over-cooked." He disappeared into the bedlam of the kitchen, returning with a basket of bread and pats of butter wrapped in gold paper.

"Get stuck in, lad," Ross said to Martin. "Nothing like an appetiser." He drank some water. "God's wine," he said. "Adam's ale."

Around them workers from the big furniture stores ate ravenously at the formica-topped tables. Their girls drank coffee and ate pastries, squeezing cream out with each bite.

Martin knifed the egg and watched the yolk spill across the meat. How were they going to pay? Do the washing-up? He wasn't particularly bothered: vagrancy made you philosophical.

Ross said: "Eat about half. Leave it to the last morsel and they can get very belligerent."

"Leave what?"

Ross speared a soggy chip and thrust it into his mouth.

"Everything to your liking, gentlemen?" the waiter asked sarcastically. He picked his teeth with a matchstick.

"Just a little overdone," Ross said. "More medium rare than rare."

"Maybe we should leave it raw like they do in the zoo."

Martin was encroaching into the second half of his steak when Ross, allowing his knife to clatter onto the plate, clapped one hand to his mouth.

The waiter hurried over. "What's the matter. Bitten your tongue?"

334

Ross regarded him magnanimously, opened his bearded lips and produced a rusty tack. "In the steak," he said wincing.

"In the steak, shit!" The waiter made a grab for the tack but Ross jerked his hand away.

"I'm afraid," Ross said, examining the tack, "that we shall have to report this to the health authorities."

"You report nothing. You're a cheat, a bum."

Ross rose with dignity. "You leave me no option."

The owner of the caff appeared. A Greek-Cypriot with soulful eyes and hands that spoke eloquently.

He spread his hands.

Ross showed him the tack. "My duty to report it," he said sadly. "Witnesses," indicating Martin and other diners.

"If you think I haven't come across this con before, you're crazy."

Ross, prodding Martin, began to make his way magisterially towards the door.

"You pay first before you make your complaint."

"If you insist." Ross reached inside his grey cardigan into a shirt pocket which Martin knew was empty.

"Okay," said the owner, "you've got away with it this time. Never again, right? No complaint, no bill."

"I'll have to think about it," Ross said.

"And don't give me that shit, right? I know a con when I see one." His hands spoke angrily.

They reached the door. "By the way," Ross said, "the steak was a little on the tough side."

The owner drew one finger across his throat. "Next time. Anywhere. I have many friends."

"Tell them to tenderise the steak," Ross said.

The owner spat.

Martin knew he should feel ashamed; perhaps he would have done if the waiter hadn't picked his teeth with a matchstick.

They walked down Charing Cross Road to the Strand, bearing right onto Waterloo Bridge. Pausing half-way across the bridge, brown water running fast beneath them, Ross pointed at the sky which was bruised over the rooftops of South London. "Maybe we should take the trains tonight."

But Martin had developed a nose for open spaces. "A summer storm," he said. "It won't be much."

"You've never kipped in the rain."

"We can always cross the street to Waterloo Station."

They continued across the bridge to the South Bank where foreigners had to be cajoled into believing that culture could survive among the streaked concrete slabs of the arts complex. In the shadows of these contradictions of aesthetic expression a shanty town was beginning to assemble for the night.

Ross took Martin to a DIY wholesalers off Stamford Street where damaged cardboard containers that had to be jig-sawed together could be obtained. Armed with their lodgings and two bottles of cider bought in an off-licence, they crossed Waterloo Road to take up residence beside the Royal Festival Hall.

Rain fell. They climbed the steps into Waterloo Station and collected discarded newspapers for sheets. "If you want to use the ablutions," Ross said, "you can jump the turnstiles. Hot water, too. Very homely. Or read a paperback in the bookstalls. There's two of them, a chapter in each. I once read a book – *It's No Sin To Be Rich* it was called – in one day starting at Victoria and finishing at Marylebone."

They went outside again and stood at the neck of the bridge. It had stopped raining but moisture hung in the air. Across the river they could see the Savoy. They descended to embankment level and staked their claim.

Music reached them from one of the penitentiary blocks. The air was warm, sky deepening to mauve to the west.

"Like this, my handsome," Ross said, wrapping newspapers around himself. "Wonder if the wing commander will be here tonight. Jones the Boat. Surprising how we pick the same residential sites."

He adjusted his sheet. "Now slip into your lodgings. Like this," pulling one section of integrated cardboard up his legs as though he were trying on a new pair of trousers. The cardboard lodged over his chest. "Then the bottom storey." He pulled the second segment over his legs. "Some sleepers tuck their heads into a cardboard box. Shan't bother tonight. In the winter, yes. But then it's favourite to find a grille with hot air blowing up your arse. Behind a hotel if you can stand the smell of stale food."

Martin, following suit, felt as though he was in a coffin.

A boy of about fourteen settled beside him and wrapped himself in newspaper. He offered Martin a brown bottle. "Jack," he said. "Milk, meths and cider. Fancy a wet?" His hands trembled.

"Not tonight," Martin said. He brandished Ross's bottle. "All right tonight."

"Suit yourself," the boy said. His hair, a plume in the centre of his skull, was shaved skin-smooth on either side. He drank from his bottle. Put a hand to his mouth as his stomach protested.

Martin heard the chatter of crowds leaving one of the grey-slab buildings. It sounded as though the evening had been a resounding success.

They were joined by Jones the Boat. He said: "Marine engineer, like to be near water."

Martin listened. He could hear the passage of the Thames, undisciplined but inexorably channelled. Like life, it seemed to him.

Ross passed the bottle of cider to him. He swigged and passed it on to Jones who drank with nautical accomplishment.

"I read," said Jones, a greying terrier in the daylight, "that there are 100,000 of us in Britain. Do you think they counted him," pointed at the boy with the plume of hair, "or him," as an old man with a bruised face climbed into his box. "Double that number, I shouldn't wonder."

"And growing," said Ross. "A new breed with the young 'uns."

The boy beside Martin placed his bottle beside him, lay down in his box and closed his eyes. His limbs twitched. He whimpered. Sweat beaded his forehead.

"Should we get an ambulance?" Jones asked in his lilting voice. "I've seen them like that before."

"Take the bottle away," Ross said.

Martin reached for it but the boy's hand beat him to it. He drank again, closed his eyes and called out for someone named Mr. Edwards.

Ross said: "As soon as he sees an ambulance he'll be off like a frog up a pump."

Down the line a pile of old blankets beneath a black umbrella heaved rhythmically as a man and a woman made love. They were said to be man and wife. There were few women on the circuit. Few West Indians or Asians.

Some of the citizens of Cardboard City were gregarious, sharing a bottle, others drew invisible curtains around them-

337

selves and there was about them a benign tranquillity that never settles upon the ambitious.

Fat drops of rain fell lazily.

"A shower won't do any harm," Ross said. "Wash the air. Keep the kickers away. Some of the youngsters like to put the boot in."

"Set fire to one poor old soul," Jones the Boat said.

The rain hardened into hail which machine-gunned the drowsing vagrants, pulping their newspaper sheets and undermining the walls of their homes.

They shrank into the cardboard. They raised their arms to their faces. Some fled to shelter; most stayed submissively.

The hail bounced high and gathered in little drifts and they could hear it on the river.

The boy with the plume of hair lay quietly, eyes closed.

The hail scurried across London and lost itself.

The girl, hair hanging wet around a white, thoughtful face, eased herself from the sodden entrance where she had dallied with her man and made her way carefully towards Waterloo Road.

The recumbent dwellers steamed in the dusk and Martin thought: What has it come to? and, without exerting himself to find an answer, stared at the emerging stars and listened to London settling in for the night; listened to the slick of tyres on wet streets and the reverent chime of church clocks and, occasionally, laughter.

As London's breathing slowed so did Martin's.

In the dawn light the boy with the plume of hair appeared to be dead, his bottle overturned, white cocktail spilled in a pool beside it. Martin shook him but his body moved loosely. He put an ear to his chest but he could hear nothing.

He roused Ross and ran to a phone box to call an ambulance. It had been vandalised. He ran through the new light to the station and called from one of the bee-hive booths in the centre of the main hall.

When he got back Ross said: "He's alive, just."

Two ambulance men took him away on a stretcher, head lolling.

Jones said: "It's his birthday today. He's fifteen."

*   *   *

338

Charlie spent the night in the open at Crystal Palace where once there had stood a palace made of glass. When he awoke he saw in front of him the National Sports Centre and it was then that he remembered why, before he had taken flight, he had run so far and so often.

CHAPTER 34

———◆◆———

The violence that had broken out in Brixton had spread to Glasgow, Bristol, Liverpool, Birmingham . . .

And while whites and blacks battled with the police and each other sociologists debated the cause of their fury. Some noted jubilantly that there was a mood of anarchy abroad; others had the temerity to discern hope – no trouble at Broadwater Farm in North London where, in 1985, a policeman had been mauled to death, not a murmur of dissent from that part of Wolverhampton where a community project provided work for a thousand of whom forty-eight per cent were black.

Some commentators recalled that there was nothing like a steady downpour of rain to quench the flames of insurrection. Fat chance, said the meteorologists, as spectators fainted in the heat at Wimbledon and bundles of gnats danced high in the evening air.

All the pundits agreed with varying degrees of conviction that the tension might be defused if Charlie won the Special Olympics. FIND CHARLIE the headlines implored.

The mood in the Portobello Road that Saturday morning was spirited. But predatory rather than political, fervour generated by the hunters of bargains.

Portobello Road is one of London's street markets keeping company with such institutions as Berwick, Camden, Dingwalls, Jubilee, New Caledonian and Petticoat Lane. It specialises in antiques, jewellery, books, coins, junk and its symphony is orchestrated by strolling players, street musicians, buskers, and one-man bands.

The coin dealer whom Martin approached was a tall and

lugubrious man wearing a deer-stalker hat who, dealing with a commodity that is easier to steal than any other, regarded Mankind with incurable suspicion.

"Jack Daniels? Of course I know him, thieving sod. Had the brass neck to try and flog me a 1933 penny. Bargain, five thousand quid! Forgery, natch. Only six of the buggers minted and they're all accounted for. Are you a punter, son, or a spectator?"

"Both," Martin told him.

"Not got a mate, have you? Oldest snitch in the book. Engage poor bloody dealer in earnest conversation while matey asks to see an Australian ha'penny, 1923, Sydney, worth three hundred quid and scarpers with it." He spread his hands protectively over the ranks of coins slotted into transparent plastic in a glass case. "Dead loss chasing him. Lose five hours' trade that way. Old Harry there," pointing at a stallholder with a mauve nose, "caught a Scandinavian bird pinching a gold bracelet. Spent all day at the nick and then they said that as she was going home next day they wouldn't charge her 'but here's your bracelet back'."

"Has Jack Daniels robbed you?" Martin asked.

"Given half a chance he would. Gold if he could lay his mitts on it. That's why none of us carries much gold, favourite for the villains. But he does pull some genuine stunts, does Jack. Pair of pattern rupees, 1901, bought for fifty quid at a country auction. Flogged them at Sotheby's for a thousand. Brought me a few tasty items, too. Nice little brockage there." He pointed at a small silver coin. "Know what a brockage is? Coin that sticks in the die. Result is that the next coin gets two heads on it like that Queen Victoria sixpence. Jack also brought me that Canadian five-cent piece, 1875, worth about a hundred quid. And that American gold 20-dollar piece, 1926D – D for Denver – worth upwards of six hundred."

"I suppose you don't know where he lives," Martin said casually.

"Sure you haven't got a mate with you?"

"Do I look like a thief?"

"What does a thief look like? Show me a member of the human race and I'll show you a thief."

"Lives in the East End, doesn't he?"

"In a squat last time I heard of him."

341

"Didn't he ever have a permanent address?"

"Only the Scrubs," the dealer said.

Hope fading, Martin said: "When did you last see him?"

"About six weeks ago. Now why would a nice upstanding lad like you want to know the whereabouts of a tea-leaf like Jack Daniels?"

"He robbed me," said Martin, inspired.

"He'll be here at 3.30," the dealer said.

"Why didn't you tell me that before?"

"You didn't ask."

"I'm very grateful," Martin said.

"Watch your pockets, boy. Some of these buggers would pick their own."

From a call-box in Notting Hill Gate Martin telephoned Heald.

*　　　*　　　*

The interrogation room has green walls and smells of lies.

Jack Daniels, watchful and contained, sits on a wooden, stiff-backed chair. Lewis patrols the room restlessly like a dog on a long lead smelling a bitch on heat. Heald, sitting opposite Daniels, massages his clumsy hands together and asks the questions that occur to him instinctively.

"Why did you pick on that particular squat?"

"It had style."

"Not because Martin Renshaw was there?"

"Martin who?"

"Come on, Jack, you knew Harry Renshaw was his uncle."

"Harry who?"

"Let's start again."

"Let's."

"You've got form, Jack, right?"

"I'm all right, Jack."

"For thieving."

A shrug. "Got a ciggie? Supposed to soften up the subject. Didn't you know that?"

He lights his cigarette elaborately, blowing out the flame of the match, inhaling, exhaling, smoke channelled in Heald's direction.

Lewis: "Have you read the health warnings?"

Daniels: "I wished them all on you."

Lewis: "Comedians aren't so funny without any teeth."

Heald: "Easy, boy."

Daniels: "Not the old tough guy, soft guy routine for fuck's sake."

Heald: "You had one conviction for stealing antiques?"

"Objection."

"You're not in court now, Jack. You're in the fertiliser."

"Shouldn't you be attending to these riots? Or hadn't you heard that this old country of ours is on the brink of civil war?"

Lewis bunches his fist in front of Daniels.

Heald: "Knock it off."

"Give me five minutes with him . . ."

Daniels: "Jesus, I thought that stuff went out with the ark."

Lewis: "We prefer coffins."

Daniels: "Maybe I *should* have called my brief." Rests his head on his hand. "No, for Christ's sake, a brief needs smarter opposition than this."

Lewis: "Ever fallen down the steps leading to your cell, Jack?"

"Cell? Never been near one."

Heald: "Come on, Jack. Those coins you were flogging in the Portobello Road . . . That job in Hythe?"

"What job in Hythe?"

"That Belgian two francs, 1930 . . ."

"Know what that's worth? Twenty pounds if it's worth a penny – unless it's a 1933 penny, that is."

"You were seen at Hampstead, Jack."

"Do me a favour."

"Jack Renshaw's shopped you."

"Jack who?"

Lewis kicks away the chair but Daniels is ready for this move which he patently considers to be as subtle as a punch in the kidneys: he remains sitting on thin air.

"Can I have my chair back?" he asks.

Heald: "I warned you, Lewis."

Daniels: "For fuck's sake!"

Heald, pulling at the cuffs of his undistinguished suit: "I can understand why you wanted to frame Martin Renshaw . . ."

"You can?"

343

"But why Charlie as well?"

"Charlie who?"

"You know Charlie who, Jack. Don't piss us about. Why didn't you keep the loot in your own room?"

"Do me a favour."

"You've blown it, Jack. You know it, we know it."

"Blown what?"

"The coins . . ."

"I should know where they come from?"

Lewis: "You *should* know, Jack. Off the back of a lorry?"

"Ever heard of auctions?"

"Your dabs were found all over the drum in Hythe."

"Coins . . . Known a few bent coppers in my time."

Lewis grabs him by the lapels of his dude's suit.

Daniels: "Knock it off, for Jesus Christ's sake. What are we doing, auditioning for *Hill Street Blues*?"

Heald: "Why did you do it, Jack?"

"Do what?"

"Stitch up Martin Renshaw and Charlie."

"Charlie the spade in the newspapers?"

"You should know, you shared a squat with him."

"That Charlie!"

"They sussed out the house in Hampstead . . ."

"And you nicked them. Good thinking."

"And you broke in . . ."

"*If* I lifted those antiques, which I didn't, why the hell would I dump them on Martin Renshaw and the spade?"

"Because there was a deal. You were paid to set them up."

Lewis spins a coin, catches it adroitly and slaps it on the outside of the palm of the other hand. "Heads you lose, tails we win. This is one of the coins stolen from Hythe. Body in the Portobello Road says you tried to sell it to him."

"Pull the other one," Daniels says.

"We could forget that . . ."

"If?"

"We could forget a lot of things," Heald says, "if you tell us why you framed Martin Renshaw."

"Don't give up, do you?"

"Once upon a time you were a respectable tea-leaf, Jack. What went wrong?"

"Once upon a time . . . That's how fairy tales begin."

344

"You disappoint me."

"And now the man's making me cry."

Lewis: "We're going to nick you, Jack. Might as well make things easy for yourself."

Heald: "Got you bang to rights with the coins . . ."

Daniels yawns elaborately.

"Why did they want Martin Renshaw out of the way?"

"They?"

"And Charlie?"

"If you'll excuse me I've got work to do . . ."

Lewis: "Thieving?"

Heald, quickly: "Those antiques, got your fingerprints on them, Jack."

Daniels: "Can't have, I wore gloves."

The silence lengthens.

* * *

Martin observed Jack Daniels's arrest from a distance and then walked to Eleanor Lubin's home in Holland Park, a short distance from Portobello Road.

Eleanor carried a brief under her arm; Danny was sitting beside a window gazing in the direction of the park where nannies, oblivious of the unrest smouldering in the city, wheeled their charges among the Caroline Testout rose and yucca gardens; of Andrew there was no sign.

Danny raised one languid hand; he looked as though he was on a high. Eleanor led Martin into the kitchen. They sat opposite each other at the table. Martin sensed a closing speech in the offing.

He said: "Where do you think she went?"

"To find William Grey for you." She poured them each a glass of lemon squash. "Home-made." She fetched ice from the fridge and dropped two cubes into each glass.

"Was she well enough?"

"She was not." Eleanor pushed at the ice with one slender finger. "Where are you living now, Martin?"

"Nowhere," Martin said.

"Rough?"

"Am I in the witness box?"

"I can understand the attractions of vagrancy," Eleanor said.

345

"Especially in the summer. A heady combination of freedom and bloody-mindedness. An escape from responsibility."

"Are you about to tell me that I've got my whole life ahead of me?"

"I'm about to tell you that Jenny has."

"Jenny is capable of making up her own mind," Martin said.

"She has: she wants to become a lawyer."

"Am I stopping her?"

"You're not helping."

"We could get a small flat together."

"If pigs could fly," Eleanor said.

"She could live here? Is that what you're saying?"

"It is preferable to a derelict school."

Martin gazed at a basket of groceries. Stilton cheese, gammon, French bread, runner beans and cos lettuce, a punnet of strawberries and a carton of cream . . .

"Are you hungry?"

"No," Martin said, "but I am filthy."

The bath was a decadence. Midnight-blue with gold-plated fittings. Martin tipped Madame Rochas bath crystals into the water and lowered himself into the scented steam. His body blushed with the heat of the soft water.

What Eleanor Lubin was implying was that Jenny was born to this life-style and he was not. Well, you can aspire to greater things. Or didn't she as a champion of justice and equality realise that?

But what should he do about Jenny? Where was she now? He wished she was here. They could talk. And make love in the hot slippery confines of the bath.

He thought about his parents. Imagined their courtship. Sad that early passions should spend themselves on either side of a fire, behind a newspaper, behind two knitting needles, in front of a television.

He thought about Joanne. The perfumed mist subsided around the bath. He thought about Jenny. He cuffed a handful of bubbles to one side of the bath.

He knew what he had to do.

He climbed out of the bath and regarded himself in the mirror. His ribs were pushing at his flesh.

He dried himself with a powder-blue towel and rasped his fingers along his jaw-line.

346

He picked up a throw-away razor – Andrew's? – and removed the yellow guard from the blade.

He rubbed soap onto his cheeks and jowels and began to shave.

He dabbed cologne on his cheeks, donned his patched clothes and, resolutely, re-emerged.

Andrew was there.

They greeted each other politely.

"Where's Danny?" Martin asked.

"Lying down," Eleanor Lubin said. "He's very tired. From resisting."

"But he hasn't . . ."

No, Eleanor said, he hadn't. But there wasn't much time.

"Seven days," Martin said. "The Olympics begin on Friday. The men's 800 metres is on Saturday."

"Think you can find him?"

He smelled eggs and bacon cooking, the sort of smell that, accompanied by coffee, you didn't want to smell if you were arrogantly resisting temptation.

"I'm going to try now. In Brixton."

"It's rough there," Andrew said. "Getting rougher. I just listened to the news on the radio."

Eleanor said: "I'm not going to try and stop you but at least I can fuel you."

There were five rashers of bacon on his plate. Two eggs, tomatoes, sausages and fried bread. And a mug of coffee.

Martin conceded defeat and began to eat.

"Okay," Andrew said when he had finished, "let's go."

"Where are you going?"

"With you," Andrew said.

"My mission," Martin said.

"I've got the car," Andrew said.

*   *   *

The old man on his way to a cricket match paused in the woods and listened to the distant and revered crack of leather upon willow. He had played once for North Middlesex on the other side of London and what he could not accept was the passing of the years; that it was more than fifty-five years since he had obtained the autographs of Holmes and Sutcliffe after their record-breaking partnership of 555 for Yorkshire against Essex at Leyton; that he had been all of fourteen when Bolton Wanderers beat West Ham at the first Wembley cup final in 1923; that he had taken a girl to Wimbledon the year World War II broke out to see Alice Marble win the Women's Singles, and that same evening at the Savoy to the strains of "Thanks for the Memory" had proposed to the girl and been accepted.

Old? No, the body betrayed the mind, that was all. He looked at the liver spots on his hands and, probing the exhausted woodland grass with his stick, took a few hesitant steps forward. Time was an illusion, was it not? The fledgling years more vivid than the present, the girl who had died twenty years ago still in his arms, interludes of particular resonance more assertive than times of great import.

He sat down on a green bench blistered with rust, fitting the stoop of his spine into the curve of its back. Butterflies flirted in the bosky air. A worried dog trotted past sniffing the city-black soil of the path.

Even the war – North Africa and France – was telescoped. And the years of jurisprudence. The old man's hands tightened on the bone handle of the stick. But not their conclusion: that was acid: that had scarred the illusion of time. He prodded his stick into the grass, hauled himself to his feet and, with a quicker tread, made his way through the oak trees towards the cricket.

A few yards from the boundary he found a wooden bench scored with initials and hearts pierced by arrows and sat down to watch the match. The bowlers were fast with galloping runs and the ball sped sweetly from the bat. Middle-aged couples sat in deck-chairs drinking tea; sunlight shimmered on the roofs of cars parked beside the decrepit pavilion.

The acid burned. Embezzlement of clients' money. Surely borrowing would have been a kinder indictment. The war, he liked to remind himself, it had blurred the demarcation lines between honesty and dishonesty. When was a partisan a terrorist? When was looting appropriating the spoils of war?

But once, before that war, the direction of his life had been straight and true. A flourishing practice – he himself had never wanted to become a barrister – and respectable riches extracted from the sublime intricacies of law. A rambling house behind holly and laurel and a spacious garden, bounded by ancient red walls, in between which birdsong was trapped. He closed his eyes for a moment but he smelled snow and the faces of the children playing in the garden were confused by swirling flakes.

If only, he thought, opening his eyes, there was some redemption he could find before experience spent itself. He followed the gaze of two of the men sipping their Thermos tea: a pretty girl with shining dark hair and inquisitorial features was approaching along the line of the boundary.

She sat on the bench. She said: "There are a few questions I want to ask you."

"You sounded like a lawyer on the telephone."

"I hope to become one."

"I've been waiting for you," William Grey said.

*　　*　　*

Heald picked up the telephone on his desk. Mrs. Clarke, mother of the boy who had been growing pot in the back garden.

"I called," she said, "to thank you."

"He's better?"

"I talked to him," she said. "Like a father," she said, "not like a mother blaming a father," she said. "We're sharing our problems and do you know something?"

Heald shook his head at the receiver.

"He dug up all his plants and burned them. Mr. Heald, did you know what those plants were?"

"Come now, Mrs. Clarke, that would have been aiding and abetting."

"Then you did! How is your son, Mr. Heald? I hope you don't mind me asking."

Heald said he was fine. An exaggeration. Stephen was coping. Give me someone else's kid and I am the Great Healer.

He thanked Mrs. Clarke for calling, replaced the receiver and read Jack Daniels's statement exonerating Martin Renshaw and Charlie.

He rubbed his big paws together. You're doing a great job, Heald. For a pig, that is.

*　　*　　*

349

Three miles away Charlie paused. At Crystal Palace he had perceived purpose. Now the evening air was hot and angry and his vision was warped. He rubbed his hands on his black, baggy trousers and stared at the disintegrating training shoes that had carried him from the city to the sea and back again. His feet burned. Flakes of ash hung in the sky. Messages dipping on warm currents reached him. Bowing his head, he tried to follow them to their source.

CHAPTER 35

It wasn't until the beginning of the last century that London colonised Brixton. Sighting green pastures across the Thames, wealthy pioneers crossed the newly-constructed Vauxhall Bridge, pushed south establishing a new suburbia and built their residences on expansive plots of land.

Then came the trains and, as often happens, a less affluent breed of pioneer followed in the wake of the colonists. They were called the working classes and for them smaller houses were built and modest stores including those in Electric Avenue which, in 1888, became one of the first shopping streets in the land to have electric light.

Between the two world wars the original homesteads became sadly neglected. Some became lodging houses for those members of the working classes who had not prospered during World War I; the others were knocked down and council flats built in their place.

The third wave of settlers arrived after World War II, West Indian immigrants who brought their meagre possessions to Railton Road, Somerleyton Road and Akerman Road where the music-hall comedian Dan Leno once lived, their numbers being swelled by other dwellers from distant shores, Asians mostly.

In 1981 the small streets such as Atlantic Road and Railton Road, known as the Front Line, and inhabited mostly by West Indians, were a battleground.

But when the smoke from the race riots cleared a sort of harmony emerged. A lot of the drug dealers split and moved to other suburbs; police reviewed their relationship with the black community; those working-class houses with their tiny fore-courts shouldering each other towards the railways were respectably dressed in coats of white and cream paint.

And Brixton prison, more famous for its escapes than its incarcerations – even three of the original convicts who helped to build it escaped – might not have entertained many more citizens, rioting near its walls, if it hadn't been for a catalyst, Eliezer Mundy.

Martin, accompanied by Andrew who had parked the Lancia a mile away, went first to Eliezer's emergency studio. But that, too, had been raided and police wearing helmets and carrying shields were fending off bricks and metal bearings. In a side-road stood an armoured personnel carrier equipped with tear gas and video cameras.

A sergeant lifted the visor on his helmet and said to Martin: "If you're Press I'd advise you to get the hell out of here. You're not popular."

"Nor are you by the look of it," Andrew said.

"With a voice like that you'll be the first to get your head knocked off."

"No one can help the way they talk," Andrew said to the closing visor. "Not even you."

A brick hit the pavement in front of them and snapped in two. Backing away, Martin approached a West Indian lounging in the doorway of a terrace house. He wore his sideburns long and his ears were plugged with the foam pads of a Sony Walk-man headset and as he stared at the fermenting rage he snapped his fingers to silent music.

Martin waved one hand in front of his face and the West Indian said: "Don't you worry, man, I can hear you. You fuzz?"

Martin shook his head.

"Press?"

Martin shook his head. "I'm looking for Charlie."

"Who ain't?"

"Where can I find Eliezer Mundy?"

"In the slammer most like. Ask the fuzz."

The soundless music changed tempo and the beat of the West Indian's fingers quickened.

They made their way past a blazing corner shop to the police station where they were preparing for a siege. But no one would say where Mundy was. "Hopefully having the shit kicked out of him," a young constable said. "He started all this."

"What now?" Andrew asked. "Are you sure there's any point to this?"

"No," Martin said. "I'm not sure."

He found a call-box on the other side of Brixton Road and phoned Eleanor. Her voice was taut.

She said: "Heald called."

"And?"

"He said it was off the record."

"What was off the record?"

"That you're in the clear."

Martin smiled stupidly out of the window of the call-box. "And Charlie?"

"Both of you," Eleanor said.

He smiled at his feet. Outside the call-box Andrew frowned and tapped his temple with one finger. Crazy, his finger said.

Martin, intoxicated with innocence, concentrated. Then he said: "So everyone must know that Charlie's innocent."

"It could defuse the situation. Isn't that the phrase?"

"They'll still say he was framed."

"But exonerated. Before he went to trial. Justice regardless of colour or creed. How about that?"

"So we have to broadcast the fact that . . ."

"The charges against him – and you – are being dropped. I'm ahead of you . . ."

The pips sounded over the line and Eleanor shouted: "Your number."

He gave it. He hung up. A long pause. The phone rang.

"They'll want to hear that the police are being sued for wrongful arrest," Martin said.

"No chance," Eleanor said. "Not in the circumstances. Stolen property found in both rooms . . . both observed at the scene of the crime . . ."

Martin said: "I'll telephone a news agency. Press Association. Tell them to put out a bulletin that Charlie's innocent."

"They'll believe you? From Martin Renshaw, co-defendant?"

"So who will they believe?"

"The police," Eleanor said. "The trouble is they've only just obtained a confession from Jack Daniels. These things take time . . ."

"Which we haven't got. Brixton's about to go up in flames ..."

"And Bristol. And Glasgow. And Liverpool."

" ... and Charlie still missing."

"What I've done," Eleanor said carefully, "is to call Heald back. Explain that a statement could prevent a lot of bloodshed, that we need it tonight. At first he said impossible. Not even a *usually well-informed source* because that would be him and he would be crucified. But he's promised to telephone God."

"And he hasn't called back?"

"Not yet," Eleanor said. "I'll phone you at that number in half an hour."

"How's Jenny?" Martin asked.

"Just got back. She seems okay."

"Danny?"

"He's crying," Eleanor said.

●   *   *   *

Dusk. In Birmingham plumes of sparks lazily switch the smoky sky as a terrace of crouching houses fired at both extremities burns. The hee-haw of fire-engine and ambulance makes a farmyard of the perspiring evening as children watch their parents salvage their homes.

In Bristol a fight breaks out in a milk-bar in the pre-pub pause. A black boy of fifteen is stabbed — by whom few can say because in the mêlée the knife is a leaping fish — and in the street outside blacks and whites advance upon each other with bladed intent.

Glasgow. The rioting is a confusion of resentments although inevitably some observers try to blame sectarian conflict.

Liverpool 8. The riots earlier in the decade appear likely to repeat themselves as throngs march through an urban wasteland chanting: "Charlie, Charlie," although here the rancour is generalised rather than racist.

In Manchester where once discontent was bloodily suppressed at the point of the sabre the protest is young and revolutionary, confined, for the time being, to the university buildings in Oxford Road. Police with riot shields lurk in the shadows of erudition emerging from time to time to manhandle a student into custody.

In other outposts strikers, infected by the anger abroad this balmy evening, clash with pickets and police and the begetters of Britain's new prosperity weep at their ingratitude.

And everywhere there are agitators abroad, Fascist or Communist, their motives singularly difficult to disengage.

*   *   *

The call-box off the Brixton Road was occupied and two girls were waiting outside it. With Andrew, Martin ran down a side street to a kiosk on Stockwell Road. He called Eleanor Lubin's number. Engaged. He waited two minutes, in the darkness, then called again.

Heald had just telephoned, she said. He had obtained permission to release a statement. Nothing official, *usually well-informed sources.*

"I'll call the Press Association," she said. "They can check it out with Heald. A quote from you would help. Call PA in half an hour." She gave him the number.

The item was carried that evening on radio and TV. Martin telephoned Eleanor once more; she told him to return to the police station. Ten minutes later Martin gave a pavement Press conference.

In the background firemen doused the smouldering remains of the corner shop. The crowd moved away from the glow and moved across the dark street to stare at Martin, the reporters and the cameramen. Police held them back.

Martin answered the questions with an assurance that surprised him. Yes, he had been scared but he had always hoped that his innocence would prevail. No, he did not know where Charlie was but he suspected that he was somewhere here in Brixton.

"Why?"

"Because he was born here. And I want to take this opportunity to appeal to anyone who sees Charlie to escort him to the police station. Tell him the charges against him have been dropped, tell him I'll be waiting for him."

"If he's found will he run in the 800 metres on Saturday?"

"He'll win the 800 metres on Saturday."

One question sank any hope of a respite in the rioting.

355

"Mr. Renshaw, do you think he's dead?"

"I hope he's alive."

A hush while *dead* expanded into *murdered*.

A metal bearing hit a camera, knocking it from the photographer's hands onto the pavement. Then a brick. Then a brand of smouldering wood from the gutted shop.

Police turned and, with batons and shields, forced the mob down the street.

They stopped beside the remains of the shop. Smoke and steam rose from the charred shell where children had bought bubble-gum and comics and the light shed by a few tatters of flame, the crescent moon and the stars, found many guises among the young mutineers: they were cowed and they were defiant, they were filled with hatred and they were disappointed that this had to be so.

Martin and Andrew walked past small numbed houses towards Railton Road beside the railway that had once brought the working class to Brixton. Street-corner groups eyed them with curiosity and hostility. No one had seen Charlie. How could they? Charlie had been murdered.

The crowd outside Mundy's emergency radio station was still hostile. As Martin and Andrew arrived a window shattered and a petrol bomb exploded inside the house. The room breathed fire. The room above began to glow. Black smoke poured into the street as the pirate studio burned. But why would the black inhabitants of a ghetto burn the property of their crusader?

It was then that Martin noticed the white faces on the fringe of the crowd. Some wore their hair long and greasily, others clipped brutishly short; a few were punks. They carried themselves loutishly and their faces were transfixed with glee. In summer there is no football so why not make the pilgrimage to Brixton for a little pillage?

The blacks spotted them. Bore down upon them. But the white faces were ready; this was why they had come to Brixton. They retreated towards Martin and Andrew, took up battle formation and presented their weapons. Knives – some with serrated blades – razors, bottles, knuckle-dusters and a crossbow.

They wore Dr. Marten boots and leather jerkins and jeans and as the West Indians advanced upon them they shouted obscenities with guttural relish.

Somewhere a siren sounded and flames crackled, yet in another dimension there was silence as the two mobs faced each other. Then the police, riot shields thrust before them, batons in their hands, eyes wary behind their visors, moved between them.

From the blacks, wearing T-shirts and jeans and trainers and, here and there, despite the heat, leather, bum-freezer jackets and lumberjack caps, came the shout: "Murderers", although it wasn't clear whether it was directed at the thugs or the police.

A masterful voice issued from a police hailer: "Please disperse, go back to your homes. Nothing can be gained from violence. For your own sakes, and your families' sakes, disperse. Now!"

"Murderers!"

A bottle shattered against a riot shield.

"Black bastards."

Bricks sailed over the heads of the police. Knives glinted. A petrol bomb exploded between the blacks and the police and flames coursed across the street.

Cameras held bravely by TV and still cameramen whirred and clicked.

From the hailer: "For the last time —" voice extinguished by a brick.

The police faced both ways. They raised their batons. No opportunity for gas here: they would gas themselves.

The flames from the petrol bomb, finding no sustenance, spent themselves.

The whites reached the police first, trying to fight their way through to the enemy. They fell before the batons as weapon met shield. But a policeman fell, too, and the whites found gaps in the ranks of judicial blue and they were attacking the backs of the police facing the blacks.

And then it was carnage.

It was Andrew who noticed the white man with bare arms and shaggy hair raise the crossbow. "That's murder," he shouted.

Followed by Martin, he ran towards the bowman. Tackled him round the legs as he discharged the arrow. The arrow, deviated by the force of the tackle, parted the hot air and struck a black youth. He fell, plucking at the arrow in his side.

A boot struck Andrew's head. He rolled clear. A jean-clad leg

tripped Martin. And the bowman was away leaving the crossbow on the granite kerbstone.

The fighting slurred. Stopped. Blacks knelt to tend the youth.
He was very young and his fingers tugging at the arrow were
slim and articulate.

The whites fled down the street leaving behind them Martin
and Andrew. Three black youths advanced upon them with
knives picked up from the debris of battle.

Martin shouted at Andrew: "Let's get the hell out of here,"
but Andrew, dazed, moved in slow motion.

Martin pulled him but he shook his head. "I can't make it."

They stopped outside a door painted pink with a brass
knocker shaped like a fist that shone brightly in the assorted
light.

And the three blacks were upon them.

They prodded the air with the knives.

One of them said: "You just killed my brother."

Martin said: "Is he dead?"

"You care?"

"I don't think he's dead."

"No fault of yours."

A knife severed a leather button from Martin's jacket. The
lapels parted.

Martin said: "I didn't shoot the arrow."

"Man here saw you. Or your friend." He pointed the knife at
Andrew. "And now we're going to kill you. Rough justice, the
only kind."

Martin remembered a conversation with Mad Bull about
wrestling. One hand over the knife-prodding arm, one under.
Shoulder down. A heave and the youth was on the pavement
behind him, knife clattering.

"Shit-head."

Another came at him, jabbing his knife.

Martin kicked his knee-cap. Another knife fell.

But the other had re-armed and two of them were coming at
them.

"For Christ's sake," Martin said, "run."

"Can't. I'll take one of them. Another tackle."

"Rugby?"

The pink door opened and Andrew fell into the house.

The blade of a knife, aimed at Martin's neck, rose and fell.

Martin dodged to one side, into the house. The door shut behind him.

Boots and fists battered the door.

A black man with greying hair and rheumy eyes said: "Don't you worry about them," pointing at the metal panels on the inside of the door and the metal shutters screening the windows. "Come to something, ain't it," he said.

"Why?" Martin asked, standing up.

"I was upstairs. Saw what happened. I've got sons your age," he said.

They left the house much later when the street was quiet. Fires burned elsewhere and the night was sharp with hatred but they made it unmolested to Brixton Road and then walked briskly to the Lancia. Andrew who was going to spend what was left of the night in his lodgings offered to take Martin to Holland Park but Martin said no, he wanted to be dropped in the Strand. He didn't say why. Andrew stopped at the Aldwych, stuck out his hand and said: "And by the way, thanks."

Martin walked up Kingsway, cutting right into Lincoln's Inn Fields. He found the plastic-sheet tent and eased himself into it. Ross patted the empty sleeping bag and said: "Your bed's made up."

Martin lay quietly for a moment. Then he began to tremble violently and his limbs twitched. But the sleep that followed as dew beaded the lawns of the dormitory was sweet.

In the morning he walked to the news-stand outside the Law Courts. He scanned the front pages of the newspapers. On the front of each was a photograph of the crossbow lying on the pavement in Brixton. The youth – and all the papers made the point that he had only been a spectator – was badly injured but he was going to live. And Charlie . . .

Where was he? the papers asked. Alive or dead?

CHAPTER 36

———— ◆◆ ————

So why had he been framed?

Martin telephoned Heald and met him on Clapham Common. They strolled together on the flat urban grass keeping their distance from old men walking their dogs and younger men wandering aimlessly and children, who should have been at school, flying kites.

Heald tapped the newspaper under his arm. "You got a good press."

"I wanted to thank you," Martin said.

Heald gestured across the common with his newspaper. "There used to be a tree there. Captain Cook's it was called, planted by one of his sons. People used to gather there to air their grievances. Pity it wasn't there last night." He turned and headed towards the bandstand. "And it's going to get worse. You want to know why you were set up?"

"Jack Renshaw?"

"Close," Heald said. He dropped the newspaper in a litter-bin. "You know this is highly irregular?"

"I did spend a week in prison."

"That's why I'm here," Heald said. "Funny places parks and commons. In winter the loneliest places in the world: in summer the friendliest."

"Walter?"

"You know better than that."

"Why should Harry Renshaw want to frame me?"

They circled the bandstand. "I only know half the answer," Heald said. "I only know what he told Jack Daniels – that he wanted you out of the way. Did he ever threaten you?"

360

"Once, when he came to take Jenny back. He told me that London was a dangerous city. I introduced him to Mad Bull . . ."

"The Uncle Harrys of this world don't like to be defied. They plan elaborate revenges. Especially in the City. How many times has a financial scandal broken on *information laid* by a high-flyer who has been out-smarted?"

"I'm flattered," Martin said.

A Chinese kite with broad wings, twin-tails and red, avian head buried its beak in the grass beside them. It was retrieved by a small boy wearing too-long jeans turned up at the ankles.

"Why aren't you at school?" Heald asked.

"It was bombed," the boy said happily.

Heald said: "And then there was Jenny. He probably thought that she was sick of the squat. That when you were carted off to the nick she would come home. That must have stuck in his craw, too: step-daughter of eminent tycoon slumming it in a squat. I liked it," Heald said.

"It was a home," Martin said.

"Your values weren't all bad. Better than Harry Renshaw's."

They drifted away from the bandstand, heading for the Long Pond.

"Why Jack Daniels?" Martin asked.

"Harry got to know him through Uncle Jack. Incidentally Daniels doesn't think Uncle Jack had anything to do with it even if he is the best house-breaker south of Watford Gap. Harry merely told Uncle Jack that he wanted a job done, no questions asked. He gave Daniels five thousand quid. Not bad, tax-free . . . All he had to do was stage a burglary in Harry's house, plant the gear on you and Charlie and tip us off."

"And then Walter puts up bail. Harry must have loved him for that."

"Uncle Jack can't have been overjoyed either. He must have sussed the stroke that Harry had pulled. Feared that, through Daniels, the wicked fuzz might nail him for the one crime he hadn't committed."

"So why did Walter bail me out?"

"From all accounts he's a decent, God-fearing citizen. Weren't you supposed to be staying with him?"

"He's a hypocrite," Martin said.

"He got you out of the nick."

"Conscience. Fear of God's wrath. He did a deal, you know."

Martin told him about Jenny's promise and their release from the undertaking when Walter told his parents about his arrest.

Heald said: "The other half of the answer . . ."

"A conspiracy," Martin said. "A long time ago." He picked up a stick and threw it for a mongrel with a clown's face.

"So why don't you put it to one of the uncles?"

"Because they're all liars."

"One of them is more honest than the others."

"Jack?"

"You're improving," Heald said.

The dog with the clown's face returned with the stick and deposited it at Martin's feet.

*   *   *

Some cities, London and Paris among them, are summer cities and they bloom accordingly; others such as Dublin and Liverpool are winter cities, sharp-frosted and parlour-bright in their season but diffident between spring and autumn.

Liverpool that July day — apart from the punished acres of Liverpool 8 where the rioters had elected to protest — was in limbo, sunshine resting in the vacuum left by the swift winds from the Irish Sea.

Even the Mersey was slovenly, skeins of colour knitting lazily in the reflections of the sky. Joanne taking Martin's parents for their regular and unambitious outing — across the Mersey to Birkenhead and back — watched the colours and became lazy with their serpentine movement.

In the wake of the red, white and blue ferry stood the august buildings behind Liverpool's Pier Head, ahead a derelict warehouse and an orange-red jetty with a glass entrance hall. The air was warm and saline.

"So," Joanne said, sitting beside them on the deck of the sturdy ship, "Martin's in the clear."

"He should never have been accused," said Martin's mother, knotting the scarf tighter under her chin in case an errant breeze took it out to sea.

"He should never have gone to London," Mr Renshaw said. He sat, hunched in reproach, staring at the Liverpool shoreline;

362

since Martin had journeyed south his features beneath his grey-ing, Brylcreemed hair had aged.

"He had to go south," Mrs. Renshaw said. "Where the jobs are."

"And end up in prison? The whole of Liverpool knows our son is a gaolbird."

"But the charges have been dropped," Joanne said.

"Mud sticks," Mr. Renshaw said.

An enthusiastic guide with freckles on her face worried a flock of middle-aged tourists onto the deck beside them. "Do you know why it's called Liverpool?" pointing across the water.

They didn't; nor were they galvanised with curiosity.

"Several theories. *Larva*, Latin for the seaweed found in the pool in the Mersey. Larvapool," she explained, freckles dancing. "Lower Pool, perhaps. Or it may just have been the colour of the Mersey. Liver-coloured . . ."

The tourists absorbed the theories stoically.

The ferry berthed at Birkenhead, discharged its passengers and took on replacements.

"Supposing he came back," Joanne said as the propellers churned the water, taking them back to Liverpool.

"He won't," Mr. Renshaw said.

"He might," said his wife.

"Well, he won't be staying with us if he does."

"What makes you think he'd want to?" Joanne snapped.

"She's right," Mrs. Renshaw said. "He shouldn't have stayed so long, our kid. But when the young 'uns can't afford lodgings . . ."

"He was supporting you," Joanne said, addressing herself to Mr. Renshaw.

"You would have preferred us to starve?"

"You could have drawn more benefits."

"I don't want charity."

"Except when it's your son's."

"We brought him up," Mr. Renshaw said. "Gave him a good education even when we couldn't afford it. When times are hard you have to look after your own."

"He could be at university now," Joanne said.

"That's what you'd like, is it? Married to an architect? Get him to design a nice up-market house in Southport?"

"Yes," Joanne said, "that's what I'd like."

"Good for you, girl," said Mrs. Renshaw who had shown more spirit since Martin's departure.

"If he comes back," Joanne said, "he's going to the Poly. Move into lodgings. Get a grant."

"One more living off the State," Mr. Renshaw said.

"Didn't anyone help you when you were a young man, Mr. Renshaw?"

"Helped myself. I didn't beg."

"And look where it got you."

"That isn't quite fair," Mrs. Renshaw said.

"I know," Joanne said. "I'm sorry."

She stared across the water at the empty docks.

*   *   *

Jack Renshaw slept late that morning, fatigued after nocturnal business at Braintree. When Martin arrived at the council flat off the Commercial Road in the East End he was drinking coffee attended by Grace who was as flamboyantly groomed as he was dishevelled.

Adjusting his black towelling robe he pointed at a chair beside a window-sized television. "Want your job back, do you? Pincher's very particular about his staff but he was over the top this time. Innocent until proved guilty, eh, Martin?"

"You know Jack Daniels has made a statement to the police?"

"Jack who?" He fingered the shiny scar tissue on his neck. "Grace, give young Martin a cup of coffee. Want some brunch? You look half-starved."

"Daniels," Martin said. "The thief you recommended to Harry."

"Don't know what you're talking about, Martin. Been sleeping rough? Meths getting to the old Uncle Ned?" touching his black, grey-needled hair.

Grace placed a mug of coffee in front of Martin and retired to the kitchen.

Martin sipped his coffee. He felt very sure of himself. He said: "Heald doesn't think you had anything to do with the antiques but he does think that, if the going gets tough, Harry might try and stitch you up. One, you know Daniels, two,

364

you're a . . ."

"What am I, Martin?" eyes dark and watchful.

"A professional," Martin said.

"A thief? Is that what you're trying to say?"

"Aren't you, Uncle Jack?"

A pause. Jack Renshaw stared into his coffee. Then he laughed. "Gutsy, aren't we. Changed a bit since Christmas. Is that what the wicked city does to you?"

Martin said: "I want to know what you and your brothers did all those years ago."

Jack wiped one hand across his face and took the humour with it. He stood up and paced the room. Stopping in front of the TV, he said: "Some stones best left unturned, Martin." His face was drained.

"How about a deal?" Martin said. "The Renshaws seem to be fond of deals."

"Every time I hear about a deal I hear blackmail."

"Information," Martin told him.

"I seem to have heard that before."

"Is it a deal?"

"Information first," Jack said.

Grace came in from the kitchen attending to her pink claws with an emery board.

Jack said: "Bit of business, girl. Go and buy yourself a mink coat."

"Chance would be a fine thing," Grace said. She opened the front door and walked onto the sunlit balcony.

Martin hesitated. What if he delivered the information and received nothing in return? But what was the alternative?

He said: "According to Heald . . ."

"Heard tell of him. Not a bad copper by all accounts, as coppers go, that is."

". . . Harry's pulling a stroke on the side."

"That's our Harry," Jack said.

"Heald's been in touch with his insurance company. They say he's claiming for more antiques than those that were recovered. But they can't do anything about it because he'll merely say that Daniels must have got rid of them."

"He always was a devious sod," Jack said.

"So the chances are that the antiques – miniatures according to the insurance company – are still in the house."

365

"So why don't I get someone to nick them? Is that what you're saying? Billy, for instance? Getting pretty devious yourself, Martin. Been keeping bad company?"

"I know the combination of Harry's safe."

The Westminster clock on the mantelpiece chimed. A child ran along the balcony screaming.

"More than devious," Jack said. "More like bloody criminal." He went to a walnut cocktail cabinet, took a glass from its mirrored interior and poured himself a Scotch.

Martin said: "Even if Harry caught you he couldn't shop you: according to him the miniatures have already been stolen."

"Did Heald put you up to this?"

"Hardly, he's the law."

"That proves something?"

"It was my idea," Martin said.

"You could go far, Martin. You could go far. But let's face it: Heald told you that Harry had set you up and Heald told you that he was claiming for miniatures that hadn't been recovered . . ."

"I think," Martin said, "that Heald realises that Harry can't be arrested for arranging the theft of his own property. I think," said Martin, "that Heald is in favour of rough justice."

"Sure, and I'd get nicked for the theft of the miniatures in the safe."

Martin said: "I don't think so. You see, Heald thinks you're honest – in a crooked sort of way."

"Tell him likewise."

"He means it. Do you want the combination?"

"In return for what happened a lifetime ago? Or so you say." Jack finished his whisky. "Forget it, I could open that safe with a tin-opener."

"But there was something a long time ago?"

"I said forget it."

"Know what I think?"

"I don't give a shit what you think," Jack said.

"I think you're ashamed."

"On your bike, Scouser," Jack said. "Tread carefully on the balcony: you might fall off it."

*   *   *

366

That evening Martin visited the night shelter in Dean Street to see if Charlie was there. He wasn't: Prince was, in the queue.

They shook hands with great vigour, held the grip, smiled with an intense shyness.

"Evening, cully, where have you been dossing?"

"Here and there," Martin told him.

"Ask no questions get told no lies. I hear you're as innocent as the day is born."

"And Charlie. I thought he might be here."

"Only a few days to go, cully. Time running out."

"I'll find him," Martin said.

"Maybe Hoover will find him."

"Who'll find Hoover?"

The queue inched forward.

"Kipping down here tonight?" Prince asked.

"Not tonight," Martin said.

"Got a taste for roughing it? Watch it. You can be as institu-tionalised to the great outdoors as you can be to a prison cell." He pulled despondently at the bead in his ear. "Fate against me yesterday. Eighty-nine miles short of 10,000. Guinness Book of Records, all that ... Remember that Pakistani collecting the tickets on the Mersey Pullman? Pulled a stroke, didn't I. Hand to the heart, frothing at the mouth ... So yesterday I don't recognise him. Same stroke, same bubbles. 'Ho, ho, ho,' says our Asian sleuth. 'Another fit, is it? Not pulling froth over this inspector's eyes, no sir.' Up I get to fetch my non-existent ticket from my other berth and up get two transport police in plain clothes and, Bingo, I'm nicked. Eighty-nine miles short. Isn't there any justice?"

*   *   *

The previous evening Charlie had reached Brixton. But the thoughts bombarding him were bullets. Houses burned, youths, black and white, snarled at each other and police, menacing in transparent helmets, made fences of themselves behind their shields. Such was the hostility of the thoughts that he lost the vision that had earlier appeared to him – the end terrace and the gentle-voiced stories in the evenings before the ugliness at night.

Once he fancied he saw Martin. With another man. Fighting with three young blacks. Then Martin's companion disappeared. Then Martin — and he knew that it was just another vision that had been dissolved by the venom in the streets.

He turned and ran for a long time until he came to a row of new houses arranged in terraces of four. They stood between neat, undivided gardens which smelled of roses and, although it was night, he could tell from the different shades of darkness that the doors were painted in various colours. Lots of blues and yellows like primroses, he felt.

He walked round the rear of them to a narrow service road. At the end of the thin back gardens stood car-ports. The door of one was ajar. He went inside. Cinders underfoot and a small car, a Mini, waiting like an unanswered telephone. He opened the door, pushed the front seat forward and climbed into the back. It was cramped but when he was curled up like a cat he was secure.

He slept.

When he awoke he could see dew sparkling on a tiny, sharp-edged lawn. Dahlias, their stakes wearing flower-pots like hats, grew on either side. Two cats, one ginger, one tortoiseshell, touched the dew and shook their paws irritably.

The kitchen door — primrose yellow — opened and a woman emerged followed by three more cats. The woman wore a wig, brown and dry, and her knuckles were humped with arthritis. She sounded lonely.

She walked across the lawn, crushing the jewels of dew. She looked into the car. Then she opened the door and said: "You're Charlie, aren't you?"

She gave him a mug of tea and three slices of toast thick with butter and coarse-cut marmalade and watched him while he ate, cats pressing themselves against her legs. Blue and white chequered curtains hung at the windows and the previous evening the kitchen had been neatly arranged for today. A tap dripped; he could fix that for her.

"Everyone's looking for you," she said.

He liked the wig. It made her look spry. He liked her thoughts, too — they were kind. He wondered if she was bald under the wig.

"I heard it on the radio," she said. "Before Derek Jameson. I get up early."

"So must he," said Charlie, taking care with his words.

"Would you like another cup of tea?"

One of her knuckles cracked as she picked up the mug. She re-boiled the kettle, waited until it whistled, heated the teapot which was the same colour as the back-door, took three teaspoonfuls of tea from a caddy bearing a picture of a king with a beard, dropped them into the teapot and poured steaming water into it. She let it brew as his mother had once done – he saw her suddenly, clearly, warming her hands on the teapot as she waited – then she poured the tea into a quarter of an inch of milk in his mug.

As he sipped it, feeling the steam warm on his face, she said: "You can stay here if you like."

"I'll mend that tap," he said.

She smiled at him and pushed her wig. "You can sleep on the sofa," she said. "Come and see."

He followed her into the sitting-room. There were pictures on the walls – a Chinese girl with a green face, a ballet dancer and waves curling on a beach which might have been Tenby which he had visited with the school before he had run away. And an audience of easy chairs around the TV. The cats jumped onto them and gazed at the empty screen.

"We only view in the evenings," she said. "We find things to do during the day, don't we." The cats blinked. "That's Iris," pointing at a fat tabby, "and that's Timothy and that's Ralph . . ."

On top of the television stood a photograph of a young man in a soldier's uniform. He wore a toothbrush moustache that made him look brave but his eyes were frightened. The photograph had turned brown but the silver frame had been polished until it was thin as paper. He knew that the young man had died a long time ago and that this was why she talked to her cats.

"I'd like to stay," Charlie said. "Just for a couple of nights. Maybe three. Depends on the tap." He smiled at her; sometimes his jokes were not understood.

That evening, after the soap opera, they watched the Prime Minister appeal for an end to the rioting which was "undermining Britain's reputation throughout the civilised world". Secretly Charlie didn't think that the queue behind the night shelter in Dean Street gave a shit about the civilised world's views on Britain.

369

Then they watched the news. The rioting had worsened. Six dead. A man with silver hair that was arranged too precisely said that if the disturbances escalated – he remembered Gosling talking savagely about *escalating* – a situation would soon arise that would not be "far removed from civil war".

He heard his name but she switched off the TV.

He said: "I'll have to go away for the race."

"Do you know where to go?" she said.

"Home," he said.

"You know," she said, touching the curls of her wig as though she were a girl, "that you can always come back."

She gave him a yellow blanket. "Harry always liked yellow," she said.

He heard the stairs creaking as she went upstairs, heard her bed sigh. He lay on the sofa beneath the yellow blanket and closed his eyes. After a few moments Ralph joined him and began to purr.

*   *   *

Jenny said: "This is William Grey."

Martin shook the old man's hand. "I hope you can help me," he said.

"I've wanted to for a long time," the old man said.

"What stopped you?" Martin asked.

"Shame," the old man said.

Eleanor Lubin poured drinks for everyone in crystal glasses.

She said: "I think we should adjourn. That's you" – Andrew – "and you" – Jenny – "and me."

When they had gone Martin sat opposite William Grey in the elegantly judicial living-room.

He waited.

They sipped their drinks.

Then William Grey told Martin what had happened.

*   *   *

A long time ago, before Martin was born.

There was Jim Renshaw with a shopkeeper's brain who might one day become another Tommy Lipton. There was Harry, avaricious and over-sexed. There was Walter even then

370

dropping sixpence in the collecting box in church and taking out a shilling.

And there was Jack. "That Jack," said the old man, "always my favourite. Not his father's son, a touch of impregnated villainy there. But style, did he ever have style. As though Raffles had slept with your grandmother in Bethnal Green. I hope you'll excuse me," the old man said.

"Get on with it," Martin said.

And so the brothers' father was sighting death with considerable equanimity. His wife was dead, only his sons to benefit from his capital which in those days was sizeable.

So what did he do? Visited by visions of eternal and bounteous tranquillity if he funded Mankind he changed his will and left most of his money to a charity, token sums to his sons.

The brothers, persuading themselves that their father was scarcely of sound mind, decided to rectify this aberration.

So they "persuaded" their father to change his bequests in front of a lawyer. "Leaned upon him," William Grey said. "He didn't stand a chance, poor old devil."

The lawyer? Their lawyer! "Me – executor of the will." Grey paused and stared into the past. "They were very forceful," he said softly. "So much so that the old man became so confused, so distressed, that he had a heart attack. Murderers, that's what we were."

Martin, knowing the answer, said: "Who was the instigator of this conspiracy?"

"Your father," William Grey said.

CHAPTER 37

Martin watched the opening of the Special Olympics that serene Friday evening in July on the television in Eleanor Lubin's home.

First an excursion into the host resort of Brighton. Its shingle beaches, Regency terraces, the bow-fronted shops in the Lanes, the Royal Pavilion and the big, belching pubs.

Then clips of previous meetings while the commentator traced their history. They owed their birth, he said, to a death – the assassination on November 22, 1963, of the President of the United States, John F. Kennedy.

As a memorial the Kennedy Foundation launched the Games for the mentally retarded and in 1968 the first Special Olympics, brainchild of Eunice Kennedy Shriver, were staged at Soldier Field, Chicago. An Olympic flag, gold on blue, flew, a runner lit a Flame of Hope, the new oath was intoned: "Let me win. But, if I cannot win, let me be brave in the attempt."

Many of today's sportsmen of supposedly superior intellects, the commentator remarked, could learn from their subsequent endeavours. "Tennis players, footballers, cricketers?" He smiled into the camera.

Cut to the stadium at Withdean on the outskirts of Brighton. A fanfare sounded and the competitors from Britain, the United States and half a dozen European countries paraded. There were thousands present to witness this festival of altruism. But of Charlie there was no sign.

*   *   *

The following morning Martin telephoned the Sussex Co-ordinating Committee in Brighton.

He told a woman with a jolly voice that there was still no sign of Charlie. Was there any chance that, if he turned up, he could still compete?

Normally it would be out of the question, the woman said. But in the circumstances rules would be waived. "We are besieged by the media," she told Martin happily.

Martin replaced the receiver in Eleanor Lubin's home. It was 9.30. The heats for the 800 metres were at 1.30 pm. Four hours. And it would take one and a half hours to get from Holland Park to Brighton.

The phone rang. Another false sighting.

Martin switched on the radio. The rioting during the night had worsened but now there was a lull. "All attention," a commentator said, "is focussed on Brighton. It seems as though the grievances of inequality and injustice have become personified in one young man. If Charlie makes it to Brighton, if he wins, then there is a chance that these grievances will be settled constructively rather than violently."

If . . . Martin, patrolling the apartment while Jenny made coffee in the kitchen, felt time dissolving. *If* Charlie got there, if he won, then Danny, who had gone to Brighton with Eleanor Lubin and Andrew, would fight the dragon. That, to Martin, seemed to matter more.

Jenny brought him coffee.

He said: "Thanks for William Grey."

"I'm sorry."

"I'm not. Harry and Walter and Jack in his way prospered from a fraud; my father didn't; that's all there is to it. My father was my conscience. Not any more."

He glanced at his watch. 11.20. He switched on the television. Special coverage of the Special Olympics. Men's and women's 100 metres, jumps, wheelchair events . . . The sun blessed the athletes as they competed with their own graces.

He watched the second-hand of his watch pushing aside hope.

The phone rang.

A woman's voice, quavery.

"I read the telephone number in the newspaper . . ."

373

"Please, ma'am, do you have any news?"

"Charlie slept in my house last night."

He heard her breathing on the line.

"Is he there now?"

"Not any more."

Hope dissolved.

"Where did he go?"

"He said he was going home . . ."

Bleeps as the money in a coin box ran out.

"Where did he go to?" Jenny asked.

"He told her he was going home."

"He's only known one real home," Jenny said.

Martin stared at her. He kissed her.

"The keys," he said.

"What keys?"

"To Andrew's car. They went to Brighton in Eleanor's car, didn't they?"

"In the kitchen," Jenny said.

"You drive."

She drove the Lancia south across the Thames, to Wandsworth.

They passed the Codgers.

Hoover was sitting under the willow tree in front of the rubble.

Beside Charlie.

*　　*　　*

12.15. One and a quarter hours in which to reach the stadium. But the cars of Saturday shoppers slowed them down in the suburbs.

Jenny gear-changed through Streatham, Thornton Heath, Purley, Coulsdon and under Merstham Bridge. Then a straight run for three miles to Hooley.

There she picked up the beginning of the M23 that carries you swiftly and cleanly through cushions of pampered countryside towards the coast.

She kept in the fast lane, foot down, ignoring the squawks of the Jaguars and BMWs that were forced to overtake in the centre lane. The road surface hummed beneath the tyres; the motorway fled behind them.

Charlie, in his baggy black trousers and white shirt, sat still, hands clenched on his knees.

"It's all right," Martin said. "We're going to make it. And you're going to win."

"I don't know," Charlie said. "I've been running a long time."

"Danny thinks you're going to win."

"Where's Danny?"

"Waiting for you at the stadium."

"The three of us," Charlie said. "Remember those days on the common?"

"I remember," Martin said.

Hoover, sitting between them, wagged his tail.

The police car, a white Rover, stopped them just past the exit for Gatwick Airport.

"Good morning, miss . . ." began a beefy young policeman with the roll of the South Downs in his voice.

Jenny prodded her thumb behind her. "That's Charlie," she said.

He pointed at the police car. "Get in," he said.

The police car sped south, flashing roof-light and siren ordering all traffic out of its way.

Past the exits for Horley and Crawley, leaving the motorway twenty miles from Brighton.

They continued along a dual-carriageway onto a two-way highway with a trout farm on one side.

Then two pillars on either side of the road, the boundary posts of Brighton.

At Patcham they turned at the Black Lion pub.

The time was 1.23.

"We'll never do it," Jenny said.

"I knew a policeman once," the driver said. "Threw tear gas into a peaceful demonstration. When he was asked why, he said: 'Because I've always wanted to.'"

He swung the Rover onto the wrong side of the road. Oncoming cars swerved and slithered out of the way.

He said over his shoulder: "I've decided to take an early retirement. Like tonight."

He drove along the road to Withdean and, at 1.28, turned right into the stadium.

The cheers filled Martin's skull.

He won his heat easily and a battery of cameras recorded him, in white vest and blue shorts, breasting the tape. But while he rested, waiting for the final, he became worried. There were so many people massed round the track, thousands of them, and all their thoughts were directed at him, swarms of them so thick that they threatened to stifle him. Breathing rapidly, he put his hand to his throat.

"Are you all right?" Martin sat on the grass beside him.

"I wish," said Charlie, "that people would think about someone else." His speech had been improving but now the words were losing themselves again.

Martin said: "When it's over – when you've won – Danny's going to be cured." He put his arm round Charlie's shoulders. "The house where you stayed last night . . . Can you stay there again?" And when Charlie nodded: "So you've nothing to worry about – you can go back to school and you'll have somewhere to stay."

Charlie fisted his hands.

"Where are you going to hang that gold medal?"

"In the squat," Charlie said. "In the next squat."

"In the house," Martin said gently. "Or in the school." He consulted the lists of runners. "There are only three other runners in the final that can get anywhere near you. An American from San Diego, a Frenchman from Afaim and a German from Pinneberg. Stay just behind them until the last bend, then get those pistons of yours going."

A man's voice announced the final over the loud speakers. "Good luck, Charlie," Martin said, gripping his hand. "But you won't need it – you're the best."

And he was kneeling and waiting for the gun and silence pressed down upon the stadium.

And then, as the pistol-shot lost itself in the silence, he was running, pistons moving easily. Through the suburbs and into the country, smelling the sea.

As the runners, still closely bunched, approached the end of the first of the two circuits Charlie was lying second.

And he was returning from the coast and the woman from the house with the green roof was handing him the towel.

Third, fourth.

And there was hatred in the streets of Brixton.

And now he was last.

He blinked and sweat stung his eyes. He was not in Brixton he was in this stadium near the sea but it was the thoughts assaulting him, joining into one great, suffocating force, that confused him.

"Charlie, Charlie . . ."

The thoughts became a roar from the crowd.

He increased his stride but as they neared the last bend the others were a long way ahead of him.

His legs were tired, too; he had been running a long time. All his life.

"Charlie!" The thoughts behind this voice, closer than the others, had a special urgency about them; they were familiar, too.

He glanced to the side of the track. Danny. Hands spread, strands of his small silken beard moving in a breeze coming in from the sea.

And they were on the common at Wandsworth. The three of them.

He passed two runners.

On the straight only the American, the German and the Frenchman were ahead of him.

"Charlie, Charlie . . ."

Wimbledon Common, too, with Hoover.

Just the American now. They were beside each other. He could hear his thoughts. *Win.* And his own. *Danny.*

He thrust his head and his chest forward at the tape and it was Danny who won.

*   *   *

It was asserted much later, after they had celebrated in the Codgers, that the landlord, on hearing about Charlie's victory, smiled but, when pressed, none of the celebrants could recall with any certainty that they had witnessed this phenomenon.

Prince was there counting the money he made from a bet on Charlie. And Gosling with his girl and words of praise. Hood, planning a sporting climax for his next novel. The anarchist subdued by this manifestation of justice. Nolan who told

377

Charlie that he had won many prizes but never a gold medal. Cuff who had found a new squat in Blackheath and Frank the Bodger who was anxious to repair it. Jesus Christ who had known anyway that Charlie would win.

Heald was there, too, pint of bitter in one big hand, smiling fondly upon Danny who had shaved off the wisps of his beard, and Eleanor Lubin and Andrew who stood a little apart from the others.

Eleanor drew Martin and Jenny aside. "I've just been speaking to Heald," she said. "Guess who's been burgled."

"Uncle Harry?" Martin asked.

She regarded him keenly. "Now how would you know that?"

"And he hasn't reported it to the police?"

"Correct, Heald heard it from a contact. Your suspicious intuition does you credit, Martin. You should become a lawyer."

"Architect," Martin said.

He took Jenny's arm and led her through the door onto the street. To the right they could just see the willow tree outside the residue of Buck House, to the left lay the common.

"Prince has lent me the fare," Martin said.

"To where?"

"Home," he said.

He touched her cheek and kissed her lips and when he stood back the questions were there in the frown between her eyes and because he didn't know the answers he turned and hurried away.

At Euston Station he bought an evening newspaper. In Brixton, Bristol, Birmingham, Liverpool and Glasgow they were rejoicing instead of rioting. "Whether or not this is a euphoric lull is yet to be ascertained," stated an editorial. "But the Gods of Sport have smiled upon us – Zeus, perhaps, in whose honour the Olympics were first held – and it is now up to those who rule this land to use their beneficence constructively."

Martin bought a single ticket to Liverpool and, sitting in a corner seat of the train, stared across the empty platform.

The train began to move. A figure on the platform, bony legs pounding, dank hair streaming.

Martin flung open the door and Prince hurled himself onto the opposite seat. "Starting all over again," he said, panting.

"Another 10,000 miles. Got a good idea for this lap." He leaned forward conspiratorially. "There's always a wheeze, cully," he said. "Never forget that."

The train gathered speed and headed north.